SWORD
IN THE
STARS

JIMMY Patterson Books for Young Adult Readers

James Patterson Presents

The Maximum Ride Series by James Patterson

The Confessions Series by James Patterson

The Witch & Wizard Series by James Patterson

Nonfiction by James Patterson

Stand-Alone Novels by James Patterson

For exclusives, trailers, and other information, visit jimmypatterson.org.

SWORD
IN THE
STARS

Sequel to Once & Future

AMY ROSE CAPETTA
&
CORI McCARTHY

JIMMY Patterson Books
LITTLE, BROWN AND COMPANY
New York Boston London

Copyright © 2020 by Amy Rose Capetta & Cori McCarthy

Hachette Book Group supports the right to free expression and the value of copyright.
The purpose of copyright is to encourage writers and artists to produce
the creative works that enrich our culture.

The scanning, uploading, and distribution of this book without permission is a theft
of the author's intellectual property. If you would like permission to use material from
the book (other than for review purposes), please contact permissions@hbgusa.com.
Thank you for your support of the author's rights.

JIMMY Patterson Books / Little, Brown and Company
Hachette Book Group
1290 Avenue of the Americas, New York, NY 10104
JimmyPatterson.org

First Edition: April 2020

JIMMY Patterson Books is an imprint of Little, Brown and Company,
a division of Hachette Book Group, Inc. The Little, Brown name and logo
are trademarks of Hachette Book Group, Inc. The JIMMY Patterson Books® name
and logo are trademarks of JBP Business, LLC.

The publisher is not responsible for websites (or their content)
that are not owned by the publisher.

The Hachette Speakers Bureau provides a wide range of authors for speaking events.
To find out more, go to hachettespeakersbureau.com or call (866) 376-6591.

ISBN 978-0-316-44929-8

LCCN: 2020932001

10 9 8 7 6 5 4 3 2 1

LSC-H

Printed in the United States of America

For all the Aris out there,
who have to hide who they are in order to feel safe.

And for the Merlins,
who need a few extra lifetimes to unveil their identity.

Stay strong, have hope, and please don't hurt yourself.

We are the best part of this future.

"On second thought, let's not go to Camelot.
It is a silly place."

—*Monty Python and the Holy Grail*

SWORD
IN THE
STARS

LOST & FOUND

Merlin crash-landed in the past with a great, undigni-fied belly flop.

The chaos of waves left him torn between gasps and muttered curses. He had rocketed through the time portal, an endless skydive without parameters or parachutes, before it dumped him in this flooded, cramped circle of stone.

"Anyone else down here?" He bobbed. "No? Just me?" He splashed around, finding rough stone, and high above, a hole punch of blue sky. This was no cavern. The walls had been hacked in a pattern that spoke of plans and intentions and humanity. He was in a well.

"Nothing a little magic won't fix." But when Merlin went to dig some up, he was near empty. Trying to keep everyone together in a time portal with completely different laws of physics had drained him. And it hadn't even worked. He would worry about that later; for now he had to get out and see if their great gamble had paid off.

He braced his arms and legs for a long climb. The well was narrow enough that he could jam himself between two opposing sides, scuttling upward and hurting his back and his neck and his dignity most of all. "Dignity is for knights," he scoffed under his breath. Merlin was a mage. A bit of absurdity came with the territory.

When he reached the top, he gripped the edge, hoisted one leg, and rolled over. He hit the flagstones of a central square with a resounding *smack*. He stood, shoved his glasses into place, and looked around.

At Camelot.

It wasn't off in some hazy distance, surrounded by dragons and dreams. The city was here, the city was *now*. A normal day in Camelot should have been bustling with crowds, crying babies, forges clanging, and those incessant flutists—a shrill reminder that music wouldn't improve for centuries. Yet all was silent, still. Layers of odors that he hadn't even known he'd missed stampeded his senses. Damp earth. Sprightly grass. Meat cooked in a godless amount of butter...

And there was *his* castle rising above the whole scene, keeping watch over the city. It was Arthur's, too, yes, but Merlin had designed it for the young king, giving it towers and secrets that regular castles could hardly dream about. It had been his highest achievement, next to Arthur's reign. Only now the castle looked small—the starscrapers of the twenty-second century had broken his sense of scale—and yet the way it stood against this perfect blue morning left a mark.

On the sky. On his soul.

He was home.

Merlin's memories should have risen up to meet him, rather

like the flagstones had risen up to meet his face, but none were forthcoming. Perhaps he was too nervous. After all, he wasn't supposed to be facing his past alone. The time portal had tried to burst his body into atomic confetti, but even worse, it had ripped his friends away from one another. He looked around for Ari, Gwen, Jordan, Lam, and Val, wondering if they'd all landed safely in the square while he alone had had the misfortune of shooting straight down the barrel of a smelly well.

All he found was one young person with a gaping mouth and fishy-wide eyes watching his every move. They had ruddy white skin and scruffy brown hair, and they said a word that sounded a fair bit like *shit*.

It was hard to adjust now that he had gotten used to the distinct Mercer accent of the future. *Not Mercer; English, the language is English,* Merlin corrected. Curse that consumer monster with its uncanny knack for swallowing culture and rebranding history! Actually, he'd gone back far enough that England didn't exist *quite* yet. The island was known as Britannia during this time. He spent a moment mentally mapping it out: Camelot's golden age had flowered just before the Norman invasion, and after the island's run-in with the Roman Empire, which left nothing but divisions and bathhouses in its wake.

"Good day!" Merlin shouted heartily, causing the scruffy kid to drop their bucket.

They eyed him, then the well. "Did you spring from the roots of the stone?"

"Stones don't have roots," he quipped, though he enjoyed the way this language lent itself to metaphor. His future-y friends had been so amused by his allegorical loquaciousness, but it was a remnant of his origins, a rare one he actually treasured. Not that he knew his *precise* origins. The farthest back he could remember was waking up in the crystal cave, ancient and alone.

"Then where did you come from?" the small stranger asked.

Merlin suppressed the desire to say *a galaxy far, far away.* "I'm from Camelot."

He was only half a foot taller than this young person, which begged the question, how old was Merlin these days? Was it possible he'd gotten *younger* since they left the future? Perhaps the portal had shaved off more of his life. A penalty for time travel? Morgana had given up her existence to send them back, while Excalibur had broken to bits. Was this his price?

He loved magic, but sometimes it was unmistakably the worst.

The kid grumbled as they sent the bucket down the well, while Merlin twisted water from the ruby robes Ari had gifted him on Ketch. He tried not to look suspicious, though that ship had probably sailed to distant seas by now. First things first, he needed to find the crowds. Ari was always at the center of the action, the others not far behind. They were her little ducklings. Thinking of Jordan and her knightly skills, he course-corrected: *lethal* ducklings. "What's happening today? Where is everyone?"

"All attend King Arthur's wedding," the kid said, sweating under the weight of the bucket as they brought it back up. "He takes his bride in the tournament ring."

Oh, yes, the ever-delightful treatment of women as possessions. He was definitely back.

Something clicked oddly. "Gweneviere? Arthur is *already*

marrying Gweneviere?" He didn't know why he was surprised. He'd commanded the portal to take them back to Arthur's eighteenth birthday season, which had been a particularly momentous time for the young king *and* a rather squishy blank period in Merlin's memories. That's when the enchanted chalice had appeared—and disappeared—and that's what Arthur's spirit had sent them back to retrieve.

"The Lady Gweneviere comes from afar," the kid said eagerly. "An exotic beauty. My friend says she's a force for good in Camelot, but my mother believes she bewitched the king."

Ah, another piece of the past he hadn't missed. The perfect storm of antipolitical, cultural, and social correctness. His friends were in for a migraine of homophobic, racist, and gender-related fuckery. He had to find them. Fast.

"Where is the wedding?" he barked, making the kid jump.

They pointed beyond the city walls, and Merlin left at a run. His path wound him around Camelot's central castle, as glowering as it was grand, with eight-foot-thick walls, stones capped with dark moss, and mere arrow slits for windows. He forced himself not to look up at the tallest tower. Another version of him might be up there, even now. Merlin had told his friends he didn't want to expose them to the horrors of the Middle Ages, which was true, but some of those horrors weren't just historical. They were deeply, deeply personal. He had to avoid a run-in with his old self at all costs.

"Shouldn't be hard," he murmured. "As long as we stay out of the castle and don't cause any scenes." How likely was it that Ari had found trouble in the few minutes they'd been apart?

Good heavens, Merlin needed to sprint.

As his breath cut short and his feet rubbed against the inside of his wet boots, he soothed himself with one of his focused to-do lists. Merlin had to find his friends, steal the chalice, and make a new time portal to return them to the night they left.

Oh, he thought, *three steps.* Always a good sign.

In the back of his mind he added less immediate, but ever-important hopes: to protect Gwen's baby, reverse his ridiculous backward aging, and release Arthur's spirit from Ari's body, allowing the dead king to finally rest. To end this cursed cycle once and for all. But surely those things would happen if they made it back to the future and irreversibly stopped Mercer.

"Piece of—" A scent wafted over him. "Delicious roasted meat."

A cheer rifled the air, and the cacophony led him through the main gates and up a dirt road slick with mud. In the near distance, atop a perfectly green hill, a proud tournament ring held thousands of people and quite the celebration. The pennants were flying, bearing the red dragon and Excalibur. More promising smells hit. His stomach roared, and he told it to stop being so Kay-like.

He pushed himself to remember the less-than-admirable qualities of this place. Even from a distance, the divisions of an unequal society stood out. Commoners huddled together on the edges of the ring, while the nobles kept comfy seats under the dyed red pavilions. If Merlin dared to ask anyone their pronouns, he might very well be treated as more dangerous than a rogue mage.

Merlin elbowed through the commoners for a better look. He was a bit grimy from well climbing, which helped him fit in with this foul-smelling bunch. Musicians lit up horns, and the crowd stilled with anticipation. Everything looked and sounded and felt like the start of a royal celebration.

He really had come out of the time portal at the right moment. It was the first bit of good news since Ketch, when for a few glorious nights he'd believe the universe was free of the Mercer Company's oily grasp and headed for the end of the Arthurian cycle. He had celebrated with Val and copious amounts of kissing.

Val. They had all gotten separated in the time portal— Ari first, then Gwen, Lam, and Jordan—but Val and Merlin had been holding on to each other, Val's brown eyes the only grounding force as every rule of physics was stripped away, and they plummeted toward a nightmare he thought he'd escaped long ago.

And then Merlin blinked, and Val was gone.

Stolen right out of his arms.

Drumbeats announced the procession as knight after knight on horseback rode into the ring. Merlin watched while they circled, noticing armor from all kinds of places. Most likely these knights had traveled for weeks to attend the event and seek favor from the king. Some of their suits were polished silver; some red, scratched, and dented; others blackened with coal. One knight stood out in blue armor, a circular dragon emblazoned on his breastplate.

Merlin squinted, both recognizing the image and drawing a complete blank as to what it meant. "I should remember more," he muttered, but then, he was seeing this wedding for the first time. His old self had boycotted Arthur's wedding— that much he *did* remember.

After the knights, women with flowers in their hair and woven around their ankles stepped forward, faces calm but unsmiling. As they formed a circle and started a complex pattern of steps, Merlin noted that it wasn't a homogeneous medieval dance crew. For some reason, he had expected everyone to be whiter than the puffy clouds above the tournament ring. A single look proved that wasn't true. While some girls were white and wildly freckled, others had smooth bronze complexions. There were pale blondes and paler redheads, as well as maidens with warm brown skin and tight black curls tumbling out of their braided crowns. One girl had a Middle Eastern set to her features and jewel-bright eyes much like Ari. One looked so much like Jordan with her thick blonde braid that Merlin did a double take. But no. Jordan would put her neck on the block before she'd throw herself into such festivities.

He went back to scanning the—also surprisingly diverse—crowd for his friends, when the star of the show appeared.

"King Arthur!" the people cried as one. "All hail King Arthur!"

Merlin's heart skidded to a stop. It had been so long since he'd seen Arthur. His first family, his *only* real family until Ari and the others swept him into their lives. At a distance, Arthur looked small, his straw hair unkempt beneath a golden circlet crown and his moves jerky with nerves. There was no command in his presence, no steel in his gaze. He wasn't yet the king of legend, but he wasn't the curious, half-wild boy Merlin visited so often in memories. He was caught between the two.

Merlin wanted nothing more than to shout Arthur's name, break through the crowds, and reunite himself with his former ward and first magical pupil, but such a meeting wasn't in the cards. Interacting with the story in the past was strictly off-limits. They were here to steal from Camelot, not make fools of themselves by bum-rushing the king.

Arthur walked slightly sideways, pulling a woman in a cream-white dress in his wake. She wore greenery in her dark curled hair, blossoms around her neck, and a decorative knot of cords on her wrist that bound her to Arthur's arm.

"Gweneviere!" several people shouted, almost reverently. Many more stayed silent. While no one would openly jeer the king's choice, dislike crusted over plenty of features. Merlin huffed and looked back to the bride. And blinked. And then blinked harder.

Gwen?

The girl he'd known as the queen of her own Renaissance Faire Planet was standing at the dead center of Camelot, her gaze defiant until she turned to Arthur and gave him an encouraging nod. Gwen looked like she fit right in, perhaps because her life had been a unique form of training for this moment. Even if her mix of European and Asian heritage set her apart enough that the youth at the well had given her the micro-aggressive title of "exotic."

The truth was that Gwen had come from much farther than anyone in Camelot could imagine. Far enough to be measured in galaxies and centuries. That's the sort of distance it took to be safe from Mercer, and they were meant to be hiding out, yet it looked like Gwen had done more than storm the castle—she'd broken down the doors of the king's heart.

In a single day? *How?*

Merlin clutched his head as he remembered that she'd gotten married to Ari in less time than that. Oh, this was bad.

Tremendously bad. He could feel the time continuum wobble. He'd have to freeze the entire stadium and steal her out of the tournament ring, and...

"Merlin!" a voice whisper-shouted. Someone snagged his elbow and he was drawn back through the crowd, away from Gwen upending the entire Arthurian cycle.

Merlin came to an abrupt stop before a familiar knight in unfamiliar clothes. They wore the same rough-spun as the rest of the commoners. Their dreads were pulled back, but they sported no piercings. No makeup glimmered on their deep brown skin. At least their smile was worth a hundred blazing suns.

"Am I glad to see you, dude!" Lamarack clapped Merlin in a hug, thumping his back. He ached all over from his portal dive and subsequent climb. "You look..."

"Younger," he said with a wince. "I know."

"At least you're alive. We thought the worst."

"Who is *we*?" Merlin glanced at the scrappy person keeping to Lam's elbow, the same kid who'd witnessed his arrival.

"He came out of the well, Lamarack," they squeaked.

"As if that were my first time at the bottom of a well." Merlin scoffed. "Hardly." He turned to Lam, only to find them looking over the crowd at Gwen, their height a great help in the effort. "What in the blazes is happening?"

"You've missed a lot, old man," Lam said without taking their eyes off Gwen.

"Missed *what*?" he snapped. Lamarack ignored him, and the mage spun back to his most pressing concern. "What happened to 'steal the cup and get out unnoticed'?" Lam quirked an eyebrow. Before they all went through the time portal,

Merlin had told them not to interfere with the past—hadn't he? There had been so much happening. An unborn baby to protect from Mercer, who wanted to claim it as a price for rebellion. A cycle of tragedy and torment to stop. Surely he'd told them not to demolish the past in the process?

Surely he shouldn't *need* to explain that one.

"You've heard of the butterfly effect?" Merlin barked. "Changing the tiniest thing in the past can damage the future. Gwen has leapt into the middle of a mythological hurricane! She and Arthur are bound to each other! Literally!" He paused. "Are they *handfasting*?"

Handfasting was a scrap of history he'd forgotten about in the great heap of time that came after it. He'd never paid much attention to anything having to do with traditions of love and romance. He'd called it idiocy, or *brainmelt* in his kinder moments, but he did remember this test of loyalty and devotion. Those who meant to marry were tied together for the length of their engagement, the knots cut on their wedding day. Most couples handfasted for a year, but Gwen had arrived today, mere hours ago.

Unless...she *hadn't*.

He flashed back to the portal's winds, everyone separated. Merlin had imagined they landed in different places, but what about different times? "Did you arrive—"

"Months ago," Lam finished wearily.

"Tell me everything," he yelled. "Now!"

His outburst drew looks from the crowd. Lam—who had lost a hand to Mercer in the future—angled to grab Merlin with the remaining one and hauled him many yards away. "We have to lay low, Merlin. We've been here *for a long time.*

Me, Gwen, and Jordan." Lam pointed to the sturdy blonde girl in the lineup of handmaidens with flowers in their hair.

"That *was* Jordan!" Merlin squinted. She looked like she wanted to hack her white dress and garlands from her body with the nearest battle-axe. Her hair hung to her waist, her cheeks the severe pink of barely restrained fury. He was afraid to ask his next question. "Ari? Val?"

Lam shook their head. "No sign of them."

"But how long have they been missing? How long have *I* been missing?"

"Four months...ish?" Lam managed. It made sense. Tracking Earth's moon wouldn't be an obvious business to Merlin's space-born friends. "Gwen keeps better track of it than I do."

"Naturally." She had an internal calendar, set to the progression of her pregnancy, no doubt. "But *four* months," Merlin said, swallowing the loss, trying to glimpse Gwen's stomach and finding that her wedding dress had a strategic shape that turned her into a formless bell. "Does Arthur know she's...?" He pantomimed having a round stomach, and then having the contents of that stomach, well, slide out.

Lam grabbed one of Merlin's hands, stopping him. "We'll explain when we're all together. Gwen will want to tell you. This place..." Lam winced. "Camelot is not what we thought."

Looking around, Merlin had to agree. And while he was delighted to be wrong about certain things—such as the total whiteness of ye olde Britain—his lack of clarity about the past was its own kind of danger. Merlin was meant to be their guide. Not just to Old Earth, but to the story itself. As King Arthur and Gwen recited vows in strong, unwavering voices, he pressed himself to remember *anything* about the original

Gweneviere. Too many movie actresses shot through his mind, and only one memory rang true: telling Arthur that he'd read the omens and that the young woman he'd fallen for was a curse on the king's heart as well as his reign.

No wonder the people of Camelot didn't trust her—Merlin had told them not to—and Arthur had claimed his first youthful rebellion by marrying Gweneviere anyway, while Merlin had kept to his tower during the ceremony like a miserable old falcon.

He would *not* glance at that tower right now. Rivers of sweat sprang up on his palms. "Gwen has put herself in horrible danger."

"She knows what she's doing," Lam said as if they needed the reminder, too.

Arthur used a silver dagger to cut the knot binding him to Gwen. They slipped rings on each other's fingers, and then the inevitable moment came when their lips met. He tucked one of her curls behind her ear. It looked fairly chaste in a picturesque sort of way. Still. King Arthur had just kissed Gweneviere. Their Gwen.

Ari's Gwen.

"This is all so wrong," Merlin whispered. Another cheer broke loose, but this time it didn't die. It grew in pitch and frenzy, twisting from celebration to something more primal. Screams shattered the moment, turning it into a riot. Swords flew from sheaths. Villagers ran, while nobles were tightly circled by their personal guards. Merlin spun. "Who's attacking?"

"It's the Middle Ages, man. Who isn't attacking?" Lam pounded him on the shoulder and rushed against the escaping masses. He kept close behind Lam, whose immense height divided the crowds on both sides. Merlin's magic was still exhausted, but he couldn't be a slouch in battle. He popped blue sparks in the face of a man who tried to stab Lam in the back.

"Get to Gwen!" Lam shouted.

It was hard to keep her in sight now that the architecture of the crowd had collapsed, but Merlin caught glimpses of her holding Arthur's hand at the center of the tournament ring. The knights from the procession had begun battling each other, no order apparent in their attack. They seemed determined to take each other apart.

"Where are Arthur's knights?" Merlin hollered to Lam as they hopped the railing and entered the straw and muck of the ring.

"Great question," they called back. "Nothing here is like the story!"

He caught sight of Jordan running to Gwen's side. She raised her skirts, kicked one of Arthur's guards in the back, and ripped his sword out of his hand before he fell. Within moments she was taking down attackers, the only one in the crowd with a smile on her face.

An avian cry sliced the sky, making both Lam and Merlin stop. Everyone looked up. Merlin's chest squeezed tight as a large falcon circled over the ring and landed on Arthur's shoulder. The king cried out, but with a spark of magic, he became a tiny songbird. Merlin had loved the trick of turning Arthur into animals, but this was no whimsical adventure. It was an escape. One that pointedly didn't include the new queen. The two birds flew high, and when the songbird tried to return to Gwen, the old falcon bullied it back to the castle, leaving her in the center of the fight, white dress a beacon for all of those who wished to hurt the king—and were now closing in.

"Dude, the old version of you is *cold*," Lam yelled.

Merlin's cheeks were ablaze, his nerves fizzing. He wanted to hide from his shame, but there was nowhere safe in all of Camelot. This place *was* his shame.

Merlin fought sudden tears. No, he would not cry when faced with medieval battle. He was a mage...whose magic was exhausted. When a knight ran at him, sword raised, Merlin crouched and hugged his knees, only to hear the unmistakable sound of someone pounding his attacker into oblivion. When he looked up, the knight with the blue armor was standing over him.

They were mercilessly tall. Merlin yelled as the knight used the back of his robes to lift him to his feet like a dog taken by the scruff. "Help Gwen!" the voice commanded.

A familiar voice. One he sometimes heard in his head. One that laughed at him when he was being foolish and cheered him on when he was being, well, foolish.

"Ari?" he shouted as the knight spun away and took on a challenger in red who swung a short sword in his right hand and a great axe in his left. Merlin watched as the blue knight leveled both with a hard swing and then charged, using their breastplate as a battering ram. Which felt Ari-like, indeed.

The red knight toppled like a turtle on his back, and the blue knight grabbed the axe out of his grip and used one hand to shove his helmet back and the other to bring the blade's arc down on his neck. In a great, foul spurt of red much darker than his painted armor, he went limp. Merlin must have been wrong; Ari was never so violent.

He tripped toward Gwen, who breathed the biggest sigh of relief at the sight of him. "I'm here, I'm here!" he hollered.

Jordan had found a sword and was protecting the queen with her entire muscled, dress-covered body. "Good, now help!"

Merlin tried to create a protective bubble, but only wound up out of breath. Gwen pulled him close as if she was now determined to protect *him*.

The blue knight swung toward Gwen, and Jordan stepped between them.

"Stop!" Jordan barked. The knight sheathed their sword and began the process of pulling their gloves free, while Jordan frowned at the dragon on their breastplate. "Who are you?"

"Your biggest fan, Jordan." The knight flung away their gloves to lift their visor.

It really was Ari. Looking and swaggering and smelling for all the world like a medieval knight.

Ari clapped eyes on Gwen, her voice clear and promising. "Hey lady."

Gwen's face flooded with happiness and tears, and Ari's was poised to do the same. They moved toward each other, but Lamarack suddenly shouted, "Yield, Sir Kay!"

"Kay?" Ari and Merlin asked in unison, both turning just as a knight pinned Ari's wrist behind her back, stole the rounded dagger from her belt, and slammed it through the chainmail beneath her arm.

Ari screamed as she fell to her knees. It was the worst sound Merlin had heard in his long, painful history. Gwen's shredded cry was a close second. He and Gwen ran for Ari while Jordan felled the attacking knight with a great blow to the helmet.

Ari tipped forward into Gwen's arms. Merlin hovered over them, inspecting Ari's wound. The dagger was in up to the hilt—which meant it had gone all the way through her chest. Now it was Merlin's turn to cry out. An hour ago he and Ari had been standing in the red sands of Ketch, imagining a future without Mercer.

Now he'd fast-forwarded to a part of their story he could not recognize.

"Heal her!" Jordan commanded.

Merlin needed a spark that could disintegrate that dagger without causing more damage. He had to seal Ari's wound and cauterize it, fast. He couldn't survive all the ages and all of the Arthurs *and* come back to blasted Camelot only to lose her. But when he closed his eyes and hummed, his fingers fizzled and went cold. Merlin had returned just in time to not save anyone.

The battle died out around them. Gwen screamed a command at Jordan. Jordan hunkered in her ruined dress, took something small out of her cleavage and shoved it in Ari's mouth, forcing her jaw closed. Merlin didn't understand what was happening. He opened and closed his useless, magic-drained hands. His power hadn't come back quickly enough.

Time was against him—it always had been.

ARMOR & ADRENALINE

Ari was hiding out in the Middle Ages, but the future was never far from her mind.

Especially now.

She couldn't seem to lose consciousness but she wasn't truly there, either. Her thoughts screamed foul memories while the Mercer first aid pill—bitter and boiling in her veins—drowned her body with adrenaline that made her, well, feisty as fuck. When the Administrator loomed suddenly, Ari swung so hard she spun and missed.

"Grab her legs!" Lamarack hollered just as someone Merlin-shaped dove for her knees, locking tight arms around her until her balance was compromised. Lam pinned one arm while the other arced in a left hook that caught Jordan in the face.

Jordan smiled, a drop of blood at the corner of her mouth and a look of dark pleasure in her eye as she hit Ari so hard that she went down and stayed down. When Ari closed her eyes, she saw an endlessly swirling taneen on fire, spinning in a tight circle. She shivered as her frozen moms were dug up from a mass prison grave. She lost her breath at the sight of so many murdered Ketchans, half-buried in the shifting red sand. She saw Kay...

She saw Kay with empty, lifeless eyes.

Ari thrashed until it all evaporated, coming back to her senses in strong arms. Sharp, real smells filtered through her. Hay, mold, horses. A lot of horses.

"This isn't how I imagined our reunion." Lam's voice was in her head, or close to it.

Merlin's voice floated down. "Have you ever seen that happen before?"

"I've never seen someone take one of those before. I've heard it can be unpredictable."

"*Unpredictable*? I think I prefer Miracle Max's miracle pill."

"Merlin, what are you going on about?" Jordan's taut words made Ari wince.

"I'll have you know that's a timeless cultural reference!"

"Shut up," Ari managed, her mouth cotton. "I'm stuck in my worst memories."

"That sounds like Ari!" Merlin knelt close, and Ari turned away, still fighting the desire to scream or punch. She peered out a window, searching the night sky and its pinpricks of stars for home. But Ketch wasn't out there. Neither was Lionel, or even *Error*. They didn't exist yet, and it left Ari feeling like she had these long months on her own. Like a futuristic ghost.

Ari closed her eyes. "Damnit, Kay. Help me, will you?"

"No doubt he'd upend Camelot for you, if he were here,"

Merlin said, finally drawing her attention to the here and now. She was lying back on Lamarack in the straw mountain of a stable.

"If I let you go, will you behave?" Lam's tone was gentle, but their hold wasn't.

"I always behave." Ari sat up gingerly, her heart still racing, tightening her chest with anxiety. She winced through the bitter aftertaste of Mercer's famed first aid pills, the kind that could regenerate major tissue damage if immediately administered but were so high priced no one ever had one lying around. Ari had only used a pill like it once before, the day her mothers and Kay saved her from the void, her body riddled with infected burns.

"What happened?" she asked.

Lam rubbed her back. "You appeared like an armored angel in the midst of battle, took a dagger through both lungs, and yet you're still with us. Thank God."

"*God*? Since when do any of you reference singular, all-powerful deities?" Merlin asked.

"Lamarack is a little too good at adapting," Jordan replied dismissively. "And you've been missing for a long time, mage."

Ari held the spot under her arm that was hot and numb. For the first time in weeks, she wasn't in her armor. Her clothes were stained and ripped, her breasts barely concealed beneath the ragged linen. "Where's Gwen?"

"In the keep with her husband, the king," Jordan said with far too much satisfaction.

"He came back for her," Lam said, "after you magically appeared in the fray, saving Gwen only to get stabbed by our resident asswipe."

Jordan narrowed her eyes. "You don't know what you've cost Gwen. Again. That pill was for her."

Ari stood too fast. Lam steadied her with a soft arm around her waist. "You had that pill for when the baby comes, in case something goes wrong." Clarity struck like a match. "Shit."

"No doubt the idiot people here will think this miraculous recovery is witchcraft and burn you at the stake," Jordan said, "but apart from that you'll be fine in a few hours."

"You make it all sound so romantic," Ari deadpanned. "Did I...hurt Gwen, too?"

"No," Lam said. "Just us. We brought you here. You called me 'Administrator' and Merlin 'Hector' and tried to attack us. Who is Hector?"

"No one." Ari closed her eyes. "I kept hallucinating. Seeing my enemies. What did I call Jordan?"

"Jordan," she said.

Ari cracked an eye to peer at Lionel's famed black knight. Jordan smirked, and Ari didn't stop her own smile. "Perhaps it was just worthy opponents then."

Merlin wandered to the large, open doors of the stable and back again.

"Why do you keep doing that?" Jordan asked.

"It's just...if Ari and I returned on the same day, Val must not be far behind. Perhaps he's in Camelot now, looking for us," Merlin said. "Perhaps I should go look for him."

Lamarack's smile was sad. "If my brother were here, we'd all know it. He's never made a single entrance in his life without significant fanfare. The same hour he was born an ice volcano erupted on Pluto so huge that a new frozen range formed. Our parents named the highest mountain after him. Percival's Point."

Merlin wrung his hands. "But then, where could he be?"

"Judging by where the portal dumped me out, anywhere." Now that Ari could see her friends clearly—Jordan in a hand-maiden's dress and Lamarack in servant's rags, she started to put together the hard truths. They must have been here for a while. And it hadn't been easy. "Tell me what's happened."

Lam turned Ari toward them. "Gwen, Jordan, and I found ourselves in Camelot during the last snow of the winter. We were freezing, starving. And desperate to find the rest of you." Ari winced, imagining Gwen in the melting snow, pregnant and searching for her. "We worked our way into the villagers' trust. Labored for them, found ways to be paid in food and lodging. It was near impossible because...because..."

"Because when you don't slot into people's expectations here, they get suspicious at best and violent at worst? Because you're used to the future, where it's no big deal that you're nonbinary, Jordan is a famous knight, and Gwen is knocked up and not here for patriarchal nonsense?" Merlin said, sur-prising Ari with robust anger. "This whole planet can kiss my ass!"

Ari held down a smile. That might have been the first time she'd heard Merlin swear. "The people here aren't welcoming, but at least they don't seem to treat us poorly based on skin tone. Didn't you say that was a bizarre, evil thing they did?"

"Oh, they definitely did," Merlin said heatedly. "But I'd forgotten that things were actually better if you went this far back. I'd even grown used to the notion that people of color were not featured in this era of European history. I don't know who started *that* lie, but Hollywood was quite talented at spreading it. Did you know that enough poorly cast movies can whitewash a time period you've lived through? Because I didn't."

This seemed like a fresh rant. "When did *you* get here?"

"I seem to be the only person who arrived on schedule. I was in the portal only today. Val was right beside me a few hours ago, holding my hand."

Lam pushed Ari's short hair behind her ear. "I almost didn't recognize you with this haircut."

"Yeah, I'm a cis guy here. Apparently that means stupid chopped hair. Speaking of"—Ari dug around the straw at the pieces of her blue armor—"Where's my breastplate? I need it. Last time someone figured out I have boobs I accidentally murdered him." She started the sentence as a sort of informative joke, but it ended as harshly as that particular encounter.

Lam, Jordan, and Merlin watched her with paused expressions. She didn't like those looks; it meant she'd have to explain the constant ragged lies she spun day after day simply to exist— not to mention the stinging absence of King Arthur's voice deep inside as if she'd somehow *lost* him when she'd left the future.

Ari found her blue breastplate and strapped it across her chest. "I think I got knocked out in the portal. The last thing I remember is reaching for Gwen. And then someone pushed me."

"It must have been my magic." Merlin sighed. "I was trying to hold us all together."

Ari shook her head. "Some*one*. I felt hands strike me. Next thing I knew, I was on the smoking wreckage of a battlefield. I stole a fallen knight's armor and found someone who'd heard of Camelot. I started walking this way, realized I was on the wrong continent, and then hitched a ride with a bunch of smelly-ass

Vikings across the water. The rest I'll tell you some other time. When we're safe back home." Ari looked anywhere other than at her friends. "Tell me the worst thing to happen in my absence is Gwen found a new unsuspecting white boy to toss around."

"Arthur," Lamarack breathed, shaking their head. "He's hard to explain."

"Oh, but I'd love an explanation!" Merlin said, his voice a slight shout. "How did all of you translate my command of *Don't disturb the cycle* to *How about Gwen marries Arthur?* We were supposed to get the chalice and get out. No parties. Absolutely no weddings. Now we've…mingled, and who knows what the future consequences will be!"

"Unless Gwen is *the* Gweneviere," Lam said.

Merlin sputtered like a teapot on high boil.

"So we've broken the time continuum?" Jordan asked. "If Gwen were the original Gweneviere, Merlin would know. He was here. *Is* here. Twice over."

They all looked at Merlin, and he washed a little green in the torchlight. "I don't exactly remember the original Gweneviere terribly well."

"Why not?" Ari asked.

Merlin squirmed. "You've met me, haven't you?" Jordan raised one careful eyebrow. Merlin pointed at it as if this were proof. "See? She's met old me. I'm a veritable monster."

"Old you can't be that bad," Ari tried.

Lamarack gave a slow blink of affirmation.

"I might have limited memory of events that transpired several millennia ago, but that doesn't prove anything about our current mess," Merlin said. "It certainly doesn't mean Gwen has been…absorbed…by the canon!"

Lam spoke up. "Gwen did this so we'd have a better standing, so we could be close to the chalice when the time comes. Also, this place is *nothing* like the stories. Camelot isn't a haven for goodness. It's all hate and fear and assassination attempts on poor Arthur. That guy is a walking bull's-eye."

Merlin paced in the straw, kicking it about. He'd rolled his sleeves up his skinny forearms, but it did little to hide the way he'd become so much smaller since the last time Ari saw him. He'd literally shrunk within his clothes. There was no denying it: Merlin was at least a year younger than he'd been when he entered the portal. "The plan remains to get the chalice."

"Right," Ari said. "When is Arthur's eighteenth birthday celebration?"

"The big party is in a fortnight," Lamarack said. "On midsummer. Morgana said the chalice would appear that night, a gift from the Avalon enchantresses."

Ari tightened the straps of her breastplate, relieved to hide the part of her that seemed to incense men to shitty behavior in this time. "We find Val, get the chalice, and go home to the same night we left. How do we portal back?"

They all exchanged looks.

Even Merlin seemed to be waiting for one of them to have an idea. "Three kinds of magic," he finally said. "That's how we got here. Morgana's, mine, and the Lady of the Lake's sword. That should be enough to make an exact jump."

"Enough?" Jordan tutted. "That sounds like a lot, wizard."

"Well, you have me," he said. "And there are bits of magic lying around Camelot. We'll find...something."

"*Something,*" Lam repeated, nice and slow.

Ari dug through the straw until she found the back plate of

her armor. She laid it out, unfolding the linen padding until she'd unearthed the remains of Excalibur. The handle and hilt remained intact, but the blade ended jaggedly after a few short inches. "Would this work?"

Merlin stared. "That depends on if Excalibur's magic is lost."

Ari held it out to Merlin, but Jordan snatched it. The sword fragment's weight seemed to grow exponentially in Jordan's grip. She dropped it back in Ari's hands after a strenuous second. "Something magical is still going on there."

Ari smiled at Lamarack. "*Something.*" Lamarack winked. Perhaps the medicine was finishing up its healing, or maybe for the first time in months, Ari could feel some kind of hope. "Merlin and I will get the chalice. Lam and Jordan, find Val. And Gwen…"

"Will distract Arthur," Jordan said. "She'll be his Gweneviere as the story requires."

"But that's just it," Lamarack said. "None of us know exactly what the story requires. Except Merlin who has so inconveniently forgot." Merlin opened his mouth but then shut it.

"Why am I always the only one who comes prepared?" Jordan sighed before hiking up her linen dress to reveal a leather strap around her muscled thigh that carried two deadly knives and a thin, rolled-up book.

Ari pinched it in two fingers as she read the title aloud. "*MercersNotes: King Arthur and His Knights.*" She handed it to Lam, unwilling to be holding anything Mercer.

"So far very little lines up," Jordan admitted. "Excalibur, Arthur, and Merlin are here. Gwen *could be* the woman described as Gweneviere. Old Merlin does hate her, and the people believe she's beautiful and 'exotic.'" Ari's eyebrows shot up; it was a miracle Gwen hadn't killed them all.

"What are we supposed to do with this?" Ari asked. "Make the time period match this story exactly?"

"Reality inspires legend, but legend is not history," Merlin said thoughtfully.

"And Mercer's slapdash quality control might bite us in the butt," Lam said, holding up a few blank pages for them to see.

Jordan snatched it back, flipping through. "I've read this a hundred times. There have never been blank pages before."

They all exchanged looks.

"So..." Ari said. "Since we came to the past, we've somehow erased part of the legend?"

Merlin cried out sharply. "What was that chapter about, Jordan?"

Jordan thumbed through it several times, and the quiet in the barn felt a bit stark. Finally, she looked up. "Lancelot. This was the chapter about Sir Lancelot. He was probably one of the knights Ari slayed so mightily this afternoon." Ari didn't have time to enjoy the first compliment she'd ever received from Jordan.

"Is this Lancelot important?" Lam asked, wincing as if they already knew the answer.

Merlin and Ari eyed each other wearily.

&

Ari was summoned to the king's court the next morning by a nervous messenger who had definitely expected to find the blue knight dead.

Merlin helped her into her armor with clumsy fingers while yammering about the future consequences of a missing Lancelot. "Arthur won't be the same. Lancelot was his greatest friend, his guiding force, his *best* knight."

"Yeah, I remember." Ari's thoughts stung with images of her brother, whose scowling loyalty had won him the role of Kay in her own futuristic version of the cycle.

"And you do know that the story of Lancelot and Gweneviere, while tragic and mildly awful, was the first tale of love in the Western canon to treat women as more than baby makers. Did you know that T. H. White, my favorite of the Arthurian chroniclers, even proposed that Lancelot was bisexual? To say that he was ahead of his time was—"

"Merlin. I need you to focus." She pointed to the spot where he'd completely botched the ties of her chest plate to her back plate. He retied them while she examined him. "Are you sure you're from this time period? You don't know how to tie armor and you can't remember—"

He surprised her with a bout of juvenile anger, kicking at the straw. "I *know* I can't remember. There's a great black hole in my head where most of this time period should be. Perhaps it's because I'm here twice over and that's completely unnatural!"

"Hey." She put a hand on his shoulder. "I'm sorry. We're all trying to figure out how this works." She decided not to add, *And it's obvious that your backward aging is in overdrive.* Ari was sure he'd noticed. Merlin handed over her sword, and she shoved it in the sheath at her belt, missing Excalibur for the millionth time. "You're worried about Val."

"So? You're equally worried about Gwen. You called her name in your sleep enough times to wake up all of Camelot!"

"Ah, you heard that?" Ari's body flushed so hard it felt like her armor was in the sun. That was no innocent dream she'd been enjoying. "We'll find Val, Merlin."

He ignored her. "Let's discuss your cover story. You're from southern France. Oh, but it won't be called that. Franks Land, maybe? You came to Camelot for the wedding, to honor the new king, but you have to go home right away. You don't believe in silly things like equality and gender freedom. You're the manliest man who ever existed."

"Of course. No codpiece can contain me."

"Your name is Sir Ironfist," he snapped. Ari snorted. Merlin's lips puckered. "Well, you try coming up with something formidable and not ridiculous. Go on."

Lamarack stepped into the stall, winking at her. They were such a sight for sore eyes after so long by herself; they'd always been her rock. "Summoned to court. This'll be entertaining."

"Sure," Ari mumbled, trying not to think about facing the person who'd turned into a damn bird and flown away, leaving Gwen in the middle of that battle to take the heat meant for him. Arthur wasn't starting out very high in her opinion. Merlin tried to give Ari one more pep talk, but she cut him off with a hug. "It'll be okay, old man."

Merlin smiled a bit at Ari's nickname for him. But it faded, fast. "I believe, here at least, I am the *young* man."

Ari donned her helmet and left the stables, heading through the main doors of the keep. The guards didn't stop her—like all things in this time, appearances meant everything. In her fine armor, she was treated like a prince. As long as no one figured out she wasn't packing man pieces, they'd act as if she had the divine right to look down on everyone. So much of this culture made her wretchedly sick. She could only imagine how Gwen was doing with it.

Gwen. Every step brought Ari closer. It sent heat through her veins, reviving the dream that had woken her up to find her legs swimming and her breath tight...

Ari found herself in the throne room without knowing how she got there. The ceiling was stories high, unusual for this era, with vaulted stone, thick beams, and dyed glass in the windows. The place hummed with finely dressed nobles. Out of habit, Ari searched for any threats, tracking the pack of knights behind the empty wooden throne. She'd only met one of them when she arrived, an old knight with creaky joints called Galahad.

Ari stepped down a fur runner, gathering attention as the room quieted, all eyes on her.

And that's when she spotted Gwen, safe in a circle of ornately dressed women, head craned to see over their protective ring. Ari wondered if Gwen could feel her taking in every single curve of Gwen's neck, cheek, lips from beneath her helmet. When Gwen blushed, Ari felt certain her lady could. Ari stopped at the center of the room, unsure of where to direct herself since the throne was empty. Arthur slid out from the crowd of nobles, as skinny and small as Merlin was these days. He grinned at the sight of Ari, which was not what she expected at all.

What the...

Arthur was little more than a child.

"You're alive!" he cried. "I thought for certain Sir Kay's blow would have finished you."

Ari genuflected. Once on her knee, head bowed, the young king lifted her arm, inspecting the spot where the rounded dagger had punched a hole in the circlets of her chainmail. Ari nudged him off, feigning pain. In truth, Mercer's pill had knitted everything back together so well she only felt tightness this morning. "Your *Sir Kay* should work on his aim. His blow did not meet its mark."

"A good thing. He was wrong to attack a defender of my kingdom." Arthur glanced at the knights with a hard scowl, and Ari watched the one called Sir Kay turn his back pointedly. Arthur beckoned her to rise and walked to his throne. He hopped onto the large seat and leaned forward, elbows resting on his knees. "Would you remove your helmet, good knight?"

Ari did as she was told, tucking it under her arm. She managed to refrain from looking back at Gwen, but only just. Ari couldn't seem to find words. Why in the hell was Arthur *so young*? Had they completely botched the time jump? By the looks of him, his eighteenth birthday—and the moment the chalice was set to appear—was solid years away.

"I surprise you," Arthur said, ruddy-cheeked.

"You have no beard," Ari said, unable to suppress a bout of what Kay had loved to call Ari Brand Honesty. "I heard you were older."

Arthur smiled, which was oddly adorable. Slightly gap-toothed and far too earnest. "You and me both, I'd say. Although how I envy your great height, Sir...?"

Shit. She'd forgotten to think of a decent moniker.

Ari gave Arthur a slight smirk.

"You conceal your name from the king of Camelot?" he asked, more curious than accusing. He stood, holding her gaze even though she was an entire head and shoulders taller than him—and most people in this time period. He circled her, and Ari felt his studying eyes everywhere. "You are odd. You speak to a king as if he is your equal. You wear the blue armor of Normandy but your skin is darker than a Northman. More like the southern Franks. You travel without servants, your accent is *very* strange, and your armor is too short at the knees. Quite the ill-made knight...Sir?"

Again, Ari merely smirked. She could not name herself Ironfist; that was a lie too far.

Gwen came forward, pushing through the ladies. She stood at Arthur's side, taking his elbow in a way that made him sort of...shiver...and Ari pound all over with jealousy. "King Arthur has asked you here, good knight, to thank you for your services in yesterday's battle. I believe you saved my life."

Arthur smiled at Gwen and then returned his scrutinizing glare to Ari. "Yes, I owe you a debt and would like to invite you to assemble a team to fight in my melee in three days' time. Alas, if you will not share your name, I must imagine you to be suspicious."

A word slid forward in Ari's mind as if pushed across a polished table by a steady hand. This was Arthur. Not the child king in front of her but the bonded presence she'd begun to doubt since crash-landing in the past.

The proffered word crystallized. Not a word; a name.

"Lancelot," Ari said, surprised to find that it left her mouth as lightly as any truth. Gwen's eyes flew wide. "I am Sir Lancelot."

DUNGEONS
&
DRAGONS

"**Stay invisible! Don't engage! Leave the legend *alone*.** Are none of you hearing me?" Merlin yelled the next morning. He'd slept on it, by request of Lam, but was still dizzy with the affront of Ari naming herself Lancelot. He'd called an emergency meeting, pulling them all into an empty tower. Apart from Gwen, who could not be separated from her fleet of handmaidens.

"Careful," Lam warned. "Merlin's going to start ranting about moths."

"*Butterflies,*" Merlin said, mentally arranging a lecture on the introductory physics of time travel.

Ari stopped him with a harshly pointed finger. "You're the one who should explain, Merlin. You said *eighteenth* birthday celebration. *Eighteenth.* That 'king' is a baby! Gwen has been married off to a thirteen-year-old!"

"Arthur always lied about his age," Merlin said, "quite unabashedly. Like most commoners in this time, he doesn't know precisely when he was born, and he was crowned at a tender age. A lot of rush to grow up. To prove that he can be a man."

"He told Gwen he's nearly sixteen," Jordan added unhelpfully.

"He *could* be fifteen," Lam said. "Val would say he's fifteen, but he'd laugh into the back of his hand the whole time."

"Arthur's celebration will happen soon, thus his true age doesn't matter." Jordan's stare sliced off further opinions. "Plus the only important measure of time is that he's young enough not to have figured out that Gwen is pregnant, yet old enough to stare longingly upon her swelling breasts with unbridled appreciation."

Merlin could follow this logic without liking it one bit.

"He doesn't know she's pregnant?" Ari asked, cringing with her eyes nearly closed. "So they haven't...?" Bless her strategic vagueness.

"It's a political match. To make him seem older in the eyes of his people," Lam said, placing their wrist on Ari's shoulder.

"He has his own chambers and sleeps in a pile of hunting dogs," Jordan admitted.

"*Aw,*" Lam said.

"Okay, but," Ari said, "this isn't about Arthur and his adorable dog pile. This is about getting the chalice and getting back to our time without messing up the story. Check that dumb book, Jordan. Are the Lancelot pages still missing?"

Jordan hiked up her skirts and pulled out the Mercers-Notes, paging through. "They've returned."

"See?" Ari asked Merlin. "I fixed it. Time continuum patched."

"For now," he said. "But if we're not meant to be part of this legend, it *will* derail."

Ari crossed her arms, bristling with challenge. "Wouldn't it be helpful if one of us knew exactly what was going to happen because he'd lived through it before?"

"You have to understand," Merlin wheedled. "This era was horrid, and not just for humans in general. I was new to the world, dropped down here with a fully formed intellect, the selfish emotions of a newborn, and no one to learn from. I spent years in a state of savage enchanted survival. And then Arthur came along. This innocent child. This spark of goodness. I believed my sole purpose was to protect him, and if that meant being the dark so he could be the light, well, I did what I believed I must. But since then—"

"You've grown a conscience?" Lam asked.

"I've blocked most of it out," he said, head drooping, the rest of his shameful words hitting the floor. "All the pain. The missteps, the cruelty...I banished it from my mind."

Merlin looked up to find that Ari had stopped listening. He waggled his fingers and cast a few sparks to get her attention back. Gods, his immature impulses were growing stronger as he aged down.

Ari didn't notice. She was staring out an arrow slit. Was more danger approaching the castle, about to scale the walls? Merlin followed her line of sight and found Gwen in the court-yard below, wearing a purple silk dress ringed in fur, Arthur following in her wake.

"I haven't seen Gwen since we left the future," Ari said, her voice somehow both breathy and tight. "I need to talk to her."

"Absolutely not!" Merlin yelped.

"We know what it looks like when you two *talk*," Lam said.

"The kingdom will erupt with adultery fever," Jordan confirmed. "In one version of these Camelot stories, Gweneviere was beheaded for her interest in Lancelot."

"I'll be discreet."

Merlin tried not to laugh. He tried very hard.

"Fine," Ari said. "I'll find a way to be near Gwen that doesn't look suspicious. Maybe I should get close to Arthur. Lancelot's supposed to be his best friend, right? His favored knight?"

"True..." Merlin said. The dark shadow of a memory rose, but he couldn't quite see what cast it. Merlin hadn't trusted Gweneviere or Lancelot when they first arrived in Camelot. He'd suspected them of some kind of scheme against Arthur. And then...a shiver raged through him. He pulled his robes tight, as if they could defend him against what came next.

"I think I remember something," he whispered.

"Good," Lam said, thumping his back like Merlin were a gassy infant instead of a rapidly de-aging mage.

"What is it, Merlin?" Ari asked.

"Right after Lancelot and Gweneviere arrived in Camelot... I tried to have them assassinated."

A great beast roared past the window.

"By dragon."

The dragon spun around the tower, parts of it visible in every narrow window at once, from its sleek head to its barbed whip of a tail. It was coming for Ari, hunting for Lancelot, because they were one and the same. Merlin felt sick and relieved at the same time. So, they *weren't* ruining Arthur's story and setting their future irrevocably off course!

"We'll be okay," Lam said, clutching Ari's arm. "You're a natural with dragons."

"Ketchan dragons! Taneens are overgrown desert lizards. That looks like a serious medieval monster."

Merlin jumped in, desperate to be helpful. "Dragons were an endangered species by this time period. Surly, yes. With inner fires that warmed their invertebrate bodies in the harsh northern climes? Certainly. Violent against humans? Hardly ever. If we break the enchantment binding the creature to the hunt, we'll be fine."

"Pretty sure it's not going to wait for that before it attacks," Lam said.

Jordan's skirts flew up, and she started handing out a small arsenal that she'd strapped to herself. At least someone here was in their element.

Lam took a throwing knife to the arrow slits, hunting for weaknesses on the dragon while Merlin spun a quick, coarse plan. "All I have to do is get to my tower and break the enchantment Old Merlin cast before the dragon gets a chance to, you know..."

"Swallow us whole?" Ari provided.

"Oh no, there's an obscene amount of crunching," Merlin said.

"You remember *that* detail, of course."

"Just keep it busy for ten minutes," Merlin said, running for the stairs. "And draw Old Merlin away from the tower!"

"You want us to lure out the guy who's trying to murder us," Ari said, voice flat.

"I would never have killed you outright," Merlin promised. "In fact, I believe I even pretended to fight the dragon so Arthur would think I was *protecting* his bride and his new knight." Merlin winced. His crimes just kept getting worse.

"We have to get to Gwen." Ari drew her not-even-remotely enchanted sword. "It's going to attack her, too." She gave him a dirty look that could never compete with how soiled he felt.

The dragon perched on the side of the castle, talons digging between the stones with a heart-crumbling sound. A second later, its tail made contact with the top of the tower. Stones flew in every direction, the roof now exposed to the sky.

Merlin stared up at the looming, green-black body. It took to the air, hovering. "I know this move," he whispered. "It's about to swoop down and snatch."

Lam and Jordan drew back.

"I can work with that," Ari muttered. When the dragon dropped toward them, claws opening like a vile black flower, Ari leaped onto the dragon's outstretched leg. She climbed the thing like a gangplank, reaching the beast's massive head and straddling its neck.

"Go!" she yelled at Merlin as the dragon reared into the sky, Ari on its back.

The sounds of catastrophe followed Merlin as he flew down the corkscrew of the stairs, watching snippets of the battle through each window as he went, always afraid to see that the story had ended prematurely with Lam pitched from the tower, or the dragon snatching up Gwen, or Ari gushing blood.

Instead Ari got a crude sort of control over the dragon by wrestling with the scale-ridge that crested its head. It pitched wildly as she rode it toward the courtyard, crashing it in a way that skidded the stones up like a bunched rug.

"No wonder Lancelot gets a reputation so quickly," Merlin said on a half-breath.

He bolted across the castle, toward his old tower. Guards and knights were running, a flurry of confusion as they tried to figure out what was attacking this time—and why. He caught a brief and yet heart-chilling glance of his old self headed toward the courtyard.

"Douchebag!" he sang.

At the very back of the castle, by the kitchens and the cold cellars, he found the door of his tower: a hearty concoction of wood, metal latches, and magic. He pushed, banged, hit the thing with a flare of blue sparks. But as he flailed, the truth came back in a slow-developing Polaroid sort of way. He'd infused the oil in the hinge with a spell. There was a magical password, one he changed every fortnight. If someone caught him before he guessed it, Ari would be killed and Merlin would be thrown to the dragon as a palate cleanser before he could say...

"Persnickety!"

He tried the door. It didn't budge.

"I really thought that would work," he said. "Fewmets! Paragon! Ensorcelled! Ovate! Scale-rot! Mange!" When none of his favorite words worked, he dumped out everything in the two-thousand-year-old junk drawer of his mind. One word shone in the midst of the mess, like a coin he'd lost long ago.

"*Kairos.*"

The door pushed itself open.

He tossed himself into a darkness that felt as familiar as an old coat. He lit his fingertips with magic; they shone white like a string of holiday lights as he ran up a treacherous staircase, riddled with switchbacks. He'd designed it long ago to stop people from bothering him before they'd even started.

He reached the steepest bit of the stairs—nearly vertical—and scrambled upward, the word *kairos* fuel to his fires. It meant that all stars had aligned, and now was the time to act. "This is our moment," he'd said, giving that word to Arthur, a birthday gift for a young king to explain why he was fated to lead Camelot out of the Dark Ages. He was the right person, at the right time.

Just like Ari was in her age.

Now she was stuck here, about to be crisped like a marshmallow set too close to the fire. And it was *his* fault. Arthur might have tempted Ari back to this time with visions of the chalice, but Merlin was the one who had to keep his friends from being killed by his wicked old self. Proving they were part of the original cycle meant one thing: their problems had gotten much bigger than stealing from the Arthurian legend.

Now they had to survive it.

He burst into the room at the top of the tower and ran to the single porthole of a window to check on Ari. She was still fighting, her arms starting to wilt with the effort of striking endless blows. The dragon had left scorch lines in the ground, great black gouts. A crowd had gathered, but Merlin couldn't tell if they were cheering on Ari or the dragon.

He turned back to his tower. Spell ingredients covered every inch of the room and were stacked upon each other. Back in the olden days, he'd hoarded as much magic as he could, testing how it worked and if he could use it. This wasn't the cozy home of an eccentric old man. It was an arsenal.

Merlin tossed aside books and stones, mortars and pestles, a set of magic-binding manacles that made him shiver. No sign of dragon-based enchantments. Outside, the cheers flared— which meant someone had gotten wounded. Judging by the size of the cheer, it wasn't mortal. He kept looking, pitching around enchanted jewelry and ogham stones.

Another cheer. More bloodthirsty, this time.

He ran to the window. Ari was on her knees, head bowed, as the dragon lorded over her. Its open jaws revealed rows of teeth. A few knights had rushed to Ari's side, but the dragon ignored them as they hacked uselessly at its ankles. The beast was on a mission.

Arthur dithered, his hand at Excalibur's hilt. "Pull the sword, you fool!" Merlin shouted. Of course, Old Merlin was right at the king's side, whispering poisoned nothings in his ear; he couldn't have Arthur dying because of his own plan to remove Gweneviere and Lancelot. Merlin's brain trembled. How could he be both trying to kill Gwen and Ari, and trying to save them at the same time? Was he the true bad guy of Camelot? The hidden good guy? The about-to-split-apart-from-time-paradox guy?

A figure burst through the crowd from the castle. Jordan pelted into the courtyard, red-faced from running all the way down from the tower, her sword brandished, hacking at the dragon with an unrestrained fury—every unspent iota of rage she must have built up over months as a handmaiden came out now, her sword hitting the scales so hard the metal *sparked*. The dragon finally swiped at her with a lazy talon, but Jordan ducked, stabbing the dragon's leg.

It turned to her with sudden interest.

"Jordan, you fool!" Merlin whisper-shouted. She was going to get herself killed, and she didn't even *like* Ari. She pitched her sword and it stuck in the dragon's thigh, lodged in a paper-thin slit in the armor of scales. The dragon roared flame, forcing the crowd back.

Jordan tried to borrow a sword from a nearby knight, and when he wouldn't give it to her, she stole it and knocked him out with a swift roundhouse kick.

"Oh dear," he muttered. Jordan would pay for that one. Merlin hoped the embarrassed knights would wait until the dragon was defeated before tackling Jordan, but they seemed to find her a much more compelling foe. Half a dozen of them wrestled her to the ground and grabbed the sword, while Ari baited the dragon farther from the crowd.

Merlin hummed, raining sparks from the window, hitting Ari's sword with a bit of magic that would make it easier to wield. Quicker, smarter, able to find the chinks in the dragon's armor. Ari had a soft spot for a good enchanted sword. The blade glowed with a rainbow sheen for a moment, and Ari looked up to the tower. He awaited her signature smile, but she only gave him a heavy nod and got on with the fight.

Old Merlin looked up, too, as if he'd felt the first ominous drops of rain.

Had he seen the sparks of Merlin's magic? Had he noticed the change in the sword? Merlin had to hurry, returning to his ransacking.

"Damn dragons!" he whispered fiercely.

"Dragons!" came a screeching echo.

He looked around and saw a dark cloth rustling. He rushed

to the end of a large table and whipped away the scrap of dusty old tapestry, revealing a large brown owl.

"Archimedes!" The bird looked far meaner than he remembered, with a harshly hooked beak and an uninviting gleam in his eyes. Even so, Merlin was delighted to find his old friend. "Do you know where the enchantment is to control the dragon?"

"Dragon!"

"Can you do nothing but repeat me?" he asked. "Gods, were you just a glorified parrot?"

Archimedes squinted and motioned his hooked beak across the room at a dusty little cupboard. Merlin rushed over and flung the thing open. Inside was an animated scene. It looked, for all the universe, like a child's primary school diorama, though it was a complicated bit of magic with several pieces in motion. Stick figures represented Lancelot and Gweneviere, one adorned with a scrap of Gwen's handkerchief and the other with a lock of Ari's short, dark hair.

"When did he even have a chance to cut that off?" Merlin asked with a shudder.

The dragon was animated by a single scale, still bloody on the underside.

He shuddered harder.

There, looking on, was a tiny wooden falcon. That piece represented Merlin, and seeing it was like being hit with a sledgehammer of déjà vu. He reached in the pocket of his robes. His own wooden merlin figurine from the market on Lionel was still there.

He threw the scene to the ground, raised his foot and tried

to stomp the enchantment apart, but only ended up yowling in pain. This called for magic. He summoned everything he could and sang an old battle song. When he flung his hands apart, the diorama split, stick figures blasting to pieces and the dragon scale shattering. Only the little wooden bird remained unharmed, tottering in the wake of the tiny explosion.

He hadn't the heart to destroy it. When his life started in the crystal cave, it was the only thing he'd had to his name. The only piece left of whoever gave him up.

He doubled over, exhausted. "Too much magic," he muttered, stumbling to the window just in time to see the dragon lift heavily on its wings, dripping blood in several places, and fly off toward the hills in the distance. Arthur grinned and lifted Ari's arm in triumph as the crowd went mad. *So much for Old Merlin's plan to rid Camelot of Arthur's favorite new knight,* he thought smugly. If anything, this had cemented Lancelot's place at Arthur's side.

Ari looked more destroyed than triumphant. She was on her feet, though, and that would have to be enough for now. Some days were for saving the universe. Some days, still breathing was all one could hope for.

"Merlin!" the bird cried. "Merlin!"

"Archimedes, do you recognize me?" He flushed with delight. It couldn't hurt if a bird knew his true identity, could it?

Archimedes screeched and extended a talon toward the stairs. Hollow footsteps sounded, and then dark-blue robes appeared, stitched with stars and moons.

"Oh," he squeaked. "*That* Merlin."

After all this time, he was facing himself. Pale skin riddled with wrinkles and liver spots. Deep, intent frown lines. Bright brown eyes. And over them, epically bushy eyebrows, over-grown and gray, which now thanks to Val had been tamed into two robust lines that had *infinite character*. Merlin knew that face from the inside—seeing it from this angle gave him a case of existential vertigo.

Did Old Merlin feel it, too? A deep sense of recognition? The old mage moved his jaw back and forth, as if chewing on week-old bread. Every moment spent waiting was a stone, weighing on Merlin's nerves. "Please say something," he found himself blurting.

"How did you get in my tower, you little carbuncle?" Old Merlin asked.

"Someone must have left the door ajar in all the dragon fuss," he said, suddenly very happy that he wasn't Ari and that lies *did,* in fact, become him. But his old self didn't seem con-vinced. He took in the destroyed diorama, the look in his eyes a shade darker than curiosity.

A hum started so low that by the time Merlin heard it, sparks were already headed toward his face.

So, *this* was what it felt like to be knocked out by his own magic.

&

When he woke, a rope was thrust into his hands, and he was lowered through a hole in the ground. He looked up, but his evil old doppelmage was nowhere to be seen—only the reced-ing face of a castle guard. Merlin hollered, but it was no use. He was in the bowels of the castle. No one would hear him.

The narrow circle of dirt opened up slightly, and he hit

solid ground. The rope was tugged back up, leaving him in a small, smothering pit that made a dungeon seem like a four-star hotel. "Oubliette!" he cried, remembering the word the French had given it much later in history. "My gods, you've put me in an oubliette."

"Hello, mage," came a voice near his elbow.

He scrambled and lit his fingers with magic, revealing several things he wished he hadn't. Sewage ran freely along one wall. Human bones were half-embedded in the dirt floor. Jordan was in her undergarments.

"You're alive!" he cried. "Well, that's something. I saw what you did in the courtyard. It was brave. And ridiculous. But mainly, brave."

The compliment only seemed to intensify her anger. "When I learned Earth history on Lionel, I heard not one mention of real dragons. Such creatures were treated as storybook villains. How did I face one today?"

"Oh, I've got this," he said, happy to have something to focus on besides the death-hole they'd been pushed into. "It's hard to see the truth of history beyond what we're taught. Whatever is passed down, we remember. When we first landed here, I had to remind myself that many existences—people and dragons and more—were revised right out of history by later scholars with rotten agendas." She looked intensely horrified, and Merlin's chest tightened in agreement. "People have used many hateful weapons over time. Forced forgetting is a powerful one."

The meaning of the word *oubliette* rose in his head, unbidden. "From *oublier*," he muttered. "To forget." This wasn't a place of punishment; it was a means of erasing enemies from existence.

"I devoted my life to a planet that sought to re-create this era," Jordan said. "Yet the codes of honor I live by are *not* honored here. If they were, no one would have pulled me from battle. Who stops a knight from slaying a monster?"

Merlin tried to shake off the sticky feeling that, today, *he* had been the story's true monster. "These unevolved grubs see a woman with a sword as an equal threat."

"Gwen assures me Arthur is different," she said. "That he sees strength in unexpected places. Yet he let his men throw me down here."

"A lot happened during the fight," Merlin said, springing to Arthur's defense even after all this time. "He'll let you out, I'm sure of it."

Jordan nodded stoically. "Mayhaps Arthur is the spark of hope that became Lionel."

"Mayhaps." He found himself back at the strange circular notion of this story. His friends featured at both the beginning and the end. They were all caught up in it—or trapped in it. With Gweneviere and Lancelot's roles confirmed, it didn't seem like a stretch to hope that Lamarack and Percival would take their original places in the story, as knights of the round table. Merlin's heart jolted at the thought that Val would be in Camelot soon—the story *required* it.

A fresh wave of sewage sloshed into the oubliette and Jordan drew back. "Will you use your magic to free us?"

"Oh, no. This is a test," he said. "My old self wants to know if I have power. He stuck me down here to see if I would escape. Which is exactly why I can't."

"You're stuck in a battle of wills with your previous self?" Jordan clucked her tongue. "The odds are not with you, mage."

"I'm just as magical as he is!"

"And less ruthless. The old man would put a child down here."

Merlin's brow furrowed, magnifying his headache—until he realized she was talking about him. "In that irrefutably harsh way that you have...can you tell me how old I look?"

She squinted. "Like you can barely mount a full-grown mare."

"Years, please."

"Fourteen?"

That was improbably young, even for his backward aging. Were things speeding up? Why was he tumbling toward infancy *so fast*? He thought of the feeling after he'd crushed the diorama. Every time his magic drained, it left him feeling exhausted. No—not just exhausted. *Aged.*

"It's my magic," Merlin muttered. "Every time I use it, I get younger."

"You only noticed this now?" she asked.

"When a person is very old, there isn't much difference between six hundred and four hundred." His voice no longer cracked over the spines of his words. It was higher, sweeter. "Between sixteen and fourteen? The alterations are...stark."

"*Oh, dear.*"

Jordan's hand went to her waist in an automatic motion—to draw the sword that she would never be allowed to carry in Camelot. "Is there anyone else in here?" Merlin asked, spinning around.

"No," she said. "I looked."

"*Merlin.*"

He knew that even-handed tone, that lovely silvery laugh.

"Nin," he said. "How are you in the castle?"

The Lady of the Lake wasn't able to leave her cave. Her bound nature had always been a comfort to Merlin.

"*My waters give me a way in,*" Nin said, the puddles at his feet rippling. "*My lake becomes the mist, clouds, and rain of Camelot. I can be where I wish, and I wish to be present for this moment. You have finally discovered that your magic is tied to your aging. Now you'll have to stop using it to help those companions you refused to leave...otherwise you'll leave them permanently.*" Nin's laughter burst with bubbles.

"I wish *you* would leave me permanently." He couldn't believe that Nin was still bothering him after all this time. He'd thought he was done with her until she grabbed him out of Ari's big standoff with Mercer, offering him one of her rigged bargains.

"*Are you sure you want me gone? I thought you might like to say hello to Percival.*"

"Val?" He fought the urge to dive headfirst into the filthy puddle. "Val is with you?"

"*Don't fret, little Merlin,*" she said. "*He's perfectly safe in my cave.*"

Val's static, distant voice called out Merlin's name through the water.

He started to shout, but Nin said, "*There, you see? All is well in Camelot.*"

And with that, the water fell still, and the Lady of the Lake was gone. Merlin felt slightly better, knowing where Val was. Having proof that he hadn't been captured or accidentally dropped down on another continent centuries before air travel.

But hearing Val's voice had kindled the need to see him again. And Nin's meddling left a bad taste in his mouth—worse than the seamy, sodden air of the oubliette.

"How do we get out of this time period without your magic, Merlin?" Jordan asked. It was, miraculously, the first time she'd ever called him anything but *mage*.

"Who said anything about not using my magic?"

"The witch in the puddle," she answered, literal to the bitter end.

He couldn't bring his friends all the way back to this time period and then leave them to fend for themselves. Magic was his only power. Without it, Merlin was nothing but fourteen going on thirteen. "I won't abandon you all to Arthur's story and hope for the best," he said, "even if each spark brings me closer to infancy." And after that? *Death by young age,* to quote Ari, once upon a time in the future.

"Ari and Gwen won't agree to this," Jordan said. "They care for you." She didn't add anything about herself—either caring or being cared for. He wondered how often she'd been left outside of their tight-knit group. But that was what she had chosen: the life of a stalwart champion, a distant hero.

And Merlin was a mage, to his bitter end.

"We simply won't tell them, will we?"

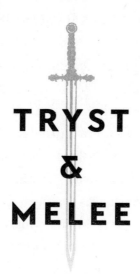

TRYST & MELEE

Ari's schemes to get Gwen alone failed, but then, Gwen had always been the true schemer in the relationship. While passing through a dark antechamber, leaving the rambunctiously feasting knights and nobles in the great hall, Ari felt a sharp tug on her armor and found herself behind a tapestry. Gwen was a sudden miracle in her arms, pulling Ari down by the chest plate, stealing a kiss so heated it left Ari spinning and steaming.

"Um, hey there."

"Three months and you say *hey there?*"

"Words aren't a high priority at the moment, to be honest."

Gwen smiled, and Ari kissed her again until the mess of Camelot faded. In her mind, Ari was kissing Gwen against a backdrop of crystal stars and vibrant galaxies. During a time when two girls in love meant two girls in love. Dragons and misogyny could fuck right off.

They parted slowly, faces pressed together. Gwen shivered. "Your armor is freezing."

"Sorry." Ari's hand cradled the back of Gwen's feverishly hot neck. "Are you sick?"

"I'm always too hot, but that could be pregnancy or the hundreds of yards of cloth I'm stuffed into," Gwen said, breath tight. "Your fingers are so cold. Feels wonderful." Ari ran her hands over every inch of Gwen's available skin. By the muted light of a distant lantern, Ari watched Gwen's eyes close, her mouth slipping open. Ari's hands paused on the warm, hard stone of Gwen's stomach. "Weird, I know," Gwen said. "But it actually makes me super horny."

"How is that different?"

Gwen smiled wickedly and pushed Ari with her body. Ari's armor crashed against the stone wall behind the tapestry. They froze. Ari's pulse pounded as they held their breath and listened, mutually grasping how much they gambled for this stolen moment.

"Jordan told me you were cast out of the portal far away," Gwen said, touching Ari's face with soft, sweet fingers. "That it took you months to get here."

"Yes," Ari whispered. "This one was the worst."

"Worst?"

"This latest chapter of being too far from you." She slid her hands around Gwen's hips, bringing her close, a few inches needing to suffice for the planet of longing in her chest. "The first time, when we were fourteen, when—"

"You kissed me so long behind the stables I actually forgot to breathe and nearly passed out? And you smiled like you hadn't ever been so proud of your own lips?"

"I mean, it's understandable," Ari frowned playfully. "I legit took your breath away."

Gwen pressed a finger to Ari's mouth. "But then *you* left, so mad at me."

Ari took Gwen's hand and turned it over, pressing small kisses down the side of her thumb toward her wrist. "It didn't stick. I crashed on your planet and accidentally married you."

"No accident. I don't have those kinds of accidents."

"Then we were pulled apart again."

"Don't skip over the places when we got together." Gwen pressed in tightly. "I don't."

She pulled out something that glimmered like metal in the low light. It took Ari's kissing-addled brain a second to realize that she was looking at a Mercer watch. Gwen turned it on, the glow seeming perilously out of place in this age of torches and tallow candles. She clicked through pictures until she landed on one of Ari and Gwen's clothes in a strewn pile on the floor of *Error*'s cabin. Ari's heart lurched with homesickness.

"You brought a Mercer watch all the way here just to look at these? Merlin will be hopping mad if he finds out. Gwen, he might actually hop."

"I needed a piece of our history. *Our* past," Gwen said. "I look at these when I miss you too much. They can be... inspiring."

Ari's eyes closed, head tilted back to make a simpering, albeit pleased, sound.

"We only have moments." Gwen's tone turned serious. "You have no idea how hard it was to dispatch my handmaidens to various tasks. They'll find me eventually. Or realize I gave them the slip and tell Arthur."

Ari stroked Gwen's neck with her knuckle. "You sure Arthur doesn't know about the baby?"

"We aren't intimate, if that's what you're digging for."

"Because he's twelve?"

Gwen scowled. "We're courting. The process can take years. What he really needs is someone who understands politics. He's in over his head. Camelot is a powder keg. Old Merlin is a disaster. I'm not sure when the chalice is going to appear, and I only have a month or two before I'm going to have *a lot* of explaining to do."

Ari's hands found the baby again, that hard, impossible place that felt both unreal and everything all at once. "We should get home before the time comes."

"And put the baby in Mercer's crosshairs?" Gwen hissed. Ari hadn't forgotten that the corporation had demanded their child as a price for the rebellion, and the rest of the damn galaxy had acted like that was a perfectly reasonable cost. "Not happening. I'm giving birth here."

"You can't, Gwen. Think of all the ways it could go wrong...even if Camelot doesn't get wind of the wedlock issue. You shouldn't have given me that first aid pill."

"I *had* to!" Gwen started to cry. Ari suddenly felt brittle. Powerless. Ari held Gwen close, apologizing until Gwen seized her feelings, smearing tears from her face with her knuckles. "We'll do what we always do, Ari."

"The impossible?"

Gwen's small smile was another miracle. "I never doubted you'd come back. Not once."

"That's progress for us." Ari kissed her, mentally reorganizing her to-do list. If Gwen needed to have the baby here, Ari would make sure it would happen. "Only two weeks until Arthur's midsummer birthday celebration. Then the enchantresses will come bearing the chalice, I'll steal it, you'll give birth, and we'll all return home to the same night we left. My moms will be waiting to help. We'll hide the baby from Mercer easily. They'll still be expecting you to be newly pregnant."

Gwen didn't say anything, and Ari could tell that she had her own plans. Her own doubts or fears or all three. For once, Ari didn't press her. She gave Gwen space, which ached with distance. "First you have to get Merlin and Jordan out of the dungeons, Ari."

"I have a plan for that, too. You'll see at the melee. Do you think you could convince Arthur to fight on my team?"

"That's a hard no. He's not a fighter."

"But don't you see? That's a problem. Arthur needs help, that much is obvious."

"We should be protecting him, not throwing him in front of swords."

Ari grew aggravated fast, tilting toward one of their infamous rows. "He has to toughen up, Gwen."

"Ari, he's afraid of everyone because people keep trying to assassinate him," Gwen said. "I wish we could tell Arthur the truth, but *we came out of a time portal to steal from you because your ancient, trapped spirit inside my wife told us to* doesn't really roll off the tongue. He might be young and inexperienced, but Arthur wants to be a good ruler in a desperate time, and even if Lionel is light-years away and Mercer repossessed my throne, I haven't forgotten what that feels like."

"So are we working with Arthur or around him, Gwen?"

"With him, as much as possible."

"And you think he can keep up with us?" Ari's voice slid

over those words much like her body longed to slide over Gwen's.

"*Ari,*" Gwen sighed, feeling it, too, pulling her close.

Footsteps echoed, and Gwen ducked from behind the tapestry, poised at the window. Ari peered out as the footsteps grew louder and then—*pop*—Gwen froze. Old Merlin hobbled by, sneering. By the time he'd turned the corner, another *pop* released Gwen from her statuelike state. She glanced around. "Did someone come by?"

Ari slipped out from behind the tapestry. "That old magical bastard! He *froze* you so he wouldn't have to talk to you. What a damn—"

"Don't forget he's our Merlin, too, or he will be someday. It's impossible to see most of the time, and it doesn't excuse anything, but...our Merlin's having a hard enough time with his body changing so rapidly. He doesn't need to suffer a literal split personality."

"You're right." Ari kissed Gwen's fingers. "You're going to be the best mom, lady."

Gwen glowed, stars shining in her brown eyes from the narrow window. "I'm scared. The good kind of scared, I think."

"I'm pretty sure that, at least, is the way it's supposed to be." Ari leaned in for a kiss, not caring that they were no longer behind a tapestry, but Gwen turned away.

"Merlin's right. You shouldn't have named yourself Lancelot. Jordan showed me the pages of her book...how they disappeared and reappeared. This is a dangerous game."

"Lancelot is the knight who loves Gweneviere. Who else could I be, Gwen?" Ari's pulse quickened. "I have to lie about who I am to survive here. My gender. My time. My planet.

Being Lancelot was the only way I could keep up this damn charade without completely losing my—"

"They don't get to be together, Ari! Not in a single one of the stories. Arthur stands between them. Their love is... thwarted. It's a tragedy." Gwen rested her head on Ari's breastplate, but Ari couldn't feel her through the armor. "And this? This is going to *hurt*."

&

Ari's sword clashed with Lamarack's outside the stables. They'd left their side open for Ari's short dagger again. She tapped Lam on their—rather striking—red leather armor with the blade's handle. "Dead. Again. Your kidneys are important, Lam."

"Remember while you've been practicing swordplay every day in this medieval paradise, I've been mucking stables." Lam hunched on a hitching post, lifting the snarling dragon of their helmet to reveal a face stained with sweat and dirt. She missed Lam's makeup and piercings. She missed their near-constant flirtations. It had always been her favorite distraction.

"Wouldn't say it's been a paradise. I killed a kid barely older than Merlin."

Lam studied her, waiting for more. "Is this Hector?"

Ari nodded. "We joined up on the road. He was a runaway. Never stopped singing but he knew all the edible vegetation and how to skin dinner." She let the rest out fast. "He saw my breasts, freaked out, went to report me for impersonating a knight. We fought and I knocked his head against a rock by accident. He died slowly." She left off the part about digging his shallow grave with her bare hands. Ari started cleaning her sword.

"The young here are never young. And the old are dead."

"What?"

Lam wiped their face. "We were still young in our future. In the eyes of the galaxy and government. Not kids, not adults. It's how we slipped through Mercer's fingers." Ari wondered where they were going with this. "Here we're adults. Middle age. Halfway to a quick death."

"Some of us have always been old at heart." Ari thought of Gwen who was queen at sixteen, married at eighteen, pregnant by nineteen. All on purpose. "I've put up with a lot since I arrived on this stupid planet, but if it's turned my lovely Lam morose, I'll never forgive it."

"Not morose. Philosophical. We can only do so much with the time we're given." They motioned to the small kid who trailed Lam like a puppy. He held up a pail of water. Ari shook her head, and he put it down sadly. "And these people aren't given much time at all."

"I won't give them a pass for forcing us into genders that aren't ours. Or thinking my vagina is a demon curse."

"Hell, no." Lam put their wrist on Ari's shoulder. "I wouldn't ask that. But see, there's Roran over there, always watching. He's trans. But he doesn't know that word or that there are so many more like him. Or that one day someone like him won't be stuffed into a dress, made to feel like he's come out all wrong."

Ari examined her sword. Lamarack had never spoken like this before, fear and anger wrestling in their tone despite their soft words. "Does he have family? Friends?"

"He has me," Lam said.

"And how are you doing with the constant misgendering?" Ari shut her eyes tight. "It's breaking me." Her body had been a liability ever since she'd crashed into this time period, needing to be a man to have any semblance of power. The constant fear of being found out was cresting toward body shame, which left her longing for Gwen. To feel her touch. To remember that they were glorious when they were naked together. Two girls burning like stars.

"The misgendering motherfucking sucks." Lamarack touched Ari's chin, bringing her out of her breath-held place of need. "But I *did* get to give Roran hope—which fills me with joy."

Ari had the weird thought that Lam was falling for this place. She threw down a rag that she'd been using, brandishing a newly shiny sword and pressing her mind back to the fight. "After the melee, you'll be knighted. It's in Jordan's book. Both you and Val become Arthur's trusted knights."

"I suppose that's evidence that he'll return soon."

"He will." Ari took her first position again. Lam chose their stance as well. "You don't want to do that. Well, it's a smart decision against me because we're a similar height, but for most opponents, your height is going to win for you. Always use it. Start high. Apparently humans aren't going to evolve above six feet for a few hundred years." They crossed blades, and she unarmed Lam swiftly. They groaned and sat down. "Lancelot needs you in fighting shape."

"And Lamarack needs you to be Ari."

Ari didn't like how close Lam was to the shifting ground of her identity. "I can't wait to be me again, back on *Error,* with a big bag of Kay's favorite chips in one hand and my love in the other." She closed her eyes, knowing what Lam meant even if she didn't want to. "Until then, Merlin is right. Gwen is right. I have to go all in. Make this real. I *am* Lancelot."

"We cannot check our identities until they're desired. That way lies grief and regret."

Ari itched to pick up the sword again, to distract herself with a fight. Fights she could win; discussions about how painful it felt to be stuck in a man's life were losing ground. "For months, I told myself I only had to get here. For Gwen, Merlin, the baby. You." Ari pulled at her short hair, missing her long braid. "Now I'm here and there's so much more to do." She sighed. "Arthur's celebration is in a couple of weeks. The enchantresses will come. Just a few weeks."

"Do you think…can Lancelot leave without changing the future?" they asked. Ari scowled hard. "Ara, this story, this king and his people, I can't fight the feeling that we need to be here, not run home with that chalice at the first chance. We can help them do better."

"But we have a whole future to save, Lam."

"Perhaps the past has something to do with that."

She hung her head. "Please don't. I can only save one world at a time."

"You're Ara Azar." Lam cupped her cheek softly. "You've already come to the aid of whole galaxies. Should be old hat by now. Kay would be damn proud of you."

Ari had been burying thoughts of Kay since his death. There was an unevenness to remembering him, as if her anger had folded into her grief and turned the ground soft, treacherous. "What would Kay do if he were here?"

"Oh, he'd be toasted," Lam said, and Ari barked a surprise

laugh. "Just permanently mead-drunk. And let's be honest, even though he's the preferred gender of this hostile island, he'd fit in the *least* well of all of us. Stomping around with that silver space rat hair, telling stories about grand things like cargo shorts and high fructose corn syrup."

Ari's laugh rolled. When was the last time that'd happened? "That hair was red when we were kids, before the gray. Remember all the firehead jokes at knight camp?"

" 'Course." Lam's best smile was out. The one that lilted to the side and showed off their perfect teeth. "And if Kay knew how serious you'd become, he'd do this."

Lam tackled her, wrestling across the hard-packed ground. Ari kicked her long legs and used the momentum to flip Lam. Unlike her fights with Kay, when she occasionally let him get an upper hand, Lam was her equal in length and strength. They tossed into the side of the stable as one, creating a great, echoing bang. She liked the weight of Lam's body, their smell. She felt a bubble of laughter that left her bold enough to knee them in between the legs but they recovered fast and pinned her.

Silent for a spell, her eyes closed and her muscles melted slightly. "Careful," she muttered. "I haven't been with Gwen, with anyone, since before I got marooned on Ketch."

Lam cursed exquisitely, and Ari laughed. "Yeah, that might be the root of your problem."

Ari kept her eyes closed. "I know. After Kay...we weren't ready. I thought we'd get together once I reached Camelot, but now there's the baby and the Arthur nonsense..." Ari didn't know where they were. Excruciatingly in love. Thwarted by cycles and stories. Either doomed or destined. Or both. "I did leave a trail of disappointed barmaids across the continent."

Lam chuckled, and that's when Jordan managed to kick them both in the ribs at the same time. Lam collapsed on the ground, holding their side while Ari yelled, "Damnit, Jordan!"

"If I had a fire hose, you'd both be blasted over the city walls."

"Good thing you don't, then," Lam said, wincing as they sat up. "How'd you get out?"

"My queen gave the child king an ultimatum. His balls or my freedom."

"*And* Jordan is over King Arthur." Ari got up, dusting her armor. This would work; it had to. "We've got your Lionelian armor in the stable. Suit up. Hide your face and curves."

"We'll need four for a proper melee," Jordan said. "Who is your fourth?"

Ari cleared her throat and motioned behind her. The king approached from the keep, flanked by half a dozen palace guards, arm in arm with Ari's wife.

Jordan nodded in appreciation and left for the stable while Lam tugged their helmet on; it was imperative that neither of them be recognized before the melee. Ari was convinced that if the people saw them fight, *and then* saw Lam was a commoner and Jordan a girl, perhaps they would see how stupid they'd been by believing only noblemen could fight. Perhaps then Ari could come out of her own gender prison.

Arthur wore a look of pure naivety, but at least he was also wearing his fine armor. "Sir Lancelot, my queen believes you can help me. Will you teach me to ride dragons?"

"Your enemies aren't going to stop trying to assassinate you unless you make a show of strength," Ari said.

"And you know the recipe for strength?"

"I do. You're going to fight with us in the melee against Sir Kay's team."

Arthur blanched. "But I've never taken a hit. Not even in practice. Merlin believes that might does not equal right."

"Might equals might." Ari looped her sword, warming up her wrist. "And that's not to be underestimated."

"Oh, gods," Lam muttered from behind her. "Here we go."

Ari winked at Arthur, causing his eyes to widen, and then she swung her sword at his polished, shining silver breastplate with all her strength. In the aftermath, the boy king lay on his back, staring at a sky as blue as his irises. Ari was immediately clobbered by six palace guards.

"I...didn't feel a thing, apart from the blasted force," Arthur murmured dreamily from the ground. "Leave Lancelot be." He waved a hand and the guards moved back.

"That's decent armor." Ari grabbed his gloved hand and pulled him to his feet. "I'm glad it's built for battle and not just looks."

"What if it hadn't been?" Arthur asked, touching the new dent across his sternum.

Ari shrugged. Gwen swore in French. And the training of King Arthur began.

&

On the morning of the melee, the tournament ring sat atop a grassy knoll like a perfectly centered crown. Its red banners bore the crest of Pendragon, waving proudly, dramatically...even though there was little wind on this blue summer morning.

Ari had arrived as early as the vendors, watching the masses file into the stadium, marveling at this view of Camelot. Like the castle, the tournament ring wore architectural glamour. Old Merlin had spared no expense when it came to demonstrating Arthur's grandeur.

Ari warmed up with a long sword in the ring. All the while her thoughts leaped from the chalice to Gwen to her friends and back again. Jordan and Lamarack joined her, both camouflaged in shining armor, identities hidden beneath their helmets. When the three of them were shoulder to shoulder, they looked out over the gathering crowds, to Sir Kay's team amassing on the far side.

"I wish we were jousting," Lam said, rotating their hand-and-a-half sword. They wore the red leather armor Mercer had "gifted" them during Ari's fake coronation. For all Ari's Mercer loathing, she had to admit that Lam looked drop-dead gorgeous in that gear, especially after they'd burned off the Mercer logo on the right breast with a hot iron. "My jousting was always better than my swordplay."

Ari snorted. "Promise me that's a euphemism."

Lam chuckled from inside their helmet.

"They won't invent jousting for a few hundred years," Jordan corrected. "That's later Middle Ages. We're in the early Middle Ages."

"There're different Middle Ages?" Lam asked.

"Hundreds of years, according to Merlin," Ari said. "We're pre–religious overhaul, apparently. Merlin said that was 'a blessing.'"

Lamarack cocked their head. "Wait, what are these ages in the middle of?"

"After people discovered science," Jordan said. "Before people wanted science."

"You're saying we're in a time of self-selected idiocy?" Lam deadpanned.

Ari adjusted her leg armor. "I'm saying we're about to fight a fake battle in a sports arena for a bunch of drunk villagers at ten in the morning. They've got a ways to go as a culture."

"Sounds like Lionel to me," Lam said.

Ari watched the crowds continue to file into the stadium. "There's more people here than the wedding," she noted. "Word is out that Arthur will fight."

"Blood is a greater draw than love." Lam's voice was poignant. "If they figure out you've chosen a handmaiden for your team, they'll riot."

Ari swung her sword to wake up her shoulder. "Lam, come on. You know pissing people off is my specialty. It's how I made Gwen fall for me."

"Speaking of the queen." They motioned with a nod of their head to the spot where the crowds were opening, creating a passage. Arthur's procession wasn't like the other knights'. His route cut straight through the heart of the tournament ring, stealing everyone's attention as he deposited Gwen on a seat overburdened with fluffy bright cushions beneath the shade of a billowing canopy. When he brought the back of her hand to his lips, Ari looked away, examining the bent joints on her gauntlets. She only hoped they'd hold up long enough for one more fight.

"Painful?" Ari expected Lam, but this time it was Jordan, come to stand beside her.

"It's painful to answer that question, Jordan, because of course it's painful."

"Pain is good. It means you're actually trying."

With that, Jordan took position. The teams were assembling and even though Ari had spent the last three days setting this in motion, she suddenly felt the weight of a seriously bad idea. There was too much hate in the air. It rose off of Sir Kay's dark expression like smoke.

From the left-center of the ring, Ari motioned for Arthur, Lamarack, and Jordan to circle in. At right-center, Sir Kay and his band weren't holding one last strategy talk but taking practice swings at the air. Ari beckoned Arthur closer. "I'm matching you up with Galahad. He's got a solid arm but aged joints. Make him bend his knees and he's yours."

"Shouldn't I be matched with Sir Kay?" Arthur countered. "I am the leader here."

"Only in name," Ari said. "He'd spank you in front of your kingdom and enjoy it."

Arthur looked down sourly. This time Ari's honesty might have dug too deep.

"I'll take Sir Kay," Jordan growled beneath her helmet. "He's the fuckwit who threw me in the oubliette."

Ari nodded. "That leaves Lam with Gawain. He's feisty. Lots to prove, although I'm not sure he's as rotten as Suck Kay."

"Sir Kay," Lam corrected.

"Yeah, sure, that's what I said." Ari was about to claim the fourth knight for herself, the unknown quantity in the group who she had a sneaking suspicion was Sir Kay's ringer, but the crowds had gone expectantly quiet. Ari had a flash of a very different time, a very different tournament ring on a planet far away. She felt the breath-held silence before Gwen had kissed her...and then gambled her entire queendom to save Ari from Mercer.

Ari looked at Gwen. The crowd was waiting while Gwen waved a bit of cloth that matched her glorious red dress. A token of her favor. Arthur started toward Gweneviere.

When Jordan gave Ari a hard shove, she snapped, "What? I'm standing right here!"

Jordan pointed. Beside Gwen—eclipsed by Gwen—a girl wearing a shade of pink that felt distinctly un-medieval stood with her own token held out. Ari hustled over and managed a wink at the girl in pink, inspiring a decent blush. Ari stiffly remembered that this was Elaine of Astolat. They'd been introduced during last night's feasting. Elaine retreated under the canopy while Arthur returned to central position, and Ari found herself stuck in Gwen's gravity. Only a few feet apart.

Ari stared straight at the queen for the span of a breath, not caring who saw the intensity in her eyes. Then the trumpets sounded harsh and high, and she jogged into the melee.

Young Arthur was nearly dancing, but Ari noted he was the only one taking this lightly. After all, it was a fake fight with blunted weapons...and real animosity. Jordan's predictable ire was glued to Sir Kay across the divide. Even Lamarack seemed ready to vent a little steam.

"First positions," Jordan said, overly formally.

"Spread out in a line, matched to your opponent," Ari translated.

They did as they were told, each fighter paired and separated by a healthy twenty-foot distance. Ari was on one end, with Lam beside her, then Arthur, and finally Jordan at the far side, facing Sir Kay, who'd started a taunting rhythm by clasping his sword against his shield.

They marched toward their opponents. Closer, closer, and finally, Arthur struck the first blow and the fight began in earnest. Ari knew it would be quick. At knight camp, they'd taught dramatic swordplay as a sort of dance. In reality, it was several strict hits, a bevy of countermoves, followed by a sword to the throat or gut.

Swords crashed and cracked. Armor sang with metal howls. And the crowd rolled about in it like dogs in mud. Ari was unsurprised to find that her unnamed opponent was more than good. He wielded two short swords, using them to fork and throw Ari's blade in the first seconds of the duel. She rolled out of the way, collected her sword, and then sealed herself into a much more aggressive stance. She tangled his blades beneath her arm in two moves, pausing with her pommel about to snap up and into the knight's exposed neck under his jaw.

He stepped away, dropping his swords. Beaten.

Ari turned back to the fight and found Arthur dueling Galahad with glee—and definitely receiving a boost in confidence and ability from Excalibur that Ari had enjoyed back in the future. Lamarack and Gawain were also having a decent fight, and actually, they were evenly matched. It was all rather unorthodox, though, as somehow they'd both lost their swords and had started to wrestle. But Lam was far taller and stronger, and ended up sort of roosting on Gawain in a way that made the crowd laugh.

Which left Jordan and Sir Kay. The ogre of a knight trundled after her, slamming his sword against hers. He was trying to pummel her into submission—very un-knightlike. Jordan was playing with him. Waiting to strike. She let him swing himself around and around, before knocking him silly and taking his sword in one swift move. The crowd roared with pleasure as Jordan raised her sword in victory.

Arthur flung up his visor with a grin on his red-cheeked face. "We've won!"

Ari grasped his forearm and pulled off her helmet, her symbol to Lam and Jordan to do the same—only when they did, the crowd's riotous cheer divided, shook, and broke.

Their anger at the sight of Ari's team made her instantly queasy. Arthur looked from Jordan to Lam and winced as the entire tournament ground toward silence. This was no longer a game, if it ever were to begin with. Ari couldn't imagine what would happen next, but she didn't have to.

In a blast of darkness, the blue sky was covered by vicious storm clouds. Ari looked around, finding strange, robed figures set around the tournament ring, hands raised as they chanted. People fled while thunder and lightning mangled the atmosphere. Arthur curled up despite his armor, making himself small, and Ari put her arm around him.

"What's happening?" she shouted over the storm.

"It's the enchantresses of Avalon!" he said, eyes wide with fear.

PUPPETS
&
POWER

From the bottom of the pit, the storm sounded like a great battle overhead. Thunder shook the oubliette, while the lightning could only be imagined through the dark. And yet, after a few intense moments, the storm was gone. As if by magic.

"That's not quite a good sign," Merlin muttered—a sentiment only magnified when, not long after, Ari stamped down the stairs above, her words dropping into the oubliette along with hard and heavy breaths.

"Merlin!"

"I'm here," he called out, sounding young and scared. He'd stopped using magic to cheer up the oubliette the same time Jordan had been let out, which kept him from growing younger while also deeply gnawing at his mental state.

"Arthur just got spanked by Avalon enchantresses in front of Camelot! They came, they chastised, and then *boom*. They disappeared. Arthur said they do this a lot. That they *hate* him."

"Oh, dear."

"'Oh, dear'? You said they were in favor of the king. You said they were going to bring him a birthday gift. Small cup, infinite power...does that ring any bells?"

"Technically, I said I've been having trouble remembering anything."

"*Merlin.*" Ari's voice fell away, followed by a sigh. "Does he know about Morgana?"

"When I took Arthur in, I was his only family. As he was mine."

"So he doesn't know that his sister loves him. *And* the enchantresses think he's a childish waste of space...how am I going to fix this, Merlin?"

"No clue, I'm afraid."

Again, Ari grew too quiet for his liking. "You okay? You taking care of yourself?"

"Oh yes, pure Bermuda down here," he lied. "You should see my tan."

"I'll try to get you out. Arthur owes me after our win in the melee. Hang on, old man." Ari's footsteps echoed in reverse, growing farther and farther away.

"Pure Bermuda," Merlin whispered into the cold, stinking black.

&

"Camelot is a medieval mess." Merlin waited for a response, but no matter how much he talked to the malodorous puddles of the oubliette, he hadn't gotten a peep from Val, or even Nin. "The fabrics are dyed these very dull shades. Everyone looks like walking bits of moss and stone. But I do know a shop where you can get a fantastic bespoke corset that..."

Footsteps cut off his chatter.

"Still down there, carbuncle?"

Merlin looked up and found a face cast in the cold, blue light of magic. *His* face—snarled by time, ignorance, and suspicion. The rope dropped, and Merlin batted it away like a furious kitten.

"Too proud to accept my help?" Old Merlin's voice rattled in the empty space. "You'd rather stay down there?"

With every sort of trepidation pulsing through him, he grabbed the rope and clung to it. Old Merlin hauled him up with ease. Was Merlin really that small now, or was Old Merlin using magic? Definitely the latter.

Which made Merlin angry at how much magic the old, stupid version of him had thrown around, not knowing it would push him toward becoming a powerless child. Not to mention too young to kiss the boyfriend he'd been waiting literal lifetimes to find.

"What do you want with me?" Merlin shouted. The hapless question wasn't exactly the power move he'd imagined opening with, but it was the best he could do, swinging on the rope as Old Merlin dangled him.

"What do I want?" Old Merlin asked, his voice sweet for one whose heart was basically a rotten crab apple. "The question, boy, is what *you* wanted so desperately that you would break into my tower." He set Merlin down and slapped on the same pair of magic-binding manacles Merlin had feared in the tower.

The old man turned to a dark twist of stairs. "Come."

Merlin tried to keep up. His muscles had grown numb, his pulse fluttering like a moth caught in a jar. When he emerged into the castle proper, even the spindly flames of torchlight were too much for his eyes. He squinted and gasped. Merlin thought his old self might be leading him to the tower. Instead, they stopped in a room with a great fire built in the hearth, a single chair set in front of it.

"Sit," the old man said, humming to summon a stool for Merlin's feet. When he didn't move, the chair scraped toward him, knocking the backs of his knees. Merlin plopped down, the chains at his wrist jangling all the way to the stone floor. He waited for spiders to swarm out of the chair, or the whole thing to burst into flames. It remained stubbornly, suspiciously, a cozy place to sit. Old Merlin hummed a ditty, and a small table arrived at Merlin's elbow, laden with food. The greatest hits of Britannia: a pile of roasted meat, a piece of thick black bread, potatoes charred on the outside and cream-white on the inside. There was even a baked apple, oozing delicious sweetness.

Merlin was prepared for torture, interrogation. He was not prepared for this.

Merlin's thoughts shot wildly toward Val. Had the Lady of the Lake remembered that he was a mortal being who needed food to keep him alive? She wasn't a hot-blooded murderess, but she wasn't exactly known for her hospitality, either. She'd kept Merlin in a bubble inside of her lake for two days while Ari and her friends were thrown into battle with Mercer. The very standoff in which Kay had died. She had said she needed Merlin alive. To what purpose, though?

The siren song of the baked apple drew him back to the

present. Merlin reached for the plate, but Old Merlin's control over his magic was complete. A single whistled note and it flew out of Merlin's reach, like a well-trained dog called to heel.

"What does the knight called Lancelot want in this court?" Old Merlin asked. "I'm told you're his squire."

"His what?!" Merlin said. "Of course I'm not his squire."

He wants to know you're not a threat to Arthur, Merlin reminded himself as his stomach turned on him. That apple smelled like cinnamon-covered paradise. Cinnamon was grown halfway around the world from Camelot. His old self had really pulled out the stops.

"It's true that I arrived with Lancelot. But I'm not in the knight's employ. We were traveling companions. Lancelot...". Merlin thought about Ari, hacking her way into the heart of the kingdom. "Lancelot wants to help this place. He could be Arthur's greatest ally."

Old Merlin cocked his head, moved a bit closer, trying to sniff out a lie. "Did Lancelot send you up to my tower?"

"No," Merlin said, thanking the truth for being so obliging. Merlin had sent himself.

"What were you doing up there, carbuncle?"

"Trying to help my family." Merlin had gone to the tower for Ari, Lam, Jordan, Gwen, the baby—and they were bound together tighter than friendship. They had fought together and fought each other. They had nearly died a dozen times, each experience bonding them like quick-dry glue. And then one of them had actually died, and the grief had been quiet proof that they would not crack apart.

"Your family?" Old Merlin said. "You will have to be more specific, I'm afraid."

The food inched closer.

Merlin searched for anything he could say that would ring true without giving his old self ammunition against Ari and the others. There was one answer waiting, one search that he'd told himself to give up on so many times—and yet it fit into this moment as smoothly as a piece of a puzzle box sliding into place. "I'm... I'm from Camelot, originally. That's why I came here with Lancelot. I wish to find my parents."

The food came within range of his fingertips, and he snatched it up, chains smacking together. The apple was still steaming, the meat glazed and perfectly tender. He guzzled a cup of the thin wine they used to give young folks.

Splendid. He was eating from the children's menu.

Old Merlin didn't yet understand that he was aging backward. He only knew that he was ancient, magical, alone in the universe. Merlin felt a tiny prick of sadness for his old self. It was filled with the most terrifying poison of all: understanding. He knew what Old Merlin felt like, and it left him nauseated. He wasn't this horrible person. *Was he?*

Merlin gulped the last of his wine too quickly and finished with a hacking cough.

"Did you think you'd find your parents in my tower, while a dragon laid siege to the city?" Old Merlin asked. "Your tale is a sock that needs darning. So many holes." The old mage sang stones to the doorways and started to brick them in. The whole thing would have looked whimsical, except it was ultimately a murder attempt. Merlin's hands flew up, his defensive sparks held back by the manacles. Which was for the best, only it felt beyond awful.

"I... I know you have magic in the tower, and I've been told that my parents are powerful. Magical, most likely," Merlin said. Nin had said that once. His parents were powerful. "Do you have a way of locating people like that?"

Merlin's sense of possibility sat up from a dead sleep. This had started out as a way of throwing Old Merlin off the scent of his friends, but what if his old self actually did have what Merlin needed to find his parents?

Maybe this *was* a puzzle box, and only both Merlins together had all the pieces.

"Perhaps," Old Merlin said, stroking his glorious beard. Gods, he could be pretentious. "But I am far too busy with this kingdom to help a scrap of a boy find his parents."

"What if you didn't know *your* parents? Wouldn't you try anything to find them?"

He hit the nerve as squarely as intended. Old Merlin paused the stones in midair. "If your parents are magical, and you are drawn to the enchanted arts...have you ever used magic?"

The fire in front of Merlin crackled. The chair pushed forward until he was so close that he felt slightly roasted. Any answer Merlin gave would seal his doom as surely as Old Merlin was sealing up the doors with the scrape of mortar. If he said yes—he was the most powerful mage in all of history—his old self would pitch him headfirst off the cliffs at Tintagel. If he said no, Old Merlin would know he was lying.

Have I ever used magic?

An answer took the long road to Merlin's lips. He thought of all the ways he'd failed his Arthurs. How his new limitations meant he was leaving Ari and her knights to fend for themselves in this ruthless world.

"Not very well," he said.

Old Merlin liked that answer. He guzzled it the way Merlin had done with the wine.

"Perhaps you can be taught a thing or two, carbuncle. I could use an apprentice." Old Merlin folded his hands over his robes, a sign that he was set in his decision. "If you train well enough, perhaps you will gain the skills to find this errant family of yours."

This was *definitely* not part of the story. Merlin didn't remember having a pupil studying at his knee in Camelot. Some things had gotten lost in the haze of time—but this? He would remember a scruffy would-be mage. Had he just tampered with the cycle? Thrown it off entirely?

"I think I'm going to..." *Have an aneurysm. Throw Camelot's first pity party. Give up altogether.* "...find Lancelot and tell him the good news," Merlin blurted, shooting up from his chair and nearly landing in the fireplace. "Thank you."

Old Merlin nodded. "From now on, you will do nothing, go nowhere, without my say."

Gods, what had he just agreed to? The stone in the doorways tumbled down, leaving rubble that Merlin could easily clear. The manacles unlocked and dropped to the floor. He ran, leaping, as that sweet, cidery old voice chased him out. "You'll most likely die, and I won't be held responsible for your idiocy."

"Of course not," Merlin said.

He was the only magician in all the ages stupid enough to get apprenticed to himself.

&

After two days of constant, non-magical chores—removing dust from books, rust from enchanted weapons, and owl droppings from everything—Merlin was finally allowed out of the confines of the tower for long enough to meet with his friends. He walked past the market in the hale, hearty sunshine, stopping to watch a puppet show in the square. One that featured everyone's new favorite knight, Lancelot.

"Can we talk somewhere less public?" Lam asked as they approached Merlin.

"Public meetings are less suspicious. Trust me, it's something I've picked up over a few millennia," he said. "Let's just hope the rest of them can make it."

"One of them is already here," came a crisp voice from behind.

Merlin turned to find Gwen, looking so different he hadn't noticed her in the throng. She wore a headpiece of twisted rags with a half-veil, and she'd shucked her queen's garb and replaced it with a simple white linen dress that did nothing to hide her bun in the oven. In fact, it looked like she was cooking an entire batch of tiny Gwen-and-Kays.

"You look different!" Merlin cried awkwardly.

"So do you." Gwen angled her head, bunching her plum-colored lips. For a moment Merlin felt certain that she knew his magic and aging were knotted up together. She'd always been terrifyingly perceptive. "Your glasses, Merlin!" she burst out. "They're gone. Too anachronistic?"

He'd lost them in the oubliette, actually. But it got worse. When Old Merlin had brought him up from the dark, he'd realized he didn't need them anymore. His eyesight had greatly improved with this last leap into youth. "Yes, that's right," he said, eager to turn attention away from him. "And you...that dress!"

"It's good to see the littlest knight on proud display," Lam said.

"I had to borrow a handmaiden's dress. Your note said to be low profile. This one is helping me fly under the radar. We're very sneaky, aren't we?" she asked the bump. Somehow that little question made the baby real to Merlin in a way that they never had been before. There was a soon-to-be-*person* in there.

The crowd roared a laugh, and Gwen squinted at the stage. "This again? They need a bigger repertoire." Puppet Lancelot was dancing, his sword positioned at the front of his pants and bouncing to the beat. It was *a lot* of enthusiastic sword-wagging.

"That joke really is as old as time," Lam said, just as Ari swaggered into the square. People's eyes didn't know where to stick—the Lancelot in the show, or the real one, shining and bold as she clanked her way toward her friends. Ari's bluntly hacked hair and sharp features complemented the intense look on her face. When she reached them, she threw an arm around Lam's shoulder and did a full-on double take at the sight of Gwen.

"Would you please take whatever you are doing down forty-two notches?" Merlin asked. "If I'm seen about town colluding with the lot of you, Old Merlin will find out."

Ari narrowed her eyes on him. "You're the one who wanted to meet here."

"He has spies all over the castle! Believe me, I'm supposed to be one of them," Merlin said, sounding peevish even to his own ears. "I got him to send me out to run errands. It's easy to trick someone if you share a number of neural pathways." Merlin pulled out a list, freshly inked. "I'm supposed to procure these...twenty-seven items before I return to the castle."

"He's got you buying magical groceries?" Lam asked. "Merlin. You made yourself into your own bitch."

Merlin hung his head. "Harsh, yet fair."

"Oh, thank gods, Jordan's here," Gwen said. "I haven't seen her since the melee."

"Does she think she's still *in* the melee?" Merlin asked as Jordan strode toward them, in full armor. A few of the women and children's faces glowed like she was an avenging angel, but judging by most of the ugly stares, a majority of Camelot had not made peace with the idea of a lady knight. "You're all amazing at not making waves, did you know?"

"This coming from a mage who wore two-thousand-year-old robes into space," Gwen said with judiciously pursed lips.

He gathered them farther from the crowd, reaching into his bag of magical ideas for an old trick. One minute they were all laughing with the show, the next they were gone, hidden behind a veil of invisibility. Merlin glanced at his body, relieved not to feel tangibly younger. "Now that we're all well met, let's not dally. Jordan, has my apprenticeship changed anything in the Arthurian legend?"

Jordan removed the MercersNotes from a small leather pouch and shook her head.

Ari squinted at the book. "Out of curiosity, Jordan, what's the last page about?"

"The greatest mystery of the legend. Arthur's final resting place."

Ari looked at Merlin. "Do you know where Arthur's buried?"

"No one does," Merlin said. "He's alive and well right now, so that's well beyond our scope." He clapped briskly, relieved to dismiss one more would-be problem. "Now. What's happened in my absence?"

"Here's an update," Ari tossed out. "Arthur and I are going to Avalon. We leave in an hour. Alone. No guards." Her eyes trailed to Gwen's and stayed there.

"You're...*what*?" Merlin fairly exploded.

"I've convinced Arthur to ask for peace between Avalon and Camelot. To invite them to his birthday." Ari winked awkwardly. When no one responded, she added, "We can't just sit around and wait! We need to make the story happen. The pages in that book could go blank at any moment."

"You wish to keep Arthur away from Gwen," Jordan said.

Ari clapped her shoulder. "It's a win-win!"

"Actually, space sounds great," Gwen said, with a pointed sigh. "Arthur...wants to make out with me." No one looked terribly surprised. King Arthur falling ass over crown for Gweneviere was *definitely* canon. "I'd say he wants to have sex, but I'm not sure he knows how sex works."

"Because he's eleven?" Ari asked.

"Every time you say his age, he gets younger," Lam pointed out.

"Which is offensive to those of us who actually age backward!" Merlin cried.

Gwen's face went through new contortions as she spoke. "Arthur has been focused on his kingdom for so long, but I think the melee made him feel more...excited...than he's ever been before."

"Yikes," Lam said.

"Wait, the melee made him horny?" Ari nearly shouted.

Jordan did a full-body swivel toward the stage, giving them her back, acting as if the puppets had become suddenly fascinating. At least they were fighting now and not wagging swords.

Gwen focused on Merlin, because of course she didn't want to talk to Ari about her "husband." "I keep thinking Arthur is as young as Ari says, and then he gets this look in his eye..."

"Like there's suddenly Prince playing in the background?" Merlin asked.

Gwen stared at him blankly. "The prince of what?"

A long lecture on the Artist Formerly Known as Prince formed in Merlin's mind, but he dismissed it. There would be plenty of time for *Purple Rain* when they got back to the future. Right now, they needed to stay focused.

"I'm sorry you have to deal with this, lady." Ari's hands slipped across Gwen's shoulders, threading her dark hair and doing something to the back of Gwen's neck that made Gwen close her eyes, her mouth tipping open as if by instinct.

"Stop it, you two! At *once*."

Ari and Gwen weren't listening. Lam looked delighted, while Jordan seemed ready to bolt and reveal Merlin's invisibility spell.

"Eyes on me!" Merlin said, feeling like the coach of an unruly sports team. "Ari, if you're headed to Avalon, you might as well kill two birds with one quest. We need the help of an enchantress. We can't involve Morgana, since that would affect the future. We must find someone willing to sacrifice some magic, so we can form the portal to take us back."

"'Course," she said. Which felt a little too easy, *and* she was staring at Gwen again.

"What did I say, Ari?" Merlin asked querulously.

"Enchantress. Not Morgana. Some magic."

A troubled look fell over Lam. They fiddled with the tie on their bracer. "And what about Val?"

"Perhaps the Lady of the Lake will release him once she knows we're close to returning."

"I really could use my best advisor right now," Gwen said. "What are your reasons for believing Nin's helping us, Merlin?"

He shrugged one shoulder. "History?" he managed. "She's always saved me from the worst of the cycle. Perhaps she's doing the same for Val."

"Why?" Lam demanded, an unexpected tone for them. But this *was* their brother stuck in Nin's cave.

"No clue!" Merlin cried. "I've never been able to figure out the Lady of the Lake." He started to explain, but the harder he tried, the more he realized he *didn't* know. So much of Nin's life had gotten lost in the fog of Arthurian backstory. She had been an enchantress once, but she wasn't human anymore. She was eternal in some way that he didn't understand. Merlin didn't even know what to call her. A magical being. Somewhere between a ghost and a goddess.

"What is her power?" Gwen asked. "What can she *do*?"

"She usually . . . watches. Keeps track of Arthur's story. Nudges things from her cave. Kidnaps me occasionally, especially when I'm about to die. Oh, and she makes magical weapons."

"Holy shit, I miss Excalibur," Ari murmured, fingers grasping the air as if the sword might appear.

"And I'm going to miss you," Gwen said, sliding both hands into Ari's. "Again."

Ari glanced at each one of her friends, and Merlin fought back a strange instinct that she was saying some kind of goodbye that was about more than jetting off to Avalon for a few days. "Merlin, can anyone see us?"

"No. This is the spell I used in the alley when we first met. Remember?"

Ari smiled sadly. "Can you three...turn around for a second?"

Merlin turned, shoulder to shoulder with Lam and Jordan. "How long should we give them?"

"Not *too* long," Lam said with a chuckle. "Or we'll never get them apart."

Merlin hummed his way through Taylor Swift's "Ours" and then turned back around. He expected to find a post-makeout hormonal haze, but Ari was kissing Gwen's wrists, silvery tear tracks on both of their cheeks.

"Be well," Ari murmured, "both of you."

She left, and Merlin watched her go, armor blaring in the midday sun. She moved differently here. Held herself differently. As if walking a *very* high wire.

"I've never seen her so serious," Lam said. "She's somehow stronger and yet more fragile. Beneath that armor, she's tired and scared. Maybe more than when we faced the Administrator."

Merlin put words to a theory that had been forming ever since she walked into the square. "She's getting lost in playing Lancelot."

"That's because she *is* Lancelot," Gwen said. "She always was, even before she knew it." Lam looked at Gwen questioningly. "I can feel it, too. I'm Gwen of Lionel, but I'm also the Queen of Camelot. It's...too much. Like being the hero and the victim at the same time."

"The puppeteer *and* the puppet." Merlin understood too well.

As if on cue, the stage erupted into a final battle. These shows were equally violent and whimsical, an unsettling combination. "Plus Ari doesn't have Kay to keep her grounded anymore," Lam said. "Believe it or not, he could always make her feel better."

"I believe it," Gwen said quietly, rubbing her stomach like a good luck charm.

Even though they were talking about difficult things, Merlin found himself relieved to have his friends around him once again. After a short while Lam had to return to their duties at the stable, and Merlin was left to shop with Gwen and Jordan, hunting down the items on Old Merlin's list while enjoying their companionship.

When the trumpets sounded and the people of Camelot arranged themselves on the main road to bid farewell to King Arthur and Sir Lancelot, he felt Gwen's fear rise. Side by side they watched Ari disappear into the dark feral woods that separated the kingdom from Nin's distant crystal lake.

Merlin had never seen the legend from this angle before. Through all the cycles, he'd been Arthur's mage, focused on

Arthur's heartbreak. But this time around he truly understood how much Gweneviere and Lancelot loved each other. Anyone who got in the way—from a rampant corporation to a lovesick king—barely stood a chance. They were the original love story of the Western canon, two girls from the future hidden in the folds of the past.

Merlin realized with a start that he was finally rooting for the other team.

Jordan loomed behind them as they made their way through the market, Gwen's bodyguard even though the queen was still in her dressed-down disguise. After finding the last of Old Merlin's items, they headed back toward the castle just as the sun sank below the horizon.

"Mage!" Jordan shouted.

It happened so quickly his brain whirled. He dropped the supplies, glass bursting, as four—no, five men swarmed out of the alleys, one jumping down from the thatch of a nearby roof. Merlin belted the chorus of "Raspberry Beret" and threw up a protection bubble around Gwen.

"Not me! They're attacking Jordan!" Gwen cried. The men flew down the streets, lashing out wildly at the knight with the long blonde braid slung over her shoulder.

"I see that now!" Merlin said, all in the time it took for Jordan to slam down her visor, draw her sword, and take out the first attacker with a hard swing. These men were not knights. They wore no colors and fought with no sense of grace. They moved at a quick, brutal, deadly pace. "Hired assassins."

"Sir Kay must have sent them," Gwen said, with a certainty that Merlin shared. He'd been bested in front of all of Camelot by a woman in armor. He wasn't going to let that stand. And he wasn't going to face her again, knowing he would lose. That would involve honor he didn't have.

Jordan cut off the second assassin at the knees—literally—when Merlin charged forward to help. Jordan saw him coming and backhanded him so hard he actually left the ground. "Don't you dare, mage," Jordan's voice rang over the dull pain in his head. "Remember, I know what it costs you."

"I'm not going to let you die in the medieval version of Street Fighter!" he cried, wobbling to his feet. Jordan had hit him *really hard*.

Her smile flared bright. "You think I can't take five men?"

They drew a small crowd as two assassins fought her at once. She led them into a corner where they lost the space to maneuver and were as likely to slash each other as they were to find their mark. Then she jumped onto a hitching post and launched herself downward, taking one of the men down with the hilt of her sword to the forehead. When they landed, the fourth one was on her, using his leverage to flip her over. He climbed over her, crowded down, her sword arm pinned so she could no longer swing.

"Jordan!" Gwen cried, palms bashing against Merlin's magical barrier.

He ran forward, ready to fling a few sparks, but then he saw the quick flash of silver. The man groaned, then retched. The attacker on top of Jordan keeled over as she swung herself out, a dagger sticking out of the man's gut. Jordan turned, arms outstretched, sword blazing, ready to take on the fifth attacker. But he was nowhere to be seen. The crowd waited. They didn't care if this girl in armor won or lost. They just wanted to see more blood spilled.

"Looks like I scared him off," Jordan said with satisfaction.

The crowd booed, deprived of their frenzied enjoyment. The knot of people around them loosened. Merlin popped the invisible bubble that held Gwen, and Jordan took her arm as Gwen seethed with relief and worry for her best friend and even better knight. Merlin didn't care whether the people of Camelot were ready to acknowledge her prowess—it didn't change the fact that Jordan of Lionel was the finest knight in any place or time.

A *thunk* sounded from far off.

Red sprayed across Merlin's vision. The missing assassin had run off to a cowardly distance and shot an arrow straight into her neck.

Jordan went down.

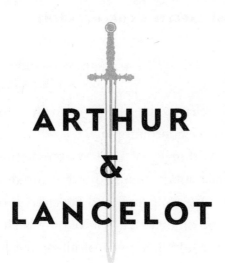

ARTHUR
&
LANCELOT

Ari couldn't help feeling that something would go wrong in Camelot the moment King Arthur left. She pushed the thoughts down, keeping her focus on the quest at hand.

Ari watched Arthur polish Excalibur from across the small campfire. She'd never seen him care for the sword before. She'd seen him train with it, fight with it, but never treasure it. Ari more than longed to hold the sword again. Merlin had taken the broken pieces when she arrived in Camelot, and the absence of the enchanted blade was never far from her mind.

Arthur's sharpening stone sang over the edge of the blade as if he'd lovingly done this every night since he'd plucked the sword from the stone. Or was this the sword handed to Arthur straight from the Lady of the Lake's disembodied arm? Jordan's book offered two possibilities—which engendered new thought on the so-called legend. Most of it had been imagined much later by romantic writers—and less romantic screenwriters—based on certain foundational truths. An old magician, Excalibur, a love triangle, a round table, a murderous son...

That was, perhaps, the only reason they had any wiggle room with the time continuum.

"You are watching me as if contemplating eating me," Arthur said, just loud enough for his timid voice to reach across the fire. "We rode long and far enough this day for me to imagine the possibility that you've only been playacting the role of a friend. Making a game of luring me out of my kingdom, away from my guards, so that you might kill me."

"Not everyone wants to kill you, Arthur," Ari said, feeling a pang for the reluctant royal. She'd been hunted by Mercer for most of her life, forced to always watch her back. "Besides, I told you the enchantresses will never take your offer of peace seriously if you arrive surrounded by armed men on horseback."

"And you don't count as such?" Arthur paused in his sharpening, staring at Ari with a daring look. "I watch you as much as you watch me, Lancelot. I know you keep secrets."

Ari studied him. "I won't keep the truth quiet if you ask the right questions."

She swore she could hear Merlin exclaiming curses at the heavens for this offer.

Arthur slid Excalibur in its long, leather sheath. "Then my question is, why have you placed yourself at my side, good knight? Why do you seek to train me, improve public opinion of me, strengthen my kingdom with allies?"

Ari stood, pacing beside the fire.

"Will you sleep in your armor?" he asked, making her pause.

"Of course," she snapped. "What if we were attacked in the night?"

"And what if I beheld your female shape?"

"My...what?" Ari actually drew her sword. Arthur pressed his lips nervously.

"You're a woman. I suspected it from the start, but after the melee, I could just tell." Arthur's serious face split with a sweet, tentative smile.

Ari thrust her sword into the ground. "So you're not surprised? Upset?"

"Everyone lies to me. The only control I have is to know how much someone lies. You're not a man, but you *are* a mighty hero." He nodded to himself as if this truth had taxed him, but not broken him. "If that is the worst secret between us, we can be friends."

Ari was dumbstruck. She felt rather acutely as if she'd acquired a little brother. He was heartfelt to a fault, trusting, loving...lonely.

Like Kay.

And like Kay, the worst dealings between Ari and Arthur would not be the chalice or Ari's ladyhood or any other subject. It would be one specific, vivacious queen.

Ari added more wood to the fire. "How far do we still have to go?"

"A day or less. We must arrive by nightfall tomorrow. That is when the door to Avalon appears through the mist." Arthur curled on the ground, punching the roll of clothes that served as his pillow. That was the other thing about this trip; Arthur had left his finery behind. He wore plain clothes, no crown. Two people on the road had already treated Arthur as if he were Ari's squire, carrying her fancy sword, and he'd seemed pleased with the arrangement.

"I believe I've underestimated you," Ari managed.

Arthur nodded. "Imagine," he said, "that you are no one. You are small and have no family. Imagine someone gives you a sword and tells you it was all a dream, your nothingness, your powerlessness. Instead, you are a king and this blade in your hands comes with a kingdom."

Arthur's voice dwindled, and Ari picked up his words, adding her own. "And with that kingdom comes thousands of voices. Those in pain, those who have been silenced or abused or even killed. You're supposed to listen to all of them. You're supposed to answer every single plea. You're supposed to take down a monster larger than galaxies with a sword as long as your leg."

"Yes. Exactly." Arthur turned his back, his voice sleepy. "And I must do it all myself. Power is the worst kind of loneliness."

Arthur fell asleep while Ari managed camp. Night was never silent in the woods, never safe. Large creatures hunted in the darkness while smaller ones hid. While Arthur slept, Ari examined him: thick blonde hair, mouth slightly open, his body all twisted up like a child.

While she stared, she felt the connection between the boy king and the ancient cursed spirit perched in her soul. This was the person who would one day save Ari's life during the Mercer attack. "Where are you buried?" she murmured to the silent voice inside. "Why aren't you at rest?"

Ari relieved the horses of their saddles and then sat against a tree, pulling a blanket over her. It was no easy revelation to feel sorry for the king, both the young man and the ancient spirit. It had been so much easier when she merely glared at the way he smiled longingly at Gwen. She wished Merlin were here so that she could ask for his advice. How had he dealt with wanting so badly to help someone who was set up for failure? And that was really it, wasn't it? King Arthur and his knights ended in tragedy. Every single version of the story agreed on that much.

Equality failed. Love failed. Kingdom failed.

That was his true legacy.

Ari pressed her memories back to the moment within Merlin's magical curtain. Ari hadn't had time to plan something romantic, she'd simply slid to one knee, her face against Gwen's chest, enveloping her entire lady—and the baby—in her arms. Gwen held on to Ari just as tightly, and they laughed and shook off biting tears. Relieved to have found each other. Blinded by the complications still between them. Ari kissed Gwen's belly, waiting to see if she got a response, but the bump was still. "She's sleeping." Gwen lifted Ari's arms until she stood back up, towering over Gwen.

"Still *she*?" Ari asked. "Shouldn't we use *they* until we know more?"

"I say *she* because I hope it's a girl." Gwen fisted her hands. Something was hurting her.

"Are you in pain? Contractions?"

"No. Ari, do you know the stories about Arthur's son?"

Ari's mind turned a corner and ran into a stone wall. Something Merlin had said when they first met floated through her thoughts like a dark cloud through a blue sky. *You don't have children, by any chance?* He'd been terrified of the idea that any Arthur reincarnations might have kids. "Gwen, the baby couldn't possibly be..."

Mordred.

Even the name made her stomach turn and her hand close on the sword at her belt.

"Mordred was the son of..." Ari had to pause and peer backward into her memories of Morgana's Arthurian lessons on Ketch. "...Someone else. I'm sure of it."

Gwen put a hand on Ari's heart. Each breath felt heavy with the weight of the space between them. "But that's just it, Ari. All the stories are different. I don't know. I *can't* know. What if I'm the one who gives birth to Arthur's son? The murderer."

"Won't happen. This kid is half-Kay, not half-Camelot, and that means the only murdering will be sandwiches. Believe me?" Ari leaned in, so close to Gwen's face that she felt that spinning inside. That perfect, out-of-control sensation of their love.

Gwen nodded many times, tears slipping free.

"I should probably kiss you before Merlin drops that curtain. I mean, can I kiss you, Gwen?"

Gwen's yes was a press up on her toes. Their lips met soft and joyous. Warm and light. Then they parted. *For the last fucking time,* Ari vowed. "I don't care that this place can't accept us together. I know how magical we are. I'm growing old with you, lady."

&

The next day, Ari's stallion reminded her of Kay, veering off the trail to snack, baring his teeth whenever Ari pointed out that maybe he was being a jackass. "We should keep to the trees," she called out to Arthur. "This road is a hunting ground for enemies to your kingdom."

"My road is that bad?" Arthur said, turning backward in his saddle.

"For commoners it's nearly a death sentence. I dodged about thirty arrows on my way through the morning of your wedding, and I was traveling with a host of knights."

"Hmm, I should do something about this road."

"Instate a guard," Ari suggested.

"Maybe."

"Do you always have to process my ideas as if they might conceal harm?"

"Do you always have to do things the moment you imagine them?"

Ari folded her arms. "If you haven't noticed, my last plan ended up with you showing off your warrior stuff. They've started calling you 'The One True King.' You're welcome."

"Yes, but that handmaiden's victory was a disaster. Surely you see that. She made Sir Kay seem less of a man. He will seek revenge."

"Jordan is a *knight*." Ari's teeth bit so hard into the word that Arthur went silent. "And she can handle anything he throws at her." Ari and Arthur navigated a labyrinth of briar bushes, directing their horses with care. "I now understand why it took you forty tries to pick a girl," she muttered.

"What was that?"

"You tell me you know I'm a woman, and then you act as if it doesn't matter. Explain."

"As long as I'm the only one who knows, I don't see the

problem." Arthur kept going, undeterred. "I told you I'm used to lies. I assure myself that a person like you, or like my queen, needs to have secrets to feel a sense of control. My mage, Merlin, is quite similar. Secrets are his safety. A condition of being so powerful."

Ari felt almost as if Arthur had grown to understand Gwen faster than she had, which was annoying. "And as you are the all-powerful king, you keep secrets?"

"They don't suit me," he said, eyeing her as if she should have recognized this about him already. "I sometimes wish they did."

Ari felt that one deeply; she ached to tell Arthur about his sister, Morgana, the extremely powerful enchantress who would chase her lost brother's spirit across human history, determined to help him, even sacrificing herself for the chance.

Maybe it would make him feel less lonely.

But she couldn't tell Arthur the future, so instead they rode out of the woods, dusk filtering over the horizon of a great, gray-misted lake at the foot of rough mountains. A small, empty boat sat rocking slightly on the shore. They left their horses and boarded, observing the quiet as if it were a threat. When she kicked them away from the rocky shore, Ari's left boot soaked through, sending a rush of shivers up her leg. They sailed into the mist, until they couldn't see any part of the woods or mountains anymore. All was gray.

"We're meant to call for them." Arthur peered into the mist. "The mists of Avalon cannot be reached by anyone other than the enchantresses. And they don't allow men inside, so we'll have to stay here. Well, I will." He tried to smile at Ari, and she scowled back. "They will come to see us. Or they won't."

"I'm no good at waiting."

"And I'm not surprised."

This time Ari's scowl slipped into a smile and Arthur seemed delighted by his success. Before Ari could say anything more, the gray mist crystallized into the shape of a person. Her brother. Ari blinked, blinked again.

Ghost Kay was watching her. Standing on the water's surface with his arms folded and his silver hair a mess. All of a sudden she swore she could taste the sterile air of *Error,* smell her brother's old rubber knight's suit...

"Lancelot?" Arthur asked.

"Something is messing with my head," she admitted, squinting. "Can you see him?"

Arthur shivered. "It is this lake. The mists belong to Avalon, to the enchantresses. The water belongs to another."

Ari looked down to face the dark, still surface. "This is the Lady of the Lake's...lake?"

"Yes." His voice was deeper than usual. "There are strange stories of this place. Merlin won't go near it."

Ghost Kay disappeared, and Ari leaned out toward where he'd vanished, rocking the boat. "Stay with me, Lancelot," Arthur called. Ari looked down at Arthur's hand on her elbow. "An enchantress approaches."

Arthur pointed to where a woman parted the mist, stepping along the dark water as if it were black glass. Her bare feet were brown, a shade darker than Ari's own skin, and the tips of her dark hair swirled around her bare legs. She wore the same slip of a dress that Morgana had in her ethereal form, only this one was tangible.

"I'm...My name is Arthur," Arthur said. "I'm from—"

"We know the boy who would be king," the woman said, stopping on the surface and staring them down with dark, fathomless eyes. "I thought that might have been obvious based on our episodic attacks."

"Yes, I just thought it'd be polite to introduce myself." Arthur had surprised the enchantress. She lifted her chin.

"We watch your kingdom expand with growing impatience for your games."

"That's why I'm here." Arthur looked to Ari for help, and she leaned back. "To ask for your aid, your blessing to my people. To build a union between us."

"Interesting." The enchantress stared at Ari briefly. "Your name we cannot know, can we? It does not belong here." The implication was that she knew Ari was not from Camelot, or even this era. She turned back to Arthur. "I am Morgause. I..."

Ari's attention rushed toward the sudden reappearance of Ghost Kay. He stepped out from behind Morgause and walked around the outer edge of the boat. He was so close that if Ari stood they'd be eye to eye, and she felt Arthur's hand on her elbow again. "Don't forget to invite them to the celebration," she said distractedly. "And tell them to bring a present."

"Lancelot?"

Ghost Kay smirked and beckoned toward the shining black water.

And Ari dove in.

&

Ari knew this wasn't her brother; Kay was lost forever. This was one of the Lady of the Lake's tricks. But Ari also knew that if she found Nin, she'd find Val. The cold teeth of the water bit into her muscles but she swam deeper until a sudden undertow dragged her down, down, down.

Merciless pressure squeezed her starved lungs. She kept her mouth tight, her eyes peering into the black depth until it began to prick with crystal stars. When she could not stop herself from trying to breathe any longer, she gasped, and metallic-flavored oxygen filled her lungs—the same scent that permeated *Error,* from the copper lines that filtered bacteria from the recycled air. Her head jerked as she glanced across *Error*'s control board.

"Good. You're up. I've got to take a whiz."

Ari looked over in slow motion at Kay. Not a ghost but her actual brother. He unstrapped from the captain's chair and ambled toward the door, tweaking her ear on his way by as if to prove that he had a body—and toilet urges to boot. How realistically charming. "I'm dreaming," she said, half expecting her mouth to fill with icy, black water.

It didn't.

She touched her chest, held tight in the cross of her seat's harness. She picked up one of Kay's tortilla chip wrappers lying on the finger-smudged console and devoured the foil's crinkling sound. Her hair was long again. She could feel the braid resting on her neck.

"This is a cruel game," Ari managed. "Lady of the Lake?" she called out.

Ari heard nothing but her own breath. She pinched herself so hard she yelled.

Ari unstrapped her chest belt and unlocked her magboots, savoring the heavy knock of her soles releasing from the grated floor, the gravity light and easy. Ari was home, on *Error,* with Kay. How could this be real?

She stepped through the cockpit to the main cabin, running smack into Kay's chest. She latched on, hugging him so hard that he squirmed.

"Dude, Ari. What are you doing?"

"How am I here? When is this? *What* is this?"

"I think you had a bad dream." Kay wasn't starved like he'd been during their last days. He was rounded and relaxed and smelled like a too-concentrated version of himself. "The fuck," he said. "Did you just sniff me?"

"You even *smell* like Kay. This is so wrong."

"You don't smell great yourself, you know that?" Kay leaned against the jutting corner of two walls, scratching between his shoulder blades, making an unsatisfied face. He exhaled as if he'd made an incredibly hard decision. "Okay, fine. You can come on board *Heritage* with me."

"Kay..."

"You've never seen it before, and you've been on *Error* for almost six months. We'll be careful and *you* won't press any Mercer panic buttons for shits and giggles. Promise you won't."

Ari couldn't find any words. It wasn't her brother or the ship now that was throwing her. It was the time stamp. Holy shit, she was back at the beginning. The day she found Excalibur.

"I suppose you want me to wear your old rubber knight's costume?"

"I thought you could wear Mom's Mercer forces uniform, but wait, the knight's costume is a way better idea." Kay popped open one of the lesser used storage panels, and the knight suit tumbled out. "You can hang out in this dusty old museum wing. No one is ever there except for Lionel nerds." While Ari stared at the suit, Kay tried to scratch his back with the edge of the storage compartment's metal door, whining dismally as he couldn't get the exact spot.

"Oh, good grief, come here," Ari said, beckoning.

Her brother leaped over the space between them in a single bound, too much satisfaction in his grin while he hunched before her and she scratched that one shoulder blade spot Kay always needed scratching. Her hand slowed after a minute, and she pressed her palm on his back, relieved by the ever-familiar—and yet so lost—sensation of his worn T-shirt, his soft skin.

"Moms would want you to get off ship sometimes." His voice was gruff with rocky feelings. "Even with how dangerous it is. No one can stay lost out here between the stars. That's what they'd say."

He spoke of their parents as if he'd already buried them. Ari had forgotten about that heartbroken tone. This was the Kay who'd spent years not knowing if his parents were alive. He didn't know that they had found a way to stay together. He didn't know that, soon, they would all risk everything to save them. His silver hair reminded her of Captain Mom. Ari wound a quick finger around a lock in the back until he barked an objection and slapped her hand away. This was her brother. Alive. Which meant she wasn't in the same time period anymore.

Oh my gods, she'd left Gwen behind in the Middle Ages.

Error's proximity alarm dinged. Kay put her in a tight headlock, squeezing and letting go so fast Ari barely felt him before he was gone again. Back in the cockpit, Ari picked up the suit. It was heavy from the extra padding Mom had ordered, for when Kay took more than his share of blows at knight camp.

"Hurry up and get dressed!" Kay called. "We'll be in the docking garage in five."

Heritage grew into focus in the front viewscreen, dwarfing her brother's messy profile—and Ari knew why the Lady of the Lake had dropped her here. This was where it all started.

And she could stop it.

Ari ran to the airlock. She threw the stupid knight costume in and hit the button to seal the inner door. Her hand paused over the second button, the one that would open the outer door and eject the costume into space and make everything un-happen. No hacking into Mercer's files, crashing on Earth, finding Excalibur. No empty Ketch, or Kay's death, or Gwen torn from her arms in that merciless portal...

Maybe this was supposed to un-happen. It'd be a new start. She'd go to Lionel, not chased by Mercer, but returning to pick up with Gwen where they'd left off with that first kiss. They could all live there, be happy.

But then, she remembered Gwen's brand-new smile. The one she wore when she touched her belly, the baby moving beneath her fingers. If Ari changed the story, there would be no series of catastrophes to lead to that small, miraculous person. Ari wished she had some way to prove that this baby wasn't destined to become some legendary patricidal maniac. She didn't have proof, but then, she didn't need it. This baby was *theirs*.

Ari's hand moved to the first button, re-opening the inner door. She lifted the rubber knight suit and put one leg in. There was a reason for this pain just as there was a reason for King Arthur's tragic story. Through the darkness, the new life.

"I'll do everything exactly the same," she told herself—and the Lady of the Lake if she were listening. "Every single thing."

Ari coughed and black, half-frozen water shot out of her lungs. It hit the floor of *Error,* which flooded in an instant, twisting her around until she was back beneath the crushing pressure of the lake, screaming a good-bye to Kay that he would never hear.

&

Ari lay on her back in a few inches of cold water. Beside her, a black lake sat silently within a great, glimmering cave. A few small, silver torches burned. She breathed hard, rubbing her face with numb hands, trying not to feel like Kay had died all over again. Her tears came fast and desperate...until the sound of *giggling* broke through her grief.

Ari opened her eyes and found a favorite memory playing out in the surface of the dark lake: back on *Error,* she was sitting in the captain's chair with her knees spread wide. Gwen, who wore nothing but her unders and that goldenrod tank top, was sitting between Ari's legs, staring avidly at the control board. This was the day before they landed on Troy. Before they met the Administrator and so much changed so swiftly.

"How do I make us go faster?" Gwen asked.

Ari took this as a cue to slide her arms around Gwen. "That orange button guy."

"There are three buttons in the orange family."

"So try all three."

"Ari, what if I crash us?"

"That's the fun thing about space. Not much to crash into."

In the dark cave, Ari could almost feel Gwen's weight through the image. New aches replaced her grief, the idea of holding Gwen like that, of being relaxed together in a tangle. The Ari in the memory guided Gwen's hand to the throttle. She helped Gwen press it forward and held on to her as the ship's speed rankled and jerked, making them burst with laughter. Ari throttled back after a few seconds, shutting off a few *no biggie* alarms, while Gwen started kissing her, and kissing her...

"On the control board, Ari?" Kay roared, appearing in the cockpit.

Ari—the real Ari who was freezing in the Lady of the Lake's cave—laughed too hard. She covered her cold lips with her hand, watching her brother chase the two girls back to the room they'd stolen from him. All the while shouting, "Next time I have a date on board, we're going straight to your bunk, Turtle! What do you think of that?! Karma is coming for you!"

Ari's laughter faded as the image fuzzed. She stood up, taking in the strange scenery. The wet rock walls, the black lake, and at its center, a small, rectangular island. She squinted; it was a funeral pyre, complete with a body laid out upon it. "Val?" she called out, voice echoing.

"Ari!" Val's voice called back from far away.

"Val! Where are you?" Ari swung around, looking for a door. Instead she found a gloriously perfect person, watching her.

The Lady of the Lake.

"Would you mind not screaming? Human voices are tedious at best." She circled Ari, showing off long limbs beneath a tightly tailored green velvet suit. Her skin was the sort of nearly-translucent white that seemed to be on the verge of glowing, and her hair was a screaming shade of red, combed against her scalp. Ari's eyes peeled a little too wide. She hadn't expected this; Merlin hadn't said anything about Nin being... smoking hot.

"Hey," Ari said, throat dry. "It's good to finally meet you."

The Lady of the Lake came so close that Ari felt self-conscious about each plate of unpolished, dented armor. The strong-lined and lean figure breathed on Ari's breastplate, fogging up the dragon Ouroboros.

"Ah, wow, you don't do small talk, heh?"

Nin peered at Ari, flint-eyed. "I don't like tears in my cave. *Salt*water is useless." She motioned to Ari's tear tracks.

Ari smudged away the remaining offenders. "That's why you showed me that memory from before Troy. To stop me from crying."

"Not a memory. A piece of time. Humans require time to march in a single direction, past to present to future. But time is a river that can flow many interesting ways, including circles. If you want to step into a different age, you need only know where to stick in your toe."

"So you really are timeless," Ari said, although her mind spun with a sudden, burning question. *That's not all you are, is it?* Ari's understanding of this being had been filtered through Merlin. And Merlin's unorthodox existence. Perhaps he had reasons to trust Nin, but Ari was drawing a blank as to what those reasons might be. Her gaze went back to the center of the lake where the funeral pyre she'd witnessed minutes ago had already vanished.

"Where's Val?" she said, fear showing in her voice.

"Unharmed, as promised. I'll be returning him shortly. Merlin is almost ready to have him back." The Lady continued her inspection of Ari. "I've never met one in the flesh."

Ari took a small step back. "Met one of what?"

"One of Arthur's human vessels," she said. "I do believe he is right. You are the last. He is finished with his grand schemes to unite humanity. Finally beaten. Poor fool." The Lady's finger traced the circular dragon on Ari's breastplate. "Do you like your armor? I had to search a few thousand years of Earth history to find it for you."

Ari's mind went black and then bright, as if someone had turned on a burning spotlight. "This armor...you picked it out for me?" She couldn't help but remember her bizarre earthly landing in the midst of battle, the dead blue knight beside her, and then farther back, inside the portal, that indelible feeling of being *pushed*. "You separated us."

The Lady sighed. "Are you trying to blame me? Is that a thing you need? I haven't been human in so long. It's easy to forget."

"You tore me from Gwen!" Ari shouted.

She smiled wickedly. "Like magnets, you two. No matter how tightly they fix together, it never becomes less amusing to pull them apart."

Merlin had been so wrong when he called her a bystander, a watcher.

At best, she was chaotic neutral in a velvet suit.

"I need to get back to my friends," Ari said. The Lady smoothed back her perfectly red hair and sighed. "If you won't let me leave, you show your true colors."

"Oh, you need me to be the *villain*. Villains are terribly commonplace, Ara Azar."

Ari knew this argument; she knew this type. "That body I saw, out in the center of the lake, that was King Arthur, wasn't it? The famed secret of his last resting place is finally known."

"*Hardly* at rest." Nin chuckled. "But then that's why you're here. To make a new deal."

"There's no way I'm dealing with you."

"Oh." She actually looked sorry for Ari. "Did you think we could skip this part? There isn't anyone powerful enough to refuse my wishes. Well, perhaps there is *one* person, but he is his own best enemy. Which is endlessly amusing, I can tell you."

"You're talking about Merlin." Ari felt around for something to hold on to. She had to get some kind of upper hand. "Then he has the power to stop you. Stop the cycle."

"The cycle is *his* prison." The humor vanished from her pristine face. "And if you wish to free him of it, you will take my deal. I will reunite King Arthur's spirit with his body. And I will send you and your friends back to your future. The only cost I require is that when you die, your body will become mine, and your soul's ventures will become my new amusement."

The fuck.

"But I'll be cursed, like Arthur." Ari stared into the dark air of the cave. "You forget we nearly have the chalice, and we'll get the magic we need to make our own portal."

"Something like this?" Nin held out a dagger bearing the Avalon crest, and Ari snatched it. "That will make your portal, and what's more, how about a show of very good faith?"

Nin touched one of the small pools, and an image swirled. Ari recognized the tower at Camelot where they'd battled that dragon, rebuilt by Old Merlin's magic. The light outside the arrow slits showed night, while inside the tower was a somber scene. Gwen, in a gold dress, weeping into the bowl of her empty hands. Merlin pressing his face hard into Lam's shoulder, who was looking down at a narrow bed bearing a very still, very dead Jordan.

Her skin was the white color of something forgotten in the sun, her neck bloodily bandaged, her sword fallen to the floor. One hand paused over the side as if her last breath had come while she was reaching for it.

Ari gasped so loudly it echoed.

"An assassin's arrow to the throat. She dies uncelebrated, without honor, and your friends lose hope, collapsing into the misery of one of the darkest versions of the Arthurian legend."

"This is happening right now?"

"There is no *now*. No past. No future. Oh, you're much thicker than young Percival."

"How in the world is this a show of good faith?" Ari asked, shaking with anger.

The Lady swirled her finger in the dark image, peeling back time until Jordan's last breath reversed, and her chest began to rise and fall. Simultaneously through the tower window, the night reversed into a purple twilight. Nin flicked her wet fingers at the air, opening a portal. "Now you have the ways and means to save your warrior. I'd call that very good faith, wouldn't you?"

A strange light glowed in the Lady of the Lake's eyes. Was this what hope looked like on such an inhumanly beautiful face? Ari didn't wait to know more. She lifted her foot, stepped into the portal and was instantly lost in the space between time.

PARTY
&
TIME

The day of Arthur's birthday celebration was finally upon them, but instead of lining up neatly, everything was flying out of Merlin's control. They weren't poised to steal the chalice and get the hell out of Dodge. They were standing in a rough circle in the tower, watching Jordan die.

Well, most of them were.

Val was still in Nin's cave—and Ari was flat-out missing. Arthur had returned from Avalon alone, announcing a new peace with the enchantresses but also keeping mum on exactly what had befallen Sir Lancelot.

Gwen and Lam were arrayed in their finest for the party, which made Jordan's stark white skin and bloodstained clothes look even worse. Merlin sat beside her on the cot they'd smuggled up to the tower, using a few sparks to help her breathe. It was paltry magic, but it made him feel better, a bit.

Trumpets blared across the city lit by a purple twilight.

Lam looked through an arrow slit to the crowds in the court-yard below. "Avalon is here. Whatever Ari did...it worked."

Merlin stood, a childish tizzy of emotions taking over his heart and body. He stamped and shouted, "This is wrong! We're meant to steal the chalice and then leave this godsforsaken place behind, once and for all!" Gwen and Lam stared at him with a pity he couldn't stomach. As if they could tell that his need to quit Camelot ran much deeper than he liked to admit. "This era is vile. It's killing us." He looked down at Jordan, immediately wanting to take those words back.

"I have to go down to the party," Gwen said as she edged toward the stairs, looking physically pained to leave Jordan. "Arthur will want me by his side. He's been distant since Ava-lon, but he needs me. Whatever happened to Ari seemed to... scare him."

"We're all scared," Lam said quietly. "She should be here by now."

Gwen, Lam, and Merlin shared a moment of fear so large it seemed to fill the tower. Then a crackle of light exploded at the center of the room. The fabric of reality tore, exposing a dark wound, and Ari stumbled through it with all the grace of a drunk antelope.

Lam rushed forward to envelop Ari in a hug that also kept her from falling over.

"How—" Merlin started, but Ari cut him off.

"No time to explain," Ari said, getting back to her balance. "We have to send Jordan to our future. *Now*."

"It's not a bad idea, in theory." Merlin had considered it: the medicine of the future would be able to heal Jordan where Merlin's magic and medieval poultices simply weren't enough.

He'd been able to put a basic patch on her wound, but it hadn't stopped the complications of infection. "The portal magics..." he said, faltering on the logistics of sending her back. "We're still down one."

"The enchantresses just got here," Lam said. With a quickly mustered smile, they added, "Should I go charm one into helping us?"

"No need. Here." Ari pushed a dagger into Merlin's hand so fast he leaped back, and it hit the floor with a clang. He looked down to find a familiar blade. It was identical to the one Morgana had wielded—and stuck him in the leg with. "That's all fired up with Avalon magic. A gift from Nin."

"Nin?" Merlin cried.

"We can talk about that later. Right now it's portal time. Merlin, are you ready?"

"But we have to wait for the chalice. Arthur should have it in a matter of hours."

Ari eyed the windows, the last of the sunset turning Camelot into a rich tapestry of shadows. "You have to trust me. We're out of time. I'm not letting her die like Kay. Send her back *now*!"

"Well, she isn't part of the Arthurian legend, so sending her back won't ruin the story. That's the good news." The bad news is that it would use up the three magics they needed to get everyone else home. How long would it take them to collect them again? Months? Years? Would Merlin even be able to do it then or would he be too busy wetting his diapers?

"It doesn't matter," he muttered, thinking of the staunch knight down in the oubliette, who kept his secret because she understood what it meant to do anything to protect your friends. Your *people*.

And Merlin's people included Jordan.

He hit a bass note, a sort of meditative chant that he'd learned from some monks in one of the long-past Arthurian cycles. The shards of Excalibur floated gently in the air, forming a circle around Jordan. The dagger glowed in the center, a bright swirling gray like the mists around Avalon.

"Why is the mage burping?" the black knight asked, eyes still closed, voice a whisper.

"It's singing," he grumbled.

"You're leaving," Gwen said softly to Jordan.

"*Not* dying," Merlin piped in, for clarity. "Back to the future for you."

"Trying to get rid of me?" Jordan asked as she muscled her eyes open.

Gwen kneeled at Jordan's side, fighting the swell of her dress and the baby hidden inside of it. "You need to get immediate medical attention. We'll...we'll be right behind you." The sunset shone on the tears trailing down her cheek.

"My parents will help you. Tell them we're on our way," Ari said. "We're coming back to the night we left. Tell them not to be surprised if we're a bit older."

"No." Jordan struggled, trying to sit up. "You could be stuck here for years. Decades." She glared at Merlin specifically. "Why are you doing this? It will cost you."

"Because we're family." Merlin glanced around. "And we need your help in the future."

"And I'm outright commanding it," Gwen said.

Jordan nodded with effort and then eyed Merlin as he sang. He worried she would blurt out what she'd learned in the oubliette, telling him not to waste his remaining magic—and years—on her. But she refocused on Gwen, thank all the gods. "As you wish, my queen." Then she looked straight at Ari. "Take care of them."

Ari bowed her head, every inch the knight. "On my honor."

Jordan laid back, arms crossed over her chest as the shards of Excalibur danced so fast they blurred. Gathering around the Avalon dagger, they became one weapon for a bright, shining moment. Merlin sang as it cut through the last of the day's perfect golden light, slicing open a doorway of deepest black. Beyond it, stars shone.

"Home," Jordan murmured, her pain momentarily shelved, as she rose to her feet with the help of Lam and Ari, and stepped into the future.

Ari spoke so quietly Merlin almost didn't hear. "Gwen, why don't you go with—"

"Ask me to leave your side and we'll be in the biggest fight of the century, Ara."

The portal resealed with a rush of wind, as if it knew well enough to obey Gwen's command. The Avalon dagger clattered to the stones, dull metal now, its magic spent. Excalibur's shards rained down as metallic dust, and Ari looked bereft all over again. Merlin clamped a hand over his face, crying out with pain. It felt like someone had reached into his mouth and ripped out several of his teeth.

"She'll make it," Gwen reassured, misreading Merlin's pain as strong emotion. "This is Jordan we're talking about. She'll...find help on the other side. We sent her back to the night that we left, so Ari's moms will be right there."

"*Mmph,*" Merlin said in what he hoped sounded like agreement. Spots at the back of his mouth were liquid fire. Four spots, to be exact. When he probed them with his tongue, he found exactly what he feared. His twelve-year-old molars had sunk. And there was no time to mourn their loss.

Ari sank onto Jordan's abandoned cot, holding her face in her hands. She was weeping.

When Gwen and Lam tried to comfort her, she pushed it all away. "I'm fine. I just...I really thought it was too late."

"Because Nin showed you the future—Jordan's death," Merlin said.

"How do you know that?"

"This all reeks of one of Nin's games."

Lam spun on him, their eyes lit with a special urgency. "You said Val was safe in her lair."

"She has a *lair*?" Gwen asked. "That doesn't sound safe at all."

Merlin owed them the truth. "Since we've gotten so close to Arthur's birthday, and the chalice arriving, I've been shouting into every watery surface for Val's immediate release and... nothing." What had seemed like an innocuous situation only a few days ago was evolving into a standoff.

"Nin told me she would release him soon," Ari said.

"Maybe she just told you that to toy with us," he countered. Ari's eyes fell on Merlin's with warning and care, as if she now knew how frightful the Lady of the Lake could be but didn't want to alarm the others just yet.

The trumpets sounded again, and Gwen smoothed her beautiful gold dress distractedly. "If we don't get down to that celebration now, we're all in trouble."

&

After sending Jordan to the future, it felt dazzlingly awful to leave the castle and find that they were still mired in the past. The Middle Ages were on full display tonight, a bonfire raging as Old Merlin set off some kind of smoky, lung-infesting fireworks in the courtyard. Merlin and his friends emerged into the haze and roar of the most intense festival he had ever seen.

And he had, against all odds, gone to Coachella with Arthur 37.

"Val would love this party," Lam said wistfully as music started up, tabers and drums and some nasal third instrument that Merlin had forgotten but sounded strangely like a synthesizer. "Forget that. He would *own* this party. Half the boys here would have been writing him sonnets by the end. Do they do sonnets yet?"

Lam had made a simple offhand comment because they missed their brother, but those words spun in Merlin's brain. How many of the boys here tonight were cuter than Merlin, and more important, not slipping backward out of adolescence? Was that part of why he had been comfortable letting Val stay with Nin so long? Because in some rotted spot in his heart, he couldn't bear the thought of Val watching him grow younger and younger until they were an equation with utterly mismatched sides?

Merlin touched the tender spots on his cheeks where his teeth had just vanished.

Ari and Gwen veered away from Lam and Merlin. "We'll find Arthur," Gwen said. "He'll be relieved that Lancelot is returned."

Gwen steered the still-ragged Ari through the crowds straight to the king, who was standing near the bonfire with Galahad and Gawain to either side. He broke away at once to embrace Ari. She returned the hug in a way that didn't look fake. Whatever had passed between the two of them on the path to Avalon, they were closer now, which only multiplied the distance Merlin felt. He used to live at Arthur's side, and now he was a mere bystander.

King Arthur raised his hand, and the crowds quieted. "Tonight, my feast is graced with one of the finest knights Camelot has ever known. Sir Lancelot is not only powerful in a fight, he has helped bring us new allies and rid our kingdom of those who would cause harm."

Merlin started. It was true—Camelot's golden age was starting to peek over the horizon, and it was largely thanks to Ari. She pushed to make things better, even when it would have been easy to make an excuse and allow the same problems to spin on endlessly.

Arthur drew Excalibur and it glowed in the firelight, orange and gold, blazing and true. Gwen motioned to Ari, and she sank to one knee, head bowed. Gwen looking on with pride as Arthur touched each of her shoulders with Excalibur's point.

"Sir Lancelot, Knight of Camelot!"

The crowd lost itself in wild cheering.

Merlin felt cold, despite the riotous bonfire. Ari was safe and the Arthurian legend was back on track. He should have felt hopeful, but between sending Jordan back and seeing this moment, it felt like he was being sealed in the tomb of this story.

They were supposed to leave.

Not stay.

Merlin grabbed Lam's arm, suddenly desperate to rid

himself of a thought. "Did you know that time circles are possible? Down in the oubliette, I was thinking about it. The later scientists of Old Earth called them closed temporal loops. Most lives march from past to future because that's what the human brain requires to understand things. But time itself doesn't care about human rules."

"So you're saying...the Arthurian cycles are one big loop?"

"I thought Ari and Gwen couldn't be in the story at both the beginning and the end. But if we're stuck in a circle, there's no reason they can't be. They sort of *have to* be."

"That's wild," Lam said.

"It's worse than wild," Merlin whispered. "I think it might be my doom."

Soon his magic would be drained, his life reduced to the rubble of childhood, and all of his friends stuck in the past. He'd never end the cycle. It would dump him here, back where it started, and leave him for dead.

But Arthur's spirit had given him hope that this story could end. Maybe it was still possible. Merlin had to get his hands on that chalice and get them out of here. *Now.*

"Carbuncle!" The word scraped against the air. "Carbuncle!" Somehow Old Merlin had picked the least musical, most anatomically upsetting word in the entire language as his nickname. "Come here, boy!"

"I wouldn't keep yourself waiting," Lam said with a pitying look.

Merlin pushed his way across the courtyard, looking for hints of the chalice everywhere he went. It didn't seem to have surfaced yet. He reached Old Merlin, who was conducting the party—literally. His hands waltzed in neat patterns, his magic ferrying goblets and cheese and great hunks of meat. People snatched them out of the air, cheering.

It all looked whimsically adorable.

It made Merlin sick.

"There are too few game pies," Old Merlin said, without so much as tilting his pointy chin down at Merlin. "Tell the kitchens to double their output."

"What's the magic word?" Merlin muttered—and then everything stopped.

From all directions, women flowed in, like cold streams moving through warm water. They had Merlin's full attention, and he wasn't the only one.

The enchantresses of Avalon commanded the crowd more fully than the king of Camelot had. Most probably feared them, but Merlin was struck with awe at the sight of these magical women. There was an untamed pride in their gazes, their bodies. They ranged in age from early teens to the most wizened eldress, and while some were as white as a stereotypical unicorn, light browns and dark skin tones were also present. Magical ladies had been known to come from all over the world to gather in Avalon. Merlin was surprised—and yet not surprised—to see that a few of them might not have been assigned female at birth. Avalon always had been ahead of its time.

Why hadn't he remembered that when he thought back on this closeminded past?

The enchantress at the forefront went to the fire, knelt by it, and whispered a few words that made it claw toward the sky.

Merlin tugged at the neck of his robes as heat flared, muttering, "Nice pyrotechnics."

The young woman who'd caused the conflagration stood tall. Her name wafted to Merlin on a wind from the past. *Morgause.* He hadn't seen her in literal ages. Crashing hair, eyes dark as omens. She was vibrantly powerful and wondrously beautiful, and the firelight sang on her soft brown skin. Still, Merlin couldn't help but feel the pinch of loss. Some small part of him had been hoping to see Morgana.

But she wasn't part of Arthur's story yet.

And in the future, she was finally dead. For the first time, Merlin's stubborn heart admitted that he might never see her again. They'd been bound together for so long that he'd taken for granted that she was part of *his* story. Maybe this was just one more sign that it was coming to an end.

No. Morgana had fought to send him back here for the chalice. And he was going to take it—for her as much as anyone else—the second it was out of Arthur's hands.

"Where is Arthur?" Morgause asked, and the people of Camelot gasped. Some of them shouted, "*King* Arthur!" But the enchantresses of Avalon recognized no king. Their power came straight from the earth. The pure stuff.

Arthur stepped forward from his pack of uneasy guards, Gweneviere on his arm.

"We are honored by your presence," he told the enchantresses.

"And we are intrigued by your notion of peace. Here, an offering to guide your venture." Morgause held out a cup. It was a small thing in life, smaller than Merlin had made it in memory. Dirty white, not the pure cream he remembered. Lined with gold, a temptation to the lips of anyone who held it. This was the chalice Arthur had sent them back to find.

This was the key to taking down Mercer. To ending the cycle.

"For a man who visited our shores without pretense," Morgause said. "A vessel made of the bones of a dragon who was slain in an attack on his city. We tracked the creature back to its cave, where it died. There are so few left, and it is deeply wrong to let such a being pass out of the world without honoring its life and preserving its magic."

Old Merlin *harrumphed* loudly from the back of the crowd. "You want the beast to keep attacking us from beyond the grave?"

"I'm not convinced that dragon was acting of its own free will," Morgause said. "Arthur might have enemies who spurred it on. Enemies who are here *now*."

Which shut Old Merlin right up.

Arthur accepted the cup. The moment seemed to stretch, nearly to the point of tearing. Merlin wondered if the old animosity between Camelot and these magical women was about to heat back up.

Then Gwen stepped forward, bowed to Morgause as a man would, and said, "Camelot and Avalon are more alike than they are different. Our lands are one land. So may our people become one people."

Morgause gave her a hard-won smile, and the enchantresses dissolved into the crowd. The music started up again. The party returned to full volume.

Lamarack entered the melee of bodies as dance patterns formed. Soon everyone was coupled off—and Lam had somehow maneuvered into a spot right across from Morgause.

"It seems I'm not the only one on a mission tonight." Merlin remembered how they'd nursed a crush on Morgana in the future. Enchantresses seemed to be their cup of tea. With just the right amount of milk and sugar.

Merlin found Arthur again, standing off to one side of the dancers, handing off the chalice with the timeless awkwardness of someone who's been given a gift they have no idea what to do with. The cup went straight into Old Merlin's hands. He turned away from the bonfire and the festivities, heading toward the castle. The chalice was in motion.

It was time.

Merlin stepped forward, so intent on the chalice that he ran directly into a little girl. She was no older than ten. She didn't back away, just smiled with a shyness that made him distinctly nervous. "Would you dance?" she asked.

"No! For several reasons!" Merlin shouted. The girl drew back as if a spark from the bonfire had landed on her skin. "I'm sorry. I'm..." But she was already running away. Merlin had gotten upset and taken it out on a child. He truly *was* as bad as his old self.

He ran away from the moment, trying to leave it behind. But it stuck to his skin. Sweat slid off him, and the dancers were everywhere, jostling him as he tried to catch a glimpse of Old Merlin with the chalice. All he saw was Lam moving in on Morgause. They broke the pattern of the polite dancing. Their bodies slid together. Enchantress and future knight had no use for the rules of this place, and together they started to—Merlin could conjure up only one word for it—grind. Merlin sparked with jealousy. He would never dance like that with Val again.

Would he even see Val again? How could they possibly get him back from Nin?

"The plan," he muttered. "Stick to the *plan*."

There was Old Merlin—already halfway to the castle gate. Merlin pelted across the party. He'd come back to this ruinous place, risked everything worthwhile he'd found in the future for that dead dragon cup. He chased it through the fug of bonfire smoke and the rude press of bodies. His vision blistered with heat spots as Old Merlin entered the castle. The chalice went with him.

And in that moment, the skies ripped open.

Rain hit Merlin hard.

Every shard of water that broke over him was a memory. No—Morgana had showed him memories. These were moments of time, full and warm and *real*. He lived through meeting Val again, on Lionel. Val asking if Merlin's sudden appearance was a set-up. Val smiling at him in *Error*'s tiny kitchen, that I ♥ NEW NEW NEW YORK T-shirt. Val staying up with him all night during the siege, not touching, the space between them deeper than dark water. Val kissing him so deeply that Merlin dissolved. Val dissolving in the time portal, right out of his hands.

He needs you, Merlin, Nin said. Now Merlin lived a different moment. Not an old piece of time. Something terrifyingly new. Val drowning in dark water. *He grew up on a planet without water, poor thing. He doesn't know how to swim. I thought I was setting him free, but he's running out of time.*

Merlin stopped. He spun away from the castle, the chalice. His heart pounded in his increasingly smaller chest, and he let out a small scream. Nin was either messing with him or Val was dying. Or most likely both. And he couldn't let that happen.

Nobody noticed him sprinting for the city gates. They were too busy dancing and carousing and eating Old Merlin's flying pies. The rain didn't seem to bother anyone else, and Lam and Ari and Gwen remained fully focused on the party, as if Nin's voice were only in his head.

Merlin ran deep into the ancient woods of Camelot, a place as twisted as every thought of Val's death. The colors of oak and ash and birch blended into a lifeless gray as Merlin reached out with his magic—to do what? He closed his eyes, branches reaching out and roots tripping him. He went back to the year on Lionel he'd spent staring at Val's dimples instead of dating him recklessly.

"Never enough time," he muttered. They'd barely gotten together when the story cracked them apart. Now there wasn't enough time for Merlin to save him. He'd never run all the way to the lake before Val stopped fighting and filled his lungs with water. Merlin clutched at his chest. His heartbeat seemed to blur at the edges. The feeling radiated outward, cold and blank. Was this what death felt like? He opened his eyes, but he wasn't in the forest anymore. He was falling through darkness. Through absence.

With a solid splash, he found himself in the shallows of a darkly glittering lake.

The lake.

Merlin didn't have time to contemplate how he'd gotten here so fast. Val was barely visible at the center of the black water, one hand grasping for the sky. Merlin cast himself away from the shore with a messy dive.

He swallowed lake water, swam harder. "I'm here," he shouted, grabbing on to Val's hand. Merlin wrapped one arm around the shoulders he knew so well and tried not to think about how much smaller he was than the last time they'd been this close. Turning their bodies, he aimed them back toward the shore. He used a bit of magic to buoy them up and focused on his kicking, not strong or steady but good enough.

Val slipped, disappeared under the water. Merlin grabbed him. Heaved him back up. Sparks filled the water, bright blue, as he expended more magic.

More time lost.

When they finally reached the bank, Merlin dragged Val past the edge of the water; he didn't want Nin touching his boyfriend again.

Val's eyes slowly rediscovered their focus. His face lit with the saddest smile in the universe. "You have freckles now."

"I...I do?" Merlin asked. He hadn't had freckles this morning. They must have been a feature of his youngest years, one that had lain in wait. Whatever magic he'd just used had cost him dearly. Whatever months he'd been clinging to that kept them close in age had slipped away.

But Val was alive. They were reunited. Anything else in the universe could be overcome.

Merlin could feel the great, foolish smile on his face. "Oh, Merlin," Val said with a wince. He twirled one of Merlin's damp red curls, then pressed a hand on his cheek. "You stupid, sweet boy. You just gave Nin exactly what she wanted."

HEADACHES
&
HEARTBREAKS

The entire kingdom of Camelot was hungover. Or still drunk.

Ari was both.

Dawn's rays seared through the high windows in the great hall, baking Ari in her armor. She sat up from where she'd slumped over on the head table, Arthur deeply asleep beside her. Looking around for Gwen, she found the chair on the other side of the king was empty. Ari got to her feet and nearly went down. Arthur stirred beside her, and she hefted one of his arms over her shoulder. He mumbled something along the lines of, "Leave me to die," and Ari carried him to his rooms as if she'd plucked him wounded from a battlefield.

Which actually worked as a metaphor because parties in Camelot were *ragers*. Ari hadn't seen anything like it since she and Kay had found their way into a twenty-four-hour lock-in nightclub on Tanaka. Once she'd deposited the one true king in his rooms, his army of long-legged, huge-pawed hunting dogs barking incessantly as she stumbled out into the same antechamber where she'd snuck behind a tapestry with Gwen.

Gwen.

Almost the entire kingdom was asleep. Could she sneak up to the queen's rooms unnoticed?

"Merlin," Ari murmured to herself, a reminder. She needed to find Merlin, to make sure he got the chalice after Arthur passed it off. And Ari desperately wanted to take it for a test drive. To know what it could do. How it could be the answer to stopping Mercer...

Ari checked the tower where they'd sent Jordan back. The cot was empty, and there was no sign of Merlin. While climbing back down the spiral stairs, her feet took her toward Gwen's rooms. Perhaps Merlin was there.

She wasn't persuading herself. No, not at all.

Ari found Gwen's guards dead asleep and decided against knocking. She pressed the door open, closed it behind herself quietly, and looked around. But Gwen wasn't in the large, canopy bed or any of the smaller chambers attached to the room. And that's when Ari stopped worrying about her headache and started worrying about the love of her life.

She shot out of the room and began a thorough search of the castle, making sure to drop in on the small hole of the oubliette, which was thankfully unoccupied. When she checked the room she shared with Lam she discovered that no, not everyone was incapacitated. Lamarack and Morgause were in the throes of an encounter so epic they both didn't notice when Ari walked in—and walked straight out again.

"Fuck," Ari muttered, shaking her head and the rather

potent images nestled therein. "At least someone is enjoying the Middle Ages."

Ari decided to try the courtyard, passing dozens of downed villagers on the way. She checked for Merlin and found the pile of Gwen's handmaidens, which at least indicated her last known whereabouts. Ari went to the stables, too hot to stay in this armor a moment longer. She retreated to the back corner where Lam kept some things and pulled off several heavy pieces, pouring cold water from the horses' trough over herself. Her headache began to ease as she remembered more of what had happened. They'd sent Jordan home; that was good. They'd laid eyes on the chalice; also good. The book still detailed Arthur's legendary adventures with his knights, and that had to be a victory. They'd made their way into the story without changing the time continuum.

Then why did something feel very wrong?

A hand slipped over Ari's shoulder, making her jump so hard she nearly punched the person attached to it. Gwen held her palms up, eyes wide. She wore one of her handmaiden's dresses, not the billowing gold finery from the previous evening. Her hair was down and curly and Ari's heart pounded.

"You scared the life out of me."

"I didn't mean to."

"It's okay." Ari rubbed the water out of her eyes. "I've been looking for you and Merlin all morning."

"I've been looking for him, too. Did he *leave* Camelot? I haven't seen him since he ran after Old Merlin. You don't think he got caught again, do you?"

"I checked the oubliette. It's empty." Ari took off a few more pieces of armor, and when Gwen started to help, Ari fell out of time for a spell, as if this were nothing more than a friendly morning on Lionel, following a fierce tournament. Gwen pulled off her layers, and Ari was exhaustingly grateful for each one. Until Gwen tugged off Ari's undershirt, and she was bare breasted before Gwen for the first time in years.

Gwen's hands found Ari's biceps and slid up to her shoulders, fingers splayed. Ari's eyes closed and the most damning sound slipped out. "Your muscles are enormous, Ari. And you're really dirty, and it's doing a whole thing for me that I do not understand but *really* want to go with." Her hands slid all the way down to the low-slung edge of Ari's linen unders, hooking into the waistband.

Ari cracked a smile. She stepped out of Gwen's reach and threw on one of Lam's clean shirts. Gwen's instant scowl was adorable. "You know we can't. Not even for a few minutes."

"I hate you."

"I know." Ari slid her arms around Gwen, and Gwen tucked her head beneath Ari's chin. Something on Gwen *buzzed* but Gwen didn't seem to care, so Ari ignored it as well. "She's going to be okay," Ari said, knowing that Gwen's thoughts couldn't be far from Jordan.

"What if no one found her fast enough?"

"She's going to be okay." Ari kissed Gwen's forehead, and then they were staring into each other's eyes, which was ever-so-much more dangerous than being topless. "Captain Mom was prowling about the night we left. She'll find Jordan."

"Promise?" Gwen murmured.

Ari leaned closer, tracing Gwen's lips with her thumb. What had Nin called them? *Magnets*. Yes, they were magnetic, and she swore she could feel their bodies lining up in the way that pulled fast and forever. Ari was painfully aware that each breath like this was a gamble, but before she could pull away, Gwen *buzzed* again. "Lady, as much as I enjoy vibrating pleasures, did you sneak something from the future back with you?"

"It's just my watch. I think it's finally broken. It's been trying to give me a news notification since last night."

"Wow, news from a distant future. Mercer has really outdone itself this time." Ari picked up Gwen's wrist, eyeing the slim piece of tech she'd hidden beneath a jeweled bracelet. "You know this is my watch."

"No. It's mine. You gave it to me on Urite. Remember?"

Ari winced. "I remember. When we got torn apart...when Morgana..." A thunderclap of a thought pounded through Ari's hangover. She pushed Gwen away, leaning over to support herself on her knees.

"Ari, what's wrong?"

"Nin. She's so motherfucking evil. I mean, she's *good*."

"Are you saying she's good or evil? I'm not following."

"She's really good at being evil. She told me that you and I are like magnets to her. That she's amused by pulling us apart. She's the one who tore me from your side in the portal. *And* she acted like she'd done it before. Maybe she was behind our separation at Urite."

"How? Wasn't that Morgana?"

"Yes and no. Morgana took me to Ketch, but once we were there, she couldn't make another portal to get us out again. She always acted weird about it. Weird because it hadn't been her magic to begin with." Gwen didn't looked convinced, but

Ari hadn't wanted to trust Nin from the beginning, and now she really didn't want to. "We have to get Val back."

Gwen's watch *buzzed* again, and this time Ari picked up her wrist to close out the notification. She clicked on it by accident and a small holographic news bulletin lit up the medieval stable. Both girls scrambled to mute it before someone heard, but then froze when they beheld the lines of bound people being marched onto Mercer police cruisers.

"That's Ketch," Ari murmured.

"Those are my people! Ari, what's the date on this?"

Ari swiped the hologram to reveal its posted information. The year was the same as when they'd left, but it was an entire season later. And from the looks of it, Mercer had regained much of its power in their absence. "Gwen, is this the date we sent Jordan back to? We must've fucked up the portal. That's not the night we left!"

Gwen was breathing so hard she'd become shiny and flushed. She started to teeter, and Ari held on to her, turning the watch off in a hurry. Ari pulled Gwen onto a pile of straw, fetched a wet rag, and used it to cool Gwen's face and neck. Gwen was holding her stomach in a way that sent fear straight through Ari. Was the baby coming? Spurred on by Gwen's panic?

"We're okay," Gwen said, interpreting Ari's fear. "We still have a month at least."

Ari pressed her lips to Gwen's forehead. "You just scared the life out of me."

"The watch must have updated when the portal was open." Gwen's red skin had paled down to a faintish milky color. "We sent Jordan back to the wrong day in the future. A future in which Mercer is back in power."

"Whatever happened, we'll fix it. We'll find Merlin. We'll... fix it." Ari kissed her, relieved when Gwen kissed back. *We're together,* she ached to say. *It's okay because we're together...* all because Gwen had refused to step into that portal after Jordan. Ari kissed her again, pulling Gwen close to her chest, holding her tight.

"Yikes. You know just about anyone could walk in on you two."

Ari looked up to find Val. Glorious, perfect, unharmed Val. She threw herself at him, wrapping her arms tight around his trim frame. Gwen pulled Ari off and hugged him, too. "Thank the stars you're okay," she said. "We were so worried."

Val turned in a circle, showing off how alive he was. He'd been in Nin's cave long enough that his usual buzzed-to-the-scalp hair had grown out into an afro that suited him just as well. "I'm damn fine, but only because this one saved me from certain death by drowning."

Val stepped out of the way to reveal Merlin. At least, the slim young boy was what Merlin might've looked like if he'd grown several years younger overnight. Ari stared at Earth's most famous mage, now swimming in his own clothes, freck-les bright on round cheeks, red hair curling in the humidity as dawn finally broke.

&

The conference was sadly born in the trench of a peat bog, where Merlin had been sent by the older version of himself to do penance for disappearing during the party. The only saving grace in this smelly business was that they were far enough away from Camelot to talk openly to one another. Not that that was happening at the moment.

"Why do I feel so sore that the old cretin didn't notice I'd gotten drastically younger overnight?" Merlin glanced up from his shoveling, and Ari looked away. "You're angry with me?"

"Not angry, Merlin," she managed. "Just...pissed off."

"Oh, that's much better, thank you."

Ari hid a small smile, hacking at the layers of squishy mess, trying to make sense of all that had gone wrong. She paused after a minute and looked up at where Val was perched on the edge, several feet above their heads, keeping watch.

"No sign of them," Val said, answering her wordless question. "You sure Gwen got the message to Lam about the meeting?"

"I'm sure." Ari went back to shoveling. "I'm also sure Lam had *quite* the night."

Merlin cleared his throat. "Should we talk about—"

"Not without the others," Ari barked. "We've had enough half-truths wafting about."

"They're coming on horseback!" Val announced, leaping to his feet, pacing until his sibling reached him. Ari scrambled out of the bog trench just as Lam leaped off the horse to embrace their brother. And they weren't alone. While Val and Lam had their reunion, Ari stared at Morgause.

"What are you doing here?" Ari asked.

Lam broke out of a hug with Val to give Morgause a hand down from the horse. Ari had only gotten a glimpse of the enchantress on her trip to Avalon before she face-planted in the lake. Now it felt so much like looking at Morgana that she couldn't help blinking a few times. They were both slender and slightly curved. They had the same intensity, like a fire that couldn't be doused. It helped that their coloring was different, Morgause's long dark hair much warmer than the black hole shade that Morgana had so eloquently rocked. "Morgause is with me. We can trust her. I think it's about time we get help from someone inside this time period."

Merlin crowed an objection from the bottom of the peat trench, and everyone looked over the edge at him. "She can't be here!"

"Are you...okay?" Lam asked, squinting at the significantly diminished mage.

"I look worse than I am!" Merlin insisted, while Val gave a sure shake of his head.

"We did something wrong," Ari said, chewing on her thumbnail. "Gwen will be here soon. We should wait until we're together." She climbed back down into the trench and Lam and Val followed. Morgause took over Val's lookout position, silent but taking in everything.

"So, what happened to Merlin?" Lam asked.

"He's been holding out on you," Val said flatly.

"We can't just talk about this with Yoko up there listening in!" Merlin said.

"Who?" Lam asked, and Merlin waved his hand dismissively. "I'm telling you we can trust her. She knows we're not from this time. All the enchantresses do. They can feel the portals every time they open and close."

Merlin was going to keep objecting, Ari could tell, but Val put a hand on his arm that settled him down. "Lam is right."

Merlin opened his mouth and Val gave him a warning look. "Merlin was just about to tell you that every time he uses his magic, he gets younger. He realized it when he arrived but didn't tell anyone."

"*Merlin.*" Ari couldn't keep the parental scolding out of her voice. "How could you keep that from us?"

"Because you needed help! And you wouldn't have let me if you knew!"

"*Of course* we wouldn't have let you. You're our family. We're not letting you sacrifice yourself!" Ari yelled. Merlin's bright brown eyes filled with tears. Ari turned away, not wanting to make him upset, wrestling with her own disappointment. She held out Gwen's watch. "I have something to show you. A news bulletin that came through while that portal was open last night." She showed them the footage, still unable to process the sight of Mercer clearly in control again. "Gwen and I think we accidentally sent Jordan back later than we meant to."

"That's…not entirely true," Val said, wincing. "Nin kept me in her cave because she's Grade-A obsessed with Merlin, but I picked up some info down there. The way this all works is that human bodies, regular ones," he qualified, shooting a glance at Merlin, "have to age in the past the same as they do in the future."

"Which means…?" Lam asked.

"Every day we're in Camelot is a day that passes in the future. We've been gone for months, so months have gone by in our galaxy. We can't return to the night we left as originally advertised. And Mercer has—clearly—taken advantage of our absence."

Ari's vision popped with bright, black spots. She dropped her shovel and held her hands over her pounding headache. They'd only left the future because they needed more time. Time for the baby. To find the chalice. To decide what to do about Mercer. And while they were missing, Mercer had the perfect opportunity to spin the future back into their control. Who knows what firestorm they'd be walking into when they finally made it back.

If they finally made it back.

"Nin is *obsessed* with me?" Merlin asked through the silence. "That's a bit hard to swallow. Not that I doubt you, but Nin is the magical, motherly, glowing presence in my life. She *saves* me. Why would she do that?"

"Oooh, pick me," Val deadpanned. "She needs you, Merlin."

"That motherly song and dance is an act," Ari added. "She didn't seem that way to me."

"What does she look like?" Lam asked. "I picture horns for some reason."

Ari cleared her throat. "Uhh…she was…attractive? In a sort of terrifying way?"

"Attractive?" Merlin spluttered.

"She wore a suit, but not a Mercer type of suit. It was cut down to…" She pointed at a scandalously low spot on her sternum.

"Funny," Val said. "That's not what I saw. My Nin has this sharp black buzzcut and she wears a lot of uniforms. Though sometimes she'll throw in a boa or a fascinator. You know, to offset it. The whole thing makes nefarious sense, really. This is her inhuman idea of *fun*. Playing dress-up to manipulate all of us."

"It's bigger than that." Ari needed to tell them about Arthur's body. About the deal Nin offered to send them all home. But she wasn't ready for them to reject the plan. She needed an emergency get-the-hell-out-of-the-Middle-Ages button, and ugly as it was, this was it.

Morgause whistled, causing them to all glance up. "The queen approaches."

Hoofbeats pounded the ground, coming to a stop above. Ari scurried out of the trench to find that Arthur had put Gwen on a dainty, prancing roan—the fool. "We only have minutes," Gwen said, putting the spurs to her speech. "I suggested taking a ride with Arthur, and thanks to Lionel's tireless horsebots I have much more practice in the saddle. He's way behind." She glared at Morgause. "What's she doing here?"

"Alternately spying and making out with Lam," Val said. "But the enchantresses should be on our side in general. They're not fans of Nin. Avalon is one of the only places Nin can't spy in on."

"Okay, I missed something. Recap," the queen commanded.

"Nin is sometimes hot but possibly evil as fuck," Ari said. "We're torn."

"What was that first part again?" Gwen asked.

"Also, Merlin might have the power to stop her." Ari took a deep breath. Now that Gwen was here, she had to say it. "King Arthur's body is in her weird cave. She's holding him hostage, making the cycle repeat." Ari tried not to stare at the child who used to be the most powerful magician in the known universe. "She said the cycle is your...prison."

All was silent in the peat bog, until Gwen spoke. "I suppose time is also passing in the future, and we can't go home to the night we left."

"How did you know?"

"We don't make mistakes like that. I knew there had to be another explanation. So I thought about all the possibilities and...we sent Jordan back wounded into the middle of a planet-wide siege." Gwen closed her eyes and took a deep, trembling breath before she could continue. "We go home as soon as possible. Before Mercer can do more harm to my people and destroy Ketch. Where's the chalice?" Merlin looked at Val. Val looked at Merlin. "I saw Arthur give it to Old Merlin at the party."

"See, that's the trick," Merlin rubbed the back of his neck, peat speckles on his face. "When I was going after it, Nin let me know Val was drowning. So I rushed to save him! Which cost me a little too much magic..." Merlin looked down at his body as if exhibiting evidence. "The old monster has had a chance to hide the chalice by now, which could make it impossible to find."

"*Impossible*," Lam repeated slowly.

"Too bad we don't know someone who thinks exactly like him," Val said in a scalding tone. It seemed to rile up Merlin in both a good and bad way at the same moment.

"That's hardly going to work! I don't remember where I put things down two days ago, let alone several millennia. Not to mention the hole where my memories are meant to be. To ask me to find something I hid in Camelot...Well, if I didn't want to keep it *in* Camelot, I'd probably stash it in my crystal cave, but—"

"Your crystal what?" Ari asked.

"Crystal cave," Val said. "It's Merlin's secret apartment that exists out of space and time. I've never seen it," he added with a clip.

"You look for the chalice there," Ari told Merlin. "I'll cover for you with the old jerk."

Val nodded his approval. "I'm coming with."

Gwen gave a sharp cry. She held her side. "Nobody freak out. It's false labor."

"Not...freaking out," Ari tried to lie as her heart beat rather pointedly. She decided against telling them about Nin's deal to send them all home at the cost of her own eternal spirit. It'd already been too much for today. Ari looked up at Morgause who was leafing through Jordan's MercerNotes on King Arthur. "Should she be reading that, Lam?"

"Oh, she can't read Mercer."

"Still." They all watched her. "Is the book on track?"

"No empty pages this morning," they said.

"So there *is* good news," Ari said. When everyone stared, she shrugged. "What? I needed some good news."

"Lamarack?" Morgause's voice slipped like ice across hot metal. She turned the book around to reveal a blank page.

Ari snatched the book. "What did we forget to do now?"

Lam exhaled through their teeth, flipping a few pages either way as if confirming their worst suspicions. "This is when Arthur finds out that Lancelot has stolen Gweneviere's heart."

&

Everyone had an opinion as to how Ari and Gwen should get busted by Arthur. Some were more X-rated than others, but in the end, Ari decided on a scenario she'd been dreaming about for what felt like years.

That evening, while the king and his nobles and knights feasted in the great hall, Sir Lancelot entered in gleaming armor. Ari walked straight through the drinking, celebratory masses to the head table where Gwen sat beside Arthur.

"My king, I'd like to dance with your wife."

"Of course," Arthur said with such a wide, trusting smile that Ari felt her first true pang. They were going to hurt him. It was the goal.

Gwen graciously got up, and Ari did her best to mimic the patterned and simplified dance styles of the time. They were not alone, dancing with several other partners.

Gwen had a worried little knot between her eyebrows. "I've been thinking," she said under the music. "This isn't just about making sure the whole stupid love triangle plays out. There are other things we need to make happen. Like the knights of the round table and...I just don't know when we're going to be able to leave, do you? We can't stay, considering the future is growing worse by the hour, and yet if we duck out on Arthur in the middle of the legend, surely it's going to break the story in some important way."

"There's going to be a moment when we can leave." Ari took Gwen's hand and placed it on her breastplate, over the spot on the Ouroboros where the dragon bit its own tail. "We just have to be ready when the time comes."

Gwen almost laughed, but it came out as mostly breath. "It's just a symbol, Ari."

"The Lady of the Lake picked out this armor for me. She bragged about it." Ari slid back the chainmail on her wrist, showing off one of her old scars. Like the Ouroboros, the marks weren't perfect circles; the spot where the circle joined itself was evident. The beginning and the end all in one. Gwen stared. "My scars match. Still think it's a coincidence?"

They went back to dancing, their awareness of each other mounting like always, drowning out the other people in the room, and then the room itself.

"So this was your idea?" Gwen murmured as they pressed palms and walked in a circle. Ari finished the turn and swung closer to Gwen, her dress swishing against Lancelot's armor. Gwen looked down at their proximity with growing suspicion. "We're to dance until he's jealous?" Gwen's eyes moved to Ari's face.

"I love you."

Gwen smiled, but then seemed confused. "That's the first time you've ever told me that."

"I know, and I'm sorry, and I love you."

Gwen nodded, emotion rushing to her cheeks, pinking her skin and brightening her eyes. "Oh, so you're going to flirt with me in front of everyone? That's it?"

"Not flirting, Gwen. My idea was to get you to talk about the future."

"I really can't think about Mercer right now."

"Not that future. *Our* future. How I love you and the baby, and I'm dying to get back to our time so we can make a home for our family." Ari smiled and a tear left one eye. Gwen traced its path with her gaze. "We don't have to live on Ketch, if you don't want to. We could go anywhere. Also, I've been thinking we should adopt Merlin. He'll act like he hates it, but we can take care of him, especially if time keeps...stealing him away."

"I've been thinking about that, too," Gwen whispered.

Ari took in the curve of Gwen's lovely neck, the way her lips parted with each breath. Ari could see it so clearly: a home for all of them. Visits from her parents. A dog. Oh, they were definitely getting a dog. "I just really want a bed that's ours. For sleeping all tangled up. For *not* sleeping," she said with a lift of the eyebrows. "A place where we aren't separated. Not by anything or anyone ever again."

"Gweneviere?"

Arthur stood in the middle of the floor, flanked by guards. Ari didn't know when they'd stopped dancing, when they'd woven their hands together and pressed their chests as close as they could be—as if they had become an illuminated illustration in an ancient text of Lancelot matched with her Gweneviere.

"Arthur," Gwen started, but the king merely took her arm and led her away. Gwen looked back at Ari while she was tugged out of the great hall, mouthing a warning.

Ari never saw the face of the knight who knocked her out cold.

CAVE
&
CRYSTAL

Merlin stepped into the crystal cave, Val right behind him. The inky portal closed, leaving them alone together for the first time since they embarked on this ruinous trip.

"So this is your cave of wonders," Val said, peering around. Merlin had always loved that brash interest. Of course, it used to be pointed at *him*. Now Val was taking in Merlin's private sanctuary.

Which was, frankly, a mess.

He'd never brought anyone here before, and suddenly it seemed like a mistake to let Val see this hidden part of him. The crystals were a splendid blushing pink quartz, natural columns sparkling in the dim light. But Merlin hadn't kept the place up through the ages. With everything he'd stashed in various nooks and crannies, it was midway between a historical museum and a level four hoarding situation.

"I only ever come here to sleep off the cycles," Merlin admitted, running about to do a lightning round of tidying.

"It's become a bit of a dumping ground for things that came to me over the ages. Though I swear I did clean it up after Arthur 28. Or was it Arthur 29? Please don't judge!"

"Too late," Val said. "I just saw the little crystal bed where you sleep. The collection of *nightcaps*? Merlin, you have like two hundred."

"Have you ever slept for a decade?" Merlin asked. "It requires extreme comfort."

"Where do you think the chalice could be?" Val asked, nudging an orphaned slipper with his toe.

"I probably wouldn't have put it in a special spot because that's exactly where someone else would check. As you can tell from looking around, my strategy was to toss things in all higgledy-piggledy."

"Did you say *higgledy-piggledy*?" Val asked.

Merlin blushed. Why did blushing feel so different as an eleven-year-old—less tingly and pleasant, more cruelly embarrassing? "The younger I get the more conversational filters I lose. Just give me a lunch box and some juice and call it a lifetime."

Merlin thought that Val might comfort him, even put an arm around his shoulder. He would take any scrap of age-appropriate affection he could get at this point. Val reached into a pile of souvenirs and pulled out a tin square. "Done and done."

It was an ancient, rusted-out lunch box, complete with Thermos. The metal was adorned with an image of King Arthur and a very powerful-looking magician with a gnarled staff. "Do you collect your own merchandise, Merlin?"

He laughed—despite himself. Despite everything.

Val still had the power to make him happy. Considering how slim their chances were of ever being a couple again, it was quite a miserable revelation. "All right, you take the right-hand chambers and I'll take the left," Val said. "Sing out when you see a magical cup."

Merlin squatted in the first cluster of crystals looking for the small, bony, gold-rimmed chalice. He hated being apart from Val for even a minute, but as the future moved on without them, it grew ever more imperative to fulfill the Arthurian legend, grab the chalice, and get out.

Would that really end the cycle, though, if Nin was the one behind it? Or would she find a way to keep it spinning on forever?

Merlin suddenly couldn't handle being back in this place, stuffed with the detritus of so many years spent chained to Arthur's story—the evidence that this cycle truly was his prison.

"Val?" Merlin asked, his voice pinging around in the high-ceilinged space. "Val, did you find anything?"

No answer.

Merlin ran back to Val's last known whereabouts. He was sitting cross-legged on the cold ground, seemingly unable to move.

"What's the matter?" Merlin asked, poking Val's shoulder. It felt like they were both hitting personal rock bottom.

Crystal bottom?

"I thought I would be fine," Val said, his eyes unfocused, his breath hard. "I *was* fine. I survived Nin's kidnapping and you fished me out of her lake but... I was terrified the whole time I was down there."

Merlin didn't know what to say; this was entirely his fault.

Val stood up, grabbing Merlin's skinny arms. "Look, there's a reason I wanted to come here with you, even though I am ready to cancel all caves forever. There are things I need to tell you, Merlin."

"Private things?" he asked, hopeful and terrified.

"Nin-flavored things," Val said.

Merlin braced himself against the smooth face of a particularly large crystal.

"The good news is, I don't think she can see in here," Val said. "Like Avalon, it's built on someone else's magic, and that makes it off-limits."

"But she can see everywhere else? Because of her water?" Merlin asked, needing to understand everything about Nin, as if this were a thirst he'd had for several hundred years.

"Wherever her water goes, she goes, too. Information trickles in that way, but that's not enough for Nin. Are you ready for the bad news?"

"How bad?" Merlin squeaked out. "On a scale from mild rubbish to total Armageddon?"

"Nine and a half," Val said. "She has a window into the cycle."

"What is it?" Merlin asked, whispering even though this was the one place they wouldn't be overheard.

"It's *who*. And . . . it's you."

Merlin's brain hit a boiling point. Nin had been watching him? This entire time?

"You're the one person she can always see. That's why she needs you in play in the cycle, that's why she keeps you alive. And she's especially excited when you're suffering. It's a little like one of Mercer's extreme reality shows, except you're the star and Nin's the producer *and* the audience. Oh, and it lasts forever."

"She's been watching every horrible thing that's ever happened to me because she...enjoys it?" Merlin's nausea rolled so hard that he wavered on his feet. Val reached out to put a comforting hand to the back of Merlin's neck like he had so many times before—and stopped himself.

"More like she feeds off it," Val said, stuffing his hand in his pocket.

"But how did she create the cycle? By stealing Arthur's body?" Merlin had been in her cave the day Arthur died—sidelined while she made him watch Arthur's demise, after which she must have stolen the one true king's body on its way to Avalon, where Morgana was waiting to put him to rest. How had Merlin not realized she was this awful much, much earlier? It was starting to seem like the one true oversight.

"Arthur is important," Val said, "but he's not the whole story. He's trapped in this like everyone else. Nin pulled some kind of power move that gives her dominion over a piece of time. I couldn't figure out how it works. She guards some things a lot more closely than others, and she did not want me sniffing around that."

So Nin really had crafted the entire cycle. On purpose. To hurt people. "I thought she was a neutral voyeur. A magical master of schadenfreude. But she's more than that, isn't she?" Merlin had barely seen Nin for centuries, and now she seemed to be everywhere. That couldn't be a coincidence. Evil time lords didn't really *do* coincidence.

And Nin was evil.

He'd thought for so long that lurking and watching was

harmless, but now he could see the truth. Not to give hate a pass, but it had the potential to be overcome. The emotion could be purged; the person who'd ingested its poison could heal and move on. Whereas sitting back and manipulating people to feed your own power? Without feeling a single one of the consequences? That was perhaps the best working definition of evil he knew.

"Look…" Val said, "There's one more thing I have to say. I know this is a weird time and that things with us are in the land beyond awkward, so this is not the right moment to bring it up, but…" Merlin crossed his fingers and waited for Val to say something about their relationship. Anything. "You're a lot like Nin, what's that about," Val said flatly.

"…what? I am *not* like Nin."

"Some observations," Val said, pacing the crystal with a hard sound. He was fully avoiding Merlin's gaze now. "You both have caves. That exist outside of time. Neither of you age like the rest of us. And please think about the portals."

"I need help to make those!" Merlin cried. "Three magics, remember?"

"Yes, but you ripped spacetime to save me from the lake. By yourself."

"You think I can make portals all higgledy-piggledy?" Merlin nearly slapped himself for that one. "You think that my magic is like *Nin's*? But…why?"

Val's amber eyes were dark in the half-light of the cave. "I don't know, Merlin. You tell me."

"I can't! I have no idea where I came from!" he cried.

"Yes, that's part of the problem. What if you need that answer?" He took a step closer, reflected light from the crystals winking into his eyes. "What if your power's greater than you've ever known? She's afraid of you, Merlin. And she's not afraid of anything else in the universe."

Val looked so wondrous, even in full cave gloom. His dark skin collected what light there was and turned it into a burnished glow. His hair had grown out into soft inches of black curls. Merlin was just old enough to understand that he wanted to kiss him. And far too young to actually do it. Nin had waited until the precise moment when big magic would take that possibility away—and then reunited them.

The Lady of the Lake wanted him alive. She wanted him miserable. She wanted him, most of all, *weak*. And that's how he felt when he looked at Val. Dizzy and helpless and far too young to deal with any of this.

"We have to find the chalice," Merlin said. It was the only thing he felt sure about.

"What if that's not enough?" Val asked feverishly. Merlin had seen him fly into this mode as advisor to the queen on Lionel. Once he saw the best plan of action, he wouldn't let anyone else rest until they were on the right path. "We need to stop Nin, and for that we need you. Which means you have to end this backward aging."

"I can't."

Val picked up one of Merlin's hands, touching his fingertips—the source of his magic. "When was the last time you actually *tried*?"

The certainty that he couldn't be fixed was something that Merlin had been holding on to for ages. He didn't know how to let go of it. "Perhaps I can give it another go," he said in a tiny voice. The entire crystal cave seemed to echo his doubt. "If that's what it takes to finish the cycle—"

"You're still playing by Nin's rules," Val cut in. "Merlin, what if you don't have to finish this cycle? What if you have to break it?"

&

They searched for hours. The crystal cave seemed to hold everything *but* the chalice. Merlin and Val eventually gave up. They worked up an impressive awkward silence as they portaled back—and the truth grew crystal clear. All things Nin aside, Merlin needed to turn his aging right-side up if he ever wanted his boyfriend back.

When they reached the peat bog again, Lam was waiting. With Morgause. They were kissing furiously. Lam stepped back long enough to wipe their lips and cast a worried glance at Merlin and Val's chalice-free return.

"I'm to escort you to Camelot," they said, holding out their arm for their sibling.

"Ari and Gwen are too busy being scandalous?" Val asked.

"It is sort of their thing," Lam admitted with a shrug.

"I need to make one stop on the way to the castle," Val said. "I have to burn the clothes I'm wearing because: Nin. I'll need something new to meet this Arthur fellow. And *someone* told me there's a place where I can get a bespoke corset."

A few weeks ago, Merlin would have begged Val not to stick out. Now he couldn't think of anything he wanted more than to walk into Camelot on Val's arm as he finally made his grand entrance.

Instead, he had to scurry in through the servants' quarters.

"Carbuncle!" Old Merlin cried as soon as he'd made it

through the kitchens and swiped a few biscuits. Which, of course, he dropped at hearing that word. "I hope the peat bog taught you a lesson. You shouldn't have left Arthur's birthday celebration. How can I depend on an apprentice who vanishes into nothing?"

That description was uncomfortably close to what he'd actually done.

Old Merlin turned around and headed back toward his tower. Across the main hall, Arthur came in with Gwen on his arm. The court didn't even smother their gossip. It flared wherever they walked. Gwen shot Merlin a look of pure misery.

She and Ari must have been exceptionally successful at hurting Arthur. It wasn't an easy task, but they were all committed to making it through the Arthurian legend as quickly as possible and getting back to their time before Mercer grew stronger. Which meant that Merlin didn't have much time at all to figure out this backward aging business.

He needed help. He needed someone with magic to spare.

Merlin looked at the receding back of the withered, worm-hearted old mage. Merlin had been amazed, disappointed, *and* relieved that Old Merlin hadn't noticed his de-aging. It would no doubt end in another interrogation. And most likely some magical experimentation. But wasn't that what he needed right now?

He ran to catch up, stopping Old Merlin at the tower door. Merlin took a mighty breath, preparing himself to pull an Ari and tell the truth. It was harder than it looked.

"Haven't you noticed anything strange?" he demanded.

"Yes," Old Merlin said. "You're getting more pesky these days. Like a fly around a rotting piece of fruit."

Funny, because you're a rotting piece of fruit! Merlin nearly shouted.

He sighed until he found a sense of calm, which was harder to summon than magic these days. "The night of Arthur's birthday celebration, I disappeared because...I was losing time." Old Merlin still looked puzzled. Gods, did he have to spell everything out for himself? "Getting *younger.*"

"And you didn't wish everyone to see your humiliations," Old Merlin filled in with surprising alacrity. He circled Merlin with his hawklike sharpness. He whipped a piece of string out of one of his robe pockets and took a few measurements as Merlin hummed nervously. What had he gotten himself into? Had he really invited the person he feared most into his personal space? "It does seem you're growing...down...rather than up."

"As your apprentice, you probably don't want me crawling around this place," he said. "It is *not* baby-proof."

Merlin held his breath. What kind of tortures awaited him now?

"This is *most fascinating*!" Old Merlin said, clapping his hands together and standing on his tiptoes, filled with the helium of delight. "Why didn't you mention that someone put a curse on you? I revel in countercurses."

"You...you do?" Merlin bumbled. He didn't remember helping people in this time, besides Arthur. Of course, he didn't remember much at all.

"Up to the tower at once," Old Merlin said, complete with impatient snapping. "No more dusting the prophetic orbs for you. We have bigger work to do."

Under any other circumstances, Merlin would have said no.

And possibly left the castle screaming. But right now, he was desperate enough to work with the very last person he would have chosen in any era, sociopathic dictators notwithstanding.

If he was going to break Nin's cycle, he needed complete control of his magic. Starting with his age. This time and place had always terrified him—but what if it held the answers he'd always sought? What if facing it was the only way to find them?

"Kairos," Old Merlin muttered. The tower door opened on its magical hinge, the stairs looming above them.

Merlin took a deep breath and said, "I guess it's you and me, old man."

SQUARE PEG
&
ROUND TABLE

Ari awoke to a bucket of water being dumped on her head. Her neck felt terrible. Her back felt terrible. The evening sun beating down on her felt, well, terrible.

She was in the stocks, head and wrists locked into worn, soft wood.

"What happened?" she asked, unable to look up, trying to figure out if what she was looking at were in fact Val's feet.

Val's voice floated down. "You are no longer Camelot's favorite knight, that's what. Hope this was your plan."

"Not exactly."

He began to pull back the mechanism that kept the wood clamped. "The good news is that your sentence has been served. One night and day in the stocks for impertinence toward the queen."

"Impertinence? That all?"

"I believe Arthur is covering for you. Even in his jealousy." Val helped her stand up, which was important because her body was stiff and her muscles felt like cement. "Tell me, did you and Gwen plan this or did you just whip out your sheer animalistic urges for one another in front of that poor young royal?"

"Worse," Ari grumbled. "I told her I loved her and we got all moony."

Val whistled. "That *is* worse." He led them toward the stable where Lam worked.

All was quiet in Camelot, and it left Ari feeling ill at ease. "Hang on a sec. I need to stretch." She stood on her own and leaned her chin way up while pulling her arms back. "That's better." Ari took in Val's sensational indigo corset and the kohl around his eyes. It was an absolute relief to see at least one of them dressed as themselves. "You look good."

"Keeps the commoners out of my way," he said. "Call it demiboy superpowers. Come on. We've got to figure out what in the hell to do next."

Ari couldn't agree more. They were about to round the corner toward the stable door when a dagger pointed hard into a notch at the side of her armor.

"State your purpose," young Roran said, shoulders thrown back and glaring mightily. The fact that the kid was half Ari's height didn't seem to bother him in the slightest.

"I'm here for Lamarack," Ari said, hoping this kid wasn't on Arthur's payroll, and that the people didn't yet know that crowd-favorite Lancelot was persona non grata.

Roran shoved his dagger in his belt. "They're meeting. I'm keeping watch."

"Ah, thanks." Ari slid down from where she'd been pressed up against the door by Roran's rather sincere blade. He took up a post in the shadows like a tiny palace guard. Val chuckled and opened the door.

They ducked inside, shutting the huge door behind them. Ari turned to find half a dozen people looking at her in utter alarm. They were all commoners, mostly muddy and dirty— but there was at least one familiar pink dress in the bunch.

"Um, what's up, Elaine?" Ari said, feeling red. What *was* going on here?

Lam got to their feet from where they'd been speaking to the small crowd and beckoned Ari and Val to the back, telling everyone to talk to each other in their most relaxed tone. "Remember, you're all united in your beliefs," they added gently.

When they had ducked behind an enormous stallion, Lam hugged her. "You all right? We heard about Sir Kay knocking the shit out of you. Gwen was *pissed*."

"I'm fine. Did it work? Did the page come back in the MercersNotes?"

Lamarack nodded, but Ari could tell there was more. "Then some other stuff went blank."

Ari groaned.

Val scowled. "We win the battles but we're losing the war, people. Why am I the only one to see that this is pure reactive and not at all proactive?"

"Hang on. I'll wrap up the meeting," Lam said. The voices in the stable rose with excitement when Lam returned to them.

While they filed out, Ari asked Val the question she already knew the answer to simply because it hadn't come up otherwise. "Chalice?"

Val shook his head.

The stable was quiet when the people were gone, and only the sounds of shuffling horses could be heard. Ari took some of her armor off, stretching her back. "Tell me you haven't started a religion, Lam."

"In a manner of speaking," Lam said. They were being shifty. Why?

"What's going on? Roran's willing to stab someone for coming in uninvited, and you're preaching...what exactly?"

Lam laughed. "Kindness, mostly. And acceptance. For all kinds of people."

"My gods, you're just...You make us all look so scrubby." Ari found herself smiling, shaking her head. Lamarack's grin glowed. "Okay, but don't get attached to this little cultural revolution. I need you back in the future beside me."

"They'll be much better equipped soon. Some of them are already using my pronouns."

"Leave it to my sibling to start humanity's first GSA." Val was undoubtedly pleased, giving Lamarack a smirk of pure admiration.

Lam pulled out the MercersNotes from a small leather bag hanging from their belt and pressed it into Ari's hand. Ari sighed with exasperation as she found the Lancelot-Arthur-Gweneviere love triangle back, but a new chapter blank. "What was here?"

"Knights of the Round Table," Lam said sheepishly.

Shit. Even Ari remembered how important that one was. It was in all the versions of the legend. "Okay, how do we fix it?"

"Stop with the fixing mentality!" Val said. "We need to set the legend floating on its own. Give it sails." Lam and Ari stared at him. "King Arthur has to go on without us.

Otherwise we'll never be able to leave without disrupting the stupid time continuum."

"How do we do that?" Lam asked.

Ari stared at the book in her hands. "We bring Arthur in on it, that's how."

"Ari..." Val's voice held such perfected exasperation. "No."

"He knows I'm a girl underneath all this armor, and he's okay with it."

"He does?" Lam asked at the same time that Val said, "He's not okay with it."

Ari stood up. "He's like me. He wants the truth, even if the truth is challenging. And I know *that's* true because deep down in me is...him!"

"And this is where you lose me." Val sat down on a pile of hay. "Cursed spirits, no thank you."

Ari turned to Lam. "I have to get in the castle. I need to talk to Arthur."

"You'll need a disguise," they said. "Sir Kay made some pretty bold statements about you not being allowed back into the keep."

"Good thing Suck Kay isn't in charge. Although, I should slip in unnoticed to avoid ending up back in the stocks." Ari turned to her childhood best friend and brought out her sweetest smile. "Val, do you have any makeover magic tucked into that corset?"

Val raised a finely shaped eyebrow at Ari. "Always."

An hour later, Ari was standing in a large wooden tub, getting her back scrubbed by Val. "Gross. Everything in this time period is gross. Did you roll around in the peat, or just make a few peat angels?" Lam came around one of the back stalls, and Ari closed her arms over her breasts. "What, you get shy around them, but not me?" Val pinched her side.

"Of course I get shy around Lam. They're *Lam*." Ari muttered, elbowing Val. She'd missed his no-filter conversations too much. Stepping out of the wooden tub, she went straight to the pile of dresses Val had procured from somewhere. "Why did you bring so many?"

"You think this is the first time I've dressed up a masc girl as a femme girl to trick patriarchal overlords? I grew up on Pluto. First things first, the dress has to actually fit. And you, Ara Azar, are not the same size you used to be. I had to estimate."

"I am much bigger." Ari looked down at the muscles she'd collected along her limbs like badges of honor. She'd been lanky in the future, but she was pretty sure she wasn't anymore. "The armor was so heavy. Took weeks to get used to it."

"Now you're strapping," Lam said, dropping a dress over her head.

"Too short. Try the green one," Val ordered.

Ari shimmied out of the dress and into the green one. It did fit slightly better, although the neckline was as wide as an ocean. "What in the world?" Ari muttered as it fell from one shoulder and then the other.

"It goes off the shoulders. Stand back." Val pushed his sibling out of the way and positioned Ari in the dress, pulling the laces taut. When Ari felt like she'd stop breathing, Val tugged the front lower and pulled the back tighter. Ari yelped, and Val added, "You're pretending to be a working girl, remember? You've got to show a little skin."

"Great." She looked to Lam. "Where's Roran?" The last

thing she wanted was to trigger him by yowling while someone stuffed her in a dress.

"He's asleep in the back. I just tucked him in."

Ari let those words sink in. Lam spoke them with such care. "He sleeps in the stables?"

"He left his family. They frightened him," Lam said. Ari felt softer inside as she imagined the fiercest kid in Camelot. Lamarack was taking care of him. Making him feel seen and loved. Of course they were.

Ari nearly shouted when Val finger-combed her hair, finding the first dozen of a thousand knots. "Well, this is going to take forever."

"Leave it down," Ari tried.

"Down and you look like Lancelot. Up and you're a lady."

"It's not that important." Ari winced as Val pulled her hair again. "I just need to get in."

"And then you're going to do what, exactly?" Val asked. Ari ignored him, and he added, "Oh, so you want to see the oubliette, too? It's just fantastic. When Merlin was locked in there with Jordan, Nin didn't blink. She *loved* how miserable they both were."

"She's more nefarious than Merlin lets on," Ari wondered. "Where is he, by the way?"

"Playing with *himself*. Don't get me started. Those two are up to something."

Ari was still and silent even though Val tugged too hard and made her eyes water. She looked to Lamarack, who nodded as if they were thinking the same thoughts, which gave her courage to voice them. "What do you think it will be like when we finally go home?"

Val was so distracted by detangling that he spoke harsh and flat. "I'll tell you *exactly* what it'll be like. Mercer will have punished the people we left behind for our absence. All of those representatives who jumped to come to our summit have probably fallen back, taking whatever bargain might keep their planets alive. Gwen's people, along with whatever's left of our friends and family, will most likely end up working in a Mercer distribution factory. And if Mercer is *really* on-brand, they will set fire to Ketch for the show alone. The last time they blew up a planet they streamed the destruction with inspired ad placement."

"Fireproof boxes and smoke detectors," Lam muttered. "I'll never forget it. Our parents bought them."

Ari's brain filled with images of the capital city, Omaira, up in flames. "Does Gwen think this will happen, too?"

Val bit his bottom lip. "She's mapped it out by now. That news bulletin was meant to reach us wherever we were hiding. To scare us. And it did, didn't it?"

"Gwen wanted to have the baby here." Ari sighed. "We thought we could go back to the same night when Mercer still thought she was only a few months pregnant. But if we go back with the baby now, Mercer will be looking for them, and I still don't understand *why* they demanded a baby as a down payment on peace. If we—"

"You can't take the baby back there." Ari was startled by the intensity of Lam's voice. "You'll have to think of something else."

Ari didn't know what to say while Val pulled on her knotted hair. She agreed with Lam, but that didn't make any of it easier. It would mean going home without Gwen. Or asking

Gwen to give up the baby for their safety. Both of which were impossible.

"How do we even get back?" Val asked softly. "It would take too much magic to make another portal. We'd end up gathering Merlin in a bunch of blankets afterward…"

Ari stopped his nervous finger-combing. "Don't worry about that part. I won't let Merlin sacrifice himself." If it came down to it, she had a way to get them home *and* free Arthur. It just meant giving up her spirit for all of eternity after she died.

Yeah, she was definitely going to keep sitting on that one.

She pulled a shawl over her still-knotted hair. "I have to go."

Lam stood and took her arm.

Val straightened her dress. "Remember, you two are about to engage in a night of utterly sinful debauchery. Sell it, or those guards *will* recognize Ari and drag her out of Camelot. Or worse. Also, Ari, bend your knees. You're way too tall in this time period."

Like Gwen, Lamarack didn't have a problem acting. They kept their demeanor set on *Drunk Flirt* as Ari awkwardly hunched over, hanging on to Lam's waist for support. The palace guards took no note of her as they both stumbled in. Ari and Lam needed only to cross the front hall to the stairs that led up to the various levels of the main keep, to the room they shared.

Halfway across the floor, Ari heard the unmistakable clanking of a knight approaching.

If it's Sir Kay, I'm going to tackle him. I don't fucking care.

Lam seemed to suspect her motivation. They spun Ari around as if they were about to start a dance and threw her over their shoulder at the waist. Ari's face was now a few inches from Lam's glorious, leather-clad ass. Lovely.

"Lamarack, were you not with a fetching enchantress last evening?" Galahad's voice. Well, that was a bit of luck. "The one called Morgause?"

Lam spoke but Ari missed it as they shuffled her into a better spot on their shoulder.

"You should seek friendship and connection with your lovers. It will lead to a better life," Galahad said, as if he were Lam's dad. Ari couldn't help smiling. "That one-lady-each-night business looks an awful lot of work from where I'm standing. My goodness, you are motivated."

Galahad walked on, and Lam hustled across the hall and up the tight stairwell, not letting Ari down even though she tried pinching them in the side. Once they were back in the small, dank room and the door was shut, Lam set her down and Ari had a full-on head rush. She grabbed her temples and wrestled her breath.

She sat hard on the bed, and gingerly touched the bruise on her jaw from where Sir Kay had knocked her out. Then she took MercersNotes out of her dress pocket and flipped it open to a random page...which happened to be about Queen Gweneviere getting kidnapped. Ari snapped it shut. "Fuck that."

"You okay?" Lam asked.

"Just need a minute." Ari and Lam were silent, until she laughed. "You're the castle heartthrob."

"Someone's got to be."

"You teaching that GSA about the glories of being polyam?"

"I only think being polyamorous is glorious for those of

us who are polyamorous." Lam peeled off their buckles and leather while they were talking and were shirtless now. "Case in point, if you had to share Gwen with anyone other than a clueless boy king, I know you'd have lost it by now."

"Your evidence?"

"Kay."

Ari winced. "That's fair."

Lam's voice glowed with a new depth. "Why do you think we haven't?"

Ari laughed in a shallow way. "Not that I haven't thought about it."

"Not that I haven't, either."

Ari dared a look at Lam in the dim room. The only light came from that veiled moon outside. "So Morgause..." Ari searched for a gentle way to ask, eyes tracing Lam's matching, delicate scars beneath their pecs. "Was she..."

"Surprised to find my downstairs has a lot in common with hers?" Lam laughed. "I believe she was delighted, truth be told."

Ari fell back on the straw mattress, and Lam sat beside her. "How the hell are you doing so well while the rest of us are drowning in medieval crap?"

"There's beauty here, Ari. There's a reason for this place. These people." Lam brushed her cheek with their knuckle. "I can't help seeing that. I loved the King Arthur story. Kay and I ate it up when we were at knight camp on Lionel, but this is so much better. It's truer. And we're making the legend happen. We're *inside* of it."

"Making it happen," she murmured. "Lam, I need you to find Gwen. Have her bring Arthur to the throne room. Alone."

&

Ari stood before the empty throne. This place was the grandest and most neglected hall in the enormous castle. The vaulted ceilings hung with wheeled chandeliers and the stone walls wore pennants and tapestries—but there was no life to it. No spark.

No legend.

Even the throne was still far too big for Arthur's young frame. She flashed back to a different Arthur. The body in Nin's cave. The aged man with a gray beard. His face worn, as if a hundred tragedies had befallen him in a span of only twenty years or so. Ari ran her fingers over the symbols that had been magically carved into the wood. Old Merlin spared no expense when it came to making sure that his boy king impressed those who visited the kingdom.

On the purple seat cushion, Ari found a worn wooden box with a clunky metal latch.

The perfect size for a chalice.

Ari's fingers twitched, and she swore she heard Kay in her head, ribbing her for her impulses, but she unlatched the box and swung it open.

It was empty.

"But Gweneviere, I—" Arthur's voice snapped to a stop. Ari spun around. Gwen had tricked Arthur here, from the look of mild betrayal on his face. How very Gwen.

"And you're not coming out until you sort this," Gwen hissed, such a boss that Arthur stepped back while Gwen shut the double doors behind her.

Ari and Arthur were alone.

"You came back. You shouldn't have."

"There are tons of things I shouldn't do."

Arthur stared at her outfit. Ari had decided against her armor for the first time since she'd arrived at Camelot. She wore a man's tunic, her arms and scars on show. She'd bound her breasts but there was no denying that her frame didn't hold the same imposing weight without the bulk of her armor. Ari opened her mouth, but Arthur beat her to it, eyeing the box in her hands. "So you found my chalice. Maybe I should try it out on you. I don't know what it does."

Ari showed off the empty box. "It's not here."

Arthur moved forward, taking the box and relatching it. "This wood is magic. The chalice is only there if *I* open it. Merlin gave it to me."

"So open it." Ari smirked, and Arthur looked amused at first, and then grouchy.

"I want you out of my kingdom."

"Why? Because I have breasts? Or because Gweneviere prefers—"

"You lie, and you...direct me. A lot." He seemed to shrink in the presence of the throne. He moved to the other side of the room, setting the box down on a large, rectangular table.

"Yeah, that is definitely not the right shape," Ari murmured before she could stop herself.

"What?" Arthur shouted so loudly it echoed. "What does that even mean? You have a problem with everything I do, including the shape of my table?"

"That's the abridged version, truth be told."

Arthur took a deep breath. His blond hair was lank today, the summer humidity missing. "What do you want from me?"

he asked, so exhausted Ari caught a flicker of the Arthur she'd seen in Nin's cave, unrested. Unresolved. A few millennia from now, his voice was going to be the only saving grace when Mercer attacked her planet.

He was only able to save her because he was lost. How had Morgana described his curse?

His soul flits in and out of reality like a bird with a broken wing.

"Arthur, I..." Ari cleared her throat. "You have an important legacy. I want to help you."

"You sound like my queen." He rubbed his eyes with his knuckles. "How? How do I make all this change? I told you in the woods, I'm supposed to answer questions that I've never even fathomed. I'm supposed to help people I do not know. It's impossible."

Ari took his hand and pulled it from his eyes. She held his fingers, almost sweetly. Arthur was clearly surprised by her gentleness and stared at her calloused palms. "You stop being afraid of what you don't understand. That's how. And you trust your knights. You make a true bond out of their loyalty."

"How am I supposed to trust any of you?" Arthur said quietly. "You're all lying. You probably want my throne, my kingdom. My wife," his voice choked up. "Well, you can have the throne. I never wanted it in the first place. But I need Gweneviere."

Ari grabbed his shoulder to keep him from staring at the throne so forlornly. She turned back to the small, magical box. "The enchantresses gave you an incredible gift, Arthur. You're supposed to use this to bond with your knights."

"How?"

"I don't...know." Ari heard Val's voice in her head. *Give it sails.* And then Lamarack's enamored whisper about the joy of *making* the legend happen. Ari reached into her pocket and felt the curled shape of the MercersNotes on King Arthur and his knights. "I have to show you something. Something to help explain why you should trust me. How you can trust me."

Only, Ari's hand wouldn't come out of her pocket. A guiding presence stilled her.

Not the book. The sword.

Ari inhaled sharply. She hadn't heard Arthur's voice in too long. It gave her hope while at the same time it reminded her how very frail and weak his spirit was becoming. Ari let go of the book and looked at Arthur. At the epic sword in the sheath at his waist.

"I hear that only King Arthur can lift Excalibur."

Arthur scowled. "You want to try my sword?"

"If I could lift it, you would trust me, wouldn't you?"

Arthur smiled, but it was a hopeless look, one that bled exasperation. How many other knights had stomped into his kingdom and demanded to try out the legendary sword? He lifted it from his sheath and struck it down hard in the stone floor.

Excalibur sliced through it with ease. Exactly as Ari remembered. Her hands hummed a little as her fingers trailed the hilt, reaching for the familiar handle. And when she lifted the blade free, her relief felt like waves crashing over rock. She'd missed every ounce of Excalibur.

And then she noticed that Arthur was looking at her with fear, and perhaps reverence.

Ari dropped the sword flat on her palms and held it out to

him. "Do you trust me now, Arthur? Because Excalibur sure does."

&

That evening, Ari returned to the throne room, armor shining. All of Arthur's knights were there, including a rather red and sweaty-faced Sir Kay. They were seated around a newly rounded table. Merlin had delightedly let them all know that Old Merlin had been—well, delighted—when Arthur asked for his help to change the shape.

Now it was time to give his knights an equal seat in his presence.

Ari sat beside Arthur, eyeing the two free seats across the table. At the same moment, the door opened and all turned. Ari beckoned in Lam, Val...and Gwen.

Arthur looked at all of them, eyes falling on Val last. Val in his corset and kohl-lined eyes. "Who are...you?" Arthur's voice was entranced, and Ari nearly busted out a laugh.

"I'm about to rock your kingdom, that's who I am." He inclined his head toward Lam. "I'm also Lamarack's brother."

"I'd like to introduce you to Percival," Ari said, barely loud enough to cover Val's predictable growl at his full name. "You will not find a sharper diplomatic mind, my king."

Arthur's eyebrow raised. Ari was being respectful for once, and Arthur had noticed. Lam and Val took the open seats while Gwen hung around in the background, fussing over tapestries and trying to blend in with them.

"I've called you all here to find out where your loyalties truly lie."

"With you, Arthur," Sir Kay said lazily, almost bored.

"Mayhaps." Arthur opened the small wooden box and there it was, the damn chalice. All bone white and gold-rimmed. "The enchantresses gave me a gift at my celebration. They told me I need only ask a question of this cup. When you drink its water, I will know the truth." Arthur held up the chalice. "I ask this magical gift, who among me is true to my Camelot?"

Arthur spoke Camelot's name as if the great city were his lover, and Ari found herself strangely moved by his passion.

"It fills with the Lady of the Lake's water," Sir Galahad whispered. "The women of Avalon were proud of this creation."

"Aye," Arthur said, handing it to Sir Kay first. "Drink your truth."

The knight huffed as though it were a ridiculous request, but sipped the liquid and instantly began to choke. He held his hand over his throat and stumbled for the door, colliding with the wall on his way out.

In the silence afterward, Arthur seemed taller, more confident. "From this day forward, Sir Kay is not welcome in this kingdom." He motioned for the next knight, Gawain, to take a drink. And they all did, the entire round table, and no one but Sir Kay had a bad reaction. The knights watched closely when Val and Lam drank, but Val nearly grinned from whatever the chalice imparted, and Lam took a steadying breath.

Finally, the chalice made it to Ari with only a sliver of liquid left in the bottom. She emptied it into her mouth, finding the water identical to Nin's lake: sharply chilling all the way down her throat.

Ari's eyesight went dark, and she gasped. She heard concerned murmurs from around the table, and then she saw a slice of time. A pure moment. Arthur was embracing her... handing her the chalice. He was giving it to her. To take to the future. And then the moment was gone.

Arthur's eyes were wide as if he needed to know what had happened to her. What she'd seen. "Sir Lancelot?"

"You have my sword," Ari said, putting a hand on his shoulder. She was going to help him with his kingdom, and he was going to give her the chalice. "My king."

Arthur took the chalice back and studied it once again. "I wonder... what is my legacy?"

Gwen's near-distant gasp was almost a shout. Ari's arm shot out to stop Arthur, but he tipped the entire chalice back and disappeared into whatever he saw. His blue eyes rolled white and his body began to shake. Ari shouted for Galahad, and the two of them lifted Arthur from his seat, laying him across the table. His limbs jumped and slammed into the hard wood, creating a cacophony of jarring bone sounds, and Lamarack and Val rushed to hold down his legs.

Ari didn't know if he could hear her through his seizure. She had a terrible flashback to when she'd met Merlin in that alley on the moon. When Morgana had gifted him a few hundred years of human history with a light tap. The way he'd cried out had felt like its own punishment—and yet that empty, whimpering silence was so much worse. The only difference was that Arthur wasn't seeing the past, he was experiencing his own future.

Did his legacy stop at the battlefield where he died upon his own son's sword? Or did the chalice show him the other

Arthurs, the endless dance of unity and despair, of might and right, equality and hate? The cycle of humanity's brightest hope ever set against its ceaseless dark?

Arthur stopped flailing, going too still. He looked dead on the crosshatched wood. Far too similar to the corpse king Ari had seen in Nin's cave. Ari shook Arthur while Gwen held his hand, testing his pulse. She gave Ari a sharp look that seemed to yell *do something.*

Ari got her hands on the sides of his face and whispered into his ear. "I'm here, Arthur."

Arthur's blue eyes shot open, and his head turned slowly toward Ari. "I saw you small and helpless. Floating through blackness." His voice sounded entire years older. "I think... that's when I met you."

"That is the past *and* the future," Ari said, surprised by the tears in her eyes.

"Help me to my feet."

She did, steadying him with an arm around his ribs. Ari found that his hands were shaking, and she placed them on Excalibur's handle. They stilled at once.

"Arthur?" Gwen asked softly. He shook his head in her direction, wincing, and motioned for everyone to leave. But not Ari. He held on to her. Ari expected a barrage of questions. Demands for explanations. Instead he set his gaze on her.

"We have much to do."

PROPHECY
&
AUGURY

Merlin couldn't breathe. It was too beautiful.

He wanted to run his hand along the grain of the dark wood, and quite possibly kiss the smooth surface. The round table here at last, and sitting around it?

Ari, Arthur, Val, Lam, Gwen—*his people.*

Merlin's friends had helped spark one of the most hopeful moments of human history. In fact, it looked better in person than it did in the legends, since nobody had gotten their grubby whitewashing hands on it yet. Several of these nobles besides Lam, Val, and Ari were knights of color. Take that, racist revisionists!

Even Gwen had a seat at the table, which of course would be edited out later. The absence of more women rankled, especially when Merlin thought of Jordan. And then there was the matter of letting nonbinary people serve openly as knights and giving more seats to common-born folk and...There was still work to do. But for the first time since they'd arrived in

Camelot, he felt it could be done. *This* was why Arthur's story needed to survive intact. This moment would give birth to so many other moments. And Merlin was right here in the middle of it, even if he'd only gotten into the room by volunteering to serve the mead.

He made a circle around the table, humming in a non-magical way, clanking down cups. He deposited a drink in front of Ari and leaned down when she accepted it with a knightly nod.

"Tell me again that this is real," he whispered.

"Arthur and I are BFFs now," she assured him. "Kind of literally on that last F, if you think about it."

Arthur drinking from the chalice had changed everything. Not just the shape of a table or the composition of the knights sitting around it, but Arthur himself. Ari had told Merlin that he'd seen his future. Not just the glory of Camelot, or even his death at the hands of Mordred, but *all of it*.

The cycles. Forty-one dead heroes. And then number forty-two, a girl from the future with a mostly broken spaceship, a smelly but lovable brother, and a mega-corporation to slay.

It was a boon to their quest to have Arthur understand his own story—although it was also a burden for the young king. His expression was covered in worried creases that hadn't been there at his birthday celebration weeks ago. His hair was still rumpled and blonde, but somehow it looked less like spun gold and more like old straw. And his eyes? They held all the ghosts of the future in two soft blue spheres. It was too much for any person to contain, let alone such a young and tender-hearted one. Arthur looked as if he'd aged as many years overnight as Merlin had, well, de-aged.

But this, too, made a kind of sense. Something had finally happened to change the boy-king into the solemn, tragic figure of Camelot. The legends often pinned the guilt on Gweneviere—because the legends were written by misogynistic tosspots. Arthur's overnight transformation didn't come from a broken heart, but an unmoored soul.

Merlin set a cup in front of the king, who rummaged up a small smile for him. "Many thanks, carbuncle." Merlin felt his face contort at the epithet. Arthur added, "Believe me, I understand. I'm the *Wart*."

Merlin broke into a giddy smile. "We have something in common!" he whisper-shouted.

"Indeed we do," King Arthur whispered back. "Merlin speaks highly of you. Do you think he'll figure out that you're one and the same, and he is in fact giving himself a grudging compliment?"

Merlin's heart nearly stopped in its tracks.

Of course the chalice had showed Arthur what became of his mage, too. Merlin was a sizeable part of his future. The only sidekick that would never leave the king's spirit behind—mortality be damned.

"May I ask you something?" For a moment, Arthur's blue eyes had their youthful glow back. The Wart had always been terribly curious. It was one of his best qualities and led to great things. After all, questions and quests had much in common. "What is it like to consort with the person you once were? The rest of us have the mercy of leaving our finished days behind us."

Merlin took a moment to consider. "Old Me is myopic at best, murdery at worst. But the more I think about it, the more

I doubt that I'm the only one keeping bad company with my past self."

Arthur laughed. "Gods, you really do sound like him."

And the king of Camelot was starting to sound a bit like Gwen and Ari. This was a very odd sort of time travel exchange program.

"You won't tell him about me, will you?" Merlin whispered.

"I swear it," Arthur said, as solemn as a freshly turned grave. "You have more than earned my loyalty, young Merlin."

The king dove back into the conversation about Camelot–Avalon relations as Merlin brought a very strategic cup to Gwen. Only the finest water for his very pregnant queen, purified in Old Merlin's tower, tinted amber to resemble the mead everyone else was drinking.

If Arthur wanted to keep ignoring the impending baby storm that was about to touch down in Camelot, Merlin certainly wasn't going to stop him. Perhaps he was allowing Gwen the space to figure it out on her own. Or perhaps his chalice vision hadn't included Gwen's assignation with Kay, also known as The Weirdest Lancelot Situation Ever.

Merlin put Gwen's cup down, expecting a secret smile or a few coded words. Instead, she grimaced, cutting her eyes toward him and quickly looking straight ahead, as if anything else would be too painful to bear. Was Gwen upset with him? Upset in general? Were Arthur's tragic feelings rubbing off on her?

Or...was she having labor pains and trying to hide them?

Merlin kept a close eye on her as he plopped down the next cup, where Sir Kay would have been sitting, had he still been welcome in Camelot—and dropped an entire glass of mead into Val's lap.

He then dove *into* Val's lap, trying to clean up the mess.

"Umm..." Val said, as the entire table looked at them. Merlin nearly died. That was part of his looming childhood it seemed; the slightest problem felt like a catastrophe of indescribable proportions.

Val waved the knights along, and the talking continued.

"It's so good to see you here," Merlin whispered. "I mean, I'm glad you made it to Arthur's court, and he so quickly acknowledged your prowess as an advisor." For some reason, the use of the word *prowess* made him turn retroactively crimson. Gods damn innocence. At least he wasn't giggling every time someone swore, right? "Are you dry? I can get you a rag from the kitchens if—"

"Breathe, Merlin," Val whispered, not unkindly. It wasn't Val's flirting voice, though. Merlin would have to figure out how to stop this backward aging once and for all if he wanted Val's romantic insinuations in his life.

Which meant enduring more time with Old Merlin.

They'd tried a few spells together the day before, but nothing had taken root. "You really are a conundrum, nothing like you in any of the books," he'd admitted, sending Merlin away so he could do more research and devise new tests.

He'd told Merlin not to return to the tower until he was called for, which meant that once the meeting dispersed and Gwen slipped him a whisper that they needed to talk, he had the freedom to do it without fear that his old self would punish him with more peat duty.

They gathered in Ari and Lam's room in the servants' quarters, a narrow slot of a space that was hardly large enough to hold Val, Lam, Merlin, Ari, and a very round Gwen. Merlin found himself smushed between the door and a concerned Lam. Apparently Merlin hadn't been the only one to pick up on Gwen's distress during the round table meeting.

"I need to talk to all of you," Gwen said. "Last night, I went to Arthur and...I asked him to let me drink from the chalice."

"And?" Lam asked, pushing with the gentlest tone.

"I asked about the baby," Gwen said. "I saw myself holding them. I *felt* them in my arms. So tiny, and beautiful, and..." They were all holding their breath now, because it felt obvious that Gwen wasn't done.

"What happened?" Val asked.

Merlin found himself upset on a level that he couldn't even fathom.

"Someone took the baby from me. Not just to hold, but... to keep. I don't get to keep this baby after they're born."

"That's not going to happen," Ari said staunchly.

"But it is!" Gwen said, strange iron in her voice. "That's how the stupid fucking chalice *works*. We already know that Arthur saw the truth of his tragic future. Why should I be any different?"

"Doesn't the chalice have Nin's water in it?" Val asked, casting around for reasons this abominable news could somehow be untrue. "How do we know that she's not just doing her best to fuck with you? Like she did with me, and Ari?"

"Arthur's spirit sent us back for the chalice," Gwen argued. "He trusts it, doesn't he?"

Val pursed his lips. A small sign, but Merlin knew it didn't bode well.

Gwen sat down on the tiny bed that Ari and Lam, the two tallest knights in Camelot, had somehow been sharing. "This feels like another horrible, unbreakable circle. My parents didn't keep me and then Mercer demanded my baby and... now this vision? It just keeps happening. This moment has always been coming for me." She whipped around to Merlin, hair straying from its elaborate knot, eyes wild. "It makes sense, doesn't it? Gweneviere doesn't have a baby in any of the legends, does she?"

Merlin might've had a dark haze where most of this time period should be, but he couldn't lie to Gwen about something that was so clear. "No."

"Unless it turns out to be Mordred," Gwen muttered.

"Mordred?" Merlin choked on the name. It was bile in his mouth.

He pitched back to the worst day in his long existence, watching from Nin's cave as Arthur lost his life to a self-righteous son he hadn't raised as his own. Each of the legends told a slightly different version of Mordred's origins, his upbringing. What if they were all hiding the same fact—that he was Gwen's love child?

Well...perhaps *love* child was a bit strong, when Merlin thought about it. He could almost picture Kay balking.

Lam enclosed Gwen in a soft, strong hug. "We're going to be with you when you give birth. You won't have to do anything you don't wish."

"The prophecies disagree with you," Gwen said, unwilling to give any ground to Lam's comfort. "And hope is only going to make this worse. What did you tell me, Ara? Hope is a lie that wants to be true."

Ari shook her head viciously, like she was arguing with her past self and losing. "Some things come true because we make them. We're here, aren't we? Making this story happen?"

"Yes, and I hate it," Gwen said. "Jordan rushed out to save me that day in the street because she knew the story. She wanted to protect me from being kidnapped, because that's what happens to Gweneviere...and she ended up with an arrow in the neck. And I haven't been kidnapped yet. So I still have *that* to look forward to."

"When we portal back—" Lam stopped abruptly as Val shot them a dirty look. And then everyone looked at Merlin and away in quick succession. Oh, they didn't want to even think about going home because they knew what it would currently cost Merlin.

Ouch.

Val cleared his throat, practical to the last. "Gwen, if you don't believe there's a way we can stop this, what *can* we do?"

"I don't know," Gwen said. "I already lost my planet. My crown. Any shred of respect that came from living in a time when women are treated equally. I thought that keeping the baby safe from Mercer would be worth all of this. Now...now all I want is five minutes before I have to go back to pretending the best parts of my life don't even exist."

Ari moved in, putting her arms around Gwen. She murmured into the queen's ear, smoothed her hair, turning this into a private moment. Gwen rested her head on Ari's shoulder, then looked up at her with shimmering eyes. There was so much love between them, so much thwarted happiness.

"Kiss her, for gods' sake!" Merlin shouted, then clapped a hand over his mouth. Apparently he'd reached the part of being eleven where he blurted out things he was supposed to chant uselessly in his head.

Gwen and Ari broke apart to stare at him.

Merlin—who knew *far* too much about holding back from a perfectly good love story—wanted to sit them down and give them a stern talking-to. Would Ari take relationship advice from an eleven-year-old? Probably not, and yet he had plenty to give.

It's not as if Gwen and Ari were aging in opposite directions. They were at the mercy of a political marriage. They were two girls who loved each other in a vicious time. Those were barriers that no love story should have to overcome, and yet Merlin knew Gwen and Ari could. He believed in them as much as he'd ever believed in Arthur, or Camelot, or the magic at his fingertips.

Ari just quietly kissed Gwen's shoulder, as if that was the most they could have. Maybe hoping for more had finally started to hurt. Maybe being ripped apart from each other so many times had torn something inside. The cycle had stopped them far better than Arthur ever could. Which meant that those tears could be traced directly back to the Lady of the Lake. When he finally broke this *fucking cycle,* Nin had a great deal of misery to answer for.

A giggle erupted from Merlin.

Val and Lam shot him genetically identical looks of disapproval.

"Fucking cycle," Merlin whispered—and giggled again.

Oh, this was far too much.

Nin was going down.

&

An hour later, Merlin was an owl. A baby owl, to be specific.

His feathers puffed out, beady eyes trained on Old Merlin.

"I thought that if I shifted you out of human form, the curse might lose its hold," the old mage said, by way of explanation. "But you're just as young as a bird as you were as a human."

"*You think?*" Merlin asked. It came out as a series of pitiful, high-pitched screeches.

"He still doesn't know you two are the same person, does he?" came a rich, hooting voice. Merlin turned to find Archimedes glaring at him. He'd flown over from his perch just to make Merlin's life worse.

"How did you figure it out, if you're so smart?" Merlin asked.

Archimedes shrugged with his entire rich, brown-black body. "You're both ridiculous, and you smell the same."

Merlin hopped away from the miserable old bird—leaping off the high table and finding, with a series of desperate flaps, that he couldn't fly.

He hit the floor, stunned but unsurprised.

Of course he couldn't fly.

He was a mere chick.

Old Merlin picked him up, his tiny owl body encompassed by the hard ridges of those ancient, cold hands. Did the vile old mage ever trim his nails? They were unevenly long, stained various colors by magical concoctions.

Merlin gratefully found himself growing, unfolding back into his eleven-year-old body, then hopping into his clothes. He bent over awkwardly as he slid his pants into place. For some reason, the concept of being naked in front of his old self was more painful than a time paradox.

"All right, carbuncle," Old Merlin said, not paying a speck of attention to the wretched state of his apprentice. He was too wrapped up in magic. He turned to a dusty red cloth that he'd hung over a portion of the tower, pulling it down with a magical flourish. Behind it was a free-standing copper tub, and a series of buckets flying in through the tower window. "I have another idea. This one took a bit of preparation, but perhaps it will reveal the truth of your condition."

A magical flying bucket tipped over, water hitting the copper tub with a gut-sloshing sound.

"What is this?" Merlin asked. "You're going to...bathe me? You're the one who needs a serious drubbing!"

Old Merlin gave him a thunderous glare.

His newly loosened tongue was going to get him killed if he wasn't careful.

"This water is from the lake near Avalon," the old mage said. "It has curious time-related properties, which might help us determine what ails you. It seems the way you experience time has been reversed by some great act of magic." Old Merlin tested the water with his hand, like a nervous parent making sure it wasn't too hot for their precious child. But Merlin was nothing of the sort. He was an experiment, and he could feel his old self getting testy the farther they went without making any real breakthroughs.

The old man dodged a flying bucket, frowning back at Merlin. "It would help to know your lineage, in the event that one or both of your parents has some kind of time magic. You don't have even the smallest hint as to how you ended up this way?"

A swallow seized up in his throat.

Merlin thought of the accusations that Val had listed in his driest tone: all the ways that he was like Nin. Their caves, their portals. In the midst of bargaining, she had even offered to reveal the identity of his parents. Had she planned to admit that *she* was his long-lost mother? A horrific *ta-da* moment?

"I have no idea how I got like this," he said weakly.

"Then it's into the tub," Old Merlin said, cracking his knuckles.

Merlin couldn't imagine undressing again, so with his robes still on he stepped into the waters of time, daintily. He didn't want anything to do with them. These were Nin's waters, after all.

She was the problem to be solved. The callous enemy to be stopped. The mother of the cycle. Definitely not *his* mother.

The moment that Merlin had settled against the bumpy copper bottom of the tub, Old Merlin set a palm to his skull and pushed him under the water. The air rushed out of his nose, hard. His ears filled with the strange, stopped-up pressure of being underwater. Beyond that, he heard a faint, sweet laugh.

"*You're finally trying to set yourself forward,*" Nin said, her warm voice suffusing the water. "*Excellent.*"

"Aren't you...supposed to...thwart me?" Merlin asked, the words mere shapeless bubbles.

Merlin came up spluttering, shaking.

"Once more, carbuncle!" Old Merlin shouted, pushing him back down.

Merlin's knees jackknifed, folding up somewhere near his nose. His robes fluttered, heavy with water. "*You think I'm your enemy?*" Nin asked softly as his air slipped away, and everything went darker than the void of space. "*You know that's not true. We've always been tied to each other.*"

"No," Merlin said, thrashing.

This couldn't be the answer. He couldn't come all the way back here only to find out that he was the son of the vicious magical entity who'd ruined his entire life.

Old Merlin let him up for just a breath. He yowled like a cat. And then—back down, his head aching where Old Merlin pressed.

The light that Merlin associated with Nin, golden and wondrous, lit the tub, and he swore he felt her fingers on his chin. Her kiss on his cheek. Was she trying to tell him that she really was his mother? Or was she messing with him, yet again?

Merlin squirreled out of her grasp, and the tub went dark and cold. *"The old man isn't really helping you with the full force of his magic, is he?"* Nin asked. *"Such a shame. Maybe that would spark something."*

Merlin came back up once more.

"Sparks!" he cried, kicking and grabbing for the edges of the tub.

"What about sparks?" Old Merlin asked, more interrogation.

Merlin leaped out of the tub while he had the chance, pacing the tower and dripping all over the stones. "The magical sparks you make, with your fingers." Merlin had to find some way to explain his idea to Old Merlin, who lived in a time well before modern physics. They didn't even know the laws of thermodynamics yet. "Think of it this way. Heat is what drives time forward. Every time it's released it creates a past and a future—an event that cannot be reversed. What is sparked cannot be *unsparked*. Once heat is released, time flows onward from there."

No turning back.

"You're brighter than you look, carbuncle," Old Merlin said.

Merlin shivered, twisting out of his robes. He didn't know if a compliment from Old Merlin was a badge of honor or a mark of shame.

There were other, deeper fears, too. Nin had pushed him to this revelation with her carefully chosen words. Why? Was she the kind of parent who gave him gifts and punished him on an epic scale? It hardly mattered now. Nothing could change the bedrock fact that Merlin couldn't break Nin's cycle until he was able to use his magic fully, and without fear of skipping backward over another birthday.

"Hit me with enough sparks to put the stars to shame," Merlin said, tilting his chin up at what felt like a brave angle.

"All right, then," Old Merlin said, pulling up his sleeves as though he relished the challenge. "...and if you're wrong, and you end up nothing but a burnt stick of an apprentice?"

"I accept that risk," Merlin said, taking a deep breath and hoarding it in his lungs.

Old Merlin sang in his harsh tenor, a Welsh song that Merlin didn't remember strictly, and yet the sound of it sank deep into his bones. The old mage's hands lit with a hundred points of light, and then they connected, a fireball headed straight for his chest.

And then there were steps on the stairs, and a voice so terrified it ripped a hole through the singing.

"Merlin!" Arthur cried.

"Yes?" they both responded, swiveling to face him. The fireball missed, crashing into a cupboard of magical ingredients and setting it on fire. Smoke poured out in several unexpected colors.

"Merlin, I need your help," Arthur said as the old mage quenched the fire with a quick counterspell. "Gweneviere has been taken!"

"Gwen?" Merlin cried.

"They raided her chambers," Arthur said. "I knew we should be sleeping together so I might defend her." Merlin tried not to scoff. Arthur's intentions were in the right place, but Jordan was the one who would have stopped any threat to Gwen—and they'd lost the black knight to the future.

"These villains left a message," Arthur said, holding up the torn scrap of a note. Merlin snatched at it, but Old Merlin got there first.

"Curious that such crude thieves would know how to write," Old Merlin said. "They must have employed someone to do this." Merlin tried to catch a glimpse of the rag that had been written on, but Old Merlin put it right under his nose, squinting and even sniffing. "I can use this to find where she's gone…" Arthur's expression tilted toward hope. "But only if you promise not to go after her yourself."

"I must," Arthur said. "I no longer ask my knights to do the hardest work in this kingdom without putting myself in the same danger. There is no honor in such inequality." Merlin could hear the echoes of Gwen and Ari in those words. He would have been proud of Arthur's evolution if there had been room in his body for anything other than fear.

"This is undoubtedly a trap to draw you in, Arthur," Old Merlin said. "If you go, your reign will end before your round table is given a chance to thrive. Don't give these petty villains what they're after. Send someone who wishes to save Gweneviere as much as you do."

"Lancelot," Merlin and his old self chorused.

They'd come up with the same answer to the equation, but they'd done different work to get there. Merlin wanted to send Ari because she would never stop until Gwen was safe. Old Merlin didn't mind tossing Lancelot straight into the maw of danger.

"Fine," Arthur said, with an even-dealing tone that matched the new maturity the chalice had brought. "But I have a condition of my own. This is the last time you dictate my actions."

Old Merlin turned away from Arthur, perhaps hiding the wince of hurt that Merlin caught. "We are in agreement."

He tossed the ransom note into a mortar and pestle, grinding it with a few black sprinkles from one of his jars. The note crumbled into a dark dust before Merlin had a chance to see it. Old Merlin ran his finger through the gritty coating on the bowl, touching it to his tongue. He closed his eyes and meditated on whatever he'd tasted before snapping them back open. Grabbing up an old map, he plopped a withered finger down on a hill in the middle of nowhere.

Arthur took the map and ran, shouting thanks over his shoulder.

"No need to thank me," Old Merlin said darkly as Arthur disappeared down the stairs, no doubt to fetch Lancelot.

Merlin tried to force himself back to a state resembling calm, but then he saw the thorny delight on Old Merlin's face. "This is our opportunity, carbuncle. We know where Gweneviere is, and we can rid the kingdom of all threats before she returns to Camelot."

"We...can do what?" Merlin asked.

He got the sense that the horrors were only about to deepen

as Old Merlin pulled open a drawer in one of his magical inventory cupboards.

"I've been conducting an augury," he said, waving Merlin forward. He found three birds with their wings pinned to the wood, stomachs slit open. Their innards had been taken out and scattered in random-looking patterns.

Not just any birds. Baby birds.

Merlin wanted to vomit. Middle Ages magic was disgusting. *He* was disgusting.

Old Merlin pointed at the organs. "The signs point to a baby that will grow up to be Arthur's great downfall."

"Not Gwen's baby!" Merlin shouted before he could stop himself.

Old Merlin folded his hands over his stomach as if that settled things. "If there was a sliver of a question that the queen carried another man's child, you've just eclipsed it. Thank you, carbuncle."

Merlin crouched down, head in his hands, stomach suddenly tight. He'd made it worse. He was always making things worse. *He* was Arthur's downfall.

"What are you going to do?" he asked, dreading the answer more than Nin's voice.

"Stealing children *is* one of my specialties," Old Merlin said with a dry, horrible twist of humor. He'd taken Arthur—but that was to save him. That was an act of mercy. Merlin had been telling himself for centuries that he'd done a good thing on that day he found a squalling infant in the fields.

This was different. Dark and unrepentant. "You can't just grab a baby and toss it wherever you please."

Old Merlin huffed dryly, dismissing the whole argument.

"I'll kill the child if I must. Whatever must be done to protect Arthur."

Merlin closed his eyes against the words, but they were still true in the dark. His old self didn't believe in any goodness but Arthur's. Still, if Merlin needed a sign that he was no longer this horrible wretch, he had it. He would never, *ever* think of killing a child, even if he believed it would save Ari someday.

"We're not the same person," Merlin whispered, a revelation that hit him with all the subtlety of a power cord. "We're *not*."

He raised his hands, and the element of surprise gave him a slight edge. Old Merlin had never seen his apprentice work magic; Merlin had been trying to keep his identity secret. But now keeping Gwen and the baby safe from this monster was all that mattered. Merlin didn't need to make peace with his past. He needed to stop the person he used to be from harming his future. He released a pent-up burst of magic at the exact moment that Old Merlin flicked his fingers.

Merlin felt every muscle in his body go stiff. His mouth was dry, propped open; his eyes couldn't force a blink. Across from him, Old Merlin had frozen as well, down to the wispiest hairs on his beard.

They were in a stand-off, and whoever managed to break it first would have a head start in the battle over Gwen's baby.

KAIROS
&
KINGS

Ari tore across the landscape, swearing and steering her horse around the worst of the overgrown wood. The sunset dropped an ominous orange light on almost everything, suiting Ari's fraught imagination a little too nicely.

Gwen kidnapped.

By who? And for what purpose except to hurt the young king? Would they realize that Gwen was pregnant? What if the baby was harmed? Ari cursed the needs of the Arthurian canon. No wonder Jordan hadn't let Gwen out of her sight.

"You wouldn't be happy with me now, black knight," Ari muttered. She almost smiled, thinking of Jordan pushing her out of the way, beating Lancelot to the place where Gwen was being held captive. Ari tried to focus on the other part of the story she'd read in the Arthurian notes—that Lancelot saved Gweneviere, and that they returned newly inseparable—but the sweetness didn't match the reality. And some of those legends bore whispers of terrible things done to Gweneviere by her captors.

Ari broke out of the edge of the wood, eyeing a thoroughly deforested landscape. It was somewhat reminiscent of Mercer's leveling of Old Earth, down to the bedrock. Here the trees had been stolen, used for timber or fire, and the ground had turned to slipping soil. In the far distance, upon a worn mound, a tower stood. Dismal and crooked—that had to be the bald spot Arthur had pointed to on the roughly drawn map.

She kicked her horse into a gallop, racing up the landscape, leaning forward to push the stallion when the terrain became muddy and steep. Finally, at the base of the forgotten tower, she jumped down and lashed her horse to a stone marker.

She took a moment to note the absence of wind.

Of sound.

Racing around the narrow, circular structure, she found a door unguarded.

It opened at her touch.

Unlocked.

Ari started to shake. She drew her sword as the last of the sunset left the sky a bruised color. Pressing into the dark of stone, she found broken chairs and tables. Abandoned items. And wooden stairs that spiraled upward.

She took them quietly, softly.

In truth, Ari was ready to murder whoever had taken Gwen. She understood that feeling now, that push to *stop* cruelty. Finish it before it could cause more harm. It was not a good feeling. It was not stable or true, and she knew that this was not what she was supposed to glean from coming back here. And yet, she wasn't going to hesitate.

No matter who had taken Gwen.

The stairs spiraled upward, upward. Ari found three

abandoned floors filled with old furniture, and when she took the last turn of the stairs and spied a shut door, her fist tightened around her sword. At the top, she took a deep breath, and shouldered the door open.

Ari thought she'd come too late. Far too late.

Gwen was lying on a small straw mattress, lifeless in the nearly black room. The lack of guards could only mean that there was nothing left to guard. Ari dropped her sword with a terrific clang, and ran to Gwen's side, only to find Gwen sitting up, reaching for her.

"Ari?"

Ari's breath came out too fast. A blast of pain that sounded wrong in her own ears. "You're all right. Oh, my gods, you're all right."

Ari kissed Gwen's cheeks, her hair. Her hands roamed over Gwen's belly, and as if the little one knew this was no time to play coy, they gave a nice, strong kick. Ari sobbed.

"Ari, we're fine. What are you...? Oh. You didn't see the ransom note, did you?"

"What?" Ari pulled back. "I couldn't help thinking the worst. Arthur was screaming, and your rooms were utterly destroyed. I thought..."

Gwen grimaced in a way that made Ari sniff back her tears and cock her head. "You are never going to forgive me for this performance."

"Excuse me?"

"I was so sure Arthur would show you the ransom note. There was a...let's say secret message in it. So you would see it and know that I kidnapped myself."

"You *what*?"

Gwen got up, pushing Ari's shaking body away. She paced the tower, rubbing her lower back. "Seriously? Did any of you actually think I'd sit around and wait to be kidnapped? *Of course not.* This was the only reasonable path. If the legend needs me to have the damsel in distress moment, then this damsel is setting her own damn terms."

By the end of her speech, she was out of breath and sweating, even though it was cool in the tower. Ari couldn't help but look over Gwen's distended stomach. Ordinarily, she wore such stiff finery. It had been an odd relief to know that she was under twenty pounds of linen and corset, turning the baby into a diamond beneath so much ruff. Now the little one was shifting and moving beneath thin underclothes, and Ari had to admit that Gwen had somehow gone from respectably round to seemingly unbalanced by her own belly in a matter of weeks.

"Gwen, please don't take this the wrong way, but did you get a lot more pregnant recently?"

"Something shifted in my body. I'm having contractions," she said distractedly. "The baby is just about ready, I think."

Ari's pulse edged up a few notches. "Just about ready like *this week* or . . . today?"

"I don't know, but I'm pretty sure I'm past due at this point. Tonight? Tomorrow? It's going to be soon. That was my cue to abduct myself."

Ari shot up and started her own pacing regimen. The top of the tower was so small that Gwen had to sit down to allow for Ari's burst of nerves. "We have to get you back to Camelot. I know it's not your favorite place, but there are actual midwives there. Val found you one that he thinks will keep your secret."

"Ari, I won't go back to Camelot," Gwen said with such fear that Ari stopped pacing. "This baby will not be Mordred, and the only way I can ensure that is if Camelot and Arthur and Old Merlin know as little about the baby as possible. I won't let this child get sucked into the narrative like we were."

Ari couldn't argue with that logic, not the way the legend had absorbed them like a sponge. "Okay, although I doubt we have more than a day before Arthur rockets out of the castle, searching for us." She sat next to Gwen on the straw mattress and rubbed her face with both hands. "So you want the baby to be born here? In this dismal tower?"

"In Avalon," Gwen corrected. "Where they'll be safe."

"Avalon," Ari repeated. "The home of the ever-so-maternal Morgana and Lamarack's hot, scary new enchantress? Is this because Nin can't see into Avalon?"

"Partly, but also, it's the seat of feminine power on this planet. My baby needs to be born there. I know that they'll help us, and I think, maybe, they'll be trustworthy enough to take care of the baby until we rid the future of Mercer."

Ari fell back on the old mattress with a soft *thump*. "That's a big gamble, Gwen."

Gwen wove her fingers with Ari's, sealing their palms together. "Yes. And that's exactly what you and I are good at. Of course, I'm not sure how we're going to *get* home. And then back again to collect the little one, but I'm not going to—"

"Nin offered me a deal," Ari said, words bursting forth from the rickety dam she'd built to keep the secret. "A way to end the Arthurian cycle *and* portal home, whenever we're ready."

"And what does she want?" Gwen stared at their entwined hands. "You, I imagine?"

"How did you know that?" Ari asked.

Gwen lifted their hands toward her mouth, kissing Ari's fingers. "People are always trying to take you away from me."

"She wants me, Gwen, but not until I die. She wants my soul. To trap it like Arthur's has been trapped for all these years. Nin seems to think that I'm the best candidate for tragic entertainment since Arthur himself."

Ari readied herself for the argument, preparing her already obsessed-upon points: that this might be the only chance to buy enough time to stop Merlin's backward aging before it was too late. To get home. And since Ari's death should be a good long while from now, they'd have decades before Nin, you know, collected on Ari's cursed body and soul.

But this was Gwen she was talking to.

"I can see why you think this is an option, Ari," she said cautiously. "But it's not. Do you remember when the Administrator tried to give us everything we wanted...in exchange for you? What did I say?"

"We don't deal in people."

Gwen nodded as if this proved her point.

"It's the only failsafe we've got, lady."

"Then we'll figure out better options."

Ari smiled; this was her love, her Gweneviere, who rode the diplomacy of any situation like a stallion she'd broken herself. Gwen's unbraided hair fell between them and Ari twirled her long, crimped locks between two fingers. She realized, for the first time since they'd crashed in the Middle Ages, they were alone.

Truly alone.

Ari stared at Gwen's velvet brown eyes, at the small dots of sweat on her nose, and the red, red promise of her lips. "I miss you," Ari said, touching Gwen's shoulder, running her hand down her arm and up again. Gwen's touch moved to the only armor-free places, Ari's neck, her cheekbones, her mouth.

"Did we forget how to do this?" Ari asked after minutes of such light stroking and paused need that her insides were melting.

"I read that sex causes labor...sometimes," Gwen said softly.

"So, you're saying we should go to Avalon and have sex?" Ari's voice had dropped to a warm, nervous tone, but she wasn't complaining.

"Yes, but we should make out before we leave."

"Perfect."

Ari's mouth found Gwen's like the swell of two great waves meeting in the center of a deep blue sea. Between Gwen's belly and Ari's armor, only their faces touched, but it was enough. Gwen's skin was Ari's one true love. She cradled Gwen's cheeks, ran her fingers into her hair, and tasted each of Gwen's lips before relearning that Gwen's tongue pressing against hers poured liquid heat straight through her.

"Well, that's fucking canon," Ari said when they finally stilled, their foreheads pressed together. "Lancelot and Gweneviere, unstoppable."

"According to our Old Earth history classes on Lionel, Lancelot and Gweneviere were the first recorded love story where a woman chose her love. She's horrifically punished for it, of course, but all the stories before that were about men claiming wives. And then after, the stories became about men and women who fight for their love against all odds."

Ari smiled. "So you're telling me Old Earth's boring romantic repertoire of 'cis boy plus cis girl equals love forever' is because two ladies from the future crashed into the past and broke their terrible mold?"

Gwen nodded, her face still so close that her nose skimmed Ari's cheek. "Despite everything that's happened, we were always supposed to come here," Gwen said, kissing her lightly. "To learn that *we* are the unstoppable ones."

&

Gwen didn't go into labor in a fit of screams or panic. It was more like running into an uncharted asteroid field. Nothing, nothing…and then nothing but hard, spinning obstacles as far as the eye could see.

The next afternoon, they were deep into their travels toward Nin's lake and the entrance to Avalon. Gwen rode on the back of the horse, a little too silent, while Ari led him along. She had taken off her armor and piled it in a blanket on the back of the horse. Walking through the Middle Ages in nothing but her pants and a shirt felt bold and dangerous. And stunningly light.

At one point, Ari stopped for a drink of water from her leather bladder and gazed back at Gwen. She was sweating, focused on something Ari couldn't see, riding her pain.

It was already happening.

"Do you know how long you have?" Ari asked, trying to

keep the fear out of her voice. They were still hours from the lake by Ari's rusty geographic calculations.

Gwen shook her head.

"Okay, so we keep going," Ari said. "Do you need anything?"

Gwen shook her head once more.

And they kept going.

When the lake appeared on the horizon, along with Camelot in the far distance and the woods between the two, Gwen whimpered loud enough to spike alarm. Ari stopped the horse and went to Gwen. Water streaked with blood had flowed from Gwen, over the horse's side and into the dark soil of the road.

Gwen was looking down at it in utter alarm. "It's supposed to be clear. I read that. It's supposed to be clear..."

Ari pulled her down from the horse, her own pulse a storm of nerves. "We're going to walk now, lady. On Ketch, the mothers always walked through the last of the pain. The transition period is supposed to be—"

"Don't say it." Gwen inhaled sharply. They walked with their arms around each other, and even though the terrain was mostly downhill, their pace was epically slow. Gwen had to stop so many times. She gritted her teeth and squeezed Ari's forearms until Ari was sure that they'd bruise. Her long hair was plastered to the skin on her neck, and Ari gently peeled it away and blew a cool breath across her skin.

Gwen suddenly doubled over, leaning low, gripping Ari by the shoulders. She swore gorgeously and then came back when the contraction was over to glare at Ari, her lips brilliant red and her face glistening. "Mistake. This whole thing was...a really, not-good mistake."

Ari tried not to laugh. "Yeah, how'd it even come up in conversation with my brother? I can only imagine how he'd react."

Gwen gaped at her. "Are you asking me about Kay? *Now*?"

Ari lowered her voice, keeping Gwen's gaze firmly locked with her own. "Yes, now."

"This is a poorly chosen distraction, Ara."

"You bet." Ari looped an arm around Gwen, judging that they had mere minutes before they would need to stop again, and kept walking. At first Ari thought Gwen might not tell her *how* the baby scheme had occurred, but then she did.

"There was this night on Lionel, well into the siege. Val wanted to have a starlit picnic with the last of the real food before we went to hard rations. He was trying to seduce Merlin. Gods, you should have seen that circus. Those boys..."

Gwen took a few short breaths and then an exaggerated long one that seemed to rip her open slightly. When she was done, she kept talking, her voice far away, wafting after the memory. "We ate the last of the non-space-dried fruit and drank the last of the wine. The four of us. Jordan was off sharpening something somewhere and Lam was more interested in hosting underground resistance rallies. It felt like a double date. Which, of course, felt wrong."

"Agreed," Ari said, allowing her jealousy to have a single, tiny moment.

Gwen smiled, and the feeling evaporated. "Val made us drink and talk about what we wanted. Not what we wanted now that Mercer was steps away from claiming the entire planet, but what we wanted *period*. All I could think about was you, how it felt like you were mine for the smallest slice of time. Like you were my family. And then I'd lost you. I told them I'd always wanted a baby. I wanted to make a family, and Val and Merlin laughed, but Kay didn't." She paused. "He didn't. He missed his moms so much. He missed you."

"An odd request," Ari whispered, remembering the words that had first introduced the idea of this baby, this new person, into her life.

"Gods, he was so dumb and smelly and cute and *never* serious, but he was serious then and it was sort of...beautiful."

Gwen didn't have to explain what that looked like. Kay had been famous for being the levity in Ari's life. The person whose life goals were locked on attaining the next bag of chips or an energy drink—until they weren't. Until he was pulling Ari back from the brink of her most arduous nightmares, the fake ones and the real alike. His own kind of hero.

After all, would Ari have had the strength to take down the Administrator in front of the known universe if her brother hadn't had the audacity to laugh in the man's face? He knew what she had to do, and he knew how to make sure that she did it.

Gwen cried out all over again, breaking Ari's vivid memory of Kay. Ari picked up Gwen and jogged the last stretch toward the gray, crystal water. "My gods, you're a beast, Ari. How are you carrying me?"

"Constant training. Lots of pent-up energy from no sex. Diet of pretty much only red meat," Ari said, smirking at Gwen in her arms. Gwen seemed faintish, and Ari didn't like it. "We're there, lady. Look."

"I'm not going to make it to Avalon," Gwen said, holding

a low spot on her stomach when Ari put her down. "The mist doesn't come until twilight. This baby is happening now."

The water, Arthur said from inside her, startling Ari so much that she stepped backward, boot sinking into the gravelly shoreline. *Trust me. Trust the water.*

Gwen stared, sweat dripping from the sides of her face. "What is it?"

"King Arthur. He spoke to me." Ari tossed a look at the water, a beautiful lake. A serene spot for new life to come into this world—or a treacherous place of no turning back. "Trust me."

"Really? You know how to pull babies out of people? Ara, you've got many of the most badass skills in the universe, but this one might be beyond you."

Ari couldn't agree more. "No, Arthur wants you to go into the water. He wants us to trust him. The last time he told me something this clearly, this directly, I was on the ship with my parents...and Mercer was firing on us."

Urgency, that's what King Arthur's voice had invoked. She began to gather up Gwen and step into the water with her, but Gwen bent over, her sweaty face pale.

"Promise me something that bad isn't about to happen."

Ari shook the darker fears away. "I think I know what he means. On Ketch, we had these birthing pools. It was supposed to be the gentlest way for the baby to enter the world."

"Hell, no." Gwen's legs gave out, and Ari had to slowly lower her to the damp shore. The sun disappeared behind the forest line, and the sky began to darken.

"Just another hour, lady. Maybe less. You can do this."

"There's got to be another way," Gwen said. "I don't want

to do this. I don't want—" She worked her hand up under her skirt, feeling between her legs. "Oh gods, is that a head? How can it happen this fast?"

The water.

What about Nin? Ari shot back.

The water.

Gwen started to groan so low and endlessly that Ari flooded with panic. She lifted Gwen's loose form and trudged into the water. Ari waited for something seismic to happen, but the water stayed just water, so clear that it bloomed with Gwen's blood.

"I don't know what to do," Ari said. "What do I do?"

"Say something. Help me."

"I love you."

Gwen scowled. "So you just pull that out now whenever you want to surprise me?"

"Surprising you is my favorite pastime."

"I hate your timing. I've always hated it," Gwen said, suddenly laughing and crying and giving birth all at once.

Ari found the baby's head with one hand, and then the shoulders, the curved back. The other hand held Gwen close in the chest-high water.

She tried not to notice the way the water chilled and turned black and swirled as she guided the baby toward the surface and Gwen's outstretched arms. The way everything was different the moment Gwen raised the tiny curled body from the water. Perhaps Gwen and Ari were too tired or scared to cry. The moment slipped from fear, to wonder, over and over. The whole universe felt too cold all of a sudden. Too frozen and hard for such a tiny warm life. Ari clasped Gwen to her chest, the baby pressed between them, the rest of this universe shut out.

&

They trudged out of the water, waiting for the mist to appear, bearing a boat to Avalon. Somewhere the baby could be hidden and cared for, safe from the Arthurian story and Mercer and Nin.

Only the mist seemed hesitant tonight, even though Ari had called for it many times, just as Arthur had done. When that didn't work, she built a fire because Gwen was shaking while she cradled the baby in a way that made Ari more nervous than she'd ever been. She tugged the blanket down from the horse and spread it around Gwen's shoulders, building the fire higher and higher.

"Ari, that's enough. Come here." Gwen's face was gray, but not as deathly as it had been when she was shivering. Ari sat beside Gwen and put her arm around her, pulling Gwen's hair back so that she could kiss her neck. "That was absolutely worse than I ever imagined," Gwen whispered. "I feel like a shell that's been cracked open and left behind."

Ari swallowed back strong emotion. "Give it a day. Maybe three. I felt that way when my moms found me. Alive, but also somewhat...gone." It hadn't been time that brought her back, though. It had been Kay. Somehow his persistence and attention had eclipsed her hurt. Well, Ari would have to do the same for Gwen.

Gwen snuggled closer to Ari.

"How are they?" Ari asked after a thick moment of not

being able to think about anything else. Gwen shook her head, her hair brushing Ari's face. "What? Is something wrong? Did the lake water do something to them?"

"No. I mean, they're perfect, but I checked. They definitely have a penis."

"The baby is assigned male?" Ari understood the problem like a thunderclap, although that didn't mean she agreed with it. "But that doesn't actually mean they're going to be..."

"I feel like I can't be surprised, but I am. And I'm scared. I've felt this coming all along. That's why I wished for them to be at least assigned female," Gwen said, voice desperate. "Maybe it's wrong to want certain things, but I couldn't help it."

Ari couldn't help but part the blanket in Gwen's arms. The sleeping baby was perfect...and so still...as if they might open their tiny pink lips and cry smoke.

Mordred.

The name *was* death. No wonder Merlin was terrified of it.

"Maybe they're trans? Or fluid?" Gwen said hopefully.

"Boys aren't so bad," Ari tried, one hand straying toward the baby's head all on its own. "Val's a demiboy. And Kay... was Kay."

"You're not helping your case, Ara."

Ari drew closer. Closer. "They need a name. That will help."

Gwen chewed on a piece of her hair while she stared. "It should begin with *K.* For Kay. Something gender-neutral so they can make their own choices."

Ari smiled softly, remembering an old joke. "Keith?"

Gwen gasped with disgust. "Oh gods, *no.* That's worse than Mordred."

Ari wanted to touch the little bundle, the soft skin. "Jordan called Kay 'Keith' this one time. Still funny to me, I guess." She smiled hopefully, looking up at Gwen's nervous expression. "We're going to be okay, Gwen. All three of us. I can feel it."

"What's that word Merlin keeps going on about? His magic word? The answer of once and future?"

"The *marriage* of once and future," Ari said. "Kairos."

"Since when do you feel so passionate about marriage?" And now Gwen was baiting Ari. Gwen was baiting Ari directly after having a baby. Gods, she loved the grit on this girl.

"I care a hell of a lot about our marriage, thanks for asking. Which is still real, and you better bet I'm going to be picking up where we left off when we get home."

"And what are you going to do until then?"

"Stare at you. Longingly."

Gwen finally looked happy, smiling and also biting her lip. "Oh! Kai for short."

"It fits. Kairos is whoever they need to be when the time comes. It's built into the name." Ari brushed the baby's round cheek and their eyes shot open. Big darkly gray eyes as gorgeous as Gwen's. Ari was holding the baby before she'd even thought to take them up from Gwen, pressing them against her chest. "I love them," she found herself saying. She closed her eyes, talking with a blush, pushing the truth out. "Gwen, they're made from us. They are our family."

"Stop it. That's too much," Gwen said, scrubbing away tears with the heel of her palm. She held her arms out, and Ari handed over the baby. Gwen held them differently. Where Ari had slung them along her chest, Gwen held the tight bundle upright, looking them in the eye as though they were a trader who'd skimped on a shipment to Lionel.

"Listen, little protégé, we're in something terrible here. And back where we came from is also...terrible. You're going to help. You understand? And if you turn evil and try to kill *any* parental figures, I'll be really, really pissed at you."

The baby yawned.

"Excellent. We understand each other," Gwen said, snuggling Kai to her chest as if the effort of holding them away had been a hero's trial.

"Gwen," Ari said quietly. "Do you want to give Kai to the Avalon enchantresses because, in a way, that means you've fulfilled the chalice vision of someone taking the baby from you, but not in some horrible way? Is this like you kidnapping yourself?"

Gwen smoothed the blanket around the baby's small face. "Maybe."

"I think it's brilliant." Ari kissed her. "And I think Kai shouldn't go alone. You could go—"

"I'm *not* leaving your side." Gwen's words were so unyielding, Ari would not fight them.

"But they can't go alone."

The girls stared at each other for a minute, speaking without words. "Merlin," they both said together. Ari added, "This will take him out of the fight before it's too late."

Gwen sighed, and Ari pulled her tighter. This plan, at least, made sense; they would send Kai and Merlin to Avalon for safekeeping, and then come back for both of them. Somehow.

They were so enamored with their little one, speaking nonsense love in tangled whispers, that they were unprepared for the moment the sleeping baby started to...glow.

"What the . . . ?"

"It's the moonlight," Gwen said, as the baby hummed with light that seemed to come from within.

"I don't think so." Ari remembered the strange swirl of black that had transformed the lake water the moment the baby was born.

A falcon circled overhead, screeching in a way that made Ari look up.

"Ari!" Gwen cried at the same moment the hideous bird dropped at their feet, wings beating against the dead leaves as it transformed. Ari's sword was with her armor and the horse. She tried to kick the bird toward the fire, but she was too late.

Old Merlin unfurled his gnarled self before them, froze Ari and Gwen, and stole the baby from their mother's arms.

MERLIN
&
MERLIN

The woods were vile, dark, and deep. Merlin ran through them at top speed, following the lonely hooting of an owl. Without turning around, he knew Val and Lam were lagging behind. It seemed that being an eleven-year-old gave him boundless energy for things like leaping through underbrush and chasing down his older, morally bankrupt self.

He would never forget the look on Old Merlin's face in the tower, as the vile mage broke out of the deep freeze first. He hadn't looked villainous and callous and craven.

No—he'd looked terrified.

Coming close enough that their noses almost touched, Old Merlin whispered, hot and musty, "I never should have let you in my tower. It was wrong to trust you. Everyone in Camelot is conspiring against Arthur."

Merlin wanted to shout that Nin was the one conspiring against all of them, and anything else was really small potatoes. But Old Merlin had already *poofed* into the form of a sleek, dark-feathered falcon and jetted out the tower window.

The next few minutes of frozen waiting amounted to torture: a mashup of his greatest fears on repeat. Fear for Ari, Gwen, the baby. Fear for himself. Fear *of* himself. But none of that was going to get Merlin out of this mess. Terror might be a natural reaction to a dark and unexpected universe, but at a certain point, giving in to it became a selfish way to live. His old self was proof of that.

Merlin's pinky finally twitched, followed by his left eye.

"Progress," he mumbled mushily. His lips still wouldn't close all the way.

As soon as he could walk, he crashed across the tower. A plan had just leaped into his mind, and it started with Archimedes. He ripped the cloth off the owl's covered perch. "Old Merlin just went out that window, and you're going to help me track him."

Archimedes blinked and looked away, beaky and superior.

"I know you understand me!" Merlin shouted.

The owl screeched so hard that he had to clap his hands over his ears.

"I'll tell Old Merlin that you've been eating the mice he keeps for auguries."

Archimedes scowled; an impressive feat considering he didn't have lips. There was no time for proper falconry. Merlin lifted his wrist, and Archimedes condescended to hop on, his claws digging into the meat of Merlin's arms a little harder than was necessary. He ran down the tower stairs as Archimedes kept screeching and clawing. Merlin wasn't going to leave the castle without Lam and Val. He didn't know what kind of ambush he was walking into with Gwen's kidnapping, and he very well might need backup if he was to focus on Old Merlin.

He panted as he came to a stop in front of the siblings, who were seated at an otherwise ill-attended round table.

"Did Ari find Gwen?" Val asked, toppling his chair back as he pushed to his feet.

"No idea," Merlin said. "But I have a bird that's going to find Old Merlin."

"What does he have to do with this?" Lam asked. "He didn't take her, did he?"

"It might be the only terrible thing he *didn't* do," Merlin said. "We have to stop him. He knows about the baby."

Lam and Val had never sworn so loud nor moved so quickly.

And now here they were, all three of them pitching headlong through the woods as Archimedes tracked Old Merlin in falcon form, farther and farther from Camelot, into the lawless woods where the fear of rogue knights and cutpurses gave way to a much deeper worry as they neared Nin's lake. Val's voice came from behind Merlin, ragged but ferocious. "If Nin had anything to do with Gwen disappearing, I will drag her out of that lake by whatever wig she's wearing, and—"

"Her hair is incorporeal," Merlin puffed, turning slightly without breaking stride.

"I know," Val said. "Just let me have one moment of righteous anger against that beautiful horrorshow."

Merlin thought of Nin taking pleasure in this latest painful twist. Coming to Camelot had only been acceptable because he believed it would shield Gwen's baby from harm, and now he was the very person who posed the biggest threat to the child—an irony that Nin would no doubt find delicious.

When Merlin broke onto the banks of the lake, he found neither Old Merlin nor Nin. Two figures were by the water, hands reaching out as if to stop someone, bodies locked in place. In the dusky light, their features stayed dark until Merlin grew close, but he already knew what he would find.

Gwen and Ari, frozen.

As Lam and Val came to a rough stop on the gravel bank, Merlin popped Gwen and Ari with a tiny bit of magic. They came back to life in stiff, shocked bursts.

"Gwen, are you all right?" Lam asked. "Who stole you from the castle?"

"No one," Ari said quickly, trying to get Gwen to sit down. "She's all right. Just, you know, she freakin' *gave birth*."

"Old Merlin..." Gwen breathed raggedly. "He took my baby!" Her rage could have lit the whole dark, pre-electric world. She staggered toward the woods. Ari met her stride and bolstered Gwen as they both stormed into a fight they were never going to win.

"You can't stop him without me." Merlin grabbed their arms, amazed at the baby fat that lined his own. "I'm finally standing up to my old self. Got off to a bit of a rocky start, but..." Gwen spun, and he half expected her to slap him or shout him down for what Old Merlin was doing—what *he'd* done, even if he didn't remember it.

"Thank gods he didn't hurt you," Gwen said, pulling him into a fierce mama dragon embrace.

Merlin feigned confidence. "I might look like a whelp, but which Merlin has actually been around longer?" He pushed his sleeves up only for them to fall back down, one torn to strips where Archimedes had clawed it.

Merlin searched the skies, but the owl must have headed back to Camelot. "Damn disloyal bird! Find someone else to clean up your droppings!"

Merlin would have to track the old mage without help from Archimedes. "We'll split up and head into the woods," he said. "Holding on to that baby requires hands, which means Old Merlin is in human form. If we take different paths, we stand a chance of catching up to him."

"Gwen is with me," Ari said, their arms wrapping around each other. "And the rest of you should know that the baby is a little...different." Ari looked at Gwen, and Gwen shook her head. "We'll explain when we get them back."

"Lam and Val, look for signs of Old Merlin, but keep a safe distance," Merlin said, desperately trying not to look at Val and leak feelings. "I'll work alone, since I'm the only one with magic."

Val stepped in front of him, stooping into Merlin's direct line of sight. "Please don't use too much."

Merlin couldn't make that promise—not even for Val—so it was a good thing Ari spoke up again. "What does he even want with the baby?"

"He won't hurt them, will he?" Gwen asked.

Merlin had always been a terrific liar, but apparently that had been a gift of maturity. "He...It's hard to say what he will or won't..."

"Everyone move!" the queen commanded, and his friends shot in three directions, Gwen and Ari keeping to the path, Lam and Val setting off into the trees. Merlin waited until they were lost among the gloom and branches before he set his lips together lightly and hummed.

His magical sonar pinged off something in the woods. A bright and untarnished magic. Could that really be Old Merlin? Merlin pushed toward it, trees rudely sprouting up everywhere he tried to step. He dodged as quickly as he could, branches giving him a sound lashing. He walked for what could have been five minutes, though it was impossible to tell time in the woods.

And then he slowed, because he heard a scraping barnacle of a voice.

"You can't keep wetting yourself, silly thing," Old Merlin said.

Merlin peeked out from behind a great oak tree. The baby was abandoned on the ground in the hasty folds of a blanket. Their little fists crabbed, their eyes screwed up as if they were working up to a truly impressive wail.

Old Merlin whirled around before Merlin could even think to freeze him. The old man's fingers shot up, a reflex that could lead at any moment to a magical first strike. "You shouldn't have been able to find me, carbuncle. I used cloaking magic that could never be detected by a mere apprentice."

"I'm not a *mere apprentice*," Merlin cried. "I'm you!"

The old mage wouldn't kill another version of himself, would he? Merlin had to believe that this last-ditch truth would save him...and not implode the entire space–time continuum.

Old Merlin looked more vexed than surprised. "At first I believed we had qualities in common, but—"

"No!" Merlin said, leaping involuntarily. "I'm not saying I'm like you. I'm saying that I'm *actually you*. We're the same person! How can you not understand that after being around me for so long? After seeing our magic is the same? Have we always been this thick?"

Old Merlin puffed a breath that made his beard leap. "You're being wildly accusative and going against my every wish. What has gotten into you?"

"I don't know, perhaps you *took my friends' baby.*"

As if on cue, the little one screamed, and sparks exploded through the clearing.

Old Merlin leaped back. Merlin fought his own surprise and swooped to grab the entire bundle, blanket trailing. The little one's weight was warm and solid, even if they did wriggle a great deal.

The whoosh of Old Merlin's freezing spell filled the air behind them as Merlin dodged, running helter-skelter into the trees. Old Merlin shouted, lighting up the woods behind him with magic and anger. The good news was that he ran much faster than his old self.

The bad news was that the infant in his arms really was soaked through with pee.

Apparently that made babies upset. This one's cries could have been heard over the English Channel, let alone a quarter mile away in the same woods. "How can you even make that much sound? You're tiny!"

Merlin found a dead-ish tree that had been hollowed out by animals and tucked in there to catch his breath. The baby was still shredding the night with wailing, though, which meant no hiding place would be safe.

A few gentle sparkles would have been a nice distraction to offer, but Merlin couldn't afford to use magic if he wanted to stay old enough to take care of a baby instead of *being* a baby. What were his skills, outside of magic? "Music!" Merlin said. "Would you like a lullaby?" He tried "London Bridge." He frantically whispered "Three Blind Mice," then cut off when he realized it was only making things worse. "Really? They couldn't do better than plagues and carving knives?"

But the truth of the past was so very ugly.

Merlin was officially out of ideas. What else did babies like? Breasts? Shiny things? He wished he still had a beard for the little one to tug on. Toys were in short supply in the middle of the night in a murder-forest.

"Wait!" Merlin fished in his pockets for the only object he'd brought from the future. He'd found it on Lionel as he and Val traipsed through the market together, eyeing all the things they'd buy for their own castle someday. A hopeful, foolish game. It made them feel like their days belonged to them, not to Mercer. Not the cycle. Not Nin, who had been watching even then, as he and Val stupidly simmered in happiness and Lionelian sunshine, taking stock of the copper pots and leather goods and anachronistic but charming T-shirts. When Merlin found a tiny wooden falcon that reminded him of the past in the warmest possible way, Val convinced him to buy it. Val had believed that Merlin deserved to be stupidly happy.

The baby gave a final-sounding roar, complete with another shower of magical sparks.

Merlin tucked the toy falcon in the little one's mouth, and the baby went instantly silent. "Oh, so you're hungry," Merlin murmured as the baby gummed the falcon heartily. "I am, too. And I do always get a bit sparkly when I need to eat." He spoke to calm his own racing heart, although he'd brought up an important point.

Where had this child come by such magic? Certainly not from Gwen or Kay.

Was this what Ari had meant when she said the baby was *a little different*?

"Carbuncle!" Old Merlin's voice scoured the woods. "Come here and I might not kill you!"

That was a blatant lie. He was going to wipe Merlin right out of the story. Maybe...it didn't require him anymore. Had he come back to Camelot to die at his own hand? What if this was truly his end, back at the beginning? What if this was how Nin won, and she was watching from her cave—the way she'd made him watch Arthur's death?

The way she watched *everything* Merlin did.

The baby cooed with delight, and their fingers glowed, tips like tiny holiday lights, bright and glittering, as if the joy of the falcon was too much.

"Hey, that's my signature move," Merlin said.

As if to prove it, sparks exploded farther off in the forest and illuminated the figure of Old Merlin crashing in their direction. "Carbuncle! I can see you! No use hiding now!"

Merlin clutched the baby close and ran deeper into the woods, avoiding all obvious paths, keeping to the soft beds of dark moss, occasionally cracking a dead stick. Had the sparks given away their location?

And how had Gwen and Ari's baby done Merlin's magic? *Twice?*

Merlin had accused his old self of ignoring the obvious.

Now here he was, doing the same thing. He found a large black oak to hide behind, stopping to catch his breath and grip the impossible. The baby's sparkle fingers had dimmed, but they glowed like tiny stars while clutching the falcon—the only evidence Merlin had ever been loved.

Perhaps because he'd just handed it to himself.

"I mean, there can't be..." Merlin's voice tiptoed toward the impossible, trying not to scare it away. "*Three* Merlins?"

The tree that Merlin was standing behind exploded, disappearing in a hailstorm of white sparks. Merlin hunched forward, his entire body shielding the baby.

Old Merlin emerged from between the trees, blazing them to nothing as he walked by. His hands were full of lightning, his eyes burning up all possibilities for mercy. "Give me the child, carbuncle. The augury—"

"It's not about this baby! You know auguries are vague as fuck!"

Old Merlin raised a hand, one blazing finger leveled at Merlin. He ducked, keeping the baby at the center of his huddled body as the magic hit the tree behind him. It sizzled like a sparkler. Merlin couldn't keep his hold on the blankets and fight back at the same time, so he ran once more, any sense of direction disappearing in the haze of fire and smoke. He came out, coughing and sagging, back on the shores of the lake.

In one direction, Old Merlin was advancing on him, stalking between the white-hot hearts of burning trees. In the other, the water of Nin's lake lapped silently. Hungrily.

Oh, good. He was stuck between a rock and an evil place.

"You don't understand the doom you're bringing on us all,"

Old Merlin growled through a smoke-ravaged throat. "This world needs heroes. It needs Arthur."

"I agree!" Merlin cried. "But I've seen the future. I've *lived* it. This baby might not be the hero you want, but you do need him. You need him so very much." If he was right about his wild doppelbaby suspicions, killing this tiny person would mean wiping all three of them out of existence in one go.

"Merlin!" Ari cried, bursting out of the woods farther down the shore, sword raised.

Gwen was right behind her. *"Where's my baby?"*

Wait, if the sparkly ragamuffin in his arms really was him, did that make Gwen his *mother*? It was too much to swallow—and yet far better than choking down the idea of Nin as a parent.

Old Merlin turned on Gwen and Ari as sparks hailed from the trees, pelting them with tiny points of fire like unholy rain. Ari took Gwen in her arms, and Old Merlin's scream lit the night brighter than his magical flame. "You two! In league to destroy Arthur from the moment you appeared in Camelot. Feeding him treachery and lies!"

Val and Lam came running, emerging from the smoke just behind Old Merlin.

"Go back!" Merlin shouted, waving them off.

"We're not leaving you with him." Ari leveled her sword, and Old Merlin looked far too happy to duel. Merlin couldn't believe that he had friends who would stand between him and his sordid past.

Old Merlin's fingers crackled, bolts of magic leaping out. Ari caught them on the edge of her blade, driven back toward the lake. Merlin ran to Gwen and handed off the tiny one. "Thank you," he whispered solemnly.

"For what?" Gwen asked, one eye on Ari as she battled the screeching mage.

"I don't know!" Merlin tried. "A lot of things, apparently!"

He turned back to Ari just as one of the old mage's bolts caught her across the face.

"No!" Merlin cried, hands sputtering with sparks.

Ari fell back heavily and landed with a crash at the edge of the lake. Lam rushed forward with their sword drawn, but Merlin got there first, throwing himself at the head of the pack.

It was time to take down this ancient nightmare.

A song roared out of Merlin's throat as his fingers fired up. He raised his hands, calling up a dragon of flame to match the one that had attacked Camelot. The sky above the shoreline filled with its long, flowing lines, its fiery breath.

Old Merlin didn't miss a beat. He conjured a fire-dragon of his own, one bright sinuous line at a time, green to clash with Merlin's orange. They met in an explosion above the water, parting to whip at the trees with their long, deadly tails. As they met again and again, the sky turned viciously bright.

Merlin flagged from heat and magic exhaustion, but in the corner of his eye he saw Lam and Val sneaking up on Old Merlin. He needed to keep the old mage distracted. He pushed harder, splitting his dragon in two and attacking from both sides at once. Old Merlin looked delighted and maddened at once. "Perhaps we *are* the same person, carbuncle! No one else could hold out against me like this!"

The sky sizzled with lightning and the first threatening drops of rain, as if Nin had opened her mouth to disagree on that point. Both Merlins paused, looking up, but the clouds grumbled once and that was it.

Old Merlin's hands went back to their wild symphonic dancing, and Merlin kept pouring out magic, because he could see no other choice. His dragons bit and reared and breathed fire, and on any other day it would have given him joy.

But today, this fight was going to end him.

He shrank so fast that he could feel it happening, his bones and skin narrowing down. If Merlin had been eleven when he'd left Camelot a few hours ago, he was much younger now. Nine? Eight? Even his mind felt different, like clothes nearly falling off. He needed to stop soon. If he didn't, he'd slip into the dark place before memories—he was risking the best of his past. The first time he'd met Ari on the moon. The last time he'd kissed Val. The golden days with Arthur, so very long ago. The new wonder of Lam's friendship. Jordan's ferocity and Gwen's bright torch of resistance. Even Kay, the ridiculous. Kay, who wasn't coming back. Merlin couldn't bear to lose the shining thought of the people he loved.

He couldn't let himself forget.

Merlin's mind lit up as bright as the stars.

Old Merlin was the one who *needed to forget*. As long as he knew about the baby, he wouldn't let this go. There was no convincing him that the child wasn't a threat to Arthur. No reasoning with his fears or the violence that followed in their wake. No winning this fight, because the old mage had hundreds of years to waste and Merlin had none.

He let out one last push of magic, his dragon splitting in dozens of fiery directions. A pack of dragons to rival the knights of the round table, each one pointed at Old Merlin's great hulking beast. Instead of attacking, they flew straight into its mouth, like a brace of arrows released down its throat. Old Merlin's dragon thrashed and burst but re-formed just as quickly. With a great swipe of its claws, it scattered Merlin's little dragons into the sky, where they fizzled into nothing.

In that moment when Old Merlin was crowing his victory, Merlin shouted, "Grab him!"

Lam and Val took hold of the skinny old mage, keeping him down. "Restrain his fingers! Cover his mouth!" With the old mage's access to magic cut off, Merlin limped forward.

Gwen was kneeling in the shallows of the lake, over Ari's unconscious body. At least the baby was firmly ensconced in her arms. "He'll be punished for this," Gwen demanded hoarsely. "The old mage has no idea what a real queen can do."

"I know what to do," Merlin said—sounding a little too much like a child bragging to his mother. "And believe me, he'll be punished."

He pushed up the sleeves of his robes, which were puddles of fabric now. His breath stuttered with uncertainty. This was something he'd never tried. But over the course of this fight, he'd gotten so young that it freed him from his old ways. Here, finally, was a silver lining of these backward aging shenanigans. Becoming a child had changed the architecture of his mind. There was no lifetime of fear holding him back.

Val had told him the truth: he had time powers.

And he had them because he was tied to the lake.

Like Nin.

Suddenly, he understood himself in ways he hadn't before. Because he'd come back to Camelot, to this moment, he'd found his lost origins. Merlin knew the place where his story began, the ways that he was different. Having that truth set him free—and in that same moment it set his magic free as well.

It felt like a rushing of dark water inside of him.

It felt like time flowing in every direction.

He closed the gap between himself and Old Merlin. "You thought you beat me," he said. "But we are more than songs and sparks."

Merlin didn't know exactly what to do—but then he remembered Morgana, touching his forehead, gifting him a few hundred years of wretched history. What he needed to do was nearly the reverse. He needed to take the past, steal the baby right out of Old Merlin's head.

He touched the wrinkles on the mage's troubled forehead.

And then Merlin was gone, spinning through the darkness. This was different than traveling through portals, behind the scenes of pure time. He was pushing into the folds of personal time—distorted and musty and strange. Still, he navigated it like he was born to the task, as instinctive as Jordan swinging a sword or Kay flying *Error*.

He crashed around in Old Merlin's memories of Camelot, finding Uther, the vile Pendragon patriarch. Merlin had gone back too far. He moved forward, through a golden age with the Wart, briefly reliving that miraculous moment of a sword pulled from stone.

Here it was: a coronation, a marriage, a baby kept hidden. Merlin tugged, absconding with any memories of the baby's existence, but they were connected to other things. It was like a root system—tug on one and the rest came up with it. Every moment the baby had touched had to go, which meant that

Old Merlin's memories of Gweneviere and Lancelot ripped away along with the rumor of their love. His own time as an apprentice went next. He felt the memory of this very fight breaking free, crumbling Old Merlin's mind when it left.

The old mage howled as Merlin took everything.

CHALICE
&
CAVE

Ari was lying on her back in a shallow pool of water beneath a black sky full of crystal stars.

Familiar stars.

She wasn't on Old Earth.

Ari sat up on her elbows, dizzy from the bolt of Old Merlin's magic she'd taken straight to the face. She tried to touch the wound, but the pain wouldn't let her. And what was she doing lying in the city center fountain? She glanced around at Omaira, the capital of Ketch. It was night, but there were still orange lights in distant windows. Signs of life. Gwen's people? Or had Nin thrust her back to a time when Ketch was still full of Ketchans?

The lights glowed brighter, spreading. Flames painted the city red, followed by screams that reached her as if being filtered through deep water. Which meant Ari wasn't here; she was seeing what Nin wanted her to see.

Ketch on fire.

"Stop this, Nin!" Ari croaked. "I'll take your fucking deal!"

Nin plucked her out of the spreading devastation as if drawing a curtain.

Ari was lying in the mercilessly cold water of Nin's lake. Her friends gathered around her, hauling her limp limbs toward the shore. "Get her out of the water!" Val yelled, his words cottony as if Ari's ears were still full of Nin's liquid time magic.

Once she was out of the lake, Gwen grabbed Ari by the front of the shirt. Ari came back to Earth gasping, mind spinning. The screams of Gwen's people on Ketch were still circling in her ears.

"Gwen," she said, out of breath. "We have to go home. Now."

Gwen spoke with measured calm, cradling Kairos to her chest. "You've had a serious blow to the head. We've all had one of the worst nights of our lives. Take a minute."

"Every minute here is lost for our future. Ketch is burning."

"Nin is messing with you, Ari," Val said. "She could have shown you months ago or years from now." Ari let him believe that could be true, but she knew Nin had gone from asking to demanding that she take her deal.

Ari beheld how small Merlin had become. He sat beside her with his knees drawn up to his chest, his arms wrapped around thin legs. She'd stopped herself from thinking of him as a child so many times in the last few weeks...but that was over now. She put a hand on his bony little shoulder, surprised when he launched himself into a hug, his head tucked against her chest.

"I'm so sorry. I'm so, so sorry," he chanted.

"That wasn't you," Ari said. "It was Old Merlin."

Merlin pulled away, chin thrust up in defiance. "And I used to be him. So it *was* me, back when I was a villain."

Gwen handed off Kai to Ari and took Merlin by the upper arms. "We are all knights and villains, commoners and kings. A true hero plays every role." Big tears rolled down Merlin's face, and Gwen wiped them away with her thumbs. "I am so proud of you. You saved all of us."

Ari looked for Old Merlin, finding the ancient magician sitting on a log beside the misted lake. He muttered fragments of magic that sent small rocks spinning in the air like a tiny galaxy.

"He's fucked up," Val said quietly. "Barely remembers his own name."

"Arthur!" Old Merlin suddenly shouted. "Arthur? Where are you, boy?"

Lam jogged over to the magician, quieting him with murmured words while Ari turned back to tiny Merlin. "What did you do to him exactly?"

"It looked awful," Val added as if he couldn't stop himself.

"I stole his memories of us. Ripped them out. Synapses were...severed. His mind is broken earth and shifting ground now, and it will be for many lifetimes."

Ari looked at Merlin anew. He was impossibly skinny, his head somehow larger, or perhaps his shoulders had shrunk. "That's why you didn't remember us," she said. "Why you didn't realize that I was Lancelot and that Gwen has always been Queen Gweneviere."

"That's why I didn't know a great many things." Merlin's high voice bled with regret. "I stole them from myself."

Ari cocked her head. "Merlin, that's different magic for you. How did you do it? It's like you channeled Morgana."

"This place has opened my eyes to a few curious realities

about my powers." Merlin looked at Ari as if he were waiting for her to do something. She smiled and tried not to stare at the way he reminded her of Kay, back when they'd first met. Her brother had also been chubby-cheeked, red-haired, and full of pouts. "The baby has strange magic, too."

"Wait, the baby can do magic?" Val asked. "Like you?"

"After they were born they sort of...glowed," Gwen said, eyeing the sleeping baby in Ari's arms. "What else can they do, do you think?"

Merlin shrugged. "I don't think there's a full answer to that one yet."

"They were born in the water," Ari said. "Do you think that had something to do with it?"

Merlin stared out at the lake. "Yes. But I don't know what it means."

"You know what it does mean? This baby *cannot* be Mordred," Gwen nearly shouted, her expression melting into relief. "Mordred couldn't do magic in any of the stories! He was a whiny, power-hungry cis boy. See? I told you I knew who my baby was the whole time!"

Merlin coughed, and Ari squinted at the tiny one in her arms. They certainly didn't look like an entitled princeling with patricidal leanings. Little Kai began to fuss, and Ari bounced them. She couldn't stop herself from staring at Merlin, gauging his years. Seven...eight? *Seven.* He was too young now to even think about calling up a portal, unless they wanted him toddling into the Mercer-ridden future.

Ari wouldn't put him in that kind of danger.

This was what Nin meant when she insisted that Ari would *have to* take her deal. The future needed them now. The baby had to be protected from both time lines...and so did Merlin. She caught eyes with Gwen, who nodded while chewing on her lips. They both glanced at the mist, the veil that separated Avalon from a harsh past and corrupted future.

Lamarack approached Ari with an unflinching smile. "Not to change the subject from one bleak emotional nightmare to the next, but we've not been introduced." Lam reached out, and Ari wasn't ready for the pride that poured through her as she handed the bundle over.

"This is our Kairos," Ari said.

Merlin gaped. "*Kairos* is my favorite word! It's always been my favorite word."

"Yes, that was how we thought of it." Ari wrapped an arm around Gwen's tired body.

Gwen held on to Ari's waist. "Kai is our perfect moment."

"Wrinkly little cutie." Val peered at the baby with amusement. "Assigned?"

"Male," Ari said.

"For now," Gwen countered. "Kai will tell us when they're ready."

Lam tried to hand the sleeping bundle to Val, and Val squirmed and held his palms up. "I'm no good with tiny and breakable."

Several of them laughed, and the circle of their impromptu joy felt as impossibly perfect as Kairos. Until Ari remembered Nin's taunting.

"We have to go," she said with certainty. "I have to take Nin's deal."

"What deal?" Val, Merlin, and Lam said together.

"A deal to buy us some time." Ari stared at Gwen. Gwen

nodded slowly. "And to get some of us home, until we're ready to be together again."

"Some of us," Val repeated skeptically. "You're planning to send the baby to Avalon?"

Ari and Gwen exchanged looks. "Trust us," Ari said. "They have to be protected."

"In this, we are agreed." Morgause stepped into their circle with sudden authority. "The enchantresses of Avalon will keep the children safe."

"Oh, where in the F did you come from?" Val yelled, grabbing his chest.

Morgause flicked a hand back toward a small boat docked on the shore. Her gaze swept them until she found Lamarack, giving them a heated smile. Lamarack leaned forward and grabbed her arm, stealing a stunningly potent open-mouthed kiss.

"Did she say 'children'?" Val asked, eyes darting toward Merlin.

Ari cleared her throat. "The enchantresses are taking Kai... and Merlin. Until we've finished with Mercer."

"But how will we get them back?" Val's voice edged with anger, and when Merlin reached a small hand toward him, Val took it firmly, protectively.

"I don't know yet," Ari said, "but it's safest if they're together. Nin can't see into Avalon, and Mercer can't reach it. It's the only place." She expected more resistance—instead she found Merlin staring up at her with those big brown eyes. "You can help the baby, and if anyone can figure out your backward aging, it's the enchantresses. Or who knows? Maybe Kai will finally be the one to do it, with whatever magic they've got."

At least, she hoped so.

A hunting horn sounded through the dark woods behind them. Everyone jumped, and Kai began to cry.

"The king is coming," Lam said. "He still believes Gwen has been kidnapped. No doubt they're following our trail with the hounds."

"Arthur!" Old Merlin yelled from where he turned circles by the shore. "Arthur! I'm here, my boy!"

"The baby has to be gone before he gets here," Gwen whispered sharply. "I don't want Kai to be part of the Arthurian cycle."

"Will you do this for us, Merlin?" Ari asked in a rush. Merlin nodded, and Ari turned to Gwen, holding Kai against her chest as if she knew how much this was going to hurt. Ari felt bright stings in her eyes, and all she could think was to move faster. Do it before they both lost their nerve. "Close your eyes, baby girl."

"I'm not baby girl. *You* are," Gwen said, eyes already closed. Ari kissed Gwen's cheek and then placed another kiss on Kai's small face. She lifted the baby and handed them to Merlin without letting herself pull their little body to her chest. Tears only broke free when the baby was safely in Merlin's arms.

"Don't let Kai out of your sight. Make sure they know we love them." Only Gwen would be able to say those words without breaking. She was turning fiercer, steady even though it had been a hundred-year-long night.

"Come back to us when you're both ready," Ari said.

"Promise," Merlin said, big brown eyes taking in Val, Ari, Lam, and finally Gwen.

The hounds bayed close by, and Merlin crossed toward the

boat and stepped into it. Morgause launched them off the shore with a push, and they were gone. A heartbeat later, Arthur's fleet of hunting dogs shot out of the edge of the woods and surrounded the company with great growling barks.

"Oh, shut up and sit!" Gwen snapped and the hounds sat obediently.

Arthur's knights poured out of the woods on horseback. Arthur was off his stallion in a rush, clambering toward the spot where Old Merlin was shouting his name incoherently. Arthur pressed the magician into the waiting arms of Gawain and Galahad before turning to Gwen and Ari. His steps slowed as he took in how they stood together, as one. He swallowed, winced. Arthur motioned to the burn across Ari's cheek. "What happened?"

"A run-in with your mighty mage. He, ugh, landed a spell wrong, I'm afraid."

Arthur nodded and turned tragic eyes on Gwen. "You're safe, my queen. I imagined the worst. The chalice gave me no memory of you beyond this night."

Gwen took Arthur's hand and kissed his knuckles. "That's because we're going home."

Arthur nodded and turned away. He walked back to his horse and pulled out the magical wooden box from his saddlebag. Ari's breath lodged in her throat. This was what she'd seen all those weeks ago: Arthur handing over the chalice. "To be honest, I'm glad you'll have this. It is too much power for my time."

Gwen embraced Arthur. "I'm sorry we had to trick you. We didn't have a choice."

"We had a few choices," Ari griped.

"We had no *promising* choice."

"There's my politician."

Gwen's glare turned to a blush. "Ari—"

"Please," Arthur said. Ari couldn't believe how much older Arthur appeared, weathered and yet ready. "My future is before me, but it's a map torn with failure. If the chalice is right, I will let you go, and then, perhaps, however you see fit to use it will set me free in this future of yours."

"The chalice didn't tell you the end, did it?" Ari asked, imagining the deal she'd soon be making for Arthur's soul.

"I saw no end but the hope for an end. What is it they will say in your time? *Rise up with hope.*" Arthur smiled sadly. "I'm only angered in that this was probably your plan all along. Work your way into my favor and then take the chalice."

Ari opened her mouth to admit as much, but Gwen threw a sharp elbow.

Arthur opened the box and plucked the chalice out. He held it toward Ari and then pulled it back. And handed it to Gwen. Gwen took it, sharpish, holding it to her chest. "What will you use it for?" Arthur asked.

"Oh, save the universe," Ari said. "That sort of thing."

Arthur smiled as if maybe he *could* understand. "And how will a little cup do that?"

"Good fucking question." Ari stared at it. "One chalice defeating a monstrous corporation and saving the universe sounds about as solid of a plan as strange women lying in ponds, distributing swords."

"No quoting Merlin!" Gwen said, choking up suddenly. Ari wrapped an arm around her and felt the aching spot in her chest that longed for their kids.

"You two really are married, aren't you?" Arthur asked.

"Going on two years," Ari said, swiftly kissing Gwen's hand. "No regrets."

"A *few* regrets," Gwen corrected.

Ari winked and turned back to the legendary king, wringing his gloves in his hands, still so unsure. "Arthur, we're..." What could she say? Sorry they were abandoning him in this medieval hellhole? Leaving him to his cursed fate and the echoes he'd face across time and space?

"I'll meet you again," Arthur said with finality. "You know when."

Ari stared in his blue eyes. *The day you save my life.*

Arthur nodded in a crestfallen way as if reliving his own future. Ari put a hand on his shoulder, remembering that no matter how small and insignificant the chalice might appear, its wisdom had changed this boy king into a legendary hero.

"You won't be alone, Arthur," Lamarack said.

Ari started, looking at them sharply. "Hell, no."

Lam held up the rolled paperback of Jordan's Mercers-Notes. "I'm staying here. To make sure that the legend is complete, so you can go home safely. Please do me the courtesy of not acting surprised."

Val hiccupped a small groan. Gwen went to Val's side. Ari shook her head. "It's a good idea, but no." She stepped close and held up the chalice. "You have to help us get back to the future and...figure out what to do with it!"

Lam didn't budge. "Someone needs to stay with Arthur. And be close in case Morgause needs any help with Merlin or Kai."

Ari didn't have a response ready for that one.

"Bye, kid." They leaned in and kissed her. It was a longer kiss than she was prepared for, and Ari opened one eye at a time in the aftermath. Lamarack crossed the shore to kiss Gwen good-bye next. When Gwen swayed a little bit afterward, Ari mouthed, *"Right?"*

They hugged their brother tightly next, while Val tried to ignore the hug and shake his head as if this weren't happening. "Ari, stop them."

"I know this trick. You're trying to disarm us with your charm," Ari managed.

Lam smiled. They held their hand out for the chalice. "What if we ask the future?" Ari gave it to them begrudgingly. They looked into it and whispered, "Am I doing the right thing?" The question made water from Nin's lake rise to the surface, but then, instead of drinking it, they just looked at it. "I don't have the same love for the future you all do. You know that. I've never found my home, my place, my reason. These people—"

"Don't understand you," Val chirped.

"But they're starting to..."

Val kept right on talking, in true sibling fashion. "And even if they *did,* so much of who you are will get erased by the stories later."

"That doesn't mean that what happens here doesn't matter." Lam stared at Ari, and she realized that this was the first time Lamarack had ever asked her for anything.

And they were asking to be let go.

Ari grabbed the full chalice back, unable to watch Lam's doubts take hold just because everyone else wanted them to change their mind. "You don't need magic to weigh in on your life." Lam smiled and Ari added, "I love you, and I hate that you're staying here."

But she did understand why.

Ari felt this night's many good-byes turn into one lump in her chest. She found Gwen's hand, and then Val's. Best to move fast, through the torturous pain of yet another parting, toward a future that needed them as much as they all needed it.

&

Ari, Val, and Gwen stepped into the lake, leaving Lamarack and Arthur behind. The unfriendly portal dumped them onto the cold, hard ground.

"It's official. I loathe caves," Val said, wiping off his pants and tugging his corset back into place. He reached desperately for a joke. "When we get back to the future, someone is eventually going to say, 'Come see these amazing cave formations!' And I'm going to be like, 'Leave. We're not friends anymore.'"

Ari helped Gwen up, and they stood, looking around at a lonely, dark tunnel that smelled of old air and damp creatures. A light came from far away, highlighting a passageway.

"No wonder she's miserable and hates people," Gwen said. "This place sucks."

"And she's *listening*," Val said, his sarcastic voice shaking a little. Ari and Gwen placed him between them. He grasped the chalice to his chest as if it were a lifeline, and maybe it was, the literal embodiment of their hope. The tunnel grew larger as they walked, the ceiling doming. Ari blinked, and suddenly she was looking at dozens of water screens. Each one projected a different story. A different century. Covering every inch of the rock.

"Are those all—"

"Great. We're in the hall of Arthurs. She's just showing off now," Val said.

One of the screens filled with Merlin's face, except he wasn't young or senile. Somewhere around forty and kissing what had to be a thirty-something reincarnation of Arthur.

Val put his hand over the screen. "Merlin wouldn't want you to watch that." Then he moved his hand and couldn't look away. "Gods, he's even hot middle-aged. I miss him *so much*," he whispered. "Does it make me stupid to still love him? He's never coming back."

Ari took his shoulder. "The enchantresses are going to help Kai *and* Merlin."

"Sure, Ari." Val shook his head before calling out. "Nin! Come out, you omnipresent Peeping Tom!"

All the screens went off at once. A sound rushed through the caves like so much water, and Ari's heart thundered at the threat of the entire place flooding. She grabbed Gwen's hand, and they ran until they came to a spot that opened up with a great vaulted ceiling.

And in the center, on a raised platform, was dead King Arthur.

Ari rushed toward him while Val held Gwen back. "Is that...?" Gwen asked.

"Yes," Val said.

"He's so much older," Gwen murmured.

"This is his body, stolen from the battlefield after his

death." Ari looked from his soiled armor to the open wound that must have come from Mordred's hateful sword. "I saw him like this in Merlin's worst memory."

Nin had stolen Old Merlin out of that last, terrible battle. She'd offered the suffering magician some mild magical fore-sight, and he'd taken it—only to have his first vision be the aftermath of Arthur and Mordred's fatal showdown. The loss of the one person he loved. And then Nin had stolen King Arthur, and his soul had taken flight. From cis boy to cis boy, until he found Ari.

Nin appeared beside Val, resting her head on his shoulder, looking as polished and potent as ever in her perfect velvet suit. "You've come back."

"No touching," Val yelled, jumping away.

Nin took notice of Gwen next, and Gwen blushed and turned toward Ari's ear. "Is she always naked?"

"*Naked?*" Ari sputtered.

"I look the way you'd like me to look." Nin smiled at Val. "A powerful drag queen for some." She looked at Ari. "A drag king for others. A soft, perfect mother for merlin." She grinned at Gwen last. "And unglamoured for a unique set."

Ari closed her eyes, trying not to envision all those things at once. "You offered a deal, and we're here to take it."

Nin turned to Ari with a needling gaze. The Lady of the Lake was a woman, and she was not. She was a person, and she was not. "Hello again, forty-second King Arthur."

"I prefer Ari."

Nin waved her hand dismissively. "Tell me, *Ari,* have you let your friends know that you've decided to give yourself to me? I hope not. I'd like a front row seat to their shock and dismay."

Val looked at Ari with sincere annoyance, but Gwen nodded.

Ari *had* to do this. It was the only way to spark new hope. "I trade myself for Arthur at the moment of my death. But only if you rejoin his spirit with his body and let him rest. Forever."

"You realize you offer me new entertainment." Nin's entire façade rippled like a disturbed body of dark water. "I've been through this particular cycle so many times. The repetition of humanity's poor choices is growing stale." The Lady of the Lake was truly terrifying if for no other reason than she reminded Ari of the blankness of deep space. Unmoved by pain or love or hope or goodness. "New crises. Won't that be fun."

"*Ari,*" Gwen tried, but Ari cast a pleading look.

"Oh, by all means, tell her how you must do this and that it is the only way to save the old, completely overrated king of Camelot whom everyone loves so dearly. The conflicted bits are my favorite." Nin perched on the edge of the platform holding King Arthur's frozen body. She propped her chin on her knuckles.

"Gwen knows why I have to do this. We all love Arthur." Well, *love* wasn't the right word. It was more like Ari needed Arthur, but love was a kind of need, wasn't it? "We all want him to be set free. We promised Morgana."

Gwen nodded, so minutely that Ari almost missed it. Val didn't seem to know what to think, his lips forming the words, *The fuck?* He looked at Gwen and when she didn't seem upset, he rolled with it. Ari turned to Nin. "You have your deal. Send us back to our time."

"More than half a year has elapsed, as you know. Where you come from, much is changed," Nin said with a sickening smile.

"Do it!" Ari shouted. "Stop playing with us."

The Lady of the Lake slid down from the platform, ice eyes sealed on Ari as she snapped her fingers. A portal opened beside Val and Gwen, tugging them in as they cried out— before Ari had a moment to reach for them. To make sure they all stayed together.

In the aftermath, no sound remained in the cave except Ari's panicked breath.

"Now, let's pull Arthur's spirit free, shall we? I have *always* wanted to try this." Nin dug her nails into the air in front of Ari.

She gasped. It felt like Nin was trying to wring the water out of her body, molecule by molecule. Ari's mouth opened in a scream that turned into a misty cloud above her head. With another flick of Nin's hand, King Arthur's soul rained onto his body, soaking into his ancient tarnished armor.

Ari struggled to her feet, emptied and scraped inside. The Lady of the Lake waved a hand behind her, and King Arthur transformed from a time-frozen dead body into a ragged corpse, and then a collapsed pile of bones. Even the bones grated to dust, and finally, all that was left was a pile of gray sand. Ari watched as the outline of a new body appeared in King Arthur's stead, faint as mist and yet just as potent.

It was Ari.

Only, she wasn't much older, like King Arthur had been at

the time of his death. She looked...the same age she was now. Ari found that she couldn't breathe. Couldn't move.

The burn on her cheek hadn't even turned to a scar.

It was still a wound.

"*Oh, yes,*" the Lady of the Lake simpered. "I always forget how hard it is for mortals to know their own demise. You're going to end very young. Not much time left, I'm afraid. Best go kiss that girl while you've got her."

HOPES
&
HEROES

The boat to Avalon was more than halfway across the lake, and Merlin was surprised that he'd made it so far without Nin smacking him overboard. She must have been satisfied with the amount of misery in the universe, for once.

He wished that he could enjoy the self-propelled boat ride after a vicious battle and a heart-wearying farewell. But even without the lapping worry of Nin's waters, Morgause kept staring at him from the other side of the little craft. She didn't force small talk—she was an enchantress, after all—but she did make him squirm, and then of course Kairos squirmed, and soon they were just one squirmy unit, making the boat rock.

As the famed mists of Avalon dropped around them like a wet, heavy curtain, Morgause's voice finally reached out. "Why did you not tell the others that you and the child are the same?"

Merlin nearly dropped the baby.

"How did you figure that out?" he piped. And then glumly added, "It's a magical lady thing, isn't it?"

"That is one way of saying it. And the question remains."

Why hadn't he told Ari and Gwen that he was Kairos? Oh, let's see. He didn't want to make it harder for them to leave. Besides, how did you tell people you'd befriended and fought beside that you were also, secretly, *their child*?

When he opened his mouth to explain, it felt like the bridge between his feelings and his tongue hadn't been built. Was this one more thing he'd lost as he got younger? "I've been looking for about a billion years for my parents and now that I know who they are it's just so...weird." Oh, how blazingly eloquent. Good job, tiny Merlin.

"Your friends do not yet see how powerful the baby is," Morgause intoned as the boat rocked. "How powerful you are."

Merlin shivered as the mists wrapped him in foreboding. And wetness. Worse than Kairos peeing himself again. "What do you mean?"

"It has long been foretold that a second child will be born in the lake of time. We've been waiting for you."

"A *second* child?"

"Nimue was also born in the waters of time. Long ago." Well, that explained why they had so much in common. Merlin couldn't wait to inform Val—if he ever saw him again. "She once lived among us as a mortal with powers much like yours. How she became what she is now remains a great mystery. But she fears one thing, and one alone. The other time child."

Merlin didn't feel empowered by this, ready to break the cycle once and for all. Instead, it felt like he was choking on a dark destiny. He had a sudden new empathy for his Arthurs.

"I can't be the hero! That's not my part to play. I'm the magical sidekick who is much more powerful and yet somehow much less important!"

Morgause didn't even dignify that with a response.

Merlin tried again. "I can't stand up to Nin before I stop myself from aging backward. I'm almost out of magic *and* time." He held up the baby. "Maybe Kairos is the one who'll save everybody. *Kairos* is our perfect moment."

Morgause gave him a look that rivaled Morgana's best acid stares, eating through his hope. "You are the one who knows how to fear Nin. You are the one who carries centuries of knowledge and mistakes from which you might learn."

"How do you know about my centuries of mistakes?" Merlin cried into the night. "Is this another Avalon thing?"

"Lamarack told me."

"While you were mushing your faces together?" Merlin really hadn't meant to say it like that. "Sorry. Sorry." The harsh truth was that Merlin knew he couldn't wave off this destiny and pass the buck to a baby. That would be nearly as bad as trying to steal one.

"There might be a way to stop me from aging backward," he said, remembering how close he and Old Merlin had come in the tower. "But I need help." When his magic had unlocked itself, so much had become clear, emerging like Avalon from the mists. His backward aging was just another form of time magic, and whoever had set it in motion hadn't given him the means to fix it alone. He could only do it with help from another lake-powered mage. Another Merlin. The mean pinch of irony came as he realized there were two in Camelot, but one had just been forced to forget him, and the other lacked motor skills.

"Kai, can you spark me?" he asked.

Kairos's eyes were shut tight, his tongue poking out of his tiny mouth.

"I'll take that as a no," Merlin said. Whined, really. "I don't have what I need here."

"You have all of time at your fingertips," Morgause countered.

Merlin breathed deeply and tried to think like a proper time baby. To be strategic, like Val would want. It was true: he could create portals. But he would have to make the jump carefully. If he aged beneath five or so, there would be no breaking this cycle. Ari and Gwen and Val would be left to deal with Nin alone.

Merlin stood up carefully in the boat. The closer they got to Avalon, the more details he could see. The gorgeous caves, the windswept cliffs, the humble homes filled with hearth fires and magic. "I thought you didn't let men into Avalon."

"We don't," Morgause said, with two meaningfully arched brows.

"Oh," he said. "Right." It would take Merlin years to get back to the threshold of manhood—if he ever made it back at all. He would have liked to spend his childhood running wild with the enchantresses. Finally getting to know and understand them. Reuniting with Morgana—definitely using the name Kairos, since she wasn't Merlin's biggest fan.

But it wasn't meant to be. Another life, perhaps.

"I'm low on power," Merlin admitted. "Would you mind helping me?"

With Morgause's magic added to his, he could make it a little farther and hopefully not vanish into babyhood in the process.

Morgause pulled out the same ceremonial dagger that all Avalon enchantresses kept strapped to their thighs, and drew a diagonal slash across her palm. Blood already dripping, she looked at the child in the crook of Merlin's arm. "The time child must be kept safe at all costs," she said. "Are you sure you do not wish to leave Kairos in Avalon?"

Merlin couldn't hand off Gwen and Ari's baby. He couldn't give away the last trace of Kay on this or any world.

Oh, celestial gods. *Kay was his dad.*

And on that ridiculous note, Merlin took Morgause's bleeding hand, and hummed. His skin started at the barest shine, and then built to a vivid beacon. The last shreds of Avalon mist parted around him. The lake below them shivered.

And a doorway carved of dark matter appeared.

&

Merlin didn't have much time in the portal to decide exactly *when* he was going. He emerged dizzied and still clutching Kairos. They were surrounded by smoke, bodily odors, and figures clad in rags. If he didn't know better, he'd think he was still in medieval Europe. But then he heard the buzzy pluck of an electric guitar and saw the stages and tents beyond the freely ranging crowds.

"We made it," Merlin whispered to Kai. "This is Coachella. There's someone here who can help us."

Kairos seemed blissfully uninterested in the chaos. Merlin pushed through the crowds, already on the hunt. Arthur 37 was set to play today. That particular Arthur—wasn't his name Dan?—would become so famous that even stadiums couldn't contain the messages of hope and love that humanity so craved, set to addictive beats. But right now, today, there was a thirty-ish Merlin around here with time and magic to spare.

He staggered around, garnering a few strange looks. Fortunately, another silver lining of being a small child carrying a baby was that people seemed determined to help him.

"Where are your parents, little guy?" a man with a monstrous mustache asked, crouching down. Merlin bubbled with frantic laughter. He couldn't begin to explain how hilariously complex the answer was. "All right, then," Sir Mustache said. "What's your name?"

"Merlin."

He nodded as if that was a fairly common name for a little kid who'd gotten dragged to Coachella. "Let's go find security, okay?"

"No, thank you." Goodness, Merlin's voice was sweet. "I just need the performers' tent."

Sir Mustache pointed him in the right direction, and Merlin headed there on swiftly pumping legs. He kept wandering off, though. It was absurdly hard not to get distracted at six. He wanted to play in those mud pits. He wanted to breathe in this good Earth air before the planet was hurt beyond repair. He desperately needed a snack.

Then—at the back of a tent, among the roadies and managers, Merlin got a glimpse of something silvery-white and flowing and unmistakable.

"Merlin's beard!" he whispered. "Kairos, it's our storied facial hair. That's going to be important to you someday."

He ducked under the tent flap, so short that nobody noticed

his presence at first. Merlin's beard was...well, it wasn't quite as grand as he remembered it. But it was there, hanging over a robe that didn't look too out of place at a hipster festival, stuck atop a frowning face that could belong to no one else.

"We really did go gray shockingly young," Merlin whispered to Kai as they grew closer. "Is that Kay's fault? I blame Kay."

"Are you here to ask for an autograph?" Thirties Merlin asked grumpily. "I'm afraid they're about to go onstage."

"I'm here for you," Merlin said, holding out Kairos. "We both are."

Thirties Merlin badgered them back toward the entrance. "Children at a rock concert. What kind of tomfoolery is this?"

"The kind where I tell you that I'm you, and I need your help."

"Ah, you're me. And who is that then?" he asked, pointing at the baby.

"Also us." Merlin snapped. "Honestly, keep up."

Thirties Merlin pushed him out of the tent just as the band started to play, the air reverberating with drums. Merlin expected the same disbelief that Old Merlin had thrown at him. But this version of him was no longer a crabby, lonely, obtuse old man. He'd had enough time to change. To shake off the effects of the mind-breaking magic that had saved Kai's life. Over the music, Thirties Merlin yelled, "And how are there so many of us?"

"We're not really different Merlins!" he shouted. "We're all the same Merlin at different points along the time line!"

"Can you prove it?"

Merlin opened his mouth and then closed it. He held up

one small hand, all five fingertips glowing. Then he danced Kai's falcon into the baby's mouth, causing the little one to also glow.

"Believe me now?"

"Yes, but...Neither of you should be here," the somber, unamused mage said, crossing his arms. "It's against the laws of—"

"Time and space?" Merlin cut in. "We've never really obeyed those, have we?"

"Time and space can suck it!" someone cried out as they passed, holding up a cup filled with an anonymous brew.

"I only need one thing, and I need it fast," Merlin shouted. "If you spark me at full strength, I believe it can set me aging in the right direction."

"Then...we've found a way to stop it!" Thirties Merlin blinked away his shock. He looked so hopeful that Merlin didn't have the heart to add that he would also take away all memory of this. It was such a quick, isolated moment that magically removing it shouldn't cause any harm, and Merlin couldn't risk derailing the future—even if it meant that this version of him would have to go through several more centuries of pain to get there.

It was worth it. Every time he thought of Ari and Gwen fighting the future, he knew how much this would all be worth it.

"Hit me," he said.

And just as the song reached an epic chorus, Thirties Merlin joined in at full volume, his hands rife with so much white fire that he nearly set his own beard aflame.

Merlin set down Kairos. Gently. And held his arms out just

as sparks flew at him, so many that his chest sizzled and his vision whited out.

When he came to, he was lying on the ground. He popped up to sitting. Kairos stared at him, looking wise and impassive in the way that only babies could manage. Strangers were watching, but Thirties Merlin didn't look worried. Everyone crowded around as if this was part of the show.

"How do you feel?" Thirties Merlin asked. "Did...did it work?"

Merlin added his voice to the song. Sparks leaped out of his hands, bright and lively, but he didn't feel the years draining with them. "I'm not getting younger!"

As the notion of finally being able to fight back against Nin grew, his sparks went mad. People clapped for his homemade light show, until the scent of smoke reached Merlin's nostrils. He'd accidentally set the tent on fire. Oh, dear. He'd have to make this other Merlin forget that bit, too.

&

"You're going to love it here, Kai," Merlin said.

They'd left the wilds of Coachella behind for the calm of Merlin's crystal cave.

Morgause had said the time child must be kept safe at all costs. There was only one place that Merlin could keep Kairos truly safe—where he could promise that, no matter what happened, he would survive it.

What he'd said outside the tent was true. Every Merlin was really the same person at different points in a long, wild story.

And it had to start somewhere.

He found the slab of crystal he'd always used as a bed and set Kairos down. The baby writhed and wailed, as if he could see the ages of pain and heartbreak that Merlin was about to cast him into. Would Gwen and Ari ever forgive him for doing this to their baby? Would he get a chance to tell them who he really was...or was he making one more hapless sacrifice for the slimmest chance at a broken cycle, a brighter hope? A better future?

Feelings fought their way up his throat, and soon he and Kairos were both crying. Kairos didn't know what was coming next. And truthfully, neither did Merlin. What if he gave up Kairos and still failed to stop Nin?

"This is not an easy thing to do, little me." He'd always wondered who had given him up, left him to face so much alone.

Now he knew he'd done it himself.

"You'll wake up here in a little while. And you'll go through this doorway to Camelot, and you'll befriend a small boy who needs you. His name is Arthur. And it won't be all bad. No, not all bad at all." Merlin tucked the falcon into Kai's fisted hand and stepped back behind a crystal column, hidden from sight. He hummed a lullaby and hit the baby with soft blue sparks. Kai's body spread larger and larger, filling up the slab. His baby wrinkles stretched into the wrinkles of an old man. A beard shot out from his chin and grew until it reached nearly his knees.

As the figure started to snore, Merlin's song faltered. In front of him was the oldest version of himself—weathered as a crabapple, abandoned before the first hope of Camelot with nothing but a little wooden falcon clutched in his gnarled hand.

All of the disgust he'd felt for his old self melted away when he saw his true beginnings. He'd started out on a path that was as lonely as any he could imagine. Yes, there had been dark patches. True, he'd made as many mistakes as there were stars in the cosmos. But he'd fought to the other side of it—hadn't he? Merlin had never stopped fighting the misery of Nin's cycle. And now he had so many people who cared for him.

Who believed in him.

Who needed him to play the hero, this time.

&

The future where his parents were putting up one last, epic fight beckoned from the end of the portal.

Merlin had never traveled this far through spacetime by himself. But he'd revisited the pain of his past and unlocked his powers. He'd stopped his backward aging, so he wouldn't slide out of existence. Now the only thing holding him back was his own fear—which was no small dragon.

Merlin kept his mind firmly on Ari and Gwen and Val as he was sucked along through the dark. Maybe it had been the influence of Nin's magic, but the portal to Camelot had felt like a ferocious, nauseating carnival ride. This was more like the little portals Merlin had created, softly dark as a night without stars.

Just as Merlin was getting used to the feeling, a clammy hand pulled him out of the darkness. When he blinked his eyes open, he was in Nin's cave.

"No!" he cried, stamping his feet. "No, no, no."

"I see you're in a hurry," Nin told him as she wisped into existence. She looked the way she always had to him—long, flowing hair to match her gown, a pleasant softness to her smile. "I won't keep you long."

She pointed to a bier that arose from the center of the lake, streaming water from the rock, a ghostly figure atop it.

"Oh, you want me to see Arthur's body so you can gloat?" Merlin cried.

"I had Arthur for centuries and you never so much as guessed it," she answered matter-of-factly. "But this is too good to hide."

She gestured to the body again, and somehow Merlin was transported onto the rocky little island, right at the side of the dimly glowing spirit. He knew this girl's scowl and dark hair better than he knew the inner workings of his own magic.

"*Ari*." The name squeezed out of his throat before he could stop himself.

Nin laughed deeply. "Arthur's spirit was exhausted by his failures. I do wonder how long Ari will last before giving out."

"Is she…"

"Dead?" Nin asked, stroking Ari's incorporeal cheek. "Yes, and also not quite." The Lady of the Lake was taunting him. She fed off his terror, his anticipation of fresh hurt.

"I won't let you begin another cycle," he shouted, filling every crack of her cave with strangled hope. He roared out magic, a fire-dragon like the one he'd pointed at Old Merlin. Nin sighed, batting it away with one finger. The movement sent Merlin flying backward as if he, too, had been struck.

He landed in the cold water. Nin had extinguished his best magic without even trying.

"You've always used magic like a child."

"And you've hidden down here like a lake monster," Merlin shouted, voice spiky with youth and pain.

"Don't be jealous because you have to live the human way," she said. "All that work to stop your backward aging and now you have to age forward in time because of that silly little body of yours."

"I could make my body older in a snap!" Merlin swam for the nearest shore, dragging himself out of the viscous black waters. "I even have practice."

"You know that won't work," Nin said. "Fast-forwarding the body does not age the spirit, which only changes as time moves and wisdom is gained. You've just given Kairos an amazing case of soul-lag. It will take him decades to catch up. But you know that already, don't you? You remember how miserable you were...don't you?" Merlin tried not to fume and give away exactly how right Nin was. "Still, go ahead and give yourself a teenage body and a child's mind before you reunite with Val. I'd love to see that festival of misery."

It was a sharp reminder that Nin was watching him. *Always* watching.

That was the next thing to fix.

Merlin threw every protection spell in the book around himself at once. Nin couldn't see him anymore—her eyes slid out of focus. She wouldn't be able to watch him. She could comb through time all she wanted.

"Cloaking yourself won't help," she said. "I know your next move. You're going to the future to save your headstrong Ari. It won't work. But it's going to be quite the show. The grand finale."

"Why do you want to watch it so badly?" he asked. She stared blankly, as if there was no answer to that question stored in her magical, glowing mind. "Why are you doing *any of this?*"

There had to be a reason, even if it was buried so deeply in the past that the enchantresses of Avalon couldn't find it. Morgause had told him no one knew how she became the Lady of the Lake. Nin was the biggest blank in the Arthurian cycle.

Merlin might be able to fight her. But he would never beat her while she was still a perfect mystery. And if she wouldn't tell him *why,* he'd have to find out for himself.

"I don't want to keep you," Nin said dismissively, while Ari's bier lowered back into the lake. The cave dissolved around him. Merlin was back in the portal, hurtling toward the future. Nin's voice grew faint. "Don't worry about me. I have a front row seat to Ari's final moments."

Merlin wanted nothing more than to save Ari, to tell Gwen the truth about who he was, to fight his way back to Val. But he was done playing Nin's game. He turned around in the portal and, with a great deal of magic, swam against the tide, back toward the actual beginning.

FIRE
&
FAMILY

Ari landed in Ketch on her feet. Her legs sank up to the shins in the shifting red sand, but she recovered fast.

The night was on fire. Smoke stained each breath, and her eyes stung until she could barely take in the sight before her. She'd come out of the portal in the dunes outside of Omaira. The cityscape was lit up against the night: red, orange, and harsh white devouring flame. Exactly as it had looked following Old Merlin's magical blow that tossed her into Nin's lake.

"Gwen! Val?"

"Ari!" Gwen's shout cut across the wind. Ari tried to yell back, to peer into the darkness of the desert around her. Instead, her eyes watered beyond sight and when she rubbed them, she irritated the burn across her cheek—the one that wouldn't even be healed by the day she died.

Fuck.

"Ari!" This time it was Val. She willed her feet to move, starting out at a jog toward the sound of their voices. How would she tell Gwen that their plan to get home had come with a new Nin clause? A particularly merciless one?

Ari ran faster, and the flames of destruction in the near distance illuminated a large, swiftly moving shadow. A taneen. A really big one from the size of its legs. The great desert lizard was sniffing her out, had probably caught her scent a mile away. It paused when it saw her, crouching low. Ari eyed the creature and recognized the broken plating.

"Big Mama?" her voice scratched. "That you?"

The taneen pounced, knocking Ari down, and she waited for the moment when its enormous needle teeth pierced her in a hundred places at once. Instead she got a great wet tongue across her arm and shoulder. Two people slid down from Big Mama's back. Val and Gwen threw their arms around her.

"How long was I gone?" Ari said, ready to hear some Nin nonsense—that they had been separated by months or miles.

"A very miserable hour," Val said, finally letting her out of the hug. "Long enough for us to assume the worst. We didn't know if we should stay where we came out in the dunes or make our way toward the city. Then the freakin' dragon found us."

"We told her to find you," Gwen said.

"Oh, no." Val held his hands up. "I didn't approach the terrifying Ketchan dragon. That was all Gwen."

Gwen held on to Ari, radiating nerves. "What is it?"

"Remember before we left, she had those eggs? She's alone now. Her..." Gwen's voice choked, her own loss vibrating through Big Mama's. "Her babies are gone."

"We'll find them," Ari said, speaking of the hatchlings, but also of their little one.

"What if Mercer—"

"Mercer doesn't kill things they can sell." It wasn't exactly comforting, Ari knew, but it was true.

Gwen took the sides of Ari's neck, directing Ari's face toward her. "What about Arthur?"

"At rest." Ari closed her eyes. "Finally."

She breathed out, looking for that place inside that had never been lonely, that had always been a listening ear or a guiding voice. She could feel the change deeply, as if the eternal candle that was Arthur had truly been extinguished and only the waxy-scented smoke remained.

One king gone from the universe, a new one rising to take his place.

One nightmarish lady in the past.

One monstrous corporation destroying this future.

Not to mention one unforgiving time lock.

Gwen could sense Ari's fear. "What is it?"

"Later," Ari said, squeezing Gwen's hand. "We have to search for survivors." Her words were eclipsed by a blast of sound and ferocious spin of air. A shuttle pressed down on them out of nowhere, landing hard in the sand so close to Big Mama that the taneen went wild, biting at the air, clawing toward the vessel.

The *very* familiar vessel.

"That's not Mercer!" Val shouted.

The headlights on the ship blinded them at first, and then lowered to a humming glow that illuminated the craft. Ari's gaze traveled to the spot beneath the cockpit's viewscreen. To the hand lettering Kay used to risk his life to touch up once a year. He'd shimmy into his old space suit, heading into the void with a fraying tether and a worn-out marker.

Error

The ship had dropped from the dark skies as if it had been looking for them. Ari thought of her moms and went wild with hope. "Whoa!" she yelled at Big Mama, who was beginning to butt the tiny starship. "Whoa!" She'd been gone too long; this taneen was no medieval horse.

When the cargo door opened, two silhouettes waited on the loading dock. Ari knew instantly that neither of these people were Mom or Captain Mom; still she ran with Gwen and Val toward the open door, caution thrown aside.

She recognized Jordan first.

No longer mortally injured or forced into a handmaiden's dress, Jordan seemed taller, broader, and stronger than ever. She wore half of her armor from Lionel, as if she'd kept the pieces she truly needed and tossed off the rest.

Ari didn't recognize the other person, but something about this big, tall, curvaceous warrior with brown skin and long black hair was beyond familiar. Ari thought she looked like... but no, that was impossible.

Gwen threw her arms around Jordan.

Ari hugged both of them. "I have never been so relieved to see you. And *Error*."

"Thank the gods you're alive," Gwen cried, kissing Jordan's cheeks.

"Alive and in a very real hurry," Jordan said, beckoning them in. "Where are the others?"

Val and Ari exchanged looks. Gwen spoke solemnly. "Lam stayed behind. Merlin is...taking care of the baby in a safe place...for now."

Jordan nodded once, but Ari saw the sudden bright sadness of Jordan's eyes. She closed the door, and Ari chased her toward the cockpit.

"We can't leave Big Mama. The city is on fire."

"She'll be fine in the desert," the newcomer said, right behind her. "We've been monitoring her since Mercer arrived. You don't even want to know how many associates she's eaten."

"I'd love to know." Val was looking from the new person to Ari and back again in a way that made Ari want to elbow him.

Jordan rushed *Error* into the sky, and then through the atmosphere to space.

Ari scanned the view for a black or white Mercer ship, her old habits sliding into place like muscle memory. "Where are they?" she muttered.

"Gone," Jordan said. "They made their point. You're lucky you arrived when you did. Had you been here earlier, you would have returned during the worst of it. The planet was overtaken by them."

"How did you know how to find us?"

"This is the spot where I came through the portal weeks ago. We've been scanning the dunes for days. I knew you'd come back when your people most needed you." She glanced at Gwen before adding, "I won't make the situation sound better than it is—"

"Have you ever?"

Jordan ignored Val, throttling faster as *Error* charged through space. "Mercer took most of the Lionelians. And your parents, Ari. They were trying to evacuate everyone and got caught. We barely evaded the nets."

"Of course," Ari said, head spinning. This was how she'd die so fast. She'd run straight at Mercer for burning her planet, capturing her parents, and claiming all of Gwen's people.

And Mercer would win.

So there really was no hope.

She found herself tripping out of the cockpit, moving through the home flavor of *Error*'s recycled air. The place had been distinctly Jordan-ized, with piles of weapons and armor where there had once been stockpiles of Kay's favorite snacks. Ari made it to the back window of the cargo bay, looking out at the orange and red stripes of Ketch. Even bombed and burning, the planet was a damn beauty. Ketch might yet become a new home, a place of life and laughter, of stinging spices and soft, vibrant cloth. Of clashing Lionelian swords and herds of roaming, wild taneens. But she wouldn't live long enough to see it.

"Good-bye," she whispered.

"Oh, we're coming back. Of course we're coming back," someone said, messing up her rather important farewell. The newcomer was definitely the warrior-type, with knives strapped down both of their long legs. "You don't recognize me. I get it. It's been a long time."

Ari turned toward them, annoyed that this person was interrupting her last view of Ketch. "Look, I just need a minute to..." Her voice dwindled as she let her mind cross the gap that had been a stone wall moments before. "Yasmeen?"

The girl's face split with a smile, wrinkling her nose and showing off handsomely spaced front teeth. "Hey, Ara."

They hugged hard while Ari sputtered words that wouldn't

add up. "How are you...Where did you...What's going on? Did we change the time line? Are the Ketchans alive?"

Yasmeen took her shoulders. "That's like a hundred questions with a thousand answers." Gwen and Val came toward them, and Gwen took in the way Ari and Yasmeen gripped each other's arms.

"Umm, introductions?" Val asked.

"Val, Gwen, this is Yasmeen," Ari managed.

"Mostly Yaz these days. She/her. I'm a good ol' lesbian."

"And I'm oh so delighted." Val held out a hand and they shook. Gwen looked at Ari in a way that demanded further explanation.

Ari stumbled on the words. "She's my...cousin."

"*Just* cousin?" Yaz draped a long arm around Ari's neck, pulling her into a sibling-styled headlock. "What? I am, like, fake dead for a few years and I lose my *best* cousin status?"

"Fake dead?" Ari and Gwen said at the same time.

Yaz seemed impressed by their synchronization; Val smirked and added, "We've got some baggage there."

Ari wrestled out of Yasmeen's hold. "Tell me how you're alive. How did you escape during the siege?"

"I should probably wait for the others."

"There are *more* Ketchans?" Ari asked, breathless.

Yasmeen's wide smile dropped. "Not as many as we wanted."

"Good. You've caught up," Jordan said, jogging over in that unhelpful way she had. "We're connecting with the Ketchan ship *Amal* in three hours."

"*Amal?*" Ari asked. "There's an entire ship?"

Yasmeen smiled again, such a crinkly, welcome sight. "We've got an entire jaysh."

"Jaysh?" Val asked. "What's jaysh?"

Gwen gripped Ari's arm, translating for them. "Army. Ketch has fighters."

"Not bad, queenie." Yasmeen winked. "Hope you're all in the mood for rebellion." She gripped the back of Ari's neck with a strong hand. "And, fuck, are we jazzed to dismantle Mercer with you."

&

Three hours was not nearly enough time, and yet it was also an eternity. Ari paced the main cabin of *Error,* having a mind-altering talk with her cousin.

Yaz let slip that a few thousand Ketchans were still alive on board *Amal.* They were the lucky ones who hadn't consumed poisoned water before the others started to die. Fleeing into space, they traveled beyond the Ridges, hiding out and waiting for the day when there might be a fight to win against Mercer. When they heard about Ari and Merlin and the battle on *Heritage,* they came back to help. "By the time we'd gotten to Ketch, you had all vanished," Yaz said. "We took care of the people left there... until the Mercer ships arrived several weeks ago."

Ari sat on the edge of the small, round table. "I can't believe we missed you by a day. It would have changed everything."

Yaz shrugged. "Doubt it. We're still massively outgunned and outmanned and out–everything else, too." Jordan grunted in agreement. These two had an interesting rhythm. Like they'd been locked up on *Error* for several weeks together. And they both liked it and hated it.

Val entered from the bathroom, swirling on the spot. "Smell me. I'm magnificent. There's a lot of bullshit on medieval Earth, but I'm saying right now the lack of showers is up there as *the worst*. No wonder those people are bored with sex. No one likes to get it all grimy."

"Were you really in Old Earth's past?" Yaz asked. "That's wild. And terrifying. That planet was hella problematic. It's why our people left in the first place."

Ari sighed. "It's worse than you know, but there are good people there, too." She thought of Lamarack, Roran, Arthur, and Morgause. And baby Kairos and little Merlin.

Jordan approached Gwen formally. "My queen. I tracked this down for you." She held out Gwen's crown from Lionel, and Gwen looked at it as if she wasn't ready for the weight of a new kingdom.

Ari took the crown for Gwen. "Thanks, Jordan."

Gwen took Ari's arm. "We should get cleaned up, too, and treat this burn before it gets infected." She touched Ari's cheek lightly, and Ari jumped a mile.

Everyone noticed.

Particularly Val, who arched his newly sculpted eyebrows.

Without a word, Gwen tugged Ari into Kay's old room. The pilot's cabin was the only place untouched by Jordan. It still smelled like him. It was still a poignant mess like him. Gwen didn't wait a moment after shutting the door before launching into her observations. "You've just found out that there are still Ketchans alive, that we might have a force to stand against Mercer, and you look like you're a brush from ultimate defeat." Gwen smiled at Ari. Not a sweet or saucy smile, but the worst kind. The *we need to talk* smile. "What happened with Nin, Ara?"

Ari sat on the edge of the bed, dropping her head into her hands. "She let Arthur go like we hoped. He's at rest now, and we're back in our time and place."

"Ara."

"I saw my body. Whatever future where my body lives in her cave, after my death." Ari looked up, too tired to cry. "I wasn't old like Arthur. I was...like this. My cheek hadn't even healed yet."

"Oh." Gwen sat down hard next to Ari. "Oh, no."

"Please don't tell the others."

"Of course," Gwen whispered.

"You don't seem shocked."

"I knew there'd be some kind of unforeseen cost, but this is too much." Gwen turned at her. "It's not going to happen."

"You should have seen Nin. She was so damn *proud* of herself." Ari dropped Gwen's Lionelian crown on Kay's bookshelf, next to the chalice. They looked good together.

"You're resigned to dying. I can feel it without looking at you." Gwen's voice grew bolder, the queen of Lionel returning after all. "You forget that our child has magical time powers. Kairos will come back for us. All grown up and ready to save their parents."

"That sounds more Merlin's style. Then again, we did leave Kai in his care." Ari closed her eyes. "Gwen, I'm going to die before Kai is able to grow up, let alone help us destroy Mercer... or stop Nin from cursing me."

"You don't know that." Gwen's voice held a warning. She

still needed to believe they'd given up Kai for a reason. That they would both live to see their baby again.

Ari reached for something else. Anything. "You know, and I don't say this lightly, we might be the worst smelling things to ever grace this room." Gwen looked up at her, expression quirked. "Come on. That shower made Val all kinds of peppy."

Gwen and Ari peeled layers of Old Earth off of their bodies. Once upon a time, this kind of scene had been foreplay. Now it felt like shedding, a necessary leaving behind. Ari tossed her medieval boots—which could have come with the slogan: all the lacings, none of the arch support—followed by her belt, pants, and soiled shirt. Gwen turned around, moving her hair over her shoulder to reveal her dress's lacings. Ari untied it, pulling the string free of each slit in the fabric until the entire piece of thick, weathered cotton opened like a set of double doors, showing off Gwen's entire back. Ari kissed her shoulder.

"No bite?"

"Later." Ari shrugged the rest of Gwen's dress off, and Gwen stepped out of the circle of it. Ari didn't press her with glances or touches or her mountain of aches. She stepped into the shower, turned it on as hot as it would go. Gwen joined her, their bodies close but not quite touching in the steam. Ari washed Gwen's hair, pulling the knots out of her curls, watching Gwen's eyes close.

"You're doing amazingly well for someone who gave birth yesterday."

"I raided the first aid box." She smiled. "Zero pain now. Just so...tired."

"Me, too."

Next, Gwen washed the grime off Ari's sore arms, her

shoulder muscles, and more. The water drained darkly from the rich soil of a planet that could no longer grow life. When Gwen made it to Ari's fingers, she kissed each one with an attentiveness that left Ari remembering better times. "What would you say to me right now if you didn't think you were about to die?"

"Go dancing with me," Ari said. Gwen laughed. "I saw you dancing once, in Dark Matter on that moon colony." Ari smirked. "You remember, lady? You totally drugged me and took me back to your spaceship like a caveman."

"Stop being cute." She put the soap down and laced their fingers. "I'll go dancing with you, but not on that ridiculous moon. There's a platform club on Tanaka with the best starscape." Gwen's body was unfurled, faceup, breasts pressing into the space beneath Ari's.

"Forgot how well we fit together," Ari marveled.

Gwen leaned the rest of the way, sealing their bodies together in the stream. Her head rested over Ari's heart. "Really? I didn't."

When Gwen left the bathroom, Ari tried to get a comb through the thick, black tangles of her hair. Impossible. She spied Val's clippers and didn't think twice as she sheared most of it away. Ari tied a towel around her waist and glanced in the mirror at her work. She looked sharper, new, older. The shave felt good, especially when she ran her hands up the back and through the messy points at the front. The circular scars across her shoulders and back were bleached from being hidden under armor for so long in Camelot. It was a strange dream already. Too unsettled and unsettling to be true.

She stepped out and felt Gwen's eyes on her. "I did a thing."

"I like it." Gwen looked over her own body, wounded. "I'm not the same, Ara."

"Well, that's perfect because I'm different." Ari moved forward, sat next to her, sliding one hand on Gwen's perfect hip, fingers tracing artistically woven stretch marks.

"I'm serious," Gwen said gently, and Ari only nodded, the tide of her feelings pulling and cresting, pulling and cresting.

"Yeah, me, too." Her voice broke until she cleared her throat.

"What I wouldn't give for something to wear that didn't once belong to Kay." Gwen sighed, holding up a shirt with several holes.

"Shall I order us something from Mercer?" Ari joked.

"Not funny. Although the convenience should never be underestimated. This is what I learned from Camelot, where it took a whole month to sew one dress. The real power is in convenience." Gwen squinted. "I've been thinking about how the Mercer boycott failed after the fall of the last Administrator. Unlike Lionel, most planets and settlements can't afford *not* to work with Mercer. We need to be prepared beyond defeating them. We need to have a plan for rebuilding the universe."

"What these galaxies need is a Mercer Company that isn't corrupt." Ari grabbed the chalice off the shelf. "I saw what happened to Arthur when he asked the right question and drank the water. It's like his eyes were opened to the entire universe. To all kinds of people. To the fight for equality. It didn't make him *see* the truth. It made him believe it was possible."

"You want to trick the new Administrator into drinking from the chalice like Arthur did," Gwen said, surprise—and approval—taking over her tone. "And how are you going to do that?"

"I'll be persuasive."

&

Amal wasn't nearly as big as the largest Mercer freighters, but she was still big enough for her docking deck to swallow *Error* as if the craft were a drop of water.

Once on board, Ari and her friends were escorted to a large, circular amphitheater full of hundreds of Ketchans. The swirl of her native tongue made the room feel dizzying, bright—like a dream. Distinctly colored thawbs marked the thirteen founding families. Even Yaz had pulled on a steely blue abaya over her black leather pants and khanjar knives. She had tossed a second one at Ari before they left *Error,* and Ari had draped the robelike garment over her clothes, trying not to imagine how much Merlin would like it.

Gwen kept close to Ari, her long curls braided into the same crown Ari had been captivated by that day she crashed Gwen's tournament. Somehow it hinted at royalty even more than the gold points of the circlet Jordan had saved.

Yasmeen introduced them to a few dozen people. All of whom seemed tentatively hopeful about Ari's presence, none of whom had known her parents or Ari as a child. No matter how relieved she was that they had returned—that Ketchans weren't gone from the universe—Ari couldn't fight the feeling of being an outsider. Maybe because she was.

In the amphitheater, an elder from each of the founding

families gathered around a circular table, and a person with a booming voice translated their messages into the Mercer language. They spoke of being in exile for so long, of coming back because of Ara Azar's public stand against the Administrator.

Ari felt a bit speechless when the room seemed to tilt toward her expectantly, all of the Ketchans waiting to hear her plan. Somehow her chalice idea seemed silly now...or perhaps too hard to explain to anyone who hadn't seen firsthand what the cup could do.

Yaz elbowed Ari. "They want to know where you've been."

Gwen spoke up. "We've been in the past. After Mercer demanded our child, we went back in time, hoping to secure a safe place for the baby to be born and to find a mystical weapon that might be powerful enough to stop Mercer's cruelty and domination."

"Excalibur!" someone called out.

"Excalibur is...gone," Ari said, her voice giving away her lingering grief for the sword. "But we have something else. Something designed to instill truth and understanding."

"What is it?" one of the elders asked, leaning over the table.

"That's hard to explain, and we're going to keep it secret until the time comes to employ it." Ari and Gwen exchanged glances; this was what they had agreed upon in Kay's old room. Secrecy could only help their cause. "Mercer mustn't know what we mean to do before we do it."

"And what would you need from us to use this weapon?" the same elder asked. "We do not have the kind of numbers we would need to face them in battle."

"But we're not helpless, either," Yasmeen said, calling out

toward the entire assembly. "We have a chance to make a difference. Now, before it's too late."

Some people cheered; others voiced that this was impossible.

Ari spoke over them. "Yasmeen is right. Mercer is powerful and impressive, but no armor is without its chink. We find Mercer's weakness, and we use our weapon." Ari took Gwen's hand. "The last time we faced Mercer, we were able to exploit the Administrator's need for a dramatic show, for legitimacy and control. We need to learn what this new Administrator values, and we will know her weakness."

A new elder stepped forward, wearing a deep-purple thawb and wrinkles that seemed almost familiar to Ari. "Forgive me, but I must know. You stepped into the past and lived there for some time. How did you return to this future without disrupting the time continuum?"

Ari glanced at Val, who cast his eyes downward over the loss of Lam, no doubt. "We were careful. And we had a sort of... map from the future that made it possible. Also, one of us stayed behind to make sure the story remained the same."

Jordan surprised everyone, speaking in a booming voice. "Of course, some things changed anyway." All of them spun to face her. "I speak of Camelot™."

"Excuse me?" Gwen asked. "What are you talking about?"

"As far as I can tell, the only thing that has changed since we went to the past is Mercer's theme park on Old Earth's moon."

"Mercer's *what*?" Val asked.

"Old Earth's moon is full of weird colonies named after the old vehicular gods," Ari said.

"Not in this time line," Jordan said, crossing her arms over her massive chest. "It's an entertainment facility. They released a new ad just this morning, an aggressive one, too. It pushed through all the pop-up blockers on *Error*."

"Run it," Gwen demanded.

One of the elders drew interesting circles on the round stone table, calling up a hologram advertisement that reached the height of the ceiling and boomed sound throughout the amphitheater. The incandescent blue made them all wince.

Ari beheld the glowing image of a sword half-sheathed in moon rock. "What the—"

"Come one, come all to King Arthur's court..." an old-timey voice bellowed, "...at Camelot™! Where all your Old Earth dreams come true!"

Ari swore exquisitely.

The commercial zoomed out, showing off the surface of a familiar gray moon—now cluttered with some abominable hybrid of the actual Camelot, Lionel, and Mercer's knack for selling *everything*. The commercial flashed a series of aerial shots. Of gift shops and rides—and employees wearing medieval garb.

"It's a demented amusement park!" Val exclaimed. "How tacky."

Gwen gasped. "Those are my people. Look! They're being forced to work there!" The Lionelians seemed to be perfectly framed in the ad, their suffering unsuccessfully masked by sparkling filters.

Ari squeezed Gwen's hand. "It's a trap. That's why they released the ad today. They must know we're back somehow, and they want us to come. To try to save your people."

The ad continued. "And as a grand finale to your stay in the land of medieval dreams..."

"I just threw up in my mouth," Val muttered.

"...try your hand at the Sword in the Stars. Pull it free and become the new Mercer Administrator! You could be the next king of the cosmos!"

Ari lost her breath. The hologram focused on a sword, showing dozens of people trying to lift it free while triumphant music blared. The commercial zoomed in until the sword was the only thing visible. It radiated light in a way that felt beyond anything Mercer could manufacture.

"Doesn't even look like Excalibur," Val noted. "Morons."

"That's because it isn't Excalibur. This is a different sword," Ari said, tingling all over as she stepped forward, drawn in.

"That sword has been lodged in the rock of the moon since humans first pioneered space," one of the Ketchan elders said. "It's always been there. Mercer has just capitalized on it. Built around it like a fortress."

"They did," Ari murmured, pulling herself closer to the ad. Why a Mercer stronghold on this small moon?

"Pause!" She stepped so close that she was face-to-face with the hologram of the sword. Her eyes trailed the hilt to the spot where she'd first read the name of Arthur's famed blade.

She pointed to the finely etched word. "This sword is *Kairos.*"

HEART
&
BEAT

Merlin stepped out of the portal and onto the edge of the lake. It had the same surface as ever: silver and gleaming, like a weapon polished and ready. But it also looked different than it had in the time of Camelot. Less defined at the edges, streams running to and away from it in all directions.

Avalon crouched in the mists on the far side, though Merlin didn't know if they called it Avalon yet—he had gone *that* far back. The air was heavy with the cries of birds.

At first, he didn't hear the woman screaming.

She had waded into the shallows, her hair like pale weeds, a man trudging next to her, carrying an iron knife.

Merlin ducked behind a screen of weeds. He didn't know exactly what he was about to witness. He only knew he'd told the time portal to send him back to the beginning of Nin's story. The truth was hiding in the past, and he was the only one who could go back to find it.

He needed to know how to stop the Lady of the Lake.

The woman crouched in the water up to her chest. Merlin peeled his attention away and found he wasn't the only one watching—an entire village had poured out to see this moment. When the woman screamed, Merlin was surprised the sky itself didn't tear open. The water thickened and darkened with blood. The knife plunged down, and a few moments later the man raised a tiny child.

It cried as hard as its mother had just screamed.

This must be the birth the enchantresses had told him about— the only other birth that ever happened in the waters of time.

The woman disappeared under the water, and Merlin worried that she had drifted into death, but after a moment she came back up, shining and wet, gasping for breath.

That's when the man started to yell at her.

They spoke a tongue that beat like a battle drum, tense and taut. Merlin was mesmerized, though he didn't know half the words they used, and the others were only kin to English. One word he picked out, over and over. *"Sunn."* At first, he thought they were talking about the sky overhead, the clouds that refused to break.

"No," the woman said softly. *"Dohtor."*

"Dohtor," the man said again, bitter as salt.

He was angry that she'd given birth to a girl instead of a boy. The man flung his hands up and argued with the heavens, as if they'd given him a bad deal. Merlin stole a word from the angry stream. *Steorra.* Was he claiming that their child had been born under the wrong stars? That the heavens hadn't aligned to give him the one thing he wanted?

The woman shook off his words like dirty water, clutching the tiny child to her breast.

"Nimue," she said, holding out her baby for everyone to admire. If they were as upset as the man in the lake, they did a better job of hiding it. Merlin felt the air fill with their celebrations as they played crude flutes and beat drums and cried out her name.

"Nimue. Nimue."

&

Merlin needed to learn everything he could about Nin if he was going to defeat her. Which meant staying here until she turned into an inhuman being—however long that took. However hard it was to keep away from Ari and Gwen and Val.

Yes, he could jump back to whatever moment in time he wanted now that he could use his powers without aging down into an embryo. But how long would he last without his friends? Especially like this—small and alone and uncared for in a time when violence seemed a given, rather than an option?

He was crouched in the reeds, on the verge of a panic attack, when someone crept up on him. Merlin whirled at the footsteps and found he was being watched. A woman with long, light-brown braids approached him with a curious look. "*Bearn?*" she asked in a low tone.

Had she just called him a bear?

"Hello," Merlin said, hoping that the greeting translated. "I'm just...here to see the baby. I'll be going now."

He didn't care how nice she looked. He couldn't trust anyone. And not to sound like a contestant on one of those Mercer reality shows where they crammed a bunch of unlikely room-mates in a spaceship together and sent one out the airlock every week, but he wasn't here to make friends.

The woman looked at him like he was speaking a babbling baby language. Merlin realized he'd just said all of that out loud. "Fewmets," he cursed.

"Fewmets?" She pointed to him, then put a hand to her chest. "Aethelwyn."

"No, no!" Fewmets was a term for dragon droppings and definitely *not* his name. But what was he supposed to call himself? He'd picked Merlin when he woke up as an old man with nothing but a tiny falcon in his hand. And then there was Kairos, the only other baby ever born in this lake. The time child, the chosen one. Did he deserve to claim that name after he'd dropped Gwen and Ari's baby at the beginning of a cruel cycle?

He pointed at himself. "Kai."

"Kai," the woman repeated. She brought food out of her pockets—dark berries and dried meat—and held it out, luring him closer like a wild rabbit. Merlin ran to her, so hungry that he acted like the desperate little kid he was.

After all of this time, was he going to be undone by snacks?

Aethelwyn only smiled and led him back to her village, fol-lowing baby Nimue's procession. The woman had a tiny hovel that she lived in alone. Merlin had years to wait out as Nin grew up, and he aged through time in his mortal body, so he dropped into the little rope bed in the corner and decided to stay. He'd promised Gwen to take care of Kairos, and in a very convoluted way, that's what he was doing.

As he learned to speak the harsh, ringing words of this

time, Aethelwyn's story became clear. Her husband and children had been killed in a raid, and she was lonely enough to take in a stray. When she asked about his parents, he fumbled for words that fit this era, and also fit them.

"*Cwene*," for Gwen. That was easy enough.

But there was no word that seemed to do for Ari. *Hero* hadn't been invented yet. Maybe heroes didn't exist to these people. There were only raiders who were right according to them, and wrong according to those they plundered and killed. They had many words for warrior—but they all meant *man*.

So Merlin chose *wine,* which meant friend.

Late one snowy night, when the tallow candles were almost out, Aethelwyn finally asked what had become of his family.

"I don't know," he said, the English words slipping out along with a few tears.

Merlin wanted nothing more than to open a portal to check on them. But he knew that if he saw Gwen and Ari and Val in trouble in the future, he wouldn't be able to stop himself from running—or rather leaping through time—to save them. And he needed to find out how Nin's story played out. How she went from a time child like himself to whatever she was within her cave. And he still had to learn his new magic backward, forward, and inside out.

So he waited.

And he watched Nin.

It was simple, really, to keep an eye on her. Even though he'd been born an outsider, the village quickly folded around him. It was so much easier to grow up as a boy. He'd always known that, but now he could *see* it, in the same obvious way that he'd seen the changes in the lake.

From the moment Nin could walk, she chased. From the second she could hold a sword—*sweord*—she swung without mercy. At eight, she beat every other village child with a sword her father had made. He was head of the village because, in a time of warriors, he made the best swords.

"A supplier of weapons," Merlin muttered.

Not that he was eager to go up against little Nimue, but she didn't ask him to fight. Her eyes swung over him as if he wasn't quite there. One of the funny rules of Merlin's portal into her past was that they couldn't seem to interact with each other.

Nimue's path was set, and Merlin was still cloaked to her.

She beat the last of the boys and ran around crowing. But when the boys sulked, Nimue's father plucked the sword right out of her hand and gave it to the brother who'd been born quickly after she was.

Nimue's mother watched this whole mess unfold with a frown. Merlin found himself rooting for this woman to snatch her daughter up and leave. Anglo-Saxon wives were allowed to divorce their husbands, a right that would later be stripped. But Nimue's mother let the moment pass. She let her small, fierce daughter be punished for her strength.

Merlin saw Nimue's face cycle through jealousy, love, guilt, hatred, as her brother swung the sword. In the end, she ran behind the huts where no one else would see her, eyes alight with angry tears. Those same eyes would later glimmer at Merlin, empty.

That was the day he left the village. He was twelve now, old enough to convince Aethelwyn he'd be fine on his own, to thank her for all that she'd done, and to carve out his own home deep in the woods.

Nimue needed more time to become the Lady of the Lake. And he wasn't ready to face her, not by a long shot.

&

If there was one thing that Nin had said in the cave that bothered him—besides admitting she'd stolen Ari's spirit to begin another cycle, of course—it was that Merlin used his magic like a child.

Living in these antediluvian woods without any Arthurs to take care of finally gave him time to figure things out. Of course, he only had a few years to master magic that Nin had been wielding for centuries. The pressure perched on his shoulders, clawing like Archimedes in a foul mood. He started out by building a shelter, impermeable to the elements but transparent, like a thick plastic tent. He fell asleep looking at the moon, dreaming of the future when he would be up there, meeting Ari.

He woke the next morning with magic on his lips. Music still felt like the best way to control it, perhaps because music itself was a measure of time. The first thing he tried to create was a sandwich. Naturally. He could feel himself borrowing matter from pockets of time where it was fallow, unused, and putting it to work.

And then it was sitting in his palm—turkey and cheddar and pickles and glory.

He never took his eyes off Nimue for too long. Every day he changed himself into a falcon and circled over the forest, keeping watch on her village with little rounded eyes. Taking on a different form required reaching for a time when his atoms didn't hold their current shape, when they could be combined with other atoms in new ways.

These were small marvels of intuitive magic, but intuition wouldn't be enough to take on Nin. He needed purpose, patience, ambition. And as the cherry on top, he needed whatever made her *so much stronger.*

He spent a year practicing before he smacked into puberty: forward, this time. In the torrent of those first months, his magic fluctuated as much as anything else. He was constantly turning himself into a toadstool without meaning to. His face sprouted reddish hairs, finally replacing the ones he'd lost, which should have made him proud, but why were they so damn patchy? Merlin became nearsighted again; and he allowed himself the indulgence of glasses—snatching a pair of horn rims from some future century, off the nightstand of a person who hopefully wouldn't miss them. He put them on, fussed with his hair, and hoped that Val would approve of the style.

That was the other distracting bit of becoming a teenager again. Merlin lost entire weeks thinking about Val. But he wouldn't save his once and—hopefully—future boyfriend by looking nice in specs. Val would tell him to be organized and systematic. To push forward to the more complex aspects of time magic. Merlin had been ripping time with a great deal of passion and very little precision, but what else was possible?

"Let's start here," he said, picking a flower, a small white variety that must have gone extinct; it didn't look like any of the ones he knew. Merlin glared at the petals, the sepals, the fuzzy pollen. He hummed like an angry bee.

Nothing happened.

You're making that poor flower self-conscious, he thought, channeling Val.

Merlin tried again, less pushy this time. He let the flower be a flower.

He let the song be a song.

He waited for the perfect moment, the one when everything changed. When it came, he hummed a little harder, and the flower wilted in his hand. He hadn't killed it, he'd simply sped past its prime. Now he hummed lighter, softer, making the flower white and lush again, then taking it all the way back to a seed. Then he had to take several naps in a row.

He could still exhaust his magic, although the longer he trained the more stamina he built. But there would always be an upward limit, it seemed. One of those irksome limitations of having a body that Nin liked to pester him about.

Not to be deterred, Merlin tried a tree next. A white oak. It should have been the tallest in the forest, its rounded leaves maroon with the deep blush of autumn. But it had fallen long ago.

"Change, you woody beast!" Merlin shouted.

That's definitely going to work, a voice sprang up in his mind. *Now you're a pimpled mage with an attitude problem.*

"Oh," Merlin whispered, dropping his hands. Here was a person he hadn't talked to in a very long time, even in his own head.

Kay.

His impossible, cycle-doomed father. The one who would have sprayed all the chips out of his mouth if he'd learned this particular, parental twist.

"Kay was my father," Merlin stated. Even the trees around

him seemed dubious. "Kay *is* my father," Merlin tried. Because that was the way of time—if something had been true once, it was always part of the story.

He didn't know how to begin missing and mourning Kay as a father. He would never be a child with a bumbling dad who captained the least likely ship among the stars. He would never be taught how to drive that ship by a frustrated and proud parent. There would be no bumbling sex talks while Kay turned magenta.

Well, Merlin *had* accidentally walked in on Gwen and Kay on *Error* once, which was even more horrifying with this new layer of meaning. He'd also stolen Kay's face in order to break into the pantry. That felt like something a person would do with their father. When he thought about it, paging through the moments of his past, he discovered that he hadn't lost everything he'd once feared missing. Yes, he'd sent Kairos back to become Old Merlin, made it impossible for him to live out a childhood with his mothers, but he had made it possible for him to find Gwen later on Lionel. To steal some golden days on *Error* with Kay. To stick it to Mercer on a quest with Ari.

He looked up and found that he'd righted the white oak tree while he'd daydreamed about his family. It had rooted itself and spread leaves toward the sun.

That night, when he lay on his bedroll under the manifold stars, he hummed a little song. He thought about hugging Lam good-bye, reuniting with Ari and Gwen, pinballing through space with Kay, kissing Val, even being righteously scorned by Jordan, and the stars spun faster and faster.

It was coming easier now.

Having a grip on this magic meant he could do something

he'd wanted to ever since he saw Ari staring at the broken shards of Excalibur. A desire that had sharpened each time he saw her mooning over Arthur's sword.

With Arthur's spirit finally put to rest, Ari was no longer the forty-second reincarnation of a dead king. She was so much more than that. Ara Azar, Ari Helix, knight of Camelot and king of the future, lover of Gweneviere, first of her name. He would do everything in his power to make sure that no one laid claim to her.

Not Mercer. Not Nin.

So Merlin created a forge, which was harder than he expected even with the help of magic, and after spying on Nimue's father for weeks, he learned to melt and combine metals to create iron. His forearms grew absurdly strong and his face covered with soot as he sent sparks into the blue sky, striking a steady beat. He sang the whole time, a song that he'd been writing for Ari and Gwen, the melody forged from great need and greater hope.

When it was done, the present shone in his hands, looking pretty and far too sharp.

"Just like Ari likes them." Merlin chuckled.

And then he opened one more portal. Instead of walking through it, he sent a gift hurtling through space, toward the very same moon that kept him awake at night, thinking of dingy dance clubs and destiny.

&

When Merlin neared the end of his teenage years, he could no longer wait for Nin's past to take its sweet time. Thankfully, he no longer had to. He knew how to speed things along now. He emerged from the woods, approaching the village, focused on Nin's story. He sang as loudly as he dared, and time bent to show him the truth.

A few years passed in a few breaths. Nin stopped trying to fight, stopped struggling to make herself heard in the village. She became withdrawn as magic started to cling to her. Flowers nudged open wherever she walked. Vines slithered toward her. At first she hissed at them, sending them away. Her father ignored her surly new silences. She kept quiet as she learned that the magic nipping at her heels was not a pest, but part of her. A power she might use. That day with the sword had taught her that any great show of force from a girl would not be tolerated.

So she practiced magic in secret, just as she'd cried.

Merlin had grown up—or rather grown down—feeling sorry for himself, nursing a hole where his parents should have been. But at least now he knew that they loved him. They would have celebrated him no matter who he turned out to be. Watching Nin grow up with parents who constantly rejected her was a different sort of pain.

Completely wrapped up in it, Merlin wasn't ready for the day the raiding party arrived. Warriors screamed their way into the village, spears raised. Nin's family and neighbors watched in horror as she raised her hand, spread her fingers over her heart, and became the center of a whirlwind of time.

She didn't control it with music, like Merlin. She tied it to the drum of her heartbeat. If Merlin had used his magic like a child, Nimue wielded hers as a warrior.

Would he have to do the same, if he wanted to get the better of her?

Nimue raised her other hand, and the first wave of raiders clattered apart like broken toys. She eased her grip, giving the rest a chance to run. But they lunged at her, shouting, and she closed her fist tight. They fell apart even faster, until they were only dust clouding the villagers' eyes.

No one cheered for Nimue as they had when she was born, which Merlin felt was hardly fair. Had the boys with the swords won the same victory, everyone would have thrown them a feast. Dark berries and deer jerky for everyone. Instead, the villagers hurled a single word at Nimue like mud, like stones. Merlin didn't know it, but he knew the way they chanted. It was the same way people would chant angrily at women with power for centuries to come.

Fear beat in Merlin's chest—and this time it was for Nin. She turned away from her village, empty-handed and headed to the lake where she had been born. The mists came to greet her, to take her to Avalon.

Days and nights bloomed and wilted while Nin learned about magic faster than any enchantress before her—too fast, according to some. She conquered the secrets of the mind in record time, but there was no celebration for the prodigy of Avalon. She sat at the edge of the lake every night, alone. She touched the water like a lover, but she never took one.

Merlin sped through more time. Nimue grew until she looked like the woman Merlin knew, but with sadness trapped in every line of her face. And because vicious cycles are vicious, the enchantresses caught wind of an omen. Another raiding party was headed for Nimue's village, stronger in numbers because they'd heard of a girl with a power greater than any sword. Merlin's heart found a wild tempo as Nimue ran over the lake, her feet barely touching the surface.

When she arrived, she caught her father by the arm, told him the omens, asked him to let her protect the village. She could have been a hero, if the word had existed. If her father had let her. But Merlin knew enough Anglo Saxon by now to understand that he wasn't just saying no to her offer. He was disgusted by it.

Nimue's father pointed to her brother—the one who still wore her sword at his belt. He said that the boy would keep them safe.

The village turned Nimue out quickly, still afraid of what she'd done. Even more afraid now that she'd been studying with the enchantresses. But Nimue didn't return to Avalon at sunset. She crouched outside the village all night. She watched the raiders come. When her brother was the first one they cut down, she didn't cry.

She shook her head and twisted her lips into a knowing grimace.

The slaughter was only beginning when Nin raised one hand to her heart. The other flew into the air, fingers twitching, as cries riddled the air. People fell to the ground without any blows exchanged. She wasn't just killing the raiders.

She was killing everyone.

Her father, her mother, the boys she'd beaten with the sword. Everyone who'd cheered when she was born and chanted her into exile when she turned out to be different. Merlin let out a pure, agonized sound when he saw Aethelwyn running for the woods. He hummed to save her, but the sound was stolen from his lips. He wasn't allowed to interfere with the Lady of the Lake's origins, and that meant he watched helpless as the woman who'd taken him in turned to a scattering of bones and hair and dust. Nin had pitched them all forward in time until everyone around her was dead—everyone but Merlin.

Gods, that felt painfully familiar.

Nimue marched somberly to the lake, one hand firmly over her heart. She walked into the water without slowing, even as it dragged at her clothes, turned her hair to weeds.

"No," Merlin said. "Don't do this." His words didn't reach her, though. And it was too late. It was already done.

The water welcomed her the way her people never had. The surface broke around her body, closing over her head. But Nin wasn't content to simply die in the water. After she disappeared from view, her heart-magic worked even as she drowned. The water throbbed, echoing her pulse, and then falling still.

In that moment, the lake changed—sealed itself off, the little rivers at the edges disappearing. She'd made the lake her own, binding it with her death as she had been bound to it by her birth. She'd stolen a piece of time and started a cycle of misery.

It started to rain, and every drop felt like Nin.

Her body washed up, gently nudging the shore. Merlin went and picked her up. She was lighter than he expected, a small part of a massive story, and yet this moment contained the beginning of every downfall.

Merlin trudged to shore and laid her body to rest. He used his hands and his magic to dig a muddy grave. As he packed on dark, wet earth, he kept expecting to be stopped. It seemed the story didn't care what happened after she died.

But Merlin did.

Nimue wasn't his enemy. The Lady of the Lake was. Nin was the spirit that Nimue left behind in the waters of time. Merlin could see it now: she was constantly remaking the tragedy of her own ending. She'd created a cycle of heroic boys with their swords so she could watch them fail.

Nin had even given Merlin the steps of the cycle. He muttered them as he smoothed over damp, rich soil that still seemed to breathe with life. "Find Arthur, train Arthur, nudge him onto the nearest throne, defeat the greatest evil in the world, unite all of humankind."

Merlin had believed he was helping.

But she'd known it would never work—made sure of it, when she had to. Nin had chosen Arthur, forging Excalibur for him in the waters of her own lake, but she hadn't chosen him because she could see the promise of Camelot.

Merlin's connection to Nin's waters gave her the perfect window to watch the story spin as the shining boy hero was cut down, his spirit set loose to try over and over again. That's why she'd kept Merlin alive, even though he might prove the only threat to her existence. She'd needed him more than she'd feared him. So, she'd kept him busy with her cycle and in the dark for as long as she could. And now she planned to start a new string of horrors that fed off Ari—she finally had a girl for a hero and it didn't even matter.

Nin didn't care.

She only needed more tragedy.

Merlin knew what it was like to be magical, miserable, and lonely. He had been through ages of pain and actual worlds of hurt. In the end, though, he'd been cared for and learned to let himself care in return. It had been the hardest work of his life, but it was worth it not to wind up like Nimue—even if the Lady of the Lake was the most powerful being he'd ever known.

And that was the worst irony of them all.

Merlin let the rain soak him through, finally grasping the answers he'd come all the way back for. He would have to die in the lake to be as strong as Nin.

It was the only way.

And there was only one task left.

"I need to return to my family at the moment they need me the most," Merlin chanted, making his request to the universe part of the song the universe itself was always singing.

Dawn rose and fell like heroes did, a hundred thousand times. Camelot came and went, the valiant strike of a match against an endless dark. Entire civilizations blinked into being and blinked out. Merlin waved his hand, humming through all of human history like it was merely the overture.

He stopped when he was alone again.

Earth had been abandoned, everyone gone in the wake of their own self-made catastrophes. The lake was still there, spoiled and polluted. The forest had been mostly leveled, and the few trees left were marked for demolition, Mercer *Ms* carved in their bark.

Merlin turned away from all of it and looked up to the stars, seeking the path he needed. He tried not to break under the gravity of what he'd just learned. He was Merlin, the great mage of Earth.

But he was also Kairos, and this was finally his moment.

MOON
&
SON

Crossing the galaxy after six months on medieval Earth was a new wonder. The endless black and nothing of space— followed by bursts of light and life at every starbus stop— created a scale of how far humanity had come. And how far it still needed to go.

Ari, Val, and Gwen smooshed against the window of the public commuter ship. Their nerves were alive. Swift heartbeats and sharp glances. Gwen had insisted that the sword was a gift from Kairos, something left in the past to make a difference in the future. Val felt staunchly more negative: that this was an extremely well-baited trap from Mercer.

Ari saw both sides, to be honest, but as her cheek started to hurt less, she could not afford to stay on *Amal,* waiting for her death to find her and Nin to make her into a new cycle.

That, and she *really* wanted to get her hands on that sword.

The bus pilot's bored voice smeared with static through the speakers. "Kemelotch stoppsh." The children on board squealed happily as the starbus docked so hard Val lost his footing. Gwen grabbed one shoulder and Ari the other, keeping him from tumbling into the surrounding passengers.

They stayed toward the back while the bus unloaded, adjusting their Val-designed costumes. He wore a hat with a jaunty purple feather, which, as Ari had pointed out, "Only draws attention instead of dispelling it."

"Yes, attention *to* the feather." He'd had a little too much fun masking Ari in a dress and Gwen in a jumpsuit as if swapping their gender expressions might alone fool Mercer. To be honest, Ari barely recognized Gwen's backside in that getup, which ended up being the one thing to jostle her one-track mind from stopping Mercer before she died. Her hands were coming alive with very specific needs.

Val gave Ari a smack that stung only because it reminded her of Merlin. "Stop it. You might not look *exactly* like yourselves, but as a couple you're unmistakable."

Gwen gave Ari a saucy look but moved to the other side of Val. "We've got exactly one hour before *Amal* arrives and all hell breaks loose. We have to be in position before then."

"Assuming they let us in," Ari said.

"Let me do my part, will you?" Val said with a dash of salt. He'd been a short-tempered mess since they'd left Merlin behind in Avalon, and Ari couldn't blame him. She only hoped she could do something to change Merlin's fate before she was gone.

They were the last to get off the starbus, entering streams of people unlike anything Ari could have imagined. Old Earth's moon was nothing like the bare silver face she'd seen from Camelot, or the hyper-neon colonies she'd once gleefully snuck into with Kay. Crowds siphoned through glass-covered walkways toward the enormous, new dome so large it made the moon appear top-heavy. One word flashed across its peak like a gleaming crown:

Camelot™

Gwen exhaled an expletive so sincere Ari stifled a laugh.

"Okay, let's be tourists," Ari said.

Up ahead, Mercer associates checked people over, sending them to the right toward the entrance to the park, or to the left for further security screenings. Ari could feel the red alarms of facial recognition software and enough heat guns to sublimate their cells on the spot. When it was nearly their turn, Ari panicked. She reached for Gwen, kissing her so heatedly that the associate deadpanned, "Honeymooners to the right. Congratulations."

Val gripped the tickets that cost way, way too much. At the turnstile, he flirted with the associate who blushed purple and let him through. Ari went next, the guard still distracted, but her relief was cut short when the associate took hold of Gwen's bag.

"You didn't go through bag check." They ripped the bag off her arm and fished through it, pulling out the chalice...and Gwen's Lionelian crown. The guard held it up and whistled.

"It's from our wedding," Ari said in a rush, kissing Gwen's neck. "We got married on Troy yesterday. The jeweler said this one is just like the crowns they used to sell on Lionel."

Gwen picked up the story seamlessly. "We're going to take pictures with the Sword in the Stars. Isn't that romantic?"

The associate smiled—actually smiled—as if they were a human underneath that stiff uniform. They placed the crown on Gwen's head and waved them through.

Walking hand in hand, Gwen whispered, "Baby girl, did you just lie?"

"Like a pro!"

"Didn't I advise you two *not* to be stuck on each other?" Val asked.

"Worked, didn't it?" Ari said.

Val chortled. "For now. And you might want to bag that crown, Gwen. Why did you even bring it?"

"For my reasons," Gwen snapped, sliding the crown back into her bag.

None of them were prepared for Camelot™. The park was worse than the ads and Ari's imagination combined. The streets were cobbled and outfitted with handmade wooden signs, a medieval paradise like Lionel in appearance, but reeking of the capitalistic starship mall *Heritage,* which was now orbiting Old Earth in great mangled hunks.

The crowds were thick and loud, riddled with feasting, yelling adults, and screaming, overstimulated children. A ride before them was made to look like a jousting ring, while a pavilion to the side boasted a sign: PRINCESS MAKEOVERS. Everything was gendered to the hilt, as if the past's hardcore misogyny was just a nostalgic throwback that had been transformed into wholesome family fun. Not to mention that the park was teeming with Mercer associates. No wonder the Ketchan elders had referred to it as a fortress.

"This place makes me sick."

Gwen tugged Ari's hand, somehow convincing Ari's feet to

move. "We have to go straight through. The sword is at the middle of the park, but we should split up. Val, get in position on the far side. Signal us if something is off. *Amal* will be here in," she checked her watch, "thirty minutes."

"Shit, getting in took too long."

"*Move.*"

Val sped off in the opposite direction with a small, affectionate eye roll. Constantly rubbing shoulders in the crowd, Ari and Gwen pushed forward until they were sweating profusely. Ari's nerves were getting the best of her.

"This will be over soon," Gwen whispered soothingly. "Pull the sword fast. From there we should have the security of the crowd's excitement until *Amal* shows up. And I have no doubt that the Administrator will seize a chance to face us... and then we use the chalice."

"What if it doesn't work like that?" Ari asked quietly.

"Do you know something I don't?"

"It's not Excalibur, Gwen. I don't have King Arthur's soul anymore. I might not be able to lift this sword, and we need to have a game plan for when that happens."

Gwen pushed her toward a small fortune-teller's booth. The attendant took one look at Gwen and dropped to her knee. "Queen Gweneviere!"

Gwen pulled the woman to her feet and kissed her on both cheeks. The woman burst into sudden tears, and Gwen moved fast. "I need you to do something for me. Take my crown to..."

Ari didn't hear the rest as Gwen whispered in the woman's ear. She nodded slowly. "Yes, my queen. Of course."

"You will be free soon," Gwen said, her commanding

presence slipping over her like a perfectly tailored dress. "I promise."

The woman disappeared, and Ari eyed Gwen. "What are you up to?"

"Giving my people some hope," she said. "Do you really think the sword won't free itself for you?"

"I don't know. I just think we should have an alternate plan." Ari looked at Gwen, truly looked at her. No wonder Mercer hadn't recognized her at the gates; she'd been hollowed by pregnancy and the Middle Ages, but she was still the Queen of Lionel. She was still so magnificent that her former subjects took one glance at her and dropped to a knee.

"Ari, we have twenty-four minutes until the last Ketchan starship covers this dome like a beacon of unstoppable change. This is what we wanted. A last stand *with* witnesses."

"It's not all I want." Ari grabbed Gwen by the hips, deadlifted her onto the fortune-teller's high table, and kissed her. Gwen's next words disappeared into the press of their bodies. Ari's mouth couldn't get enough, her hands pulling Gwen's hair back as she tasted the skin of her neck, the edges of her breasts. It was sweet but also desperate.

Gwen gripped Ari with her arms and with her legs. And she didn't let go. Neither of them did. "We're going to make it through this," she said in Ari's ear.

"Okay," Ari's voice was rough. "But do I have to wear this fucking outfit?"

Gwen laughed warmly, cupping Ari's cheek.

Val's voice floated up from Gwen's watch. "Ari? Gwen? What in the hell is happening? You should be at the sword by now."

Gwen stared at Ari's costume, and she started to peel off the jumpsuit. "Slight change of plans. We're going disguised as ourselves."

"That makes *zero* sense!" Val hollered.

Ari slipped out of the dress, glad she'd convinced Val to let her wear her own clothes underneath. Gwen pulled the dress on. It was too long at the hem and far too tight in the bodice, but that only created a stunning amount of cleavage. When Ari stood again, Gwen's hands slid up her forearms to her shoulders and chest in a way that left Ari prickling with the best nerves. "Ready?"

"With you? Always."

They wove their fingers together and stepped out of the tent—to a waiting crowd.

Apparently Gwen's fortune-telling subject wasn't great at keeping secrets because a host of Lionelians were waiting, most of them wearing half medieval gear, half Mercer work uniforms.

And they weren't alone.

Ari's parents were there. They held hands and nodded proudly. Ari passed them as they started a procession toward the sword, reaching out to clasp hands with Captain Mom. Thank the celestial gods they'd made it this far. She tried to tell them with her eyes that it would be okay, they had a plan.

Mom winked.

The fortune-teller returned to Gwen's side and handed her something small that Gwen swiftly slipped into her pocket. Ari went to ask, but Gwen just shook her head. The group formed a protective circle around Ari and Gwen, escorting them to the sword.

Val radioed in, rushed and whispering. "Mercer's definitely onto something! They're gathering in ranks!"

Together, and growing in number with each shouted hail, the Lionelian resistance made their way to the center of the park where a host of armed associates barred the path. "Let them through! Let them try the Sword in the Stars!" people shouted until the crowd became a small riot.

Ari kept her hand in Gwen's as the associates scrambled, motioning to each other, radioing for help. Just behind them, beyond the circle, Ari saw the glittering hilt of the sword that was either a gift from their child or the most tempting trap ever laid.

And then Terra, the new Mercer Administrator, appeared, parting the crowd in her matronly gown. Ari could feel the chalice tucked in her pocket. What would happen if she could get Terra to drink from it?

What question would Terra have to ask?

Terra smiled. "Ara Azar and the former Queen of Lionel, welcome. What an interesting choice to come to us and be condemned to death, but then, public executions do match our medieval theme, don't they?"

Boos and angry shouts rippled through the crowd.

"*We* will try our hand at the sword," Ari said, turning her eyes on Gwen. "Both of us. If we fail, you can kill us."

The crowd quieted with a snap.

Terra appeared annoyed. She flipped a hand at them. "Go on then. Try your luck."

Ari didn't like her willingness. It felt almost like she knew something. The girls entered the ring of dozens of heat gun–toting associates. They approached the flat, worn piece of the moon that bore the blade, and for a few moments, the charade fell away.

Ari felt herself smile as she looked over the golden hilt and silverish handle. It reminded her of the blue cast to her armor in Camelot. Her eyes took in each letter of *Kairos*. She looked at Gwen and found her smiling too, brown eyes bright. "You first."

Gwen slid her fingers over the handle. She gripped it tightly, and Ari swore it moved at her touch. But when Gwen pulled, the blade stayed, firm and tight in the soft, ashy lunar soil. Gwen stepped back, exhaling with slight disappointment. "Told you," she whispered. "Kai made this for you."

Ari didn't stand on ceremony. She took the handle and went to raise the sword as if it were Excalibur—and it didn't budge.

The crowd began to roil with disappointment. Ari thought she heard Val cry out. She closed her eyes and cursed, tugging once more with both hands, to no avail. This time when she looked over, Gwen's eyes were dark with fear.

Terra came forward with such a simpering smile that Ari felt a lash of hatred. This woman might be playing her role differently than the first Administrator, but in the end, they were the same monster. "What a pity. But I do like the neatness of our bargain. Would you like to be hanged, or perhaps the firing squad? Not exactly period appropriate, but who cares."

All at once, the dozens of Mercer associates surrounding them aimed their weapons. Ari stepped back and into Gwen. Her leg bumped the hilt of the sword, and she could have sworn it moved.

"Wait. A moment to say good-bye," Ari said with as much confidence as she could muster.

Terra waved permission like a bored emperor.

Ari turned to Gwen, but Gwen beat her to it. "Don't you dare say good-bye to me."

"Gwen, what if Kai made the sword for us? *For both of us.*"

Gwen squinted, and then her eyes grew large. They reached for the sword together, both of their hands fitting around it perfectly.

They drew it high above their heads in one seamless motion. The crowd erupted in screams of delight. Ari couldn't help beaming at Gwen, who appeared wickedly happy with the sword aloft, cheering along with her people and the thousands of patrons.

When the chaos finally died, Terra had the audacity to look only mildly impressed. She stepped so close that Ari felt the buzz of the chalice. Of what they still needed to do. "Look at that. You've bought yourselves a grand, storied exit after all."

Ari charged, pressing the sword to the Administrator's throat.

Only, the sword passed through her. As did Ari.

The crowd went viciously silent.

Terra smiled.

"You're not even here," Ari sputtered. "You're a hologram."

"Is that what you think?" Terra laughed. "Well, Arthur never was that intelligent, so I shouldn't have hoped you would be. Time to collect on our bargain, I think." She snapped at the associates and the heat guns around them began to charge with a whining, climbing sound.

"Nin?" Gwen said, horrified. "You're *Nin?*"

Terra vanished with a smile, and Gwen ran for Ari.

Ari asked the cosmos for one last piece of hope: that she would reach Gwen before they were murdered by dozens of heat rays. Their arms closed around each other as the shots rang out—a cacophony of extraordinary violence. Thousands of blasts and then...*sparks*.

Ari felt like she'd been coated by sand. Only not quite. She opened her eyes slowly, finding herself covered in...rainbow glitter? It poured off them, creating a puddle of bright color around their feet.

And standing between Ari and Gwen and the wall of associates was Merlin.

&

A portal closed behind Merlin with a snap, which was surprising, but even more surprising was his age. He'd gone from seven back to seventeen. Possibly older. His hands were posed toward the associates' heat guns.

"Holy shit!" he shouted. "You were nearly incinerated!"

"Merlin?" Gwen said as the Mercer weapons began to reload.

Merlin snapped his fingers and every single living thing on the moon, apart from the three of them, froze. "Note to self, *the moment they need me* is a tad too literal. Next time I'll try for *an hour before the moment they need me*. Although, let's not hope for a next time."

"Slow down, Merlin," Ari said. "You're talking like your robes are on fire."

"Sorry, sorry," he blurted without actually putting the

brakes on his speech. "It's just, I've been waiting for this meeting for, well, *forever*. I've been living alone in the woods, which isn't exactly a whetstone for keeping social skills sharp. Oh, wonderful, you got my present!" He pointed to the blue sword in Ari's fist, looking like a little kid who'd finger-painted a surprise for his mum and was suddenly afraid she wouldn't like it. "It doesn't have the same properties as Excalibur, but she's quite magical and—"

"Merlin!" Gwen said, stopping him. "How did you freeze thousands of people at once?"

Merlin laughed as if she'd told a good joke. "I didn't freeze them. That would take copious amounts of magic. I stopped time. Think of it like a pause button." He mimed pushing a button. "Doesn't require much power, it's only a little maneuver. I can reverse time, too, but," Merlin whistled, "that's a bit trickier."

"You hit pause on this whole battle?" Ari spoke slowly and blinked hard.

"I think I paused the entire universe, truth be told. That's, um, the only way Nin wouldn't butt in. It won't last forever so we should probably catch up quick."

"Merlin, *where's* my baby?" Gwen asked, shaking rainbow glitter off her body in sheets.

"Oh, I'm...Well, I never did work out how best to explain this." Merlin looked to Ari, whose understanding was coming in fits and starts, unlike Gwen's, which was rigidly stuck on her tiny, baby Kairos.

Ari stared at Merlin's red hair, graying at the edges, or really turning a silver that was reserved for a certain space rat lineage. Like Captain Mom. And Kay.

"You?" Ari asked, carefully. He nodded with such hopeful brown eyes. Gwen's eyes in color and Kay's in shape. She turned to Gwen. "Do you remember when you said Kai was special? That our magic time baby might come help us at any moment?" Ari spoke slowly, half confused, half shocked.

Gwen was impatient. "Of course, but—"

"What if he already did? What if we met Kai years ago... and he's been with us all along?"

Gwen looked at Merlin for half a second and then back at Ari. "*What?*"

"We *have* been flying around the cosmos with a backward aging magician like it's no big deal."

Gwen put her hands on her hips, making a fresh cloud of glitter fall to the ground. "I don't understand what you're saying. How could Merlin *be* my baby?"

Merlin held up a finger. "Technically I'm not. Or, I was, but that was a few millennia ago. See, the baby became Old Merlin, and then aged down, and down, and down to...well, me." The girls stared until he added, "And then aged back up a bit. Toddling about, entranced by my own boogers, wasn't for me, not when I knew there was an alternative. I hope you understand."

"My baby turned into *Old Merlin*?" Gwen shouted. "The mage who stormed around Camelot telling everyone that I was a scheming harlot? That's ridiculous. It's horrendous. It's—"

Merlin closed his eyes and spoke fast. "I turned the baby into Old Merlin, started him on his path in Camelot. That's why the old version of me was so feral. I might have looked like an old man, but I had an infant's understanding of the world. It was all hunger and fear. And that's why I formed a desperate tether to the one person I loved."

"Arthur," Ari said, head down as she touched her new sword lovingly. Gwen shook her head, which only freed more sparkles. "Glitter, Merlin? Really?"

"It was the first thing that sprang to mind!"

"How could you, Merlin?" Gwen asked, scolding in a way that felt *distinctly* parental. "How could you do that to Kairos?"

"I did it to myself, point of fact," Merlin said, the truth etched on him as pain. "I knew that, no matter how much I suffered by living through the cycle, I would survive it and find you eventually. Any other choice could have kept us apart forever."

"You're telling me you put yourself through all of those monstrous, lonely lifetimes to come back to us?" Gwen peered at him from all sides.

"I had to. You're my family."

Gwen grabbed his hand, pulling it close to her face. She examined each digit as if counting and inspecting a newborn's fingers. "Are you really mine?" she asked. "I should know. I should look at you and just know."

"Our family does stretch the imagination a tad." Merlin smiled crookedly. "Although, the first time I saw you, you seemed familiar. I thought maybe it was because Old Merlin had had those run-ins with you back in Camelot, but now I think I was remembering your voice. Your face. I know most people don't remember their birth, but I'm not most people."

Gwen let go of his hand. "I'm really confused right now. I think I need a minute."

"I understand. I had about fifteen years to think it all through." Merlin plucked a soft pretzel out of the hands of a frozen person. "Time travel is horrible on the blood sugar."

Gwen watched him devour it. "Oh, gods, he really is Kay's baby."

"He has your eyes," Ari said. "Kay's hair. Can't believe I never noticed before."

Gwen shook her head. "How do I explain to people that I have a seventeen-year-old baby?"

"I'm closer to twenty now," Merlin said, rubbing his stubble proudly.

"My baby is older than me," Gwen deadpanned. "Sure, why not." She rushed at him, nearly picking him up despite their size difference. Ari's relief wrestled with her panic. Time might be on pause, but a hundred weapons were still pointed at them.

"I'm going to stop Nin," he said into Gwen's shoulder, holding her tightly. "I know how she became so powerful."

"Do you also know she's been pretending to be the new Administrator?" Ari asked, sheathing the beautiful sword in her belt.

Merlin opened and closed his mouth. "What? She has no body. It's part of the problem, truth be told, although it does keep her locked in that cave, which is a help."

"Well, she's figured out how to use Mercer's technology to be here now, as a hologram of some sort." Ari cursed. "There have been signs all along that she's been dabbling with humanity in this time period. I should have seen it."

"That's why she wanted my baby..." Gwen touched Merlin's scruffy, lightly bearded cheek. "Why she wanted you. If

Mercer had taken you, you never would have been born in the water. You never would have become the powerful Merlin who will stop her."

He grimaced. "I haven't done it just yet."

Ari's thoughts were sudden and bleak. "The water."

"What was that?" Merlin asked.

"The poisoned water that killed nearly all the Ketchans… that was Nin, too!"

The silence was new darkness.

"Wait, there are Ketchans still alive?" Merlin said. "That sounds like good news."

Gwen spoke up. "They went into deep space hiding years ago and came back when we took a public stand against Mercer. Only we'd vanished to the past before they arrived." She turned back to Ari. "How could Nin do that? I thought she was bound on Old Earth."

Ari grabbed at her skull, roughing up her short hair. "I should have seen this before! The way she showed off how easy it was to drop me in the fountain on Ketch. She was *laughing at me*." Ari pointed at Merlin. "You said her power is in every atom of that lake. When I first pulled Excalibur from that oak, there were Mercer machines harvesting the trees and bedrock. They would have gone for the water, too, wouldn't they? All of the resources? They sucked up Nin's lake and launched her into the cosmos. She probably reached everywhere in no time. Infiltrating the universe one drop at a time, controlling things from her cave, unlimited power via Mercer's same-day shipping!"

Ari looked over the thousands of frozen faces, and then up through the massive crystal dome at outer space. Soon *Amal* would arrive, but it wouldn't matter because Mercer wasn't the bad guy after all. They were the weapon.

"Look, we probably only have a minute before the universe starts rolling again." Merlin spoke quietly. "I know this sounds bad, yes. It sounds awful, but I also know how to defeat Nin. That's where I've been so many years, spying on Nin's backstory. Waiting to find out the secret to her power."

Ari caught the way Merlin's voice fell on that last part. No triumph or gloating. Whatever he knew was costly. "What is it, Merlin?"

He ignored Ari. "I'll need the chalice for my plan. Arthur was right on that score."

Ari took it out of her pocket but didn't hand it over. "Tell me what you're going to do with it first."

"Beat her at her own game." Merlin stared at Gwen, attempting to keep the caginess out of his voice, but Ari heard that too. She might not be genetically related to Merlin, but he had a few of her heroic loner tics.

Merlin interrupted Ari's thoughts by turning to her. "I know the deal you made to free Arthur. He's at peace now. I felt it even in the past...a deep release as if time itself was relieved." Merlin sighed sadly in a way that told her he'd also seen her body beneath that lake. He knew they were all running out of time.

Even for someone who could pause it.

And just like that, people started to blink, and move, ever so slightly.

"What can we do to help you, Merlin?" Gwen asked in a rush.

"Keep the Mercer baddies off my back. Distract them?"

"Well, the Ketchan starship due any minute should do just that," Ari said. "How will you get Nin to show herself again?"

"I don't need her to come to me. I'm going to her." Merlin gave himself away by wrapping his moms in a huge, emotional hug. Gwen held on, but Ari's mind started to whirl.

Whatever Merlin was about to do was possibly—or even purposefully—fatal.

Merlin came out of the hug with the chalice, and all of a sudden, the Mercer heat guns were revving up again, and the entire amusement park broke open with chaos.

Gwen started shouting to the Lionelians, getting them in ranks, protecting the tourists. *Amal* appeared overhead, causing screams of fright and then pure shock.

Ari stood in the middle of it, guarding Merlin's back while he asked the chalice a murmured question and poured it out into the hole where the Sword in the Stars had been plunged into the soil. "What's that supposed to do?"

"Quiet, please. I'm concentrating."

Ari watched Merlin hum a few different notes, eyes closed, focused on something that seemed to be inside of him, or beyond him, or both. The small puddle began to grow.

After a few minutes, it was as big as a bucket and still getting bigger.

That's when the black Mercer starships arrived in pairs. The view of the cosmos was blocked out, and *Amal* was hopelessly surrounded. Ari heard shots, far away at first, then coming closer. "Hurry, Merlin."

"Not something to be hurried!" he sang. A series of associates broke through the Lionelian blockade, and Ari threw them down with her new sword, loving the way it sliced the air. It was shorter than Excalibur, but sharper, too.

Gwen was fighting alongside her people with nothing but a replica bow and arrow. The Lionelians were strong and mad, but the associates had the numbers. When an entire block of them moved in, Ari had an impossible choice—continue to protect Merlin or rush to their aid.

A hacking sound fired from above, like a spaceship with a smoker's cough, and then *Error* tore into the dome, landing on an entire battalion of Mercer associates.

The loading bay opened, and Jordan leaped out swinging dual axes, Yaz right behind her with her knives. Jordan immediately took a stray heat gun hit to the armor, bucking slightly and then swinging her ever-buff arms with furious precision.

Ari found herself screaming out a short cheer that caught Jordan's attention, and the black knight grinned hard and cheered right back. Ari couldn't think of anyone she'd rather have at the head of the resistance, swinging heavy weapons. And loyalty really had won the day—because Jordan would never let anyone hurt Gwen. Which left Ari free to keep Merlin alive.

His puddle had grown as large as a bathtub. It gained depth, spreading up Merlin's legs, contained by an invisible force. "You're drawing Nin's lake?" Ari asked. "Can she not exist in space or something?"

"She's not remotely vulnerable unless we can get in her cave, and we can't make her open it. Nothing can. Unless I'm as powerful as she is." The water had grown huge, looming over Merlin like a liquid doorway.

An entrance to drowning.

Ari turned to fight two more associates as her thoughts clicked into place. Whatever Nin had done to make herself so immortal, so ethereal, so powerful had cost her humanity. And Merlin was about to make the same sacrifice.

People screamed as the park was suddenly awash in red light. The Mercer ships fired on *Amal,* all at once. Ari had to do something to save the last Ketchans, but there was only one thing that would stop Mercer mid-attack: bad PR. Like not saving the thousands of tourists in their stupid park.

Ari launched her blue sword skyward. It flipped as it flew, magically enhanced, striking the enormous dome and causing instant fractures. The last time the dome had broken on this particular moon, the cracks gave way to searing, boiling sunlight. Not this time. This time, the surface was turned away from the sun and the instant cold of the void roared through the cracks. "Run," Ari shouted to Gwen. "Get everyone to safety!"

Gwen herded her people and the tourists toward the emergency lockdowns.

Merlin looked at Ari, eyes blown wide. "What did you do?"

"Remember when we met? Right here?" Ari smiled. "Unless you count that other time. The time I watched you take your first breath."

Merlin sputtered, fighting tears. "You're making this harder than it already is!"

The shattering cold of space pushed through the crack in the dome, prying it wide. Everything was freezing, starting with Ari's confidence, and ending with the lake. It solidified with a sickening crack. The dome above gave way, the cold pouring in along with the silver of the stars. Ari's sword shot out toward space, and she shouted.

Merlin's magic snapped into place, creating a bubble to keep out the cold and leave her with oxygen. He called the sword back to her hand in the same motion. She held it tightly, but she held on to Merlin tighter. Until she couldn't. He sealed the atmosphere around her skin like a space suit and pushed her away.

"Stop! Merlin, *stop!*" She propelled herself toward him, which was increasingly hard in the limited gravity.

Merlin hummed until the water returned to the state of a liquid doorway. "I'm sorry," he said, tears muffling his words. "Don't make me say good-bye!"

She got a hand on his shoulder and held on to his robes. Her mind spun with ways to make him stop. "But we just got you back."

"There's no other way to get Nin to open her cave!"

But there was. And Ari knew it.

Merlin went to step into the water, and she pulled a low blow.

"You didn't even see Val yet," she shouted. Merlin's resolve cracked ever so slightly, and she grabbed him by both shoulders. "You're the hero now, Merlin. Not the martyr." Ari put a hand to his cheek. "Our perfect moment. Our beautiful Kairos."

And she pushed her sword through her own chest.

SWORD
&
STARS

Merlin's tears froze along the rims of his eyes.

"This is *not* what I made you the sword for!" he cried, as Ari fell to her knees, blood suddenly everywhere.

Gwen screamed and rushed back toward them as the rest of the crowd disappeared toward evacuation pods. Val must have already made it out; Merlin didn't see him at Gwen's side. Ari's distraction had been only that—a ruse to keep him from carrying out his plan.

He magically sealed Gwen into an air-suit as she knelt and frantically searched through the folds of her dress. She came up with a tiny pill, as white and hopeful as the first sight of the evening star.

"Is that what I think it is?" Merlin asked. "How did you procure it?"

"I knew Ari was going to get hurt doing something exactly like this, so I traded in my crown." Gwen forced the pill between Ari's lips and broke it by pushing Ari's teeth together.

Ari choked, which pushed blood from her wound, and for a second Merlin truly thought she might get better, might come back swearing and spitting and ready to fight like last time. Instead, she slumped all the way to the ground. Her eyes were two blank screens, staring up at the broken dome.

"No, no, no," Gwen said, her voice strangely empty. She must have thought her contingency plan would work—just as Merlin had been sure of his own scheme to save her. And now she was dying, just like Nin had promised she would.

Ari's body started to vanish.

Gwen looked to Merlin like he might be able to stop it.

"Nin is collecting her," Merlin said helplessly.

Which meant she had to open her cave.

That's what Ari had died to give him—a way to get to Nin.

But there was no way Merlin could stop Nin from creating a new cycle with Ari's spirit. His magic wasn't as powerful as the Lady of the Lake's. Ari had ruined the only plan to make him strong enough. If Merlin cast himself into the body-sized bubble of the lake and bound his death to it *now*, Ari would have died for nothing.

With only seconds until she was completely gone, Merlin shouted, "Get Val off this blasted moon! Keep each other safe!" This wasn't the way Merlin had dreamed his reunion with Gwen—with any of them—would play out. Even with all of time at his glowing fingertips, there was never enough when he needed it most. Merlin threw his arms around Ari's quickly disappearing figure. He felt her dissolve right as the moon's dome cracked into a final collapse. Merlin closed his eyes and caught a ride with Ari's body.

He smelled Nin's cave before he saw it—damp and close,

like all of the misery Nin had inspired over the centuries had been trapped down here and distilled into a particularly strong odor. Wet dog and stale dreams.

When Merlin opened his eyes, Nin was standing over Ari's body like a beautiful vulture.

Nin didn't seem to mind that Merlin had appeared in her cave, but then, he was still cloaked to her. He undid the spell and waited for her to notice.

"Oh, good," she said, with the first genuine smile she'd given him in centuries. It was terrifying. "Even when I can't see you, Merlin, you remain as predictable as a tightly wound Swiss watch. Your desire to save this shiny hero brought you here just in time for the end of this show. And the beginning of the spin-off."

Merlin scrambled to his feet and raised his hands, his magic grabbing for the first thing it could find. A scattering of loose stones rose into the air and flew at Nin—passing through her incorporeal body and hitting the cave wall.

"That's it?" Nin asked with a canned laugh. "That's how you're going to fight me after all this time? Sticks and stones?"

"I don't want to fight you, Nimue," Merlin said.

A shadow passed over Nin's calm for a moment so tiny that only another time child would be able to isolate it. It seemed that sticks and stones wouldn't break Nin's bones, but that name just might have hurt her.

"I'm tired of fighting, *Nimue*," he said, pressing harder on her past. "But I've been caught in a circle of your making with very little choice about it for centuries, and I'll be damned before I'll let you start a new one with Ari."

"Oh, you've already been damned," Nin said. "By your

own choices. You blame me for the universe's troubles, but are you so sure I'm the author of this sob story? I've never once taken dominion over a single mind or a body. I've only given people choices, never taken them away."

"Like when you kidnapped Val?" Merlin asked, ripping several stalactites from the cave's ceiling and sending them to impale Nin.

Nin sighed and blinked out of existence. She came back, glowing and pouring a cold whisper right into his ear. "I saved Percival from the time period you were afraid to lose him to. I kept him away from your twisted old self. I let him watch over you in safety and comfort and I even made snacks. Really, I thought you would thank me."

"Should I thank you for nearly drowning him, too?" Merlin asked, turning to Nin only to find that she'd blinked back to Ari's side.

Nin shrugged. "You saved him. One of your finer moments, really. You got to play the hero, and it was *adorable*." Merlin shuddered from the cold of this place, from the deep freeze of Nin's soul. "We both know how the stories of heroes end. You won't be able to save Ari. Back to the safety of being the magical lapdog for you, Merlin. Back to your true place in the cycle."

Merlin flinched and unleashed a torrent of magic. Sparks hit the walls of the cave like dynamite, sending rocks in every direction. The water crashed, the lake churning up. But Nin didn't look a bit worried. She was perfectly implacable. She was *winning*.

Merlin should have sacrificed himself to the lake without making a glitter show of saving his family first. Now Ari was dead, because he'd been too human. Because he'd loved them too much. He looked down at Ari's body. There was still so much color left in her cheeks—was that a side effect of the Mercer pill?

"She's gone, Merlin," Nin said. "Or should I call you Kairos?"

The hurt of that name—that person he'd never gotten to be—crackled through him. His magic burned, looking for another way to take down this master manipulator. Merlin wasn't strong enough. No one was.

No one rivaled Nin. Except...Nin herself.

Merlin sang a door into existence. A dark, starry portal right in the middle of Nin's cave. He closed his eyes and fished through the past. Merlin found what he was looking for easily, because he didn't have to stray from the path of his own history. When he opened his eyes, Arthurs were pouring out of the door. Forty of them, to be exact, stolen from moments when they were doing unimportant things. Sleeping, trimming their beards, training to fight the smaller-but-no-less-evil evils of their day.

Nin shook her head as her cave filled with manly muscles and varying historical hairstyles. Gods, Merlin had forgotten Arthur 29 had muttonchops.

"*Heroes?* I thought you would have learned that lesson by now, Merlin. Heroes are just well-armed boys that everyone uses to make themselves feel better about doing nothing in the face of horrors."

"That...can be a painfully accurate description at times!" Merlin shouted. Nin's eyebrow rose even as she floated softly above the surface of the lake. "But heroes can also give people hope to keep fighting. And these Arthurs aren't the draw, I'll admit. If I can't touch you, maybe forty swords made with your own hopped-up magic can."

That was the one thing all forty of these Arthurs had in common—besides the soul of an ancient king and a shared gender, of course. They all carried Excalibur.

"Arthurs!" he cried to the confused horde of warriors, kings, and celebrities. "It's me!" They turned to him, and just in case the dislocation of being stolen from time was a little too much for their minds—gods, he'd have to make them all forget this later—he added, "It's Merlin the mage!"

There was a strange chorus in which many Arthurs shouted that he looked too young. One tried to fight his way to the front to get closer to him: a dark-haired man who'd clearly been ripped away from a dream, judging by the mussed hair and the sleepy eyes.

"Oh, Art," Merlin whispered. He'd conjured his Arthurian ex-boyfriend into this fight. "Listen to me! Nin is the reason you've been trapped in this story. You must use Excalibur to stop her." The Arthurs looked at one another, and perhaps the spirit inside them recognized each other, because they all stilled and shared a moment before rushing at Nin.

She was floating above the water, but Merlin could fix that. He pulled more rocks from the cave walls, creating bridges for the Arthurs to rush across. Every time one got close enough to attack her, she flicked a finger and his sword froze. "Merlin, I made those swords. You think I can't stop them? You think I can't make them do any little thing I please?"

All of the Excaliburs rose in the air, danced a little jig, and returned to the hands of their owners.

Nin sighed heavily and then every Arthur disappeared at once, along with the Lady of the Lake. When she reappeared, she wiped her hands clean as if all of those boy heroes had left a sticky residue on her incorporeal skin.

"What did you do with them?" Merlin asked, suddenly terrified.

"Sent them back where they were meant to be and convinced them it was a horrible dream," she said. "Really, Merlin. Always expecting Arthurs to do your dirty work." Her glowing face morphed, expression stretching until it took on a familiar cast. A crown rose from her incorporeal brow. "I notice you didn't include the first Arthur in that little brigade," Nin said, tugging at one of his wayward golden curls. "Too soon?"

Merlin's heart skidded over the next several beats.

"Oh, you must be rather distraught, having just watched Ari die."

Merlin's heart was no longer rampaging. Now it was on fire. "She wouldn't *be* dead if you hadn't put your hand up Mercer's rear and used them as your own personal puppet!"

"I don't usually have to become so...involved," she said, sliding back into her original form. "But Ari makes things difficult, doesn't she? You're mad at her *right now*. You're furious that she killed herself and stopped you from carrying out whatever plan you'd concocted to save the day. People don't ever listen when you want to save them, do they? They would rather do the same wrong thing, over and over again. They would rather *die* than let you be right."

Nin's words doubled in intensity. Merlin couldn't help thinking they weren't only about him. They were echoes of that day when she'd tried to save her people. The day when she'd been stopped instead of hailed as a hero.

She changed, skin shading darker and hair growing shorter until it was cropped nearly to her skull. Her smile stretched until it was Merlin's favorite smile in the universe—stolen right off Val's face. "You know who's easy to get along with? Percival. I really did enjoy his company. How long has it been since you've seen him?"

"You know," Merlin said, hands spitting sparks.

"I just want to hear you say it," Nin said, spreading her hands generously wide. "You and I have all the time in all the worlds."

"It's been fifteen years," he ground out, trying to keep more magic from exploding out in a fireworks display of anger.

"Such a lovely, round number." When Nin smirked, she looked exactly like Val. And when she came nearer, Nin's fingers on his neck felt exactly like his. "If you left now, you'd get a whole mortal lifetime together."

The temptation of seeing Val again, of truly having a future with him, was almost too much. "I don't run away anymore," Merlin said, clenching so hard he thought he might break. "And I've stopped taking your bargains, remember?"

Nin changed once again, as if she was rifling through a deck of cards, looking for the ace. She settled on a face that Merlin's heart had always known—a face that held secret hints of his own. Dark curls tumbled down as Nin grew curves. She adopted a scowl, half serious and half sweet. "What about your lovely mother? Shouldn't you get back to her? Haven't you waited all this time to return to her? She would hate to think of you here, watching this new cycle be born."

Merlin gasped, terrified at just how good she was at this game.

"I told you I knew who your parents were," Nin said. And then her face changed again, and somehow she was Kay, cocky and stalwart and wearing those mythical cargo shorts.

"Gwen and Ari gave me a great gift when they brought you to my lake to be born. You were the perfect window to watch humanity fail itself. Your dedication to these little Arthurs has been deliciously comical. Your suffering has brought me so much life...such as it is."

Nin gestured down at herself, her true form flickering. "You can't hurt me, Merlin. You can't even touch me. You might as well go now, because it's about to get much sadder. You thought you knew tragedy? Imagine how much worse this will be with a girl like Ari. She'll pick the strongest, the bravest, the stubbornest as a home for her spirit. She'll search for her lost love. But it won't work, Merlin. You know that. Every single one of her would-be heroes will fall."

She glanced toward Ari with Kay's face, but Nin's terrible calm. The Lady of the Lake was going to take Ari now, claim her.

Merlin's throat seized around tears. "Can I...can I say good-bye?"

Nin shrugged Kay's shoulders.

"You know, Kay hates when people borrow his face," Merlin muttered.

"You have two minutes," Nin said, gesturing toward Ari's prone figure. "Don't disappoint me. Make them truly awful, Merlin."

He nodded, tears blazing down his face. As he passed Nin

and she could no longer see his expression, he nearly broke into a dance of glee. He'd time-magicked those tears, stolen them from a moment when he'd been truly sad. Because Merlin had glimpsed the truth behind Nin's gloating. She would only be messing with him this intently if she were afraid. That meant there was still a way to stop her. He only had to find it.

Merlin walked to Ari on the bier. He kneeled at her side, blinking at the dried blood on her shirt. Merlin peeked and found that the spot where Ari had stabbed herself had all but healed. The Mercer pill must have worked on her wound. But she still wasn't breathing.

And Nin was still a big, immortal problem.

Merlin laid a hand on Ari's heart, hummed, and sparked. She jolted up, then quickly went back down. No breath.

The winds in the cave picked up, blasting Merlin away from Ari. Nin looked furious. Good. He *wanted* her furious. He wanted her small and petty and fighting and caring and... human.

Merlin closed his eyes, in the grips of a new idea. He sang as loud as he could, filling up every crevice of Nin's cave with his deepest contralto, belting out the beginnings of Cher's master-piece, "If I Could Turn Back Time."

"What are you doing?" Nin seethed, as her glow dimmed and flared.

Merlin kept singing her backward, the same way he'd brought the tree in the woods to a seed. This whole time he'd been assuming he had to become as powerful as Nin, to step up to her level of existence. But what if he had it all back-ward, in true Merlin fashion? What if he didn't need to be less human to fight Nin? What if he needed to bring her down to his size?

As Merlin hit the chorus, Nin started screaming. Her face contorted, its perfection dropping away. Her golden hair was back to its reedy paleness, her skin the sort of milky blue-white that would have occurred naturally if she'd spent too long in a cave. She dropped out of her gentle float, hitting the rocks. Her hands came up bloody and Merlin gasped.

Nimue was back.

But Nin was still fighting to regain every second, every year, every century.

"You know, this was much easier with Morgana," he gritted as he fought.

The cave spat rocks like bloody teeth. The water started to boil.

Merlin reached the end of the song, and Nimue was still Nimue: the young woman who'd lost herself in her anger, but had not yet given up her humanity.

"What are you doing?" she asked, looking up at Merlin with a flash of disgust. Her voice was small, a cold drop of water where it used to be a raging tide. "You'll never be able to keep me like this. You'll drain your magic and then..."

"Then what?" Merlin asked. "You'll be Nin again?"

He rushed over to her, fingers blazing with the threat of sparks, his hand closing around her startlingly real neck. "I'm afraid you'll be too dead for that."

Nimue laid a hand over her heart. A whirlwind of magic started up, time pushing at Merlin, trying to age him prematurely. He could feel his skin prune, his hair shoot longer. He sang and reversed it; she screeched and he sprouted gray hairs. They were fighting now, but for the first time they were matched. Merlin's magic was depleted in a way that Nimue's wasn't, but she was so out of practice at being in a body that she stumbled like a new colt.

"Boy," she spat. "Are you going to kill me? That's what men do. That's what men have always done. They kill and burn and take, and they stuff their ears against the screams, but at the end of the day they want to be remembered as *good*. So they write stories about their shining deeds and all are made to watch and listen and love them."

"You're right!" Merlin said, tossing boulders from the cave into Nimue's whirlwind so she had to evade them, throwing off her attack. "Everything you're saying is spot-on! You could actually go further with it!" He nodded at Ari's body, nearly forgotten on the bier. "Humanity is trying to get better, though, and this time *you're* the one holding it back."

Nimue faltered—which gave Merlin the perfect opportunity to push her down, pinning her to the rocks of this odious cave with a blast of light and heat so fierce it shone like a sword, ready to slice.

Nimue closed her eyes.

But for some reason, Merlin wasn't magically stabbing her.

He would have taken out Nin, destroyed her. But this wasn't Nin.

"Heroes aren't what you think," he said. "It's...it's not just one boy and his pride against the world. Or it doesn't have to be. If we give more people a chance, if we give them each a moment, those moments will add up."

Merlin stepped back. He'd finally stumbled over the answer, after all of these centuries. "That's why *you're* going to be the hero this time, Nimue."

"What kind of trick is this?" she asked flatly, still lying on the rocks.

"No trick," he said, holding up his magical fingers to prove they weren't about to spark her into nothingness.

Nimue had done terrible things. So had Merlin. But he'd been given a chance to get better—a chance that she was never given.

To change this story, really change it, he had to finally break *this* cycle.

The only catch being that if he was wrong, Nin would come back and they would all be doomed. But he was no longer the mage with a gnarled heart who would do any dark deed for a moment of safety.

He hummed the tones of a song that Morgana had always liked, and a dark doorway lit up with glowing white runes.

"What are you going to do?" Nimue asked roughly, getting to her feet. "Let the enchantresses of Avalon finish your job for you? They hate me as much as you do."

"They feared you, Nimue. You never let yourself be truly one of them. You stood off to the side, powerful and alone." He winced. "I know what that's like."

"You don't let me go," she said faintly, as Nin's glow fought its way through her pale, ordinary skin. "That's not how this story ends."

"You can't see the future anymore," Merlin reminded her. Nimue blinked hard, and Nin's glow receded. She was no longer fighting Merlin. It looked more like she was fighting herself. "This door is your second chance," he rushed, needing to convince her before Nin came rushing back. "Leave this future. Use your magic to live in this body. Live out your life as an enchantress, powerful and respected, as you always should have been."

The Lady of the Lake's warm, round tones slipped out of Nimue's thin lips. "There's always a price. What is yours?"

"That's a very Nin question, and I don't appreciate it," Merlin said. "The only thing I want, in this exhausted universe, is a guarantee that your eternal counterpart won't come back."

"Getting rid of one powerful spirit won't make all people good," Nimue said.

Merlin sighed. "I've lived through enough of humanity to see the stunning range of mistakes that we can make. At least without Nin, we can make some new ones."

Nimue looked from the doorway to Merlin, and back again. "When I died, I bound the waters of time. Unbind them, and Nin will never be able to return." She looked around the cave as if it were a nightmare trying to sneak up on her. "She wants to come back. Do it quickly."

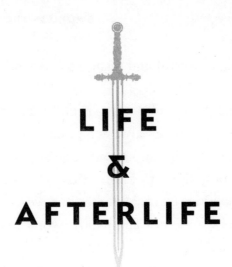

LIFE
&
AFTERLIFE

"**Motherfucking assballs of unrelenting space whores!**" Ari yelled and jumped to her feet. She leaped down from the stone pyre and started kicking and punching it until her knuckles bloodied and feeling returned to her legs in the form of new bruises.

"Ari?"

She swung around and found Merlin staring at her. "Hey, old man," she managed through the pounding of her pulse, the racing of veins. "Thanks for the jump start."

"You . . . you're alive again."

"Have been for a few minutes. I was trying not to interrupt your victory there. Do you know how hard it is to lie still when your heart is on fire?" She spun in a full circle, unable to stop herself. She really needed to beat the tar out of something. "Didn't that less salty version of Nin tell you to hurry?"

Merlin nodded, beckoning her closer, but also seemingly wary of her adrenaline-fueled state. "We have to destroy the lake, so Nin can never return." His finger cut the air, opening a portal that looked like an oily curtain.

Ari grabbed his hand and rushed him through.

The surface of Old Earth's moon was a true wreck. Pieces of the dome clung to the frame high above them. The litter of Mercer's medieval abomination was floating into space. The surviving tourists were streaming into *Amal*'s docking hangar in a series of escape pods. *Error* sat in the middle of the post-battle scene like the most misfit victor in the history of humankind.

Merlin resealed them both in magical space suits, pulled the chalice out of his robes and knelt by the puddle he'd created, which was now a small skating rink of black-hard ice.

"So this is why Arthur wanted us to go back in time for a cup," Ari said. "To access her water anywhere."

"I told you he grew into a wise and helpful ruler." Merlin tipped the chalice, and a bit of Nin's lake water poured out— and kept pouring. He closed his eyes and sang the song of the spheres, a strange collection of notes that represented the movement of the planets and stars in the heavens. Ari hadn't heard it since she was a child.

Merlin's fingers coaxed every atom from wherever they hid in the water stores throughout the known galaxies. He didn't stop when the bubble was as big as his body this time. From all throughout the universe, the waters of Nin's lake gathered. They rained down through the dome, filling up the crater of the abandoned theme park, smoothing over Camelot™ until it was one more bad memory to add to Ari's store.

Ari watched for Nin. She found the blue sword called Kairos and cleaned off her own blood on her pant leg. When she finished, she found Merlin on his knees. The lake stretched out before him. The cold of space had already frozen it solid.

"Every single atom present," Merlin said, breathing hard.

"And how do we destroy it?"

Merlin huffed. "Now what do you think I made that sword for if not destroying closed temporal loops?"

Ari blinked hard, but she didn't need to be told twice. Together they walked onto the slippery, mercury-silver surface. When they reached the very center, the ruined dome above gave an unfettered view of the stars. Ari held up Kairos, the sword catching the light and turning into a wonder of glittering blue.

Ari stabbed the sword into the lake at the same time that Merlin sang a note so high and clear that it seemed to turn into pure energy, shattering the surface into millions of shining pieces. The waters of time lifted around them—gently floating, finally freed. They sublimated somehow, turning from shards of seconds into the wisps between heartbeats.

And then they were gone.

Merlin slumped to the lunar surface, legs folded beneath his robes. His magic was fading with exhaustion, and Ari felt the flicker of the bubble that kept the air in and the cold out.

Ari was still radiating with adrenaline from the first-aid pill, and she shoved the sword in her belt and scooped Merlin up in her arms. "My gods, you're a lot heavier than you were a few weeks ago."

"No 'you were a baby just yesterday' jokes." Merlin rested his head on her shoulder, and Ari didn't care if he was twenty times the size he'd been the last time she cradled him; this was their Kai. But he was also her Merlin and connecting those dots stung in the best way. "Ari, you were fatally injured moments ago. How are you carrying me?"

"It's either this or punching everything in sight." Ari took slow, long steps toward *Error*. She locked eyes with Jordan through the cockpit and moved toward the airlock entrance to the ship, waiting for it to open.

"I can stand," Merlin said. Ari hesitated, and he added, "I'd like to be standing on my own when I see him again."

Ari put Merlin down on unsteady feet. The outer door opened, and they wedged themselves into the tiny space designed to be a sort of waiting room between outer space and inner home. "Last time we were in here together we were fucking with those Mercer ships, on our way to Troy. Remember?"

Merlin nodded, his reddish-gray hair falling in his eyes. "I got loose. I thought I was going to be lost to the cosmos forever and you grabbed me and hauled me back in."

Ari squeezed him, hoping that the airlock took extra seconds to fill with air. "That's what moms are for, Merlin."

Merlin locked bright eyes with Ari in the tight, small space. He didn't have to say it.

"I know, old man. Me, too." She wrestled him into a hug, and when the inner door swung open, they blinked through tears at Jordan, Val, and Gwen.

Gwen rained her hands over their faces, kissing both of their cheeks and adding her own tears to the party. Her hands found the bloodied slice in her shirt, and she swore until Ari wrapped her up in her arms.

"I'm okay, lady. I'm okay." Ari pulled away.

"I'm never going to forgive you."

"Really? I thought this one was pretty good payback for the

time you kidnapped yourself. Get it? I knew I had to die so I set my own parameters. You inspired me."

Gwen's eyes flared. "You didn't know I had that pill."

"True," Ari said, kissing her. "But I knew both of you would save me. Sorry, I don't want to miss this." Merlin and Val were meeting each other all over again, and Ari turned Gwen's chin with a soft knuckle so that she could watch, too.

Merlin held both of Val's hands. He was trying to find words and failing miserably. Odd nouns were just popping out. Val leaned in to kiss Merlin, and Merlin leaned back a little. "I have to tell you something! It might change your mind about...me."

"If this is about you being the magical time baby, and the fact that your moms are my best friends, I've already come to grips with it," Val said, leaning in even closer.

"You have?" Merlin's eyes were huge. "I mean, you know?"

"Someone had to do the parenting math on all this non-sense. The second Gwen gave birth to a glowing baby, I was pretty damn sure." Val tossed a look at Ari, who had definitely not figured it out and felt a fair amount of parental shame on the subject. "Of course, you can't just *tell* someone their lost baby found their way home a long time ago."

"Next time," Gwen growled, "*try*, Percival."

Val's scowl turned to a laugh, and Merlin caught his lips in a kiss. Ari's whole body hummed with happiness at the sight of the two of them.

"What is the status on the evil time lake?" Jordan asked, as if the effort of holding back had been a serious trial. Her shoulder was bound, but she still had a ready weapon in each hand.

Merlin took offense. "Evil? Time cannot be evil. But it can

hold on to the pain of its past. We've put an end to all that. We've set it free."

"Merlin took care of Nin," Ari said. "And then we broke the lake apart. Now we only have to worry about Mercer."

"Hardly," Jordan scoffed. Everyone stared until she elaborated. "You both pulled the Sword in the Stars. Technically you two are now the Administrators of the Mercer Company."

The sudden silence was a small explosion.

"I abdicate," Ari said automatically. "Gwen's got this one."

Gwen wove her fingers with Ari's in agreement. She turned back to Merlin. "What about the pieces of time lake? Can they ever rejoin?"

"They will go everywhere," Merlin said. "Not bent to the needs of one story, but naturally flowing into new legends."

"Your magic is entirely too sexy," Val breathed, and Merlin blushed as red as his hair. He smiled at his friends, just as a bright spark of magic shot out of him, firing around the small spaceship.

While everyone ducked, Jordan clapped her hands around the light. She held her cupped palms out, and they gathered around. When she opened her fingers, the magic stayed put, lighting up the center of their family like a brand-new star.

&

Several moons of time—and literal moons—later, Ari checked her watch. Gwen was supposed to have met her an hour ago. Her shuttle from Troy was late. Ari waited on the balcony of the little nightclub on Tanaka, the vivid view of a neon-green water planet before them.

She fussed with her outfit for the hundredth time, and Val put a light hand on her wrist. "You look epic. She'll be here. Relax."

"Easy for you to say," Ari said, eyeing the way Merlin was attached to Val, arms around his waist, his chin resting on Val's shoulder. "You two already have your happily ever after."

"It's got to be Mercer BS that's holding her up," Merlin said. "This is the cost of putting her in charge of the universe."

"She's only interim Administrator. She's setting up something she calls an 'elective congress' to oversee the first age of the Mercer Trading Company."

Merlin made a terrible face. "Sorry, just got a bad historical taste in my mouth."

"What?"

"Remind me to talk Gwen through the better examples of democracy…as well as the ones where fascism leaked in and trumped everything else."

Val and Ari watched Merlin shiver away whatever he was remembering. "I don't actually envy how much you know about humanity and all of time in general." Val's arms were looped around Merlin's shoulders.

"This is what I get for not going with her," Ari said, typing a quick message to ask if Gwen was all right. "The lovebirds in action."

"Time away from each other does build up the missing," Merlin said, nuzzling Val's neck.

"If you take even one portal away from me before I'm ready, you'll be sorry, mage. Very sorry." Val wore a solidly no-nonsense look.

"Wouldn't dream of it," Merlin said, placing a light kiss on the back of Val's hand.

Ari groaned and turned away, glancing out the picture window on the balcony. "You'd better get that out of your system before she arrives. I might not go full mama bear on you two, but she's likely to punt the PDA out of the nightclub."

Ari's watch buzzed, and she warmed throughout at the short message on the small screen. *ETA five minutes. Ready for me, baby girl?*

Ari looked up and found Merlin and Val in the sort of hands-everywhere kiss that no parent cared to witness. Most of the time, when she looked at Merlin, she saw her best friend. The person she'd crawled through history and across space with, surviving side by side. This time, however, when she looked at him she was seeing entirely too much tongue.

"That's it. Out! Go dance. She's almost here."

Val looked back at Ari, dark eyes gleaming while Merlin breathed heavily, the collar of his shirt opened up, no doubt by Val's teeth. They led each other with a double set of locked, entwined hands, off the balcony and through the curtains that led to the thrumming bass of the club.

Ari sighed and fussed with her short hair. She stared out into the endless black nothing, the stars twinkling through like the kind of hope that had always been, and would always be, too expansive to be snuffed out. Not by any evil company, or disgusting Administrator, or uncaring time enchantress, or even grief.

Ari felt Gwen before she saw her. Arms circled her waist, and Gwen's cheek rested on her shoulder. "Missed you," Ari managed, feelings swelling into each word. "Too much."

"We're in recess for a few weeks. Long enough to go home with you for a spell."

"You're going back to Ketch with me?" Ari turned around in Gwen's arms, leaning against the glass and pulling her tight. She wasn't ready for how Gwen looked. Short shorts, dancing flats, a goldenrod tank top that slipped off one of her shoulders like a silky bedsheet. But that was nothing compared to her powerful, certain eyes rimmed with determination and the kind of charcoal liner that Lam seemed to be born wearing.

Ari drew light fingers down her cheek. "Nice eyes."

"Lam taught me. Forever ago." She tugged at Ari's cuffed sleeves and biceps. "This is a nice look. Val?"

"I am his living doll. You'll know I'm back in control of my wardrobe when—"

"You wear the same sword and ripped-up pants for two weeks straight?"

Ari smiled dreamily. "I loved those pants. Although, I come to this date unarmed." She showed off her waist, belted but unsheathed. Gwen's hands moved fast, stealing Ari's hips and pulling them toward her. The hunger in her eyes was momentarily stunning.

"We could go back to my ship," Ari whispered. "Like right this second."

"You promised dancing." Gwen tugged Ari by the hand, pulling her toward the dance floor. Ari watched as Gwen's gaze skimmed the crowded space until she found Val and Merlin. Val danced with his thin, toned arms in the air, closely shaved head thrown back. Merlin danced like he had yet to be introduced to his lower half, like—

"Oh my gods!" Gwen placed her hands over her face. "He *dances* like Kay."

"I see it," Ari said, laughing as they began to move with a strong beat. "Kinda wish I could un-see it."

"I know I promised I wouldn't overly mother him, but someone has got to teach that boy how to dance."

"We'll bring it up carefully, but yes, this is a solemn duty we should not avoid." Ari watched as Val grabbed Merlin's fist-pumping arm and locked it down. "I have a feeling Val will be all for it."

A new song started, a slower one, and Ari hooked Gwen's arms around her neck and pressed her lips to Gwen's ear to speak over the music. "Is it too weird? Seeing him and knowing he was—is—the same little person we fell in love with on Old Earth?"

"Not weirder than some of the things we've been through," Gwen said, although her tone tilted sad. "I do miss my baby, though."

"Yeah, but I've been thinking about this one. Kai turned into Old Merlin. And when Old Merlin got mad at us, he turned a *dragon* on us. Perhaps it's not too much of a loss not to raise a super magical, wickedly headstrong child. He could have portaled us anywhere in time and space simply for giving him a time-out."

"He could still do that."

"Yeah, but now Val would make him undo it." Ari pushed Gwen's hair back. "How about we have another one. In like six...teen years?"

Gwen laughed. "Sixteen years sounds perfect."

The song shifted again, tuned to something that seemed

to be a particular hit at this club, as everyone screamed and raised their arms. The flicking, whirling colored lights shut off, and a shade over the entire ceiling pulled back, showing off deep outer space. The dancers went wild as the only light in the club came from a thousand silver stars.

Ari kissed Gwen, tasting the past and the future and the wide, daring universe all at once.

BEGINNINGS
&
ENDINGS

Six Months Later

Merlin walked through the bustling market on Ketch, wearing brand-new robes.

His first, ancient set had been confiscated, and the second pair—the one Ari had gifted him—had gotten wet in the lake of time and never dried right. Besides, they smelled like Nin's cave.

These were his *I-survived-battling-an-ancient-tragedy-monster-so-I-deserve-nice-things* robes. They were a little bit of every color shimmering together, with planets stitched onto the hems. He swirled them around his feet while he moved between the stalls, as he did every morning, watching an entire world come back to life. At first, the silence had seemed too much to fill. Now the blaze of sunrise had to compete with the shouts of the hawkers and the smells of roasted dijal, a bird that was distractingly delicious when you put it on a stick and smeared it with yellow-orange spice.

Merlin finished up his second breakfast as Gwen and Ari rounded a sharp corner in the market. Ari looked at home here in a way that she never had anywhere else, striding through the market wearing the Ketchan clothing she'd salvaged from her birth family's home, with the obvious addition of Kairos— the sword, not Merlin—at her hip. Gwen would have looked like her regal self anywhere. She wore a queenly corset over a T-shirt and dark trousers, one thin braided crown wrapped over her head and the rest of her curls hanging loose.

Every morning that Merlin woke up and ran into them in the market felt like walking straight into the dream that had kept him going for all of those years in Nin's past.

Gwen greeted Merlin with the same hug she did every time she saw him, one that always seemed like it was half for him, and half for the baby he used to be.

"Where's Val?" she asked.

"He told me he had to go on a secret mission," Merlin said dryly.

"I'd be fine with no more secrets or missions," Gwen scoffed, though Merlin knew that wasn't true. Her missions were only beginning. She left Ketch once a moon to travel to Troy and from there, to other worlds where she brokered trades to the broken universe. Merlin loved seeing Gwen the way she was always meant to be, the way Camelot would never fully let her—wielding political power as smoothly and confidently as Ari swung around those magical swords.

Val, who was never far from Merlin's side these days, ran over with an armful of glass globes. The returned Ketchans and the Lionelians who now lived here had filled the market-place with their traditional arts in an effort to keep them from dying out, lost to Mercer's dark age.

"What are those for, precisely?" Merlin asked.

"For the library," Val said.

"There is plenty of illumination! The sunlight here does wonders," he said, trying not to blush at just how much of that last bit was about Val's glowing muscles, his dark hair that caught the golden light and held it.

Six months had given them plenty of time to come back together, in the most epic ways.

"If a library doesn't have enough lighting, do you know what it starts to look like?" Val asked.

A *cave,* Merlin mouthed, as Val shouted the same thing.

A roar sounded at Merlin's heels, and he turned with his fingers ready to spark.

"Merlin, stop!" Ari shouted. "They're looking for me."

Two young taneens were trailing them, one nipping actively at Val's shoes, the other looking up at Ari with the boundless love of a baby.

"Are they allowed in the city limits?" Val asked.

"They get a little impatient," Ari admitted. "I promised to train them for knight camp."

"You're not going to have those children fighting dragons, are you?" Merlin asked with a gasp.

"Of course not," Ari said, scratching the smaller of the taneens until it panted in delight. "They're going to ride them."

Merlin's heart buckled at the thought of such danger. He might be a mage, and finally in control of his buried time powers, but he was no longer tangentially immortal. With Nin gone, there was no one to keep plucking him out of near-death experiences. Someday, he would die. But first he had to live, which meant getting used to a certain number of dangerous ideas, especially with Ari in his life.

"Be back tonight!" she shouted over her shoulder as she ran after the taneens.

"My wife, the sexy dragon trainer," Gwen said as if presenting her to the whole universe. Then her voice dropped to a confidential tone. "I finally feel like I can let Ari go without worrying I'll never see her again."

"Good," Val said. "Because Troy is a mess and they're going to need you in full retinue, *with* the black knight. You should go let Jordan know."

"Who's going to run knight camp?" Merlin asked.

"Yaz can take care of it for a few days," Val said. "Though I have to admit those tiny knights are very attached to Jordan."

In addition to helping Gwen on her more dangerous diplomatic missions, Jordan had forged another purpose—to train a new generation with honor. So far, most of them were failing due to her impossible standards for swordplay. Merlin had been more than willing to enchant their blades, but Jordan had shot that offer right out of the sky.

Ari grew small in the distance as the taneens took off. She always came back from her training sessions sweating and happy-swearing. "Being a hero looked good on Ari, but I think this is her true form," Gwen admitted with a quiet glow.

"I don't think anyone is meant to play the hero forever," Merlin said.

He thought of Nimue, living out a quiet life in Avalon. Her heroic moment would never be met with parades or universe-wide celebration, but most heroic moments weren't. Each was a single drop in the great flow of time, but every drop mattered. And the right one, at the right moment, could change the water's direction entirely.

Ari disappeared, and Merlin wondered how long he had before she returned. He was planning something that required utmost secrecy. He felt the pull to go work on it, but first, there was his actual job to tend to.

Val and Merlin walked back to the great home that used to belong to Ari's family. She had decided to take a new, smaller home with Gwen, and gifted this palatial dream with its tiled walls and spilling greenery to the city of Omaira as a library.

And she'd put Merlin in charge.

He had entire floors dedicated to myths and legends and their children, fantasy and science fiction. He had a beautiful room filled with books of Old Earth photography. There were dictionaries and encyclopedias and as many cookbooks as he could smuggle, which he kept in what used to be the kitchen, now labeled KAY'S ROOM.

"Much better," Val said, lighting up the first of the globes as he placed it near the door that led to one of Merlin's favorite rooms. A very special collection. "I see you've expanded the Arthur section *again*."

"There are so many versions, I really must be exhaustive!"

"You really must stop time-hopping and stealing books!" Val said. "What if you go back and some caveman whacks you over the head and I never see you again?"

"There's nothing worth stealing in the Paleolithic," Merlin said. "So you have nothing to fear. Though, cave paintings are often considered the precursors to the first developments in literacy, and I *could* do a quick—"

"No!" Val said. "This is already too much."

"Nobody misses these," Merlin promised as Val climbed a ladder up the stacks to hang another globe. "I only pinch books nobody is using. And I do good works, too. I rescued quite a lot of manuscripts from the library of Alexandria before it burned down. And I had a lovely chat with the librarian. She wasn't even worried when I walked out of a black spot in the wall. People in ancient times were much more open to magic."

"I guess everything goes in cycles, hmm?" Val said, perusing the new selections despite his complaints. "Look at this!" He pulled out a slim volume. "Tolkien wrote an Arthur story?"

Merlin peeked over from where he'd been shelving a delicious new acquisition, a book of short stories by Kat Howard with an Arthurian novella. Nin made an appearance in that one. Morgana was rather central. And the Arthur mantle was taken up by a headstrong college girl with a lovely girlfriend and a very loyal dog. Yes, Ari would enjoy that.

"You know Tolkien?" he asked, as Val paged through the book.

"Of course I know Tolkien," he said. "Mercer used to sell replicas of that evil ring. They thought it was funny. One company to rule them all." Val cocked his head. "I just looked into the future and you looked a lot like Gandalf."

"And?"

"I was into it," Val said. Merlin blushed his way to the film section. Val rolled the ladder over. "What is this old film you've hand-labeled *Trash King Arthur*?"

"Oh, that one. It's notable for being as far from the actual story as humanly possible. Percival *is* Black, though."

"Damn straight, he is." Val ran his fingers over the neatly filed volumes. "Someone really should write the rest of the story. You know, the cycles that came after the first Arthur? All the way to the end, with your magical sword sticking Nin's lake into a billion icy bits? Seems like a pretty huge omission if you ask me."

"Actually, a pair of twenty-first-century authors came rather close!" Merlin said, skimming through the books and pulling out one with an electric pink, glowing Excalibur on the cover. "They got a few things lopsided, of course. I *am* a good dancer."

Val artfully dodged that one. "What's this?" He pulled out a folder filled with shiny silver discs. "A whole television show with your name on it! Should we put the lights down low and watch?"

Merlin pursed his lips. "Quite fun in places, that one. I do like the dragon. But, well, they had a tendency to make it seem as if Arthur and Merlin *could* be love interests, only to pull out at the last possible second."

Val quirked an eyebrow, a double entendre no doubt simmering behind his smirk. When he spoke, it was more frustration than amusement. "*Ugh,* why would anyone do that?"

"It was called *queerbaiting,*" Merlin said, the word like a stone in his shoe. "And it was sadly common in that age."

Val made a disgusted face and a retching sound to go with it.

Merlin had to agree. He'd heard the arguments. That they were *just stories.* But he knew, from deep personal experience playing a role in one of the most enduring legends in Western history, that stories were never just a string of pretty words on a page or attractive strangers on a screen. They climbed inside your head, reordered things. Tore up parts of you by the roots and planted new ideas.

Magic, really.

And not always the sparkly kind.

Merlin had told himself stories. He'd said he wasn't a hero because he'd stood beside brave men and played the enchanted sidekick for so long. He had given in to the idea that because he'd once been lonely and lost, he always would be. He'd believed that love was for fools who couldn't see the inevitable ending. That hope was always going to die, spitted on the end of someone's sword. But the tales he'd told himself weren't just wrong—they were dangerously wrong. They were pain and fear buffed to a shine until they glittered like truth.

Now Merlin's old stories didn't just sound like piffle. They sounded like exactly what Nin would want him to believe. It was time for something new.

"Queerbaiting, hmm?" Val asked, coming down the ladder to slip into his waiting arms. "I feel a sudden, intense need to make out with you."

Merlin felt a smile breaking through, bright as the glint of Ketchan sun. "Righting the wrongs of the past again, are we?"

"Something like that," Val said, pulling him close. Suddenly Merlin was glad they'd brought new lamps into the library, because they made it easy to see the dramatic dips in Val's smile, the dark starburst of lashes above his amberbrown eyes.

Their lips touched, and just as Merlin left the world behind,

Val pulled back and pointed at the dust motes that had stopped falling halfway to the floor, the curtains that were no longer rustling in the breeze.

"Kai," Val whispered. "You froze the universe again."

"That *does* seem to happen when we kiss."

They pushed toward each other, slower this time, and to be honest Merlin didn't mind if they altered the fabric of reality with how good this felt. Maybe reality could do with some altering. At their sides, their hands swirled around each other and then locked. They kissed for so long he couldn't tell if it was measured in minutes or hours. When they eventually pulled apart, because the universe rudely *had* to keep existing, Merlin knew they would be back at it soon enough.

Finally, a cycle worth getting caught up in.

&

Merlin didn't ask Val to come with him to the cave where *Error* was hidden, for obvious reasons. The empty sandstone loomed around him, the ship sitting idle since its dramatic entrance in the battle of Camelot™.

Merlin had an idea. A gift for Ari and Gwen. It was their three-year anniversary, and he figured that their love child was on the hook for a top-notch present after all they'd been through.

It was going to take a great deal of magic. The first step in the plan was to page through the past until he found the right moment to steal a few specific items. But when he opened a portal, that wasn't where his feet and his whims had carried him.

He emerged into a small home on Ketch. He padded down the hall and peeked through an open archway into the living room, where Gwen was sitting with her feet tucked up on a bright couch. Ari was on the floor, slashing around a foam sword.

They were both older, Ari covered in tattoos and Gwen's curves back at full strength. They were laughing, waiting. Ari held out the sword, paused, and then a tiny girl burst into the room on the shoulders of a slightly older Merlin. She held Kairos aloft, her little hands just big enough to clutch the hilt.

"Do you have that, baby?" Gwen asked, leaping up to help her. "It's heavy. And sharp."

"She's got it," Ari said, showing her how to hold it, and then sliding seamlessly into the role of a knight in the arena. Merlin—thirties Merlin—roared and steered the girl forward.

Gwen stood up on the couch just as the girl's hold on the sword wilted and shouted, in a plummy royal tone, "Avalon is the winner! Ari comes in a close second! Now the queen says it's time to feast!"

"Mama! Queen Mama! Kai Dwagon!"

Slightly older Merlin roared once more, politely, and put her down as Ari grabbed the sword in a bit of seamless family choreography. Avalon rumbled into the kitchen unexpectedly, caught sight of Merlin, and shouted, "The 'nother dragon!"

Merlin slipped out of the future, and back into the cave. This wasn't the first time he'd checked up on his soon-to-be sister. They were still ten years away from her arrival, and sometimes it was hard to wait. Avalon was too perfect, and Merlin liked knowing that Gwen and Ari would get the baby that he'd never go back to being for them.

But this moment wasn't his gift to them. Some truths people had to come to in their own time. After all, you couldn't just *tell* someone they were going to have another magical baby. Not that he'd seen her do magic yet, exactly. But she *could* pick up the sword. And her name *was* Avalon.

"Back to the real plan," Merlin said crisply. He closed his eyes, cast his mind outward and hummed, looking for just the right time to steal from the past.

"Not stealing," he corrected himself. *"Borrowing."*

ONCE & FUTURE

Merlin had put blindfolds on both of them. Ari managed to get hers pushed up so that she could see a sliver below the bottom, a great shot of her boots, but then Gwen elbowed her until she pushed it back down.

"What do you think he's up to?" Ari asked. "Anniversary present?"

"It's a surprise, Ara."

"I don't like surprises."

"But I do," Gwen countered. "Let him have his fun."

"What about *my* fun?" Ari said, abandoning whatever Merlin was about to show them for a few stolen kisses. Blindfolded kissing *was* a good time as it turned out, and Merlin had to clear his throat several times before Ari released Gwen and went back to the ready-to-be-surprised position.

"Step this way. Lightly."

Ari and Gwen walked hand in hand into a portal while Merlin kept a leading grip on the back of her shirt. She wouldn't lie; her heart trilled. Traditionally speaking, every time she went through a portal, something rotten happened, but she trusted Merlin, and she knew where they were the moment they arrived. Copper in the air. Dim light. Metal grating underfoot. She couldn't wait for Merlin to say so and tugged her blindfold off. "We're on *Error*."

Ari dropped Gwen's blindfold, too, so that she could see what Ari was seeing.

Merlin threw his arms out before *Error*'s main cabin. Strings of bright lights crisscrossed the entire space while the small table was bursting with food from what looked like several different worlds and eras. "It's a throwback party! Happy anniversary!"

"Surprise!" Val yelled, followed by a full-mouth echo from Jordan who was currently making serious business out of a cupcake with a tiny Excalibur sticking out of the top.

Gwen smiled, crushing him in a huge hug.

Val wore an interesting grin as Ari gave him a hug. "Give me a heads-up, will you? No, let me guess. My parents are going to pop out from some place, and we're all going to drink and hang out until—"

Ari's words disappeared. A long-fingered hand clapped over her eyes. She would have known that hand anywhere—even if the smell was now mingled with horse and fire and leather armor. She spun around and right into Lamarack's chest.

Ari was shouting. She had no control over her excitement as she hugged Lam again and again while they laughed. "How is this even possible?"

"Magical time baby," Val crowed. "Kai nicked them from Camelot for a few hours. *Surprise*," he finished, poking Ari in the side. "Now we can have a *real* party, huh?"

Ari found a few smudges of gray at Lam's temples and a brand-new wrinkle to their eyes. "You're older! How long has it been on your end?"

"Seventeen years," Lam said, placing their wrist on her cheek. "You look the best you've ever looked." They smiled to Gwen. "I imagine you have a lot to do with that."

"Keeping Ari busy is my favorite esteemed position." Gwen embraced Lam, and they lifted her off her feet.

Lam looked around the spaceship as if they were in a waking dream. "Arthur and I were on our way through Mirkwood. On a quest to free Gawain, and this person jumped out from behind a tree. I nearly ran him through, but Arthur stopped me."

"I did nearly get killed," Merlin said solemnly. "I have improved my tactics since then. Don't surprise past humans with portals. It's a grand rule."

Ari felt the universe tilt. Or perhaps it was just the spaceship. Val was on her left, Lam on her right. Jordan was checking out the controls, and Merlin was staring at her straight on with the most tentative, hopeful smile. "Thank you, Kai."

"I couldn't think of a better present than to bring us all together, even if just for a night."

Ari felt a familiar stab. This was her family, and they were together...minus one.

"*All* of us," Merlin added, his brown eyes bright with excitement.

The entire cabin turned quiet while Ari looked around. There was no way...was there? She pushed through them, rounding the empty cockpit, heading straight to Kay's room.

She burst the door open.

Kay was passed out on his bed, half fallen off the mattress, boots stuck to the floor and head thrown back. The rest of her friends were right behind her, uttering their own surprised noises as they collided with her back.

Merlin cleared his throat. "So, here's a rather enormous condition of the night. Kay is alive, yes, but he's also, um, trashed. Too wasted to remember this tomorrow, which was my exact plan!" He looked to Ari and Gwen. "I stole him from the after-party of your wedding to Gwen, which is why we're having the party here and not on Ketch. I should warn you, though, he's still rather disgruntled by the idea of your marriage, which isn't the best way to celebrate your anniversary, but—"

Ari couldn't wait a second more. She leaped onto the bed and shook her brother by the shoulders.

"Hey!" Kay shouted, more alert than anyone would have guessed even if his gray-silver hair was standing straight up. "Where's that Lionelian whiskey?" He pointed to Gwen. "She knows what I'm talking about."

Gwen clapped a hand over her mouth.

"What are you all looking at?" Kay smacked his own face. "Did someone draw a vagina on me when I passed out?"

Ari pulled him to his feet and they returned to the cabin where Merlin set the music blazing with a well-aimed spark. Drinks appeared in every hand. Ari watched as Lam and Kay tried to outdrink each other, and Jordan and Gwen leaned shoulder to shoulder.

Merlin walked by Kay for the second time and gave him a squeeze. Kay elbowed him off, but Ari saw the secret smile, the way Kay never really minded the love, and in truth, he had always been one of the minor gods of it.

Merlin stepped over to Ari. "Are you happy?" he asked tentatively.

"More than you know."

"I don't think we can do it again. Even this is a little risky, but..."

Ari put an arm around Merlin's shoulders. "You know I like risk. Things have been a little boring since we overthrew the all-seeing time enchantress and straightened out Mercer."

"Val keeps telling me that boring is good."

Ari and Merlin traded a knowing look and then turned to watch as Val, Gwen, and Jordan talked and laughed together. Lam and Kay were arm in arm, mid–drinking game.

"Living up to your name, Kairos," Ari said, wrestling the idea that time was fleeting. A river that could only ever sweep them away. They'd have this night and then their lives would keep moving, changing. But wherever they went—wherever hope went—new legends would draw mighty swords and fight for better futures.

ACKNOWLEDGEMENTS AND

RESOURCES

The *Once & Future* duology is an absolute dream that would not exist without the support of Sara Crowe, Sarah Davies, Aubrey Poole, and the powerhouse team at JIMMY. Additional thanks to Alex Abraham, the O&F Street Team, and our little in-house mage, aka Maverick.

M'k, now that the official business is out of the way, we would like to toss out some love to you, dear reader. Especially if you happen to be a teenager, and *especially* if you happen to be a queer or questioning person. We think it's a little odd that resources tend to only show up at the back of books filled with loss. Hope can be just as tough, just as slippery to hold onto— we know. We fight that good fight every day.

So here are people who are ready to help, whether you need immediate support, or you just have some questions:

> *Trans Life Line: a hotline run for and by trans and nonbinary people. Learn more at www .translifeline.org or call 877-565-8860 in the US or 877-330-6366 in Canada. Check the website for info on hours.*

The Trevor Project: a hotline run for and by LGBTQ+
people. Learn more at www.TheTrevorProject.org
or call 866-488-7386. Available 24/7.
National Suicide Hotline: crisis support for anyone at
any time. Call 800-273-8255.
Not OK App: a free app download trusted by mental
health professionals with one-click support.
Available 24/7.

This world isn't what we want it to be. Not yet. But it isn't as horrible as it sometimes feels or appears. We wrote these books because we believe in a better future, and stories that light up the stars with possibilities, connecting all of us to a greater universe.

Remember, this time we're the heroes.

Cori & Amy Rose

ABOUT THE AUTHORS

Amy Rose Capetta and **Cori McCarthy** met while earning MFAs at Vermont College of Fine Arts and fell in love soon after. They are the authors of more than ten acclaimed novels and live in the mountains of Vermont where they champion queer teens and raise a young hero.